WATERLOO PUBLIC LIBRARY
33420014447461

BEAT THE DEVILS

Josh Weiss

GRAND CENTRAL
PUBLISHING

NEW YORK   BOSTON

This book is a work of historical fiction. In order to give a sense of the times, some names of real people or places have been included in the book. However, the events depicted in this book are imaginary, and the names of nonhistorical persons or events are the product of the author's imagination or are used fictitiously. Any resemblance of such nonhistorical persons or events to actual ones is purely coincidental.

Copyright © 2022 by Josh Weiss

Cover design by Philip Pascuzzo. Cover copyright © 2022 by Hachette Book Group, Inc.

Hachette Book Group supports the right to free expression and the value of copyright. The purpose of copyright is to encourage writers and artists to produce the creative works that enrich our culture.

The scanning, uploading, and distribution of this book without permission is a theft of the author's intellectual property. If you would like permission to use material from the book (other than for review purposes), please contact permissions@hbgusa.com. Thank you for your support of the author's rights.

Grand Central Publishing
Hachette Book Group
1290 Avenue of the Americas, New York, NY 10104
grandcentralpublishing.com
twitter.com/grandcentralpub

First Edition: March 2022

Grand Central Publishing is a division of Hachette Book Group, Inc. The Grand Central Publishing name and logo is a trademark of Hachette Book Group, Inc.

The publisher is not responsible for websites (or their content) that are not owned by the publisher.

The Hachette Speakers Bureau provides a wide range of authors for speaking events. To find out more, go to www.hachettespeakersbureau.com or call (866) 376-6591.

Print book interior design by Abby Reilly

Library of Congress Cataloging-in-Publication Data has been applied for.

ISBNs: 978-1-5387-1944-2 (hardcover), 978-1-5387-1943-5 (ebook)

Printed in Canada

MRQ-T

10 9 8 7 6 5 4 3 2 1

For my mother, Hillary—"Livin'!"
For my father, William—"Don't laugh, it's true!"
And for my grandparents: Lillian and Al Givner &
Miriam Revah-Slucki.

Inspired by the Holocaust survivor Elias Weiss

I have here, in my hand, a list of two hundred and five people that were known to the Secretary of State as being members of the Communist Party and who, nevertheless, are still working and shaping the policy of the State Department.
                    —Senator Joseph McCarthy (R-WI)

I have to turn my head until my darkness goes...
                              —The Rolling Stones

My fellow citizens:

I stand before you today, humbled and extremely grateful that the American people saw fit to elect me as president of this great nation. I will do everything in my power to live up to the pedigree of this, the highest office in the land. To protect you from threats both foreign and domestic.

Today, if you'll allow me, I would like to touch upon the dangers facing us here at home. We are locked in a life-or-death struggle against a great evil. And what is that evil's name? Communism. I have witnessed its growing tendrils firsthand and know, just as you do, that something must be done.

The fact that I stand here today proves that. This is our day, our celebration.

The Democratic party, the party of Communism, has attempted to stymie my efforts toward making this country great by ridding it of Stalin's proxies. They tried to silence my necessary warnings through a combination of censure and mudslinging. They and their rag known as the *Daily Worker* have used my surname to birth a phrase that I shall not utter aloud here, so as not to evoke the tarnishing and insulting intimations it carries.

If getting a bit rough with Communists is un-American, then I must plead guilty to being un-American.

Needless to say, the Democrats, with their lynching bees and slander, have shown themselves to be under the complete domination of the Communistic Frankenstein, which they themselves have created. They shouldn't be called Democrats; they should be referred to properly as the "Commiecrat" party.

The true, democracy-loving people of this great land have woken up from the Commiecrat spell—a dangerous form of witchcraft known only to a select few who walk among us with names like Rosenberg, Sobell, and Greenglass. These foreign parties look like us—oh yes, make no mistake about that—but they do not share our ideals of democracy and capitalism. They are wolves masquerading as sheep, pilfering our scientific secrets and poisoning the minds of today's youth with the godless ideology of the USSR and its satellite states. They are a parasitic force upon our American way of life.

House committees and hearings have proved to be ineffective when it comes to weeding out the traitors. Those countermeasures do not go far enough! I can pick out anyone in this crowd gathered here today and ask them: "Are you now or have you ever been a Communist?" Whatever answer they might provide is beyond worthless because if that poor soul does worship at the altar of Joseph Stalin... well, you know what they say about the Devil being the father of all lies.

A Communist cannot change their ways any more than a leopard can change his spots. The momentum of their past acts, I believe, carries them onward. Macbeth put it best: "I am in blood stepped in so far that should I wade no more."

Swift and thorough action must be taken to prevent a catastrophic decline of American society and its foundational principles. I promise, with every fiber of my being, to crush the vise of Communism and deviancy, and that begins with purging our government of any subversive agents that might wish to do us harm.

A man chosen by the American people to guard the watchtower of freedom is expected to fulfill certain responsibilities. Unless that man has the intelligence to recognize the traitors and—if I may use a word that we use in Wisconsin—unless he has the *guts* to name them, then he should be taken down from that watchtower and should not be representing the American people. I will always give up the names of traitors and Communists, no matter how important the positions in which they are discovered.

And the battle against the Marxists does not end at our borders. Even now, the conflict in Korea rages on with no end in sight. Even now, the Red Menace mocks the United States' inability to stem the flow of Communism at home and abroad. How many American men must die to satiate the bloodlust of the Soviet Union and its Bolshevik allies? Mothers who have lost sons are now wondering why we didn't follow General MacArthur's sensible theory of hitting back hard. Some say that if we hit back with excessive force, if we try to win this war, we might make the Chinese Communist mad. Now, why we should worry about making someone mad when they're blowing the heads off our boys, I don't know.

No more, my fellow citizens! No more! No more shall the hammer and sickle loom over this great nation like a threatening rain cloud. There are brighter days ahead. I promise this to you... or my name is not Joseph Raymond McCarthy.

—President Joseph McCarthy's inauguration remarks
(delivered January 20, 1953)

PART I
July 1, 1958

What sort of day was it? A day like all days, filled with those events that alter and illuminate our times...and you were there.

—Walter Cronkite

CHAPTER 1

In the beginning, there was the shovel and then there was the darkness.

That's where the world ended for Morris Baker, but it's also where it began. It was the impenetrable darkness that roused him from a paralyzing abyss of memory. Well, the darkness, and the ringing of that damn telephone.

It was Tuesday. He knew it was Tuesday because an empty bottle of peach schnapps lay on his nightstand. He always drank peach schnapps on Monday nights, just like his father before him...except that his father hadn't been a vicious drinker.

Who was he kidding? Morris Baker drank peach schnapps every night and most of the day, for that matter.

He knew he had woken up on a Tuesday because the government-issued Norman Rockwell calendar sticking to his grease-stained refrigerator told him so. The picture for the month of July consisted of two "proud" Americans—a husband and wife—in conservative swimsuits lounging on a tropical beach, clinking their martini glasses together.

In the distance, a sad-looking couple dressed in drab, gray uniforms were bound in chains that bore the hammer and sickle insignia of the Soviet Union. Set against the cloudless blue sky above the two couples in red, white, and blue lettering were the words THE FREEDOMS OF CAPITALISM! traced in a bold black outline.

Baker saw two identical versions of the calendar, thanks to the schnapps, but he was just able to make out that it was the first day of July and that...*Shit!*

The phone was still ringing. He rolled over and stretched his arm off the bed, blindly feeling around for the receiver as the naked woman lying next to him stirred faintly.

Baker fumbled with dirty socks, a crumpled chocolate bar wrapper, and a neglected guide called *How to Recognize a Communist in Ten Easy Steps*, published by the government's official newspaper: *Counterattack*. Since David Schine was a Jew, his once-prominent *Definition of Communism* had been rendered "incomplete, inaccurate, and in dire need of updating for the safety of the nation." Finally, Baker found the phone with his callused fingers.

"Yeah?" he grunted. His mouth was dry and sour from the schnapps, which also turned his head into a pounding drum of bad life decisions that paraded by with each beat. He looked up and squinted, sucking in a hiss of discomfort. Daylight exceeding the recommended dose for his hangover blasted his constricted pupils.

"Baker, hope I didn't wake you," said his partner, Brogan Connolly, from the other end. He didn't sound very apologetic.

"No, I was having an early brunch. Lucille Ball is here. I really am preoccupied at the moment. Please do call later." He'd lived in America for over ten years but still couldn't shake his Czechoslovakian accent, which turned words like *was* and *the* into *vas* and *zee*.

"Not interested in your lip, Baker," replied Connolly. "I need you in Echo Park, pronto. I can hear that slur in your voice, by the way. Put the damn schnapps bottle down and get over here."

"Vat—what—is it that couldn't wait for me to actually be on duty, Connolly?"

"Two stiffs, double homicide."

"So? Vee"—*we*—"get homicides all the time. It's our department for Christ's sake."

"First off, his name is Jesus. Secondly, don't take the Lord's name in vain or I'll be forced to teach you a lesson with the Dublin Twins. And yeah, we get murders all the time, but it's not every day that you come across a journalist for a big-time network and a washed-up motion picture director. Can't make heads or tails of it. Just thought you'd wanna know."

Suddenly Baker was no longer so focused on his schnapps-induced headache. The woman next to him turned over with a muffled grunt. The covers slipped down, revealing her pale breasts. For a moment, Baker considered hanging up the phone.

"You still there, Baker?"

"Yes, yes. Keep your head on." The idiom tasted foreign on his lips. "What's the address?"

"Nine Eighty-Four Altivo Way. Right off Echo Park Avenue."

"Okay. Anything else?"

"Just get your chopped-liver-loving ass down here, all right?" Connolly abruptly hung up.

"Connolly, you Irish bastard," Baker groaned, placing the receiver back into its cradle on the floor and rolling onto his back.

"What is it?" mumbled the woman.

"Work call," Baker said. "Go back to sleep, Liz."

She was snoring again in seconds. The shafts of light forcing their way through the uneven blinds were casting early-morning shadows that reminded Baker of a barbed-wire lattice. The errant thought invited an intense wave of nausea into his gut. He sat up quickly, not ready to start the day by cleaning up a puddle of regurgitated peach schnapps and pinto beans. He sat on the edge of the bed, mentally coaxing his stomach to relax and continue its regularly scheduled programming.

"Well, as long as I'm up," he said, stretching and opening his mouth in a satisfying yawn. Baker stood and started to get dressed. Before heading out, he grabbed his gun, which sat atop a stack of unopened letters from a West German court. The words DRINGEND! URGENT! were stamped across the envelopes, but Baker, who had received the messages over a period of several weeks between May and June, was in no hurry to open them.

CHAPTER 2

The California sun seemed to be free of its cage as he made the drive out to Echo Park from his studio apartment in the heart of Chinatown. Nobody ever seemed to bother anybody in Chinatown. Well, that wasn't entirely true. Good, "patriotic" Americans hated the chinks just as much as they hated the kikes, and there were drunken raids on Chinese shopfronts from time to time. These domestic pogroms often resulted in someone losing more than just their livelihood.

Still, living among the Coolies could made a Yid *somewhat* invisible. And besides, living alongside the Chinamen just felt right; there was an unspoken form of kinship with the Jews, was there not? They were, after all, two peoples who, at points throughout their histories, had amounted to nothing more than expendable labor forces and were, at present, now despised for their shared association with Communism.

Truthfully, Morris Baker didn't fit the stereotypical Jewish look, no matter how many jokes Connolly made to the contrary. His nose was thin, but it wasn't a crooked beak like so many of his kinsmen were said to possess. His eyes were a murky dark brown and (not surprisingly) noticeably sunken since the end of the war. In fact, the only feature that hinted at his heritage was a head of curly brown hair so dark, it looked black in all but the most selective of lights.

The sky was nothing like the Rockwell illustration on Baker's refrigerator. It was a deep, unpleasant shade of orange as the sun mated with the Los Angeles smog. The intense morning rays caused amorphous shadows among the forest of palm trees in Echo Park. At this hour, they looked more like deformed monsters than the botanical landmarks of warm weather. Despite the fact that it wasn't even eight o'clock yet, Baker's white shirt was already soaked with a healthy layer of sweat. He cursed himself for stupidly forgetting to put on an undershirt and neglecting to shave the shallow stubble creeping up his neck. At least his hangover was abating . . . sort of.

Looking out the open window of his pale-green Continental Mark II—whose noisy Y-block V-8 engine never shut the hell up—Baker saw a cluster of lotus plants shooting out of the Echo Park lake. The mottled growths resembled the periscopes of a bright-green submarine armada. The gibberish of Huey "Piano" Smith's "Don't You Just Know It" was coming out of the radio. Just like the country he now lived in, the lyrics made no sense to Baker.

"*Aw yeaaah, baby!*" said the disc jockey once the song had ended, letting out a wolfish howl. His voice sounded as though he had the unusual habit of gargling gravel most mornings. "*Don't ya just love that one, folks? Even the Reds can't resist a tune that good! This is KPXM Los Angeles, where we're playin' all the jiviest jams of yesterday, today, and tomorrow, baby! Aww yeaahhh . . . !*"

A new song began to play, but barely made it to the chorus before it was replaced by a garbled Shakespeare reading somewhere out of range. "The fault . . . Brutus . . . not in our stars . . . in ourselves . . . resist . . ."

"Piece of junk," said Baker, turning off the radio with a flick of the wrist.

Soon, the erstwhile Echo Park branch of the LA Public Library system came into view. The building resembled a multilayered cake, assembled from an appealing combination of white and orange bricks. Big black letters sat atop the entrance like blight on a potato farm: HOUSE UN-AMERICAN ACTIVITIES COMMITTEE OFFICES: LOS ANGELES DIVISION. Cleared of its books and shelves, the library was now a place where suspected Communists and deviants were taken to be processed, interrogated, and, in some cases, unofficially disposed of. People could still make it out alive, of course, but their psyches and fingernails were never the same.

The deafening roar of a supersonic jet overhead brought Baker back to his senses. For a moment, the thunderclap blurred out the Continental's overworked engine as the jet hit Mach 1. Baker snapped his head up just in time to see a white cloud bloom from the tail end of the aircraft as it sped off into the morning sky. Its scream became more and more muted by the second. For ten years, man had been able to break the sound barrier, and for ten years, he wouldn't let anyone on the ground forget it.

"Oy, we get it already," Baker shouted at the jet, his brain threatening to roll over like a dying dog.

It was only a five-minute drive from his apartment on North Hill Street to the former library and then another nine to the address Connolly had provided via Glendale Boulevard, which took him through Effie Street and then to Echo Park Avenue.

Altivo Way was a small street right off the avenue, boxed off by palm trees and bushes, and lined with bungalows. It gave the impression of an exclusive, colonized jungle that was both comfortable and expensive. The city proper was slightly visible between all the scrub, and Baker wryly warned himself to look out for hungry tigers waiting to pounce from the trees.

The house at 984 was curious in that it resembled a ranch. Upon further inspection, however, Baker could make out several lower levels that reminded him of the wooden puzzle boxes sold in the various shops and stalls across Chinatown.

He pulled up next to the house, noting that several sleek black-and-white Chevy Delrays were already parked outside. The circular crest on their bodies read CITY OF LOS ANGELES, FOUNDED 1891 and featured the state and American flags. A uniformed officer (a newbie named Thomas or Travis, Baker couldn't recall) was leaning against one of the squad cars, keeping an eye out for any nosy neighbors trying to catch a morbid glimpse of the crime scene. For added measure, a spiderweb of yellow police tape crisscrossed the entire lawn, and for the second time that morning Baker thought of barbed wire, a whole fence of the stuff running off into the horizon in either direction. Once again, he repressed the image.

Some Altivo Way residents, still in fluffy bathrobes and satin pajamas, were standing curiously on their lawns and driveways, craning their necks to see what all the fuss was about. Thomas/Travis acknowledged Baker in the way that nearly everyone on the force acknowledged him: by spitting on the ground. He was used to it by now. Any qualms he may have had about forgetting the little shit's name were forgotten.

"Top of the morning to you as well," said Baker sardonically.

Strolling up the stone walkway to the door of handsomely carved driftwood, Baker noted the gold calligraphed *H* on the house's mailbox. The brass doorknob was gleaming with indelicate smudges, no doubt a present from the uniformed officers who first arrived on the scene. Their hastiness and stupidity had probably destroyed any evidence of fingerprints. Baker turned the warm knob and walked inside.

The slight Irish lilt of Brogan Connolly boomed out of the darkness: "About time, you Hebe son of a bitch! Now we can finally get started!"

CHAPTER 3

N ice to see you too, Brogan," said Baker with a smile.

Brogan Abraham Connolly was a large, loud, and foulmouthed—but (mostly) good-natured—Irishman with flaming red hair and muttonchops that had gone out of style sometime after the First World War. His bright-green eyes took prominence over his hair, but it was usually his mouth that was most recognizable.

Baker would have pegged Connolly as an anti-Semitic bigot long ago if he hadn't seen firsthand proof that Connolly hated everyone the same—regardless of race, religion, or ethnicity. Hell, Connolly sometimes hated a person if they looked at him funny. Between them, Baker and Connolly had closed more cases than anyone else in the department and, therefore, bonded over this common ground more than anything else.

Their very first case together involved tracking down Raymond Neff, a particularly sick individual who had been abducting the youth of Los Angeles, molesting them, killing them, and burying their corpses in Death Valley National Park. Baker, who had seen children murdered countless ways during the war, was fed up with Connolly discounting his theories about the killer as "Hebrew hogwash" and even requested to be paired with another detective.

It was a stroke of luck that the two of them, leaving a nine-hour stakeout of a play park in Los Feliz, stumbled upon Neff trying to squash a particularly fat child into the trunk of his car. Baker left Neff with a broken arm and an eye so swollen, it had to be surgically removed before the man's state execution in the gas chamber. The violence against Neff earned Baker a month's suspension and docked pay, but it also earned him Connolly's respect and friendship, even if the latter did sometimes take umbrage at Baker's excessive drinking. Since that time, they'd worked as a seamless unit, constantly teasing each other like immature schoolboys. No other plainclothes detective would dare touch a case when the dynamic duo of Connolly and Baker was already on it, not unless they wanted to duke it out with the former.

"I was just telling Mickey here that if you hadn't shown up within the next five minutes, we'd send out an APB on a big-nosed Sheenie drunk fitting your description," said Connolly, chuckling.

Also present in the dimly lit hall were uniformed officers Mickey Sheehan and Kelvin Bletchley, both of whom were giving Baker nasty looks.

"I was asleep when you rang. You have," Baker said, his accent turning the word into *half*, "to give me time to get dressed, or I'd show up with my shirt on backward and my, how you Americans like to say? Yes, my pecker out," replied Baker, his eyes finally adjusting to the house's weak lighting. He now realized he was standing in a wide hallway painted canary yellow and adorned with film posters housed in thick frames: *The Maltese Falcon, In This Our Life, Across the Pacific.*

The beautiful, toughened, and pudgy faces of Bogart, Astor, de Havilland, and Greenstreet all stared back at him with sharp glances, while dramatic tag lines declared: EXPLOSIVE! BLAZING! and BOY, WHEN BOGART BOFFS THOSE JAPS...YOU CAN FEEL IT!

Although he wasn't a frequent attendee of the movie houses, Baker knew who Bogart was. Everyone in this town (and the world, for that matter) knew who he was: McCarthy's key propaganda tool in fighting Communism. He was still the iconic and manly symbol of American grit, especially after surviving a nasty battle with throat cancer a few years back.

Most recently, he'd played a key army general in the exemplar of sci-fi horror schlock: *It Came from Planet Communist! In head-turning 3-D!* While not a big fan of the drivel they played on screens these days, Baker killed an afternoon watching the picture and found the blue-and-red paper glasses far from head-turning. Headache-inducing was more like it.

Baker didn't recognize any of the films on display in these posters. Granted, he had arrived in America after the war and perhaps some of these had been made before his emigration, but he surely would have heard of them if they involved Bogart.

Most of the films these days (under the supervision of the government's Department of Motion Pictures) were basically the same: An unsmiling Communist, be it spy or alien, tries to ruin the American way of life and the brave Republican, capitalist, and democracy-loving hero stops them cold in their tracks.

Baker's slight confusion must have played on his face. Connolly piped up again in his gruff voice.

"I was confused for a second there too, Baker. Haven't seen these films in over ten years. In fact, no one has! Hueys banned them in '53, shortly after McCarthy took office. Didn't want people watching stuff that didn't keep them on their toes. You know how the story goes."

Baker straightened. "I assume the maker of these pictures is around here somewhere without a pulse?"

"Right down here, as a matter of fact," said Connolly, pointing to a brighter room off the darkened hallway. Baker headed in that direction, briefly noticing a kitchen at the far end and a set of stairs that led to the house's lower levels.

"By the way," he began. "What schmuck touched the doorknob with his bare hand?"

"That was Tommy outside. Kid doesn't know his gun from his dick yet," Connolly responded. "I've done some light dusting myself, but it's been goose egg so far. Whoever did this, they knew what they were doing. Right through here."

Baker walked through the slightly arched opening of the room toward which Connolly had directed him. A sudden flash exploded before his eyes, partially blinding him. Tiny lights popped and subsided, giving way to the blurry form of a man holding a large camera.

"Christ!" growled Baker, prompting an indignant squawk from Connolly. "You could warn a man!" He rubbed his eyeballs with knuckles that felt like sandpaper.

"Sorry, Morris," said crime scene photographer Philip Lathrop, already unscrewing the flashbulb from his cumbersome Graflex Speed Graphic camera and replacing it with a new one. "Didn't see you there. You check the lighting in here? It's absolutely perfect!"

Baker let out a small sigh. Of all the photographers the station had to send, it was the one who fancied himself an "art-eest." To call Philip H. Lathrop a perfectionist was an understatement. He sometimes forgot he was taking pictures of corpses—not actors and models.

He'd have made one hell of a cameraman for the motion pictures if the background checks weren't so stringent and the president's cronies (along with their snot-nosed kids) didn't get first priority.

"I hadn't noticed," replied Baker, his vision returning. Lathrop was right, the lighting in here was pleasant and easy on the eyes. It lazily funneled into the space through high glass windows situated on both sides of the wood-paneled room.

The place was also handsomely furnished with spindly-legged Czech armchairs and a brown rectangular sofa. All the lavish seating faced a color RCA television set supported by gold-tipped appendages. Sitting atop an immaculate glass coffee table was an overflowing ashtray and a small pile of hardcover books, the top one of which teased a history of tramp steamers. A crystal decanter of amber liquid sat next to the books, half empty.

A polished record cabinet, complete with a top-of-the-line Zenith stereo system, sat in the corner to the left of the television. The player was still on and a faint crackling could be heard from the speakers—a sure sign that a record had reached its end. Baker wasn't sure why, but he didn't like the lonely sound.

The bodies of two very dead men were huddled in front of the coffee table. One of them was slumped over in a Barcalounger upholstered with black leather. His hair was graying, his face deeply lined. The heavy bags under his eyes looked as if they were relieved to finally rest after so many sleepless nights. He wore high-waisted pants, house slippers, and a plain white undergarment shirt that had a nasty red stain in the chest area.

The second man was not as recognizable, because he was lying facedown on the white carpet, a pool of his dried blood clinging to the fabric. He wore a slim-cut, navy-blue suit (which made it hard to see any bullet's entry or exit), and the tan soles of his wing-tipped shoes faced the ceiling. Next to the body was a suede ottoman with a slight indentation. The man's final sitting place.

Baker turned to address his partner. "How'd you find out about this?" he asked.

"Neighbor heard shots and called us," replied Connolly, scratching his freckled nose.

"We speak to the neighbor yet?" Baker asked.

"They hung up before we could get a name or number. Probably didn't want to get involved any further."

That figured. These days, no one stuck out their necks more than was absolutely necessary. "Have you ID'd them yet?" Baker asked in a calm and measured tone. He was too used to death to be fazed by the ghastly scene before him.

"We believe so. The fellow on the chair there," Connolly said, pointing to the Barcalounger's corpse, "is John Huston. Was a film director before the industry came under government regulation. Hasn't worked in movies in over a decade, but he directed all those pictures you saw out in the hall there. Wasn't too hard to get a fix on who he was. After all, it's his house!"

"It is?" asked Baker.

"Didn't you notice the *H* on the mailbox before you walked in here? Thought your people were smarter than that, Baker. But yes, it's Huston, all right, and this is his humble abode. Nice place, too, if you ask me."

Philip snapped another photo of the crime scene before Baker posed his next question. "And this one?" He pointed to the man on the floor. Connolly reached inside his checkered jacket pocket and pulled out a square piece of brown leather, which he threw to Baker.

"Found this on him," said Connolly. He produced a pack of Pall Malls, pulled a cigarette out of the box with his yellowing teeth, and lit it with a match he struck on the wall. Baker caught what turned out to be a very worn leather billfold. Opening it up, he found $150 in cash, a bent photo of two young teenage girls, and a New York driver's license issued to one Walter Cronkite. He quickly sucked in a breath of air and almost choked on it.

"This man is *the* Walter Cronkite?"

"You could be on one of those quiz shows with brains like that, you know? You're a regular Charles Van Doren," said Connolly, now puffing away on his cigarette. "Yes, he's an on-the-ground reporter. Or *was*, I should say. Did some coverage on the nuclear drills in Korea and also had that educational show. What was it called again? *You Are Here?*"

"*You Are There*," Baker corrected his partner. Cronkite was an ambitious young journalist with a no-bullshit approach to reporting the facts as they were, even if those facts were long since established. *You Are There* presented famous historical events as though they were occurring in real time. It was discontinued once McCarthy took office due to a blatant lack of anti-Communist content, but Baker made sure to catch every episode. He admired Cronkite, who reminded him of Edward R. Murrow, another journalist who fought hard to report the truth until the president had him discredited and driven to suicide.

"Right, right," Connolly replied, waving an impatient hand through the smoke cloud of his Pall Mall. "The real question is . . ."

"What is he doing all the way out here when he should be in New York?" said Baker. "Have we reached out to CBS yet?"

"I radioed in to Gladys. She's calling the network and the family."

"Anything else on the bodies?" Baker said.

"Not a thing. Well, nothing except this."

Connolly fished inside his jacket pocket again, pulled out a small blue object, and tossed it over to Baker. It was a travel-size notebook. Baker immediately flicked through its dog-eared pages, which were cramped with potential sign-off phrases that took up every last inch of space. Some were even scrawled sideways in the margins, but nothing seemed suspicious about a brainstorming journalist. Baker checked the very last page but saw nothing about Huston or anyone else.

"Strange, no?" he finally said.

"What's strange?"

"A big-time reporter and not a notepad on him? Other than this, I mean. I've never seen a newsman without one on their person. You've seen that putz Sullivan skulking around our offices. If Cronkite was interviewing Huston or doing a piece on the film business before it was regulated, shouldn't he have come prepared with something other than a little diary of catchphrases?"

"Good point," said Connolly.

"And what point would that be exactly?" asked a cool voice from behind them. Baker instinctively pocketed the sign-off notebook. He and Connolly turned around to see two strangers in long trench coats and wide-brimmed fedoras standing in the entrance to the living room.

"Shit," Connolly whispered in a voice only Baker could hear. "Hueys."

Baker recognized the agents of the House Un-American Activities Committee by the copper pins affixed to their lapels: a clenched fist embossed with the Stars and Stripes. While it was way too hot for the wardrobe choice, trench coats were always worn by Hueys, who wanted to look as intimidating as possible. It was a little trick they'd picked up from the Gestapo.

"May we introduce ourselves?" said the fellow on the left. He had a strong chin devoid of any stubble, and his suit under the heavy over-coat was of a light-gray color. It gave him the appearance of a storm cloud that had gained consciousness. "I am HUAC Inspector Hartwell and this is my partner, HUAC Inspector Waldgrave."

Waldgrave was about two feet shorter than Hartwell, but what he lacked in height, he made up for in bulk. He had almost no neck and his beady eyes shifted back and forth in their sockets, making him look like a wary caveman being hunted by some primeval beast. Framed between the two government inspectors was a nervous-looking Charles Ward, LA's chief medical examiner.

"And why, may I ask, are McCarthy's Boys on our crime scene?" asked Connolly in a voice that couldn't hide the snarl behind it. He was playing a very dangerous game. Pissing off a Huey almost never ended well for the instigator, even if the instigator was an officer of the law. Out of the corner of his eye, Baker could see his partner's hand hovering over the area of his jacket that concealed his double-action revolver.

"Due to certain circumstances that you need not bother yourself with, Detective Connolly," said Hartwell, "this investigation has come under government jurisdiction. Inspector Waldgrave and I have been assigned to the case." Hartwell turned to Lathrop, who looked like he was about to faint. "Mr. Lathrop, you will forfeit all the film you have taken here today to the HUAC offices on West Temple Street." He then turned to Charles, who was cowering in fright, his leather bag of medical instruments clinking ever so slightly. "Mr. Ward, you will submit your postmortem report straight to me, is that understood?"

Charles nodded, eyes wide.

"Where are the usual Hueys on the Echo Park beat?" asked Connolly, tempting the fates once again. "What were their names? Kirk and Weston?"

Hartwell looked over at Connolly. The inspector's cheap smile was still there, but his eyes were now cold. Clearly, Hueys didn't like the nickname their adoring fans had concocted for them.

"Kirk and Weston were reassigned to the Midwest office," he replied icily.

"What's that crackling?" asked Waldgrave in a low grunt, speaking for the first time.

Everyone turned their heads to the record cabinet. Hartwell strolled over to it and pulled back the dust lid.

"Ah, Wagner's 'Ride of the Valkyries.' Are you a fan, Detective Baker?" he asked with a cruel smile. His fury at being called a Huey was gone, the barbarous glee of his station returning in full force. Hartwell pulled the needle off the record, and the faint pops and crackles stopped with an uneasy abruptness.

For the slightest moment, Baker's veins seemed to constrict, and the darkness threatened to overtake him. It wouldn't look good if he passed out here, right in front of these two bastards. He swayed a little but fought hard to keep his face calm as he took a deep breath and looked down at Cronkite's body. He had heard the Wagner composition before, of course, but that was in another life when it was called "Ritt der Walküren." The room's original calming aura was gone. It now felt desolate and dreary, the outpost of a drafty and lice-infested barracks.

Baker pulled out his pack of Kools—the menthol helped hide the alcohol scent on his breath, plus he sappily liked the commercial with the ice-skating penguin ("your mouth feels clean, your throat refreshed!")—and used the lighting of one as an excuse not to answer the Huey's question... *Wait, what was that?* Cronkite's right hand wasn't splayed out like his left. It was curled tightly into a fist. How had it taken Baker so long to notice?

25

He had one chance. "Damn!" He dropped his lit cigarette next to Cronkite's body and knelt down with his back to the HUAC agents. "These stupid, slippery Jew hands of mine!" he announced theatrically as he pried the dead man's rigor-mortised fingers apart—not without some difficulty—to reveal a small and crumpled piece of paper. He quickly swiped it up and stashed it in his pocket alongside a pack of matches. Baker stood to face Hartwell and Waldgrave again, placing the lit cigarette in his mouth as he did so. This time, he smiled back.

"Well, it was nice to meet you two gentlemen. My partner and I will be leaving now. Good luck with the investigation."

Connolly's jaw dropped comically.

"Smart kike," murmured Waldgrave, motioning for Philip to hand over his camera with one incredibly beefy hand.

Baker grabbed his partner by the jacket collar as Charles opened his medical bag and began to examine the bodies. They trekked back down the hall, past the film posters, and out into the morning sunshine.

Bletchley and Sheehan were smoking with the young officer Baker had seen when he arrived. Once he and Connolly neared the Delrays and a newly arrived black 1940 Cadillac V-16 (the HUAC vehicle of choice), Connolly rounded on Baker.

"What the fuck was that about, Morris? Just gonna be a lapdog for the Hueys, then? Gonna let them step all over you? That's our damn crime scene and you know it, for Christ's sake!"

Connolly quickly crossed himself. Baker puffed on his Kool and looked back toward the house, just to be sure they were truly alone.

"His name is Jesus, Connolly, and please don't take the Lord's name in vain," he said, reaching into his pocket and bringing out the crumpled piece of paper. "I needed to put on that act so I could get this out of Cronkite's hand and away from those two stooges."

Connolly stared at him, then laughed. "I knew something was going on. You'd never give up a case so easily. You're one shifty Yid, you know that? Next thing ya know, the Liberty Boys will come recruiting."

"Don't start on those stupid radio broadcasts again." Baker smoothed out the paper and puffed on his smoke. "Look at the top here. Perforated. Mr. Cronkite had another notebook with him after all. The question is: Who took it and why?"

Connolly whistled. "Well, I'll be damned," he said. "What does it say?"

Baker looked down at the page, and his stomach once again threatened to bring up last night's schnapps and beans. He didn't let the surprise and shock show on his face but placed his thumb over the very bottom of the paper and held it out. Brogan only saw the three words scribbled hastily in the center of the page.

"It says 'Beat the Devils,'" Baker said, his mouth going dry. Suddenly he no longer wanted his cigarette. He flicked it away in the direction of the other officers.

"Any idea what that could mean?" Connolly scratched his sideburns in thought.

"Not a clue," Baker said, "but we're gonna find out." He was already turning away and removing his thumb from the bottom of the page to reveal one more word in splotchy blue ink: "Baker."

CHAPTER 4

"...met with President McCarthy in Miami yesterday afternoon to voice his thanks for the aid the American Expeditionary Force provided to Cuba in crushing the Communist insurrection that attempted to seize control of the small island nation. In addition to thanking the United States, President Batista stated that he was eager for closer relations between the two countries. As a sign of good faith, he will allow the US military to place Jupiter missiles in Cuba for the protection of both freedom-loving countries. The public hangings of Fidel Castro, Che Guevara, and the rest of their band of miscreants will be televised live on NBC this evening at six o'clock local time. The event is sponsored by Colgate toothpaste. Remember: Three ways clean is Colgate Clean! Following his meeting with Batista, President McCarthy urged the American public to remain wary of the Red Menace. Please do not hesitate to report any Communist, subversive, or deviant activity to your local..."

"HU-*AC* office," finished Baker, putting a strong emphasis on the last two letters as if he had something vile stuck in his throat. There was nothing about Huston and Cronkite on the news yet, but the day was still young. He toggled the radio dial and was informed that traffic was still closed off near Griffith Park on Los Feliz Boulevard and West Observatory Road for "important road work." Since he didn't live near Griffith Park, which was also far away from the LAPD headquarters, he wouldn't have to worry about it. After a coin flip, Connolly agreed to stay back and loiter around the crime scene, see what else he could sniff out. Baker, meanwhile, was headed back to the office to write up a report.

Baker turned the radio dial again, a bit more aggressively than he should have, and it popped out of its socket and onto the carpeted floor. "Fuck!" he bellowed, the go-to American curse dissolving into the air. Now he was stuck with nothing but garbled static. Perfect.

It was ten o'clock and the sun, which had finally dissipated all of the smog, was now on full blast as he sped past tall palm trees and neon signs that lined Sunset Boulevard. The signs were nocturnal creatures. At this hour, they sat blind and asleep, waiting for the sun to dip low in the sky so that they could wake.

On almost every corner, yellow posters stained black with the trefoil symbol of radioactivity indicated the entrances to public, underground fallout shelters. A large and sun-faded billboard at the end of the street showed a smiling Bert the Turtle. His ridiculous safari hat and bow tie firmly in place as he reminded folks to "duck and cover" in case of a nuclear attack. Other phrases like OH MY! *DANGER!* and YOU MUST LEARN TO FIND SHELTER! were pasted across the billboard in screaming red text that was beginning to crack and peel from the intense California heat.

Beat the Devils.

What the devil did that mean? And why in the world was Baker's name written on that page? Somehow he didn't think that Cronkite, a man he'd never met in his life, was setting himself a reminder to pick up a fresh loaf of bread on his way home. Not that he'd ever make it home now.

Baker did feel a little guilty about not telling Connolly about his name showing up on the note, but something deep within his brain (the raw animalistic part that had helped him stay alive during the war) told him to keep his trap shut. It could be a coincidence. But Baker couldn't shake a growing sense of foreboding that made him shiver.

What person would want to kill an out-of-work movie director and a young CBS reporter whose career was nothing special?

Something just didn't add up. Baker was resolved to get to the bottom of it, no matter how many Hueys got in his way. That particular Huey, Hartwell, knew about Baker's past. That business with Wagner was proof enough. *Not surprising*, he thought. HUAC—while a much younger government organization than its contemporaries—made the FBI and CIA look like uninformed rubes, mainly because they had no shame in their unscrupulous methods guaranteed to extract skeletons from any closet. And if a person was squeaky clean... well, a skeleton or two would just have to be planted.

He turned right onto North Beaudry Avenue, took a left at West Temple Street, and made another right. The entire trip from Huston's house took an hour. Now Baker was looking at the sharp-angled headquarters of the LAPD at 150 North Los Angeles Street.

Completed just three years earlier, the Police Facilities Building was designed by out-of-towner Welton Becket, who was fast becoming the city's prodigal son of architecture. The 398,000-square-foot structure had cost a pretty penny (just over $6 million to be precise), but that paid for all the amenities like crime labs and recording devices hidden in the jail cells. The building was an officer's wet dream. It centralized LA's police facilities for the first time in the city's history.

Baker steered the Continental into the underground parking lot and pulled in amid the patrol cars, his own vehicle a lone speck of pale green in a stark sea of black and white. He took the radio dial and jammed it back into place. The static was immediately replaced with more incomprehensible nonsense: "Alarm...dismay...allies abroad... considerable comfort...enemies."

* * *

In the lobby, he passed a bank of pay phones and the Joseph L. Young mosaic, which depicted the state's famous attributes: palm trees, iconic buildings (such as Grauman's Chinese Theatre), rolling hills, and the rippling waves of the Pacific Ocean. Like Baker, Joseph L. Young was a Jew. Since the capture and execution of the Rosenbergs five years ago, people had carved hateful slurs into the mosaic so that KIKE and TRAITOR stood out like open wounds on the artwork that spanned the lobby's marble pillars.

The Rosenbergs' betrayal gave McCarthy all the gleeful pretense he needed for rounding up possible enemies of the country by the hundreds and deporting them deep behind the Iron Curtain, while harshly restricting the rights of those he had not. There was even talk of resurrecting the old Jap internment camps out in the desert. The president's position also emboldened groups across the country to destroy Jewish businesses, synagogues, and community centers with impunity. It had gotten so bad that American Jews no longer affixed mezuzahs to the doorposts of their homes.

More often than not, Baker wondered if it was still worth continuing to fight the good fight. This town, like so much of the country, was sinking further into the bubbling morass of hatred and iniquity with each passing day. Soon Los Angeles would not be able to pick itself up out of the muck. Baker found himself rubbing his left forearm and the blue-ink tattoo etched upon the flesh there.

Of course, not everyone bought into the government's carefully concocted anti-Communist propaganda. Every so often, little bits and pieces of resistance slipped through the cracks of media censorship. The Liberty Boys broadcasts were very popular these days. Every so often, mysterious and barely audible announcements telling the nation to rise up against McCarthy would hijack the radio waves. Connolly and many others liked to believe in an underground organization dedicated to fighting the administration, but Baker actually agreed with the government on this one. The Liberty Boys broadcasts were most likely coming from some crackpot ham radio enthusiast in his basement.

* * *

As per usual, the building's sprawling office space was a hive of activity. Phones rang nonstop, officers jotted down notes or referenced sepia-tinged albums of wanted fugitives, and pretty young secretaries clacked away on their Smith Corona Silent Portables, which, despite their name, were not very quiet. Ignoring the usual dirty glares from his colleagues, Baker grabbed himself a cup of coffee. As the caffeine coursed through his body, he began to feel more awake, more like himself. The schnapps hangover would soon be gone...until he decided to take another dive into the bottle.

He passed by the paunchy, toad-like portrait of President McCarthy affixed to the center wall and reached his desk, whose metal top was covered with unfinished reports, memos, and the latest quarterly memo on the number of Communists in the State Department. The government, it said, "is happy to report" that the number was down from fifty to twenty-five. The figure was constantly fluctuating to scare and/or pacify the American public. With the Fourth of July coming up, Baker guessed the lowering of the number was meant to emphasize democratic pride and increase spending for the national holiday. Baker's desk stood out from those of his fellow officers because it featured no pictures of friends or family.

Sitting down, he spied a short note on top of the clutter, which was written in the slanted handwriting of his and Connolly's new secretary, Gladys: "Miss Short came by to see you. Asked you call her immediately.—G."

"Oy vey," groaned Baker, running a hand through his dark-brown curls. He wadded up the note in his palm and threw it into the wastebasket before finding a blank report form. Placing it in his Lettera 22, he began to type:

HOMICIDE INVESTIGATION REPORT

July 1, 1958
Case no. 766533
Prepared by Detective Morris E. Baker

This morning, Detective Connolly and I responded to a call in Echo Park, which led us to the bodies of two deceased men at the address of 984 Altivo Way. Both victims were killed with two quick gunshots to the chest at point-blank range, although

Charles Ward should be able to provide a more extensive answer in his autopsy report (more on that below). Detective Connolly conducted a preliminary dusting of the scene but discovered no apparent fingerprints.

Upon further inspection, the men were identified as former film director John Huston and CBS journalist Walter Cronkite. The house in which they were discovered belonged to the former. The LAPD was informed that a crime had taken place by a concerned neighbor, who reported gunshots, but the caller did not disclose their name, number, or address. Why these men were together, especially with Cronkite being a New York–based reporter, is unknown at this time.

Inspectors from the local HUAC office by the names of Hartwell and Waldgrave arrived shortly after myself to take control of the investigation and bring it under federal jurisdiction. Detective Connolly and I left the scene in their able hands, while Philip Lathrop handed over his photographs of the bodies. Charles Ward will turn in his autopsy report directly to the HUAC inspectors now in charge of the investigation.

There. That should satisfy any Huey eyes that were almost certainly planted in the station. Baker settled back in his chair and started pulling out his pack of Kools when a sharp voice made him jump. "Baker!"

It was Dashiell Hanscom, a vice detective who harbored a particularly nasty hatred toward the Semitic crowd. His nose was always bright red, not from the blistering LA sun, but from a terrible addiction to cocaine. He sniffed and leered at Baker. "Parker"—*sniff!*—"wants to see you in his office straightaway"—*sniff!*

"Did he finally decide to give me that raise I've been begging for?" asked Baker, smiling innocently.

"Yeah, you'd like that, you moneygrubbing"—*sniff!*—"son of a..." mumbled Hanscom, not catching on to Baker's sarcasm. Baker swiped his newly finished report from the typewriter, waved it around to dry the ink, got up, and strolled over to the desk of Gladys Hargrove.

"Gut morgn, Gladys," he beamed, placing his report on her desk. "Could you please file that away for me?"

"Right away, Detective Baker," she replied with a giggle. She always seemed tickled by Yiddish.

Gladys was a pretty, twenty-something member of the LAPD typing pool with a pale complexion and a blond bouffant haircut. She'd been with the department for the last six months and was also one of the few people in the office who treated Baker like a human being. Oftentimes she'd get coffee for him in the mornings or, if he was working late, stay behind to keep him company as he typed up reports. These were little kindnesses that had been absent from his life for quite some time. He still struggled to understand why Gladys was so different from the rest. Today she wore a white blouse patterned with daisies tucked into a brown velvet skirt that stopped just above her knees. The outfit accentuated her hourglass body and perfectly rounded breasts and— not for the first time—Baker imagined her out of those clothes and in his ruffled bed.

"You got my note about Miss Short? She was quite insistent you call her right away," said Gladys, bringing him back to reality.

The image of Liz swam to the forefront of Baker's mind. His headache teased a thrilling comeback. The caffeine high from the coffee was already wearing off and his bowels were starting to rumble. He really needed some schnapps.

"Yes, I did. Thank you, Gladys. Um, Detective Connolly said he called in earlier about getting in touch with the professional and personal contacts for a Walter Cronkite. Did you get a chance to do that?"

"I did," Gladys answered a bit glumly. She pulled a piece of paper from the top of her desk and began reading. "I spoke with Mr. Cronkite's wife, Mary Elizabeth. She was quite upset, poor dear. She's all right with the city detaining the body until arrangements can be made for a funeral. I also spoke with a Mr. James Aubrey of CBS, who was quite shocked by the news. He said Cronkite was away for a week or so on family leave. He couldn't imagine what he was doing all the way out here without his wife and daughters, or why anyone would want to kill him."

"What about John Huston? Did you speak to his next of kin?"

"I didn't get the chance. The Hueys took over just as I was finishing up my call with Aubrey. They said it was no longer necessary to speak with anybody related to the case."

"Do me a favor, call all of Cronkite's people back and give them my home and desk numbers and tell them to get in touch if they like. Do the same with Huston's camp if you can reach them."

"Not a problem, Detective."

"Thanks, Gladys. Oh, and one more thing." He lowered his voice. "Please ask Cronkite's people if he ever mentioned the name Baker."

Gladys gave him a questioning look but didn't press the matter. He left her typing and headed for the office of William H. Parker, Chief of Police.

CHAPTER 5

Willliam H. Parker had become the LAPD's chief of police eight years earlier and spent his tenure trying to sweep the streets clean of murder, corruption, drugs, and prostitution. Although all of them had a nasty habit of sticking around, especially among his own underlings, Parker liked to believe in the best of every man. Not even the likes of coke-snorting Dashiell Hanscom was exempt from Parker's benefit of the doubt. Good old Dash was supposed to be attending rehabilitation sessions on Parker's dime. The chief ran a tight ship that held officers accountable for their actions. The ones he found out about, anyway.

What Baker really liked about his boss was the fact that the chief didn't give a shit about catching Communists. On several occasions, not all of them private, Baker heard Parker decry: "This nonsense with the Russians. We've got enough on our plates without having to hunt down some sad little pamphlet maker squatting in a condemned tenement. Let the termites take care of him!"

It was a wonder the chief hadn't been picked up by the Hueys for such talk. But Baker knew better. William H. Parker was good at his job and even better at keeping some semblance of normalcy in a fractured city that was a melting pot of ethnicity and celebrity. The arrests and intimidation on the part of HUAC could only do so much. Parker was the man McCarthy could count on to keep Los Angeles from erupting into outright revolution.

While he could be gruff at times, the chief was the kind of honorable man who would almost certainly have statues and buildings posthumously named in his honor. He was the latest in a long line of honorable American stock. His grandfather, for instance, had served in the American Civil War.

Baker knocked on Parker's office door and heard his boss's drawling voice say, "Yeah? Come in."

He opened the door and walked inside the cozy space just as the chief's personal driver, Officer Daryl Gates, was on his way out with a large stack of papers cradled in his arms. "Remember, sir," Gates said to Parker over his shoulder. "You have a tee-off time with Governor Brown at two. Last time you forgot, and the governor wasn't all too chipper about it."

"Yes, yes. Very good, Daryl," replied Parker. He sat behind a grand wooden desk, its spotless organization a reflection of the way he ran the police force. "Ah, Baker," he said upon seeing him. "Thank you for coming. Have a seat."

He gestured to a chair upholstered in a drab maroon fabric and Baker sat down, taking a look around the office. Baker had been in here so many times, perhaps it was time the chief started charging him rent. Inwardly smiling, he recounted all the times he and Connolly were reprimanded for their unconventional police work. Parker screamed himself hoarse after the duo apprehended Merl Mencken (dubbed "the California Castrator") in Encinitas without warning the San Diego precinct beforehand.

Baker noted the black-and-white photos of Chief Parker in his army uniform, receiving a slew of medals: the Purple Heart, the Croix de Guerre, and the Order of the Star of Italian Solidarity. There were also snapshots of the chief shaking hands with Mayors Bowron and Poulson. Sitting squarely behind the chief were the framed portraits of President McCarthy (wide forehead, receding hairline, double chins, the whole nine yards) and Vice President Richard Nixon (a California native whose slightly crooked nose and sweaty sheen were ever-present, even in a photograph).

Daryl Gates closed the door and Parker shook his head like an annoyed water buffalo covered in gnats. "Good kid, that Daryl. Good driver, too, but a little high-strung. Still, he could have my job someday with that work ethic of his."

Baker shifted in the chair, which squeaked and groaned under his weight.

"Tell me," began Parker. "How long have you been on the force?" That was Parker, always switching from one subject to the next without warning. It was the mark of a good policeman, though. He knew how to catch people off guard, make them slip on their own tongues.

"Eight years, sir," Baker responded. "Joined the LAPD around the same time you became chief."

Parker leaned back and steepled his fingers. "Quite right. Quite right. I seem to remember taking a chance on a promising young Jewish boy who wanted to fight crime and do some good in the world. That sound about right to you?"

"Yes, sir, but—"

"Giving a chance to a Jew, when many consider your kind to be no-good subversives, when you've acted rashly more than once on the job. I don't mind telling you, Baker, that you've been a right pain in my ass. Many people in this town—hell, this country—would like to see you strung up on a tree branch, make no mistake about it. But do you know why I took you on? Why I let a so-called foreigner join my police force? Why I stand up for you when the Hueys are on my ass every few months to give you the boot?"

"Because you have a quota to fill?" asked Baker sarcastically.

Parker chuckled.

"Not quite, Baker. Not quite. I let you join because I saw a broken man, a man who had lived a thousand lifetimes before he showed up on my doorstep with the hope of being a cop. I fought in that war like any good American worth his salt did. I fought on the beaches of Normandy and took a bullet from the damn Krauts, but you...well, you took much more from them, Baker, didn't you? I could see from the minute you applied to the academy that you had spent too much time squashed under the fascist jackboot. And I didn't fight in that war and take metal from those goose-stepping bastards to turn away a lost and tortured soul. I believed in you, just as firmly as I believe Bert the Turtle's duck-and-cover method is full of maggot-squirming horseshit. Taking you on, I told myself, was making it all worthwhile for the world we'd rebuild from the ashes of war."

Baker was at a loss for words. "Sir, that is quite a touching sentiment, but I don't underst—"

"The fact that you are an excellent detective is just the icing on the cake."

"Sir, what are you say—?"

"I'm saying," said Parker so forcefully that his glasses slipped an inch down his nose, "that I don't want you pursuing this double homicide case any further. And that goes for your partner, too."

Baker was astonished at how quickly word had traveled. "How did you know about the case, sir?"

"How do you think? The Hueys love shoving their jurisdiction so far up my ass, it's coming out my ears! I got a call thirty minutes ago from a prick named Lonergan that they were taking over the investigation. Smug sons of bitches." Parker let out a deep sigh. "Nevertheless, I know your stubborn track record, Baker, and it'll do no good to fuck up a government investigation. It'll just bring you a lot of pain and the Lord knows you don't need any more of that. You may fancy yourself one of them, what are they called? Freedom Lads?"

"Liberty Boys, sir, but—"

"It doesn't suit you, mark my words," Parker interjected as if he hadn't heard. "I'm just looking out for you, Baker. Do I make myself absolutely clear?"

Sticking his nose where it didn't belong, minding his own business. Baker knew these survival instincts all too well.

"Crystal, sir," he said, wondering whether he should bring up the fact that his name appeared in a note left behind by a dead man. But that same, indescribable instinct kicked in again. He kept silent.

"Good," grunted Parker. "Now get out of my office. I'm giving you the rest of the day off. Hell, take the rest of the week, if you like. Relax and forget you ever saw that crime scene. Do that, and I guarantee you'll live a long and happy life. As for me, I've got eighteen holes of golf waiting."

Baker got up and walked out of the office.

"Take care, Chief, and happy Fourth of July," he said.

"You too, Baker, and don't forget what we talked about."

"Yes, sir," responded Baker. But *forget* wasn't really part of his vocabulary, and never would be.

CHAPTER 6

Liz was waiting for him in the parking lot, leaning against the Continental, her arms tightly folded against her chest. Elizabeth Short wasn't gorgeous in the traditional sense. Her face had strange curves, her nose was a little bulbous, and her lower teeth were a little crooked. But her full black hair and ruby lips could make her attractive in the right situation. As always, a string of pearls was strung around her neck and dipping into a canyon of sizable cleavage.

"Morris, dear," she cooed in her semi-whiny drone. "You barely said goodbye to me this morning. Did Gladys let you know I came to see you?"

"She did. I was going to call you as soon as I got home," said Baker, quickly putting his arms around her in a cursory hug and giving her a peck on the cheek.

"You sure you haven't been avoiding me?"

"Not at all," Baker sputtered. "I've just been busy with work, is all."

Liz held up the crumpled note Gladys had left on his desk, the very one he had thrown into the waste bin. Her green eyes were blazing with triumph.

Baker looked Liz full in the face, embarrassed at being caught in the lie.

"Okay, I forgot, nu? Sue me."

That got them both laughing, and Baker kissed her again, this time on the mouth. When they broke apart, Liz was smiling, all trace of annoyance vanished.

"I've just been thinking about that drive we took up to San Francisco last weekend," she said. "I thought we could maybe do something similar for the holiday this weekend?"

"Uh...sure," said Baker. He immediately corrected course when Liz showed signs of firing back up for an argument. "Yes! Absolutely! In fact, Parker gave me the rest of the week off. Why don't I come over tonight?"

Liz's face lit up. She and Baker had been going—well, it couldn't be called "steady," but they'd dated pretty regularly for almost ten years now. He met her in 1947, not long after he first arrived in Los Angeles. At the time, he was working as a newspaper delivery boy while he waited to hear back from the LAPD about being accepted into the academy. On his way home through Leimert Park, Baker spotted Liz strolling along and immediately had to know her name.

He convinced her to get dinner with him, and their relationship took off from there, but Baker's affection for the woman had considerably dwindled across the intervening years. He still couldn't fully explain why he kept coming back to Liz. The thought of ending things here and now occurred to him, but she was talking again.

"Oh, what a wonderful idea!" Liz squealed, delivering a kiss to Baker's cheek. "You can help me run lines again!"

Oy vey zmir, anything but that. Liz harbored dreams of becoming an actress, but there was only one drawback: The woman had no talent. If Baker was given a nickel for every time she'd asked him to run lines in her shitty apartment behind the Florentine Gardens nightclub, he might have been able to retire to a beachfront property in Malibu.

"Great," he heard himself say, his mind already reeling back to the Huston-Cronkite case. "Can't wait."

"Perfect," Liz said. "Shall we say nine thirty?" Without waiting to hear if that time worked for him, she turned to leave, but pivoted back on her heel almost at once. "There is one more thing, Morris."

"Yeah?"

"Well, we've been together for quite a while now, and . . . it's just you haven't told me you loved me yet. I was just wondering . . . do you not love me because I'm a shiksa?"

The question wasn't asked in anger. Liz sounded more like a child asking why she couldn't stay up late and watch *Father Knows Best*. Baker was startled by the inquiry. Being romantically involved with another Jew was something he hadn't thought about since before the war. He wasn't a practicing Jew, or even a proud one, so why should this shock him so greatly? No sensible answer (or even a simple lie) presented itself.

When he did not reply, Liz looked down, clearly crestfallen. "It's okay," she said, "we can discuss it some other time. See you later, Morris." With that, she walked away and into the gloomy depths of the underground garage.

Baker shook his head and lit up a smoke. A shroud of guilt descended on him. Had he really never told Liz he loved her in the last decade? He hadn't even noticed. Was he simply incapable of that emotion? Was he just too broken, or did his inability to say the words *I love you, Liz*, indicate that he didn't truly feel that way about her?

Despite having closed more cases than any other homicide cop in his department, Baker couldn't formulate a proper conclusion to this one. He climbed into his car, started the ignition, and heard Frankie Lymon declare over the radio that he wasn't a juvenile delinquent. In a daze, Baker drove out of the chilly parking lot and into the summer sun.

CHAPTER 7

He was naked and out of breath. Running circles in the frigid winter air. His lungs burned and saliva congealed in the back of his throat like swamp water. All he could do was run. One more lap over the ground of frozen mud and he could rest, could stay alive, could prove that he was healthy enough to be spared from the gas chambers.

"Ritt der Walküren" was blaring over the speakers, mocking him. It was a song for the mighty, they said, but he was gaunt and weak. So weak. And yet, he was still running, still breathing... still living...

* * *

Baker was slumped over the Continental's steering wheel. A small spider's thread of drool dangled from his lip, slowly dripping into the pool accumulating on his trouser leg. He could not remember how he had gotten this way, or even where he was. Slowly, he looked up and reality came crashing back as a cloud of acrid black smoke billowed from the hood of his car. Pain shot through his neck and forehead.

46

There was a smear of blood on the steering wheel. A tender touch told him there was a thin gash on his scalp.

He must have crashed the car. Luckily, nothing seemed to be broken. He took a medicinal swig of the schnapps he'd picked up on the way home. The bottle was almost full, so the crash could not have been caused by alcohol. Besides, Baker had long since mastered the ability to function while hitting the bottle.

It was the darkness—at least that was his term for it. Everything would go black and he'd wake up, completely unaware of what had happened, as if only a split second had passed. Most of the time, he got lucky and it only happened while he was in the solitude and safety of his apartment. But sporadically, he'd be in situations like this and end up hurting himself. He'd once nearly bit his tongue clean off during an episode and had to endure two weeks of Connolly's incessant teasing over his temporary speech impediment. By some miracle, it never occurred on the job—not once in eight years. More important, his blackouts had never hurt anyone else.

He'd lived with the issue since the end of the war. He knew that if he went to a doctor with it, he'd probably be removed from the force. It was bad enough that he was a Jewish police officer; he couldn't imagine what the Hueys would say if they found out he could lose complete control of his faculties without warning. And if he couldn't help people as a cop, what was the point of persevering in this topsy-turvy world?

Holding one hand to the gash on his forehead and wincing, Baker pushed open the door and spilled onto the pavement. One look around—which caused pain to shoot through his neck again—revealed he was on North Broadway in the middle of Chinatown. A magnificent red pagoda stood in the distance, a sentinel from another land. A Communist land.

The Continental's momentum had been stopped by a metal pole, but the engine continued to work overtime, not understanding that the rest of the vehicle was at a standstill. Thick clouds of black smoke continued to furl out from the under the hood, but Baker wasn't too worried. The car had done that before, even on its best days.

The soothing bars of "A Thousand Miles Away" by the Heartbeats crawled out of the radio as if nothing was wrong. It played for a few moments before it was sharply cut off by an incoming Liberty Boys broadcast: "We must not confuse dissent with disloyalty," said a deep and ominous voice. "We must remember always that accusation is not proof, and conviction depends on evidence and due process of law. We will not walk in fear of one another. We will not be driven by fear into an age of unreason..."

"You okay, mister?" A group of Chinese youths were warily approaching Baker. Cars were slowing down to assess the damage, their drivers hoping to catch a sight of gore, but no one completely stopped or got out to offer help. In this town, no one was willing to do you any favors unless there was something in it for them. It's how the whole country was these days. That said, children could still be counted on to be kind before they became jaded like their parents.

"Yes, I believe so," said Baker, wiping more blood from his head with an oily handkerchief he pulled out of the glove compartment. The boys wore shabby plaid sport coats with high-waisted trousers, while the girls were in flowery sundresses that looked secondhand. There were five kids in all, and they couldn't have been older than nine or ten.

"Mogwai wreck your car, mister?" piped up one of the kids, a flat tweed cap perched on his small head at a slanted angle.

"Mog-what?" Baker asked, still dabbing at his aching and bleeding head. The damn head wounds always bled the worst. Out of the corner of his trained detective's eye, he noticed a hunched figure leaning against the side of a laundry across the street, their face obscured by the shadow of a large-brimmed fedora. There was no mistaking it— they were watching him. Or they could have just stopped to watch the wreck without getting too close. McCarthy's damn paranoia seemed to be rubbing off on him.

"Mogwai. Uh, demon," the kid said. "You know, a devil? They like to wreck machines."

Baker gave a wan smile. He reached into his jacket for a smoke and felt his fingers brush against the paper containing Cronkite's last words in his pocket. He threw the bloodied handkerchief back into the car and lit up a Kool.

"Maybe, kid. It just may be."

* * *

The car had suffered a nasty dent and the paint was scratched away in some places around the front bumper, but it was still able to carry Baker home in one piece.

His apartment building was situated on North Hill Street in the heart of Old Chinatown. It was a quiet street just off the main drag of North Broadway, which ran the length of the area. Not many Coolie-haters ventured this far in to abuse the people they despised so much. Even so, Baker knew that the collection of shops and apartments had armed guards standing just out of sight in case any McCarthyites got a little too tanked and decided to have some fun.

Baker waited for a high-speed railcar to hum by before he pulled into the lot designated for residents. The small white building in which he lived was covered in the blackened residue of soot and smog. The stucco facade sported a collection of large Mandarin characters: 天堂公寓 or, as Baker learned after three years of living here, PARADISE APARTMENTS.

"Paradise" was the greatest overstatement anyone could make about the place. The slightly bent palm trees arching over the entranceway gave those who entered false hope that they were about to enter a nice—perhaps even glamorous—place to live. For the cockroaches, rats, and mold, it was a veritable oasis. For the humans who inhabited it, however, there were not many praises to be sung. Nevertheless, Baker didn't complain. He'd had worse lodgings before. Much worse.

After parking, he walked across the pockmarked pavement and through the front glass doors marked with golden zodiac signs. The sharp smell of lemongrass and sweet scent of stewed plums immediately hit his nose. Since moving here, Baker had become a fan of cuisines from the Orient and the waft of aromatic air made his mouth water on cue, like that of a Pavlovian dog. Not that Baker had ever once been invited to dinner by one his neighbors. He usually frequented the local restaurants. He was probably the only white person—let alone Jew—in this entire building, and probably the entire neighborhood.

Crossing the stained maroon carpet of the lobby (which was torn up in places, revealing the cold hard concrete underneath), he made it to the cracked marble staircase to the second floor. The elevator hadn't worked in years and besides, the enclosed, caged space made him anxious. His landlord, Mr. Eddie Huang, could be heard arguing with his wife, Marlena, in rapid Mandarin inside their apartment, which meant all was right with the world except for...

Apartment 2D, the former residence of the Liu family. As Baker neared it, a bone-chilling draft seemed to sweep up from under the door of the empty unit like a disturbed apparition and, for the third time that day, the darkness began closing in on him.

Traitor, hissed the Lius from the back of Baker's mind. *Where were you when they came? You did not speak up, you coward...*

Baker shook his head from side to side, not in an effort to clear it, but to make a gesture that said there was nothing he could have done. Fighting back nausea and the threat of passing out, he ran down the hall, unlocked the door to his own apartment (the 2A upon its wooden surface had fractured long ago), and escaped to the safety of the mess within.

Stained and wrinkled shirts littered the floor along with the discarded cellophane from cigarette packs, empty schnapps bottles, and Hershey's chocolate bar wrappers. The apartment was not extravagant by any means. His bed was in close proximity to the grimy kitchen, and the tiny bathroom sat right next to the squat icebox. At least the Huangs weren't too cheap to pay for indoor plumbing and Admiral kitchen appliances. He walked over to the deep sink and cleaned the gash on his forehead. Most of the bleeding had stopped by now.

On the counter was his meal of the night before: a half-eaten turkey sandwich, a baked potato, and a can of pinto beans. The pat of butter on the potato had melted from the heat, and a thin film sat over the beans. The place was fully alight with afternoon sunshine and mercifully devoid of barbed-wire shadows. Baker hoisted the blinds all the way up and took in the window's rather bleak view of the abandoned seafood restaurant across the street. With no tenant to maintain the building's well-being, its outer walls were covered in blasphemous graffiti that condemned the president: *Murderous McCarthy! Resist! Long Live the Liberty Boys!* These messages came courtesy of the neighborhood youth, though their parents would tell them that such actions only brought more violence to Chinatown if any McCarthy supporters or Hueys happened to see the slander.

Baker pulled off his gun holster with a sigh of relief. The snub-nosed revolver had been digging into his back ever since he'd hastily left that morning. He placed the gun back onto the pile of West German letters he was ignoring. Trudging through the floor's detritus, Baker plopped onto the bed, which belched out a small flurry of duck feathers into the air. Mixed with the accumulated dust and crumbling plaster of the place, the feathers helped create a mesmerizing beam of debris.

Staring up at the cracked ceiling, his hands behind his head, Baker tried to unscramble all that had happened since Connolly summoned him to Echo Park. A former big-time director turns up dead with a reporter for one of the biggest news networks in the country. And not long after the cops show up on the scene, Hueys take over and even the headstrong Parker plays along. And then there was the most head-scratching piece of the puzzle: Cronkite's note. Was the reporter referring to him when he scribbled "Baker" at the bottom of the torn page—and if so, why? It made no more sense to him than the words "Beat the Devils."

It would be maddening if Baker tried to put everything together without the department and all its resources. There was also the fact that meddling any deeper on his own would probably get him fired, killed, or worse: chucked in a HUAC interrogation room where death was the least of a guy's worries. He flipped onto his stomach, rolled off the bed, walked over to the small Zenith television sitting on the kitchen counter, and flicked it on. Its alien-looking antenna needed to be jiggled for a moment before a black-and-white picture of thatched huts came into focus. Harried villagers in gas masks and men in radiation suits ran on- and off-screen as the cheery, transatlantic voice of Walter Winchell spoke over the clearing static:

"Teams from the Nuclear Negation Administration continue to run exercise drills with Korean citizens in the zone near the thirty-eighth parallel. Meanwhile, the head of America's anti-Communist armed forces in Asia, General Douglas MacArthur, assured the South Korean government that the next attempted invasion from the North would constitute an act of war and would allow the United States to exercise the nuclear option ..."

Winchell was just another one of McCarthy's media puppets. Ever since Murrow had been kicked off the air and disgraced from journalism (thanks, in part, to *Red Channels*), his toadies had taken it over like a swarm of locusts and turned it into a barren wasteland of repetitive anti-leftist rhetoric.

Baker turned the television knob. Some no-name reporter for the local station was droning on in a monotone voice, which he probably thought passed for seriousness.

"The bodies of former film director John Huston and up-and-coming CBS reporter Walter Cronkite were discovered dead in the former's home this morning."

Attention piqued and heart racing, Baker turned up the volume.

"According to an official government statement, the two men, who were also romantically involved, had ties to a left-leaning writers' guild from pre-regulated Hollywood. Local HUAC officials have confirmed that Huston and Cronkite had been under federal surveillance for some time in the hope that they would be eventually placed under protective custody, away from 'unsavory parties' who might wish to do them harm. Sadly, those unsavory parties reached the two men before the brave HUAC inspectors could. The double homicide has been ruled a crime of passion..."

Of course, one of the government's favorite ploys: passing off the death of political dissidents as a homoerotic affair gone wrong, with some Communist ties thrown in for good measure. The Bolshies were "a godless people," according to the president. "If they had their way, there'd be men marrying men, women marrying women, children marrying dogs. Complete chaos!" McCarthy had declared during a recent speech in Philadelphia.

Still, the stratagem of branding Huston and Cronkite as a pair of Commie-loving lavender lads was effective. It painted the Hueys as sympathetic for wanting to place them under protective custody. It made no sense, considering that the entire administration encouraged violence against subversives and homosexuals—both real and imagined. Baker considered whether HUAC was behind the murders, but quickly shot down the theory. Something like this wasn't their style. They usually liked to do all the dirty work at their headquarters, where no neighbors could report screams or gunshots to the police.

He realized that it wasn't the *how* or the *who* that bothered him, but the *why*. He'd never heard of Huston until this morning, so the man couldn't have been particularly outspoken about the administration. Then there was Cronkite, an honest and dependable journalist. Had his ambition to make a name for himself put him onto the trail of a deadly story?

Another turn of the television's knob yielded a speech McCarthy made at the recently built Lambeau Field right after America had sent a man to the moon earlier in the year. This was followed by the usual educational "Man in Space" program produced by the Walt Disney Company. A stern-faced man with neatly parted hair and a thick German accent explained the efforts being made to further space travel as he pointed to the diagram of a rocket ship:

"The training methods for future spaceflight and the special equipment needed for survival are much like those of present high-altitude flying..." said the scientist, whose syllable-extending English was a forced struggle against his native tongue.

Baker was never much one for the sciences. One more knob twist.

A rerun of *I Love Lucy* was playing on CBS, the one where Lucy and Ethel accidentally board a plane for the Soviet Union and thwart a Russian plot to invade the United States. The friends stumble back into Lucy's home in the very same drab Communist uniform depicted on Baker's refrigerator calendar. Ricky takes one look at the hammer and sickle patches on their shoulders and raises his eyebrows.

"Lucy, you got some 'splainin' to do!" he shouts.

"I sure do, comrade," replies Lucy, looking into the camera as it closes in on the exasperated expression screwed onto her face.

Cue audience laughter.

Baker had seen the episode half a dozen times. There were no new episodes since Desi had been deported to Cuba. He turned off the television and the picture was compressed into a small band of white light before disappearing completely. He returned to bed and flicked through Cronkite's tiny notebook of sign-off phrases and sipped schnapps for a while before nodding off.

* * *

Shadows were lengthening in the apartment when there was a sharp knock on the door. Baker was lying facedown and picked his head up from an expanding pile of schnapps-infused drool on the stained sheets. He was drunk and disoriented from dreams about blazing fires and shovels. But when the knock came again, he shot up like a bullet. Sharp raps on the door had never meant anything good back in the small shtetl where he was born and raised. It also didn't mean anything good in McCarthy's America.

Baker silently crept to the door and picked up his revolver off the end table. A few coins of loose change skittered to the floor.

"Who's there?" he said in a croaky voice.

"Courier service," came the chipper reply from the other side of the door. "I have a message to deliver to a...Morris Ephraim Baker of Paradise Apartments, Chinatown. Apartment two-A, an individual of Judaic Origins."

Baker winced at the last few words, but slowly undid the chain and bolt and pulled the door open. A young man, no older than twenty, was waiting just outside his apartment. His baby face was red from the heat.

"What's this all about?" asked Baker.

"I'm not sure, sir," said the kid. "I was just told to deliver a letter to this apartment, to Morris E. Baker. Is that you?"

"Yeah, that's me."

The kid nodded happily before rifling in the courier satchel draped over his shoulder and pulling out a creased manila envelope. He handed it to Baker.

"There you are, sir."

"Who do you work for, kid?"

"Shelton Courier Service, sir. People leave letters, documents, tele-grams with us, you see. We can deliver them right away or delay them."

"Delay them?" Baker said, eyebrows raised.

"Yes, sir. If someone wants a letter, document, or object delivered at a later date, say, after they pass on, we can do that. That envelope," he explained, pointing to the one in Baker's hand, "has been in our possession for a little over two years with explicit instructions to deliver it to you upon the death of the client who wanted it sent."

"I see," said Baker, not totally understanding who would want to send him something after they'd kicked the bucket. He had no family and no real friends to speak of, unless you counted Brogan, Liz, and Hollis Li—the genial proprietor of a local Chinese eatery. He rummaged in his pocket and pulled out a quarter, which he held out to the young man.

"Oh no, sir. I couldn't," said the boy. "They pay me quite well as it is. It's my uncle's business, you see. He treats me right."

"If you're sure, kid," replied Baker, putting the coin back in his pocket. "What's your name?"

"Oliver Shelton, sir."

"Well, Oliver, keep up the good work."

Oliver beamed. "Thank you, sir. I'll try! Oh, and sorry about the 'Judaic Origins' thing. It's a federal mandate."

"Think nothing of it," said Baker. Oliver headed off down the hall toward the still-shouting Huangs.

Back in the solitude of his apartment, Baker took a generous swig of schnapps before ripping open the envelope. Inside was a sheet of cream-colored paper, neatly folded into thirds. In large black typeface it read:

Dear Mr. Baker,

I regret to inform you of the passing of Professor Arthur X. Scholz, MD, PhD. The reading of his last will and testament shall be conducted the morning after the delivery of this note at Los Angeles City Hall at nine o'clock sharp. Please check with reception for specific room details upon your arrival. *Do not be late!*

Sincerely,
Laremy Dinsmore Fenwick, Esquire

Baker turned over the paper. Nothing else was written on it. A quick look inside the envelope didn't reveal anything else, either, but the meaning of the paper was quite clear. Some professor had left Baker something in his will. He couldn't recall ever meeting an Arthur Scholz, and yet, Scholz had thought of him before his death. A little over two years before the fact. The phone rang just then, making Baker jump again, and the paper he was holding swayed gently to the floor like a feather.

"This is Baker."

"Baker!" It was the ferrety voice of Los Angeles Medical Examiner Charles Ward. "Glad I caught you at home. I've just finished taking a look at the stiffs you and Connolly were investigating this morning and—well...I'd rather not say over the phone."

Baker smiled. Tapping phones was a specialty of the Hueys, but it didn't make much difference now. Charles had just said he didn't want to talk over the phone, which meant immediate suspicion for anyone listening in on their call. Not the smartest move, but giving up use of the phone entirely out of paranoia meant the Hueys had won.

"I'm on my way," said Baker, slamming the phone back in its cradle and swiping up his jacket in one fluid motion.

Fuck the Hueys. Never, in his entire policing career, had Morris Baker given up on a case. Nothing felt right around this murder, especially now that Charles—one of the jumpiest people he knew—wanted to talk about it. He was so preoccupied with his thoughts that he didn't even glance at Apartment 2D as he made his way down the hall.

CHAPTER 8

The tiles in the surgically clean morgue beneath City Hall reflected the dizzying fluorescent lights that shone down on the frigid room of the dead. The long bulbs popped and sputtered as if they, too, were about to pass on. This was the lair of Charles Fitzpatrick Ward, a portly man who wore a pencil mustache in the style of Clark Gable. Unlike Gable, however, Charles gave quite a damn about a lot of things. Like grime, for instance. He was an easily frightened individual who detested being referred to as "Charlie," and Baker often wondered why he had chosen such a macabre profession.

Some people in the department liked to joke that if Charles saw his shadow in February, there'd be six more weeks of winter. Morris Baker was not among this group. He liked Charles because the man was kind and honest. The only decoration in the examiner's sterile workspace was a bouquet of freshly picked white roses sitting in a vase of blue glass.

"Well, Charles? What have you got for me?" Baker asked, pacing back and forth across the waxed floor, which caused his shoes to slip and squeak. Damn, it was cold in here. He lit a Kool to warm up and remembered that if he didn't cut back on the smokes, his body would be lying down here someday soon.

Charles was standing on the far side of the room by two metal slabs covered in white sheets. They were bathed in the warm orange glow of an extendable lamp affixed to the wall. Big toes, white as chalk, were sticking out from under the sheets with identification tags tied to them. The medical examiner nervously rubbed together his hands, encased in thick black rubber gloves, and adjusted the rubber apron covering his sizable lower half.

"Over here, Morris," he said, walking to a thermostat dial and cranking it all the way up. A steady blast of frigid air blossomed into the room, drowning out the deadly stillness of the morgue. Charles then walked over to the transistor radio that kept him company during the lonely hours of work and turned it on to the highest volume, so that Chet Huntley and David Brinkley were practically shouting the details surrounding the public execution of Fidel Castro and his band of Cuban rebels in gruesome detail.

The Hueys had bugs in almost every municipal building in the city. Every civil servant in Los Angeles eventually caught on to the ruse, holding sensitive conversations in hushed tones or else obscuring them with running water, clacking typewriters, or industrial blast chillers meant to keep dead bodies from decomposing. Baker, who was pacing just to keep his blood from freezing over, walked over to stand beside Charles. The medical examiner began to whip the sheets off the naked bodies of John Huston and Walter Cronkite, gently folding the canvas against the lower half of their lifeless abdomens.

The rest of Huston's body was just as wrinkled as his face and dotted with large, hair-sprouting liver spots. Cronkite's body looked much younger and fitter with no real distinguishable features other than being extremely pale and covered in patches of brown hair. Long V-shaped seams stood out on the dead men's chests where Charles had cut them open for autopsies. The eyes of both men were closed, but neither looked peaceful. In particular, Huston's mouth was contorted, his brow furrowed, as if he had died in a state of utter disappointment.

"What do you see?" asked Charles, his words carried off in a whisper of chilly steam from the air-conditioning.

"A coupla dead guys," replied Baker, taking a puff of his smoke.

Charles frowned, clearly not satisfied with that answer. He held out a finger and wagged it over the bodies. "Look closely at their chests."

Baker took another look. Sure enough, he saw two small, identical holes in the same location on both bodies—right over the heart. It looked like Charles had cleaned the wounds. They were hardly noticeable upon a first glance. On Cronkite's younger, less wrinkled frame, the hole stood out more prominently.

"So? They both took metal to the chest. Probably died instantly," said Baker. He checked his watch. He was due at Liz's place in half an hour. "I worked that out for myself already."

"Oh yes," said Charles. "Punctures right through the heart right around four or five this morning. But look, Baker. The holes on both bodies are in the exact same position. How many times have you been able to get a perfect shot like that two times in a row? The odds are low."

Charles had a point. It was the sign of an exceptional gunman.

"Okay, I admit it's impressive, but let the Hueys figure out whodunit. They have the case now. I like you, Charles, so in the words of Chief Parker, 'Drop it.'"

He didn't really mean that. Wasn't his presence here proof that he wasn't going to let this go? If so, why was he discouraging Charles? Did he not want to drag anyone else down with him? Perhaps, but the fact that Charles, usually so excitable and cautious, had braved the telephone and summoned him down here was confirmation that Morris Baker wasn't alone in his suspicions.

Charles's eyes widened in shock, clearly thinking about Huey torture methods. Baker felt guilty for scaring the poor guy. Even so, he was a bit disappointed in what Charles was telling him. Crack shots, especially among dangerous gang members, were a dime a dozen in this town.

He was just about to leave when Charles spoke up again.

"But the bullet wounds aren't the only interesting thing I found, Detective. I removed the bullets from the bodies," continued the examiner. "There were four in all. Nothing unusual there, but I sent them off to the lab for analysis. You know, to see if there was anything we could learn about the make of the murder weapon, but the report yielded something more curious than that."

"I'm listening," said Baker.

"Well, the lab reported traces of uranium-235."

The half-smoked cigarette Baker had been keeping between his lips dropped from his mouth and onto Charles's clean floor, but the medical examiner hardly noticed. Baker inconspicuously crushed it under the sole of his shoe.

"What?" he asked, trying very hard to keep his voice casual. "You mean the stuff they use to make A-bombs?"

"The very same!" declared Charles, holding up another finger. Baker half expected him to shout, *Eureka!*

"But isn't that stuff dangerous?"

"Only in very large amounts. These bullets had incredibly faint traces of uranium. Quite harmless, of course, but curious all the same. Lionel at the lab didn't know what to make of it, and neither do I. That's when I thought of you. I think you'll agree with me when I say I don't like the Hueys very much. You've always been nice to me, Baker. Everyone finds it creepy down here and they can't stand the sight of dead bodies. People just want my findings and leave without looking me in the eye. You're different, you stay and talk. The bodies don't affect you like the rest. I think if we want any truth out of this, you need to find it."

Baker was flattered. He'd never considered Charles a close friend, but he was still a reliable man who could be trusted to do his job. Now he was talking about mucking up a government investigation, something that could land him in a HUAC interrogation room with his head—or more likely his testicles—in a vise. Baker knew that Charles Ward was decent, but now he knew that the man was also brave, no matter what jokes were made at his expense.

Charles, like Gladys, could be trusted to do the right thing, even if the prospect frightened the pants off him. It seemed that after all these years, he'd finally grown a pair; a pair that could very well be sliced off by those two yutzes Hartwell and Waldgrave.

"Thanks for telling me this, Charles," Baker said, placing a hand on the man's shoulder.

Charles nodded in appreciation. "I'll be submitting all the evidence to the HUAC offices as ordered," he said in a quavering voice. He looked around the room as if he expected to spot a Huey microphone being reeled into the ceiling on a fishing line. "But I think you should do more digging, Detective. Off the books. If we keep turning a blind eye to all this shit, there's no hope for any of us." He turned back to face the two dead men. "We could always use a little more truth in the world."

* * *

A few hours and several excruciating pages of Shakespeare dialogue later, Morris lay wide awake in Liz's bed, contemplating what Charles had said. Liz fell asleep while excitedly detailing their weekend plans up north. She never could keep her eyes open after they made love, an act that carried a lot more passion for her than it did for Baker. These little sleepovers were merely a distraction for him, a thin barrier that helped keep the demons at bay when the sun slipped below the horizon. Quieting those monsters, however, was becoming more difficult; he was slowly building up a tolerance to the comfort Liz once brought him.

Just before dawn, he slipped out of bed, got dressed, and quietly left Liz's apartment, leaving her with sweet and unbothered dreams of San Francisco.

My dear brother, Eitan:

How's the weather up there in Canada? Getting frigid yet? We're
having a lovely autumn down here in the States, but winter is certainly
on the way. All the leaves are gone now. I'm not sure if the news
has reached you yet, but Beth Tefillah burned down last night. You
remember having your bar mitzvah there when we were kids? Of
course you do! I recall giving you a healthy-size bruise on the neck
with all the candy I was pelting at you.

Sadly, our cozy little shul is no more. Some of our Gentile neighbors
had a little too much to drink for Thanksgiving dinner, and the
bedlam erupted from there. Kristallnacht: American Style. It went on
all night (you wouldn't believe the noise!), and Fanny wouldn't let the
kids play outside today. She was too frightened, and I have to admit,
I'm scared myself.

Some of the congregants and I tried to put out the fire, but it was
too late by the time we got there. The worst part is that the arsonists
didn't even flee the scene—they just stood there, torches in hand, and
watched our shul burn to the ground. They didn't bother to cover their
faces, either. And you know what, Eitan? I *knew* some of them.

This wasn't some fringe group of fanatical McCarthy supporters.
It was members of my own neighborhood mingled with members
of those HUAC offices they've set up all over the damn place. The
president decried the violence this morning, but he was so vague. I
don't think he mentioned the word *Jew* once and I nearly jumped out
of my skin when he said local HUAC inspectors were looking into
the incident. How did he describe them again?...Oh yes, he used the
phrase *good old folks*.

I wish I could say McCarthy is just a bigmouthed loony, but I remember they used to say the same thing about a certain chancellor over in Europe. He's only just started his second term and there's talk of him trying to repeal the 22nd Amendment so he can run for a third. Can you believe the chutzpah?

I feel so powerless right now and thought writing to my big brother would do some good, like sucking the poison out of a snakebite. As Bubbe used to say: "This too shall pass."

With God's help, we will all be okay. If not, we may have to join you up there in the Great White North. We'll shoot some moose together. Did you know they are kosher? Now, that's a steak I'd like to try!

My best to Lillian and the kids.
Your brother,
Joel

PART II
July 2, 1958

My opinion was that if we had a common enemy,
we should get together commonly.

—Julius Rosenberg

CHAPTER 9

LA's City Hall was a giant white obelisk shooting into the sky. The tallest building in the city, it was designed by three different men and finished in 1928 with concrete that contained sand from all fifty-eight of the state's counties and water from twenty-one of its historical missions. Similar to the Paradise Apartments, the entrance was framed by two palm trees, but that's where the comparisons ended. City Hall's interior was much grander, not to mention cleaner. Over a dozen American flags affixed to the multi-arched entranceway flickered in a slight breeze that did nothing to alleviate the heat of the day. It was going to be another unrelenting scorcher.

Baker stood outside the building ten minutes before nine o' clock, sweating like Alger Hiss under oath. He had phoned Gladys, asking her to tell Connolly that he'd be late to work. While he technically had the rest of the week off, Baker knew he'd be a lot more productive in the structured environment of the office. Otherwise, he'd just be lying on his bed, staring at the ceiling, sipping schnapps, and drunkenly trying to work out why Huston and Cronkite were murdered.

For the reading of Arthur Scholz's will, he chose his nicest brown suit, a white cotton shirt, and a blue knit tie that hardly fell below his sternum. His brown penny loafers were shined, their tassels bouncing with every restless movement of his feet. The little sleep he was able to muster in the night was disturbed by visions of faceless creatures with razor-sharp teeth that feasted on the cries of people long since dead.

He was so dazed, in fact, that he almost overlooked his tail. No one wore long trench coats in this weather other than the Hueys. Maybe it was some Huey dick following his movements, making sure he didn't dig any further into the case. One thing was for sure: It was the same spectator from yesterday's car accident. He'd been followed all the way from Chinatown. Under the guise of tying his shoe on the bottom step of City Hall, Baker gave them a cursory glance. The fellow was tall, and his face was obscured by the hat's wide brim. Baker could shake a tail like that, no problem, but that wouldn't be necessary. They couldn't follow him into the will reading, so there was no point in staging an elaborate getaway.

Taking off his own fedora, Baker strolled up the marble steps, under the oval arches, and into the shade of City Hall's large, chapel-like interior. The dented IWC watch on his wrist told him it was five to nine. Leaning against the right-hand wall were the mismatched HUAC inspectors from the day before: Hartwell and Waldgrave. Both were smoking and speaking in hushed tones until Hartwell clapped eyes on Baker and sneered.

"Why, Detective. What brings you to City Hall today on this fine morning?" Hartwell asked. "I would think once in twelve hours would have been enough."

So, they knew he'd been here to see Charles last night. "I could ask you the same thing," Baker said scathingly. "Except I don't have time for the chitchat."

Hartwell raised his eyebrows and held up his hands in a mocking gesture. "Ya hear that, Gene?" he said to Waldgrave. "Sounds like this Hebe's in quite a hurry." Turning back to Baker he added, "Please, don't let us keep you, Detective. We're all busy men, aren't we?"

Baker began to walk away, then turned back around. "You know, police officers need to visit City Hall to consult with the district attorney and make sure the city's laws are being upheld. Not that you two would know anything about upholding laws."

Hartwell adopted a self-satisfied smile. "Easy, Detective. That mouth of yours might just get you *blown up* one of these days. Now scat before my generous mood wears off and I book you right here on the grounds of being a mouthy Shylock."

Baker flipped Hartwell the bird before walking away. Their narrowed, suspicious eyes followed him across the lobby to the reception desk, where a tired-looking secretary informed him that the reading of Scholz's will would take place in conference room 1-E. He took a right and found himself in a spacious hallway, passing oaken doors with golden letters and numbers glued to their exteriors. There was a faint buzz of conversation coming from behind the door marked 1-E. A plaque next to it read: GENERAL CONFERENCE ROOM. He turned the knob and walked inside to find a scuffed rectangular wooden table with twelve metal seats placed around it. Half of them were filled.

"Ahhh, Mr. Baker. Thank you for coming. We're all here now, I believe." This was said by a plump man in a magnificent seersucker suit standing at the head of the room. A straw hat with a red, white, and blue band rested a few inches from the man's considerable belly.

Despite his girth, he crossed the room in a few swift waddles. He held out a pudgy hand of sausage fingers for Baker to shake.

"Laremy Fenwick, attorney-at-law. Pleased to meet you, sir, or Detective, I should say," he said, enthusiastically pumping Baker's hand. "Death wills, living wills, I do them all, my good man. Just give me a ring if you ever need one."

The lawyer chuckled and pulled out a lacquered business card from his inner jacket and handed it to Baker. Baker frowned, thinking that this was no place to be marketing legal services. They were here to honor the last wishes of a dead man. He tucked the card into his over-stuffed wallet and flashed Fenwick a mechanical grin. The overweight attorney waddled back to the head of the table and used a polka-dotted handkerchief to wipe the sweat off his many-chinned face, reddening from that little jaunt across the room. "Please take a seat, Detective," he said.

Baker sat and glanced at the other people gathered. There were five of them in total: four men and one woman. The woman wore a thick black dress and while a matching veil covered most of her face, Baker could still see heavily lidded eyes, dark skin, and beautifully chiseled facial features. The four men looked to be of varying ages and were dressed in immaculate black suits. Their faces looked solemn, but there was no hiding the anticipation in their eyes.

Two of them, extremely handsome with sleek blond hair and mesmerizing blue eyes, had to be brothers. The third was unshaven and had a high creased forehead. The fourth was the most well-kept of all the men. He wore round, wire-rimmed spectacles and sported an out-of-date mid-contour haircut that caused Baker's stomach to twist with inexplicable revulsion.

"Well, then!" boomed Fenwick genially. "Shall we get started?" He produced a crocodile-skin briefcase from beneath the table, clacked it open, and pulled out a sheaf of papers held together with a large paper clip. Placing a pair of gold pince-nez on his nose, the lawyer made an uncouth noise in his throat and began to read:

"I, Arthur Xavier Scholz, being of sound mind and body, do hereby declare the following to be my last will and testament:
    "Article One:
    "To my sons, Albert and Carl..."

The two blond-haired, blue-eyed men perked up.

"...I leave my house on Thirty-Three Ninety-Six Mandeville Canyon Road in Brentwood Park. May it bring you both joy and comfort as it did for me. To them, and their families, I also bequeath half my fortune of one point six million American dollars. May they spend it wisely."

Albert and Carl nodded to indicate their understanding and sat back, apparently relieved their father had left them something of substantial value. Fenwick then turned to the woman with a warm smile:

"Article Two:
    "To my wonderful maid, Valentina Vasquez, I bequeath the other half of my fortune of one point six million dollars. You were extremely faithful over the years, and I hope you can use this money to live a long and happy life."

It was subtle, but Baker detected slightly jealous looks from Scholz's sons. Valentina nodded and pulled out a handkerchief from a clutch purse in order to dab at the tears beginning to fall from under her veil. Fenwick then spoke to the unshaven man with the high forehead:

"Article Three:

"To the University of Southern California, I leave the publishing rights to my academic papers and findings. May they be useful in teaching future generations of physicians and nuclear physicists to come. May the department send my dear colleague, Roger Danforth, to collect the papers. Die Luft der Freiheit weht!"

Roger nodded and rubbed his scruffy cheek with a knowing grin. Fenwick finally turned to Baker and began to read:

"Article Four:

"To my dear, old friend, Detective Morris Ephraim Baker..."

Baker had never known an Arthur Scholz. What was this fella playing at? Was this some sort of elaborate put-on?

"...I leave my photograph album, which chronicles my various sojourns and adventures in the far-flung jungles of Africa, the 'Dark Continent' as it is sometimes called. I had a devil of a good time and hope he has the same enjoyment, albeit of a more vicarious nature, from the photographs contained within its pages."

Fenwick reached into his briefcase once again and brought out a beige vinyl photograph album. He waddled over to Baker and placed it in front of him. Baker showed none of his confusion but accepted it with a small nod. He looked over the table and saw the man with the mid-contour haircut staring at him none too kindly. Baker looked away.

Fenwick shimmied back to the front of the table and adjusted the pince-nez as he scrutinized the will once more:

"Thank you all for coming today. I know you must all be saddened by my death, but please do not spend too much time wallowing in sadness. I had an enjoyable life full of eventful memories. I would rather you live for today than mourn my departure from this world. After all, death is just another part of life."

Baker's eyes widened. That last line kicked something to life, as though his brain had finally gotten an intransigent motorcycle to co-operate. He couldn't explain why that string of words sounded so familiar. The connection was hazy and before the thought could form into something solid, Fenwick pushed on:

"And that should do it. Thank you all again for coming," he said, stowing his eyewear into a small leather pouch. "Now, Carl, Albert, Valentina, and Roger. I have the various deeds and paperwork here that just need your quick signatures. If you wouldn't mind staying to take care of that, then we can all go our separate ways. Detective Baker, you are free to leave."

Fenwick smiled at him before turning his attention to the paper-work. Baker took one final look around the room. The man with the mid-contour haircut, the only person in the room who had not been acknowledged in Scholz's will or by Fenwick himself, was still giving him an appraising look. One a lion might give a gazelle before ripping out its throat.

* * *

He was halfway across the lobby when Fenwick came waddling after him, his face red again. "Detective!" he called. "Detective, there was one last-minute proviso in Arthur's will I forgot to tell you about." The lawyer leaned in close and under the guise of shaking Baker's hand whispered, "Arthur wanted you to know his time of death, which was at six p.m."

Baker nodded, and Fenwick walked away.

* * *

Sitting in his car outside City Hall, Baker sipped schnapps and flipped through the album Scholz had left for him, noting the will's verbiage. "I had a *devil* of a good time." There was that word again. Three dead men and they'd all fallen right into Baker's lap.

MEMORY MAKERS was written in thin gold lettering along the bottom of the album cover, which was quite worn despite its plastic lamination. A postcard depicting a breathtaking view of the city from the Griffith Observatory was affixed to the first page.

GREETINGS FROM LOS ANGELES, CALIFORNIA! the postcard declared in large, blocky letters. Baker peeled it off with some difficulty and turned it over, but it was blank. Baker shrugged and put it back. You could get postcards like this at any airport or tourist trap in LA.

The photographs contained within the album were monochrome and sepia snapshots of a dapper man (presumably Scholz) riding elephants and holding up tiger pelts. Why would he leave such a thing to Baker? They'd never met and what's more, Baker had never been to Africa. He wasn't very adventurous, unless you counted his emigration to America.

He could look more into Scholz; there was nothing illegal about inheriting a few old pictures as far as he knew, unless McCarthy decided that Jews couldn't inherit property anymore. Based on the way the political winds were blowing, that wasn't such a far-fetched idea.

He hid the album under some loose upholstery beneath the Continental's driver's seat. The engine turned over and he peeled away from the curb with a loud screech of tires.

CHAPTER 10

Baker was accosted in the LAPD lobby by Andy Sullivan, part-time reporter for the *LA Times*, part-time writer of *Variety* gossip, and full-time pain in the ass for anyone unfortunate enough to have information that he wanted. As per usual, Andy was wearing his hat with the big PRESS card stuck in its band. Andy sometimes acted as if the size and boldness of the letters printed on the card were equivalent to having a big dick. Even if that were the case, it didn't give him the right to go around smacking people with it.

"Sooo, Baker," said the bothersome muckraker, flipping to a fresh page in his spiral-bound notebook. "What's this I hear about two showbiz stiffs you found up in Echo Park yesterday mornin'?"

"Andy," Baker began, "if you want the story, go to Echo Park, knock on the HUAC office door, and ask the Hueys nicely for answers. It's their problem now. Besides, didn't you catch the news on TV yesterday?"

"Come on, Baker. You know full well the Hueys won't give me a single comment! And do you really think this is another Monroe-Hopper case? I mean, lightning don't strike the same place twice.

There's something you're not saying here, and I bet it's a scoop the trades would slurp up like sodee-pop! Just imagine the headline, 'Disgraced Film Director Found Dead in Own Home!' and then the deck, 'LA Homicide Detective Speaks Out, Doesn't Buy into Official Government Reports.' We've known each other how long now? Six, seven years?"

"It feels like a hundred lifetimes to me."

"Come on, Baker. Out with it!" Andy's pencil was poised on the notepad, ready for the story to come pouring out of Baker's mouth. But the detective only smiled.

Andy's face fell.

"Are you gonna give me something or not?" he said. "It can be off the record if you like. Off, on, in between. It don't really matter to me. Take your pick, Baker."

"Even if such a story existed, and I'm not saying it does," said Baker, "but if it did, it would never make it past the censors with the case now in the hands of HUAC agents."

"True, Baker," said Andy, a salacious grin spreading across his face. He began to rub his thumb, pointer, and middle fingers together slowly. "But ya grease enough palms, you can print almost anything. You of all people understand the power of money, dontcha, Baker?"

Baker responded to the unsubtle remark on his Jewishness with another grin. "Andy, why don't you head back to New York. I think the rats who raised you are missing you something awful. Have a nice day," he finished with a wave of his hand.

"I won't forget this, Baker! Ya hear?" Andy called after him. "You can sit on it all you like, but I'll get that scoop with or without you!"

"Sure you will," Baker called back airily. "Putz."

* * *

Office activity was in full swing when Baker walked in at half past ten. He would've been there earlier, but he'd doubled back on his usual route in order to give his tail the slip.

Three vice cops were attempting to calm a screaming prostitute, who was waving around her feathered boa as though it were part of some bizarre mating ritual. Meanwhile, Dashiell Hanscom was bending below his desk, pretending to tie his shoe as he filled his inflamed nostrils with bumps of cocaine.

Connolly was resting his feet on his desk, blowing Pall Mall smoke rings. "You know," he smirked when he saw Baker, "if I was given the rest of the week off, I wouldn't be within ten miles of this place. Got a screw loose, Baker?"

Baker shrugged. "What else am I gonna do? Get a tan? Not really my thing. Sorry I'm late, by the way."

"It's all right," replied Connolly. "Gladys gave me the ol' heads-up. What took you?"

"I wanted to delay looking at your ugly Irish mug," said Baker, pulling out his own cigarettes and lighting up. Connolly's smile faltered.

"Well, looking at Cliptips isn't exactly like watching a burlesque show, pal." He stroked a finger down one of his red muttonchops. "As much as I'd love to sit around all day smoking and trading pleasantries, Baker, shall we get some work done or would you like to count the money in your wallet first to make sure it's all there?"

"It's empty," replied Baker. "Fucking your wife doesn't come cheap."

At first, Baker thought Connolly would punch him, but then he leaned back, snickering. Attacks on his personal character were one thing, but insulting his wife and kids could lose a guy some teeth from the Dublin Twins.

"Not a bad crack for a Hymie such as yourself," Connolly said. He blew another smoke ring into the air. "I've been thinking, Baker. I know I came off a little hot yesterday, but I gave it some thought and I actually like my balls where they are, so let's just drop the Huston-Cronkite thing, eh? I say we start making more inquiries into the Bersinger murder. Her husband and daughter are planning to move east, get away from the memory of the thing. Let's go knocking and see if we can't get some leads before they skip town."

"All right," said Baker, who was only half listening. His mind was on the short note Gladys had left on his desk: "No one in Cronkite's camp knows anyone by the name of Baker."

"I said, what are your thoughts on cheeseburgers for lunch?"

Baker snapped his head up to see Connolly eyeing him suspiciously. "What?" his partner said. "Think your God won't approve of that lunch option?"

"Cheeseburgers are fine."

"Nothing like some good dismemberment to get you in the mood for lunch," said Connolly, grabbing his hat off the desk.

* * *

John Bersinger and his daughter, Anne, proved to be a fountain dry of information, so Baker and Connolly headed over to Merv's Diner for double bacon cheeseburgers, fries, and ice-cold Cherry Cokes.

"I mean, who is that fucked up?" asked Connolly, stuffing a handful of greasy fries into his mouth. "Jesus, I mean, yeah, people are killin' each other all the time. The Hueys make it a weekly habit, but cuttin' 'em up like that? Christ!" He was so busy eating, he forgot to cross himself.

Baker took a long swig of cola, which he had surreptitiously spiked with schnapps. He'd finished his meal and was thumbing through Cronkite's small book of sign-off phrases. Cronkite had scratched out such gems as "You stay classy!" and "That's all, folks!"

"Mrs. Bersinger was, like you Americans say, in the wrong place at the wrong time," said Baker. He would have loved to forget the anguished faces of Betty Bersinger's husband and daughter as they were forced to relive details of the grisly murder, depicted in Philip Lathrop's stark black-and-white photography.

"You can say that again!" Connolly said, now using his fries to scoop up melted cheese that had fallen from his burger.

At the counter, a group of greasers was causing a ruckus at the counter with the diner's brusque owner, Merv Pachenko.

"Look Daddy-O," shouted one youth with a head of duck's ass hair. "We ain't payin' for this meal. You got that?"

Merv, a muscular man with a thick mustache and a grease-stained apron, leaned over the counter and tilted his head toward the kid.

"Yeah? And who is 'we' exactly?"

The lead greaser puffed out his chest and primped the collar of his black leather jacket.

"The Gypsies, man! You dig?"

"Oh, I dig, all right," Merv said with a nasty smile. He twirled his mustache before bringing up a sawed-off shotgun from under the counter. "Let me introduce you to my friend. If you don't pay up, he'll carve out a hole in your chest where there shouldn't be one. *You* dig?"

The greaser's chest deflated and his friends ran out of the diner like scared rats fleeing a doomed ship. They slipped and stumbled over one another on the waxed floor as "Rock Around the Clock" by Bill Haley & His Comets played from the jukebox in the corner.

One fleeing Gypsy called over his shoulder, "Sorry, Eugene!"

Merv's triumphant smile got bigger. Poor Eugene, the once mighty leader of the Gypsies, looked like he was about to wet his tight Levi's.

"That'll be a buck fifty, Eu-Gene. And please be sure not to get any piss on my newly waxed floor."

The kid's face was beet red. Everyone in the diner roared with laughter. Eugene produced a worn dollar bill and two quarters from inside his jacket and threw them on the counter.

"Fuck off, man. I'm never coming in here again." The greaser walked out of the diner, readjusting the jeans over his crotch.

"Have a nice day! Nice doin' business witch youse!" Merv called after him, putting the shotgun back under the counter to general applause. Baker and Connolly had been here enough times to have gotten to know Merv Pachenko. He was a tough guy who'd fought the Krauts and the North Koreans and would still be in Asia had it not been for a land mine that had taken his left leg during the razing of an enemy village. He gave Baker a quick wink and began wiping off the counter.

"Fuckin' kids," murmured Connolly, crunching ice between his yellow teeth. "Disrespecting their elders and stuffing themselves into phone booths. Can't stand 'em."

"Don't you have children?" asked Baker.

"Yeah, two little angels," he said, his expression softening. "And if they ever acted like that, I'd beat a new personality into them." He crunched ice for a few more seconds before speaking again. "Gonna have kids someday, Baker? Don't tell me you're some kind of lavender lad. I'm barely over the fact that you're a Mocky."

Baker laughed and held up his middle finger.

"Kids? Me? I can barely take care of myself!"

He had given some thought to having kids, but ultimately decided that it would be a cruel joke to bring an innocent person into a world like this. He slipped a dollar onto the table and got up.

"Let's go," Baker said, glancing at the bulletin board hung on the wall near their booth. Among the notices and flyers, he saw a familiar news clipping: "American Man Becomes First Person to Walk on Moon!"

Under the grainy picture of Francis Gary Powers planting the Stars and Stripes on the moon's cratered surface, the story was illegible, covered in scrawls of anti-Soviet sentiments:

WHAT NOW, SPUTNIK?!

SPACESHIPS ARE MADE IN THE U.S. OF FUCKIN' A.

AMERICAN SCIENCE > COMMIE SCIENCE

BETTER DEAD THAN RED!

Baker and Connolly walked outside into the blazing heat and into the pseudo-shade of Connolly's gray 1957 Eldorado. Connolly turned on the radio and let out an "ooo" of delight as a choppy message came through:

"... Liberty Boys speaking ... Our president ... proved ... that anyone ... exposes him, anyone who does not share his hysterical disregard for decency ... human dignity ... human rights guaranteed by the Constitution, might be either a Communist or a ... Resist, my fellow Americans. Rise up! Rise up! Resis—"

The broadcast cut out and was swiftly replaced by Ritchie Valens expressing his love for Donna. A smiling Connolly raised an eyebrow at Baker, who simply shrugged.

"Crock of shit," he said. "I've heard more inspiring speeches from Nixon."

Soon they were cruising back to headquarters.

* * *

He and Connolly decided to call it a day on the Bersinger case when no leads turned up. They spent hours poring over Charles's medical report, bouncing theories (each one wilder than the last) off each other until they were sick of looking at photographs of Betty Bersinger's mutilated body. They would try again tomorrow, but the odds of them catching the killer were shrinking every day. With the national holiday so close, a general malaise hung around the office. No one felt like doing much.

Connolly lost the report-writing coin flip and was currently hammering away on his typewriter, mumbling anti-Semitic slurs the entire time. Baker had his feet up on the desk, enjoying a Kool, when he noticed a commotion by the front of the office. Like deer sensing the danger of an incautious hunter, every policemen and secretary in the place popped their heads up.

Gladys was trying to keep pace with a woman in a tight magenta dress and a black mesh veil striding up the rows of desks with a young girl in tow. The girl—and Gladys—looked utterly perplexed.

"Ma'am, please!" Gladys called. "You can't just walk in here."

"My husband is dead. Now please leave my daughter and me be," replied the woman. She stopped walking and addressed the room at large. "I'm looking for a Detective Baker or Detective Connolly! Baker or Connolly, are they here?"

Morris and Brogan comically raised their hands in unison. Finally, looking somewhat pacified, the woman approached their desks and lifted the veil from her face. She pinned it to a fascinator that matched her dress. Her radiant presence seemed to dim the lights in the office, which accentuated her alabaster skin, full red lips, black parted hair, and stunning dark eyes. This was a perfect specimen of the opposite sex. Baker guessed that he wasn't the only guy in the room whose slacks were beginning to feel a little too tight.

"Boys, please," she said in a sensual voice, and Baker's heart melted just a little bit more. "I'm flattered, but I'm not your headmistress. Put your hands down. I just came to talk."

Connolly was already offering up his chair and pack of cigarettes to her. "Of course, of course," he simpered. "I'm Detective Brogan Connolly and that there is my partner, Detective Morris Baker. What can we do for you, Miss...?"

"Soma. Enrica Soma"—she rolled the *r* in *Enrica*—"and this is my daughter, Anjelica. Anjie dear, say hello to the nice homicide detectives."

Anjelica said nothing. She burrowed her face deep into the magenta fabric of her mother's dress.

"Of course, of course," repeated Connolly. Baker had never seen his partner act this way, not even in front of his own wife. "And talk we shall. A pleasure to meet you both. Gladys! Go get Miss Soma a cup of coffee. She is a guest in our offices."

"Oh, I couldn't impose," began Enrica.

"It's nothing," said Connolly.

"Well, in that case..." said Enrica, who had already swiveled around to face the flustered secretary. "A splash of cream, two sugars. And I mean a splash, Gladys, dear. If there's too much, I won't drink it, and that's a promise."

There was something so finite about the instructions. Gladys—sharp as a tack—took it as her exit cue, hurrying off to get the coffee.

"Now," began Connolly, turning back to the woman, "how can my partner and I assist you, Miss Soma?"

Soma fished inside her crocodile-skin handbag and pulled out a long cigarette holder. She took a deep puff and said, "It's about my husband. Well, ex-husband, now, I suppose. Until yesterday, I was Mrs. John Huston."

Baker's ears nearly stood up when he heard this. He sat forward and blindly felt for a notepad and pen. "You were married to John Huston?"

"Indeed I was," said Enrica, who dug in her handbag once more and pulled out a silk handkerchief embroidered with her initials. "Poor Johnny. Poor, poor Johnny." She sniffed solemnly and dabbed at her eyes, which had become over-bright with the promise of tears.

"Mrs. Huston," Baker probed. "May I ask how you heard about your husband's passing?"

"Well, it's obvious, isn't it? I saw the police tape around our house. Anjie and I had been back east to see my father for a few weeks. Johnny said he was working on a new project and needed space to think. I mean, I was thrilled—ecstatic really—to hear that he'd be working on another picture."

"We noticed the old film posters in your home. He hadn't worked in quite a while, is that correct, Mrs. Huston?" asked Connolly.

"You can just call me Enrica, boys," Enrica said. "And you are correct, Johnny hadn't made a film in quite some time. We were married in 1950 and it used to be—in the early days—that I wouldn't see him for days or weeks on end. He was either pent up in his study writing his next screenplay, on location filming, or at the studio cutting the thing together. Oh, he loved all steps of the filmmaking process. He believed in the art of the craft, not what ideology you believed in. He refused to start making the tripe they turn out these days. Johnny was a true artist and he stood for artistic integrity until the very end..."

Baker took advantage of the ensuing lull to ask another question. "So, what did he do then, Mrs. Huston? I mean, Enrica. What I mean to say is, and please excuse me if I am overstepping, but this city isn't the cheapest place to live. Detective Connolly and myself were at your house and it—again, please excuse me—well, it didn't look like your family was starving."

She smiled at this and said, "Very astute of you, Detective Baker. Yes, it's true. Johnny was out of a job these last few years, but we never wanted for anything after he left the industry—or was kicked out, whatever you please. Anyway, we had some money saved up from all his old Warner contracts. You remember the Warner Bros., don't you? A shame what happened to them. As for me, I went back to modeling and ballet. I was once on the cover of *Life* magazine, did you know that?"

Without waiting for an answer, she pressed on: "Johnny, he was never the same after McCarthy came along. Filmmaking was his entire life. He tried to write some screenplays, but the president's new studio system wouldn't buy them. So, to answer your question, Detective Baker, I became the sole breadwinner while Johnny stayed home and raised Anjie and our son, Tony. Tony's with a friend right now. Anjie would be, too, but she wouldn't stop crying when I tried to drop her off."

"Of course," said Brogan. "These are trying times. Please continue."

"Yes—so a few weeks ago, Johnny says he's working on a new project and that it's going to be revolutionary. I was so thrilled, I didn't think twice when he asked me to take the kids to my father's place in New York, so he could have the place to himself and really get down to work. We were on the East Coast with my father and if you don't believe me, you can look up Antonio Soma in Manhattan. He's a well-known restaurateur and he'd be more than happy to corroborate my story."

"And your mother?" asked Baker, who was scribbling on his notepad like a crazed maniac.

"Died before the war. Anjie here is named after her. May I continue?"

"Surely," said Connolly.

"We came back from our trip because the kids dearly wanted to watch the fireworks with their father. But we couldn't even pull into the driveway because the house was surrounded with police tape and crawling with federal agents. I tried to get something out of the men guarding the house, but they would only tell me that a murder had been committed and if I had a question I could 'inquire further at my local HUAC office.' They wouldn't even budge when I said it was my own damn house! Can you imagine?"

Gladys brought the coffee, and Enrica thanked her and took a sip. "Ooo, Gladys, dear. There really is too much cream in this."

"Oh, I can go get you a fresh cup," offered Gladys.

"No, dear. I tire at the thought of you trying to get it right. That will be all."

Gladys took the cup from Enrica and stormed off, slamming the coffee into a nearby waste bin with such force, droplets shot onto the tie of an unsuspecting Dashiell Hanscom.

"Luckily," continued Enrica, "a police officer was still on the scene, cleaning up the tape, and heard me yelling. He offered to escort me off the premises, which I refused at first. But the look on his face was kind and understanding, so I agreed. Once we were down the drive and out of earshot, he let slip that you two had briefly been on the scene the day before."

"Please accept our condolences, Enrica," preened Connolly. "And please excuse my bluntness, but did you attempt to follow up with the local HUAC office? I believe it is right by you in Echo Park."

"Anjie, close your ears." The girl obeyed. Erica turned back to the detectives.

"Those sons of bitches? Ha! I don't trust them as far as I can throw them, which is to say not at all. They won't let me see my husband's body. Johnny didn't trust the bastards, either. He gave up his entire career just to spite them. Look, I've been hearing the reports—Johnny may have been a lot of things, but he was no homosexual. And I can say that with one hundred percent certainty. He was no Commie-lover, either, but like I say, that stuff didn't matter much to him."

"And do you have any idea of who would want to kill your husband or why Walter Cronkite was at your house?" asked Baker.

"To that, I don't have an answer," she said, looking frustrated. "Johnny didn't have many friends, especially after he left the business. As for me, we might have had our differences, but I would never wish Johnny dead, so you can rule Enrica Soma-Huston out as the killer right now, boys."

"And Cronkite?"

"No idea. Maybe he was helping Johnny with his new project? I can't say for sure what he was doing in our home. I only ever knew him from television, same as everyone else."

She turned back to Anjelica and signaled it was okay to pull her fingers out of her ears.

"Enrica, you have been very brave in coming to us," said Baker, lowering his voice conspiratorially. "However, I must ask you not to speak of this meeting with anyone outside of this group. It could be dangerous for all of us if anyone knew we were attempting to encroach on a federal investigation."

She pushed air out of her nose derisively. "Please, Detective Baker. Do you take me for a fool?"

"Of course n—"

She abruptly stood. "The children and I are currently staying at the Ambassador Hotel, room five-C. I can't bear to stay at the house after what happened—not that those Huey louses would even let me if I wanted to. If you call me with more information or questions, which I fully expect you to do, say you are Bartolomeo Vanzetti calling for Nicola Sacco and they will put you through. Good day, Detectives. Come along, Anjelica."

Anjelica just stood there, staring up at Baker and Connolly with wide, sad eyes. For the first time during the visit, Baker heard the girl speak.

"Are you gonna catch the bad people who hurt my daddy?"

"We're going to try our best, young lady," he said. Anjelica beamed up at him, showing off a pure and toothy smile that only kids are able to genuinely muster.

Once Enrica and Anjie had left, it was like Connolly had been lifted from an enchanted spell. His abrasive demeanor returned in full force.

"Jesus." He crossed himself for taking the Lord's name in vain. "You get a load a' her? Sure, she's good-lookin' and all that, but asking us to go against the Hueys? It's like asking a man to go to the gallows, thread the rope around his neck, and pull the lever."

"Mhmm," replied Baker, who was looking over the frenzied notes he'd taken.

"Christ, Baker"—another cross—"you're not actually thinking of helping her, are ya? Please tell me all that stuff you said was just a way to get her out of here and cover our asses."

Baker looked up from his notes. "Oh, yes, yes. Nothing to worry about, Connolly. Our posteriors are well protected."

"Damnit, I know that look in your eye. You actually wanna help her. Those schnapps must have scrambled your brains more than I thought. I don't want my life ending early 'cause of some Smokestack Dust Bunny like you. Whatever you're thinking of doing, keep me out of it, okay?"

Baker barely heard his partner, already thinking about what Enrica had said. She had confirmed his suspicions: that the rumor about a Communist-tinged love affair between Huston and Cronkite was a steaming pile of shit. The Hueys may not have carried out the murders, but their taking over the investigation made the whole thing stink of a cover-up.

But what was there to hide exactly? Why would Huston send his wife and children across the country if he was just pursuing a motion picture? He was clearly working on something that required the help of a fact finder with integrity. Someone like Cronkite. It was important enough that someone had killed them over it, which meant Huston sent his family away for protection.

Two families had lost fathers. How many families, including his own, had Baker seen torn apart and murdered? He'd become a police officer to do some good and help people. Seeing the look on Anjelica's face convinced Baker that he would not stop looking into this.

A conversation halfway across the room broke his reverie. Harold Peterson, a potbellied plainclothes detective, was interviewing a sobbing woman in a red-and-white polka-dot dress.

"O-L-I-V-E-R. Yes," she sniffed into a handkerchief smudged with mascara.

"And you're sure the last time you saw him was yesterday, Mrs. Shelton?" asked Peterson, not looking up from his notepad.

"Yes," Mrs. Shelton said. "He left after breakfast for work. His uncle runs a courier service, you see. Clark—his uncle, I mean—said he'd sent Oliver on a route in the late afternoon and he never came back. He didn't call me right away, because he thought Oliver had just gone home for the day."

"And where was this final errand in the evening?"

"Clark said the route was all over the city, but it ended in Chinatown. That's all he told me. He takes his client privilege very seriously and said he couldn't give the exact address unless a warrant was provided. Theodore, Oliver's father, was furious when he heard that, but Clark just wouldn't budge. Is there anything you can do?"

"An address of that final delivery would be very helpful in narrowing the search, Mrs. Shelton. I'll put in a call to City Hall as soon as we're done here and request that warrant. It may take some time with the holiday coming up and all."

Baker needed some air. He had to get out of here, although he could not exactly say why he did not simply go up to this woman and tell her that he was the final person on her son's delivery route. Perhaps it was the fear that as a Jew, he'd be instantly blamed. If he tried to say that the only thing he'd done to the boy was try to tip him, the Hueys (and there was no doubt they would interrogate him) would only focus on the fact that a penny-pinching Yid like him offered the boy a single quarter.

Harold Peterson finally looked up from taking notes. He looked tired. "I'll take the photo you brought along and we'll put out an APB to all officers and...say, Baker, don't you live in Chinatown or thereabouts?"

Baker turned around with as casual a look on his face as he could muster. "Yes, Peterson. I do," he responded "What do you need?"

"See this kid anywhere near you last night?" He held up a black-and-white photograph of a smiling young boy—the one who'd delivered the summons to the reading of Arthur Scholz's will.

Baker put on a thoughtful frown and furrowed his brow for added effect. "Nope. Sorry, Peterson."

"Ah, well. Just thought I'd check," said Peterson, turning back to the boy's mother. "Now, what's the best number to reach you at?"

Baker didn't hear her phone number. He was already up and heading for the exit. With trembling hands, he pulled the flask of schnapps out of his pocket.

* * *

Baker was back in his car and on the fast track to getting drunk. Parked in the lot of his apartment building, he lounged in the driver's seat, scrutinizing what Arthur Scholz had left him, trying to keep his mind off Oliver Shelton.

He looked at every picture. No one could deny they were beautiful and expertly taken. They depicted vast Saharan landscapes; native, spear-clutching tribesmen; lions, giraffes, gazelles, and zebras—all of them looking up at Baker from the past. Others showed Scholz smiling, arm in arm with strangers; Scholz holding up a large-mouthed rifle in one hand and some limp, tusked beast in the other. The late doctor-professor was no doubt handsome with a strong cleft chin, thick eyebrows, and an even thicker mustache. In other men, the mustache would have given off a sense of advanced age. For Arthur Scholz, it just made him look younger and more handsome.

There was just one entry in the album that seemed out of the ordinary: a blurred something just out of focus with bright-orange blotches. It looked like someone had made a mistake while developing the film. In all likelihood, it had been exposed to light at the wrong time, but if that was the case, why include it with all the other photographs?

Baker took another sip of schnapps. He reached forward to pull the blurry photo from the small triangular paper fastenings that kept it in place. Before he could lift it, there was a tap on the window. Slightly annoyed, Baker turned, ready to tell the person to buzz off, when he found himself looking into the barrel of a gun.

CHAPTER 11

B aker wasn't scared. He'd had guns—many of them—pointed at him before. He stared at the firearm (a strange-looking pistol) and then up at the person holding it: someone with a long trench coat and a wide-brimmed fedora that obscured their face in shadow. Baker's tail from earlier.

He smiled and rolled down the window of the Continental. "Afternoon, my good man. Awfully hot today, isn't it? What can I do for you?"

The gunman didn't say a word, only motioned with the gun for Baker to get out of the car. Baker lifted his hands as well as his eyebrows. "All right, all right. But you might want to put that away. You could put someone's eye out."

Baker was quick. He slammed the door out into the stranger's midsection, causing them to double over. They grunted in pain and shuffled back a few steps. Baker wrenched the pistol from their grasp, turning it around on them.

"Didn't your mother ever teach you not to stand so close to car doors?" Baker said. "They can be quite dangerous. Now let's see who you are and then we can move on to why you've been following me around."

The hunched figure slowly straightened up and pulled off her hat. Baker actually took a step back and lowered the pistol. It was a dame, and one of the most beautiful women he'd ever seen. She had silky blond hair, and like Baker's, it was curly. The brilliant-green eyes that stared back at him were sad and resilient. Her nose was dainty and well shaped, the work of a divine sculptor.

"My God," he breathed in Yiddish, and then repeated it in English.

"Well?" she asked, and there was something in her voice, an accent or inflection that Baker couldn't immediately place. "You going to shoot me or what?"

"Shoot you? My dear lady, what do you take me for? I'm a gentleman. I want some answers before I pull the trigger."

Was that a smile he saw flicker across her face? Whatever it was, the woman swiftly replaced it with a scowl. "You'll get nothing out of me," she said.

"Well, that's not fair. We hardly know each other. How about we take a walk, you and me, Miss...?"

Miss No-Name stared back, silent and unyielding.

"All right, miss. After you." He looped an arm around hers, as if they were about to go for an evening stroll. He also placed her bizarre pistol into the supple flesh of her right side below the armpit. "No sudden moves if you please."

Baker steered her toward the Paradise Apartments. Once inside, they walked over the stained carpet and up the marble stairs to the second floor. The Huangs were, for once, totally silent, but lazy Swing crackled from behind their door. Something by Benny Goodman or Glenn Miller. Baker unlocked his apartment, gently pushed the woman inside, and closed the door with his foot, never breaking eye contact with his guest.

"Sit," he said, pointing the gun at his bed. She crossed the messy room and sat on the mattress, which creaked and sent up its usual cloud of dust and feathers.

"It stinks in here," she murmured. There was that inflection again on *stinks*, which sounded more like *steenks*.

"Yeah, well, I never said I was a florist, did I?" said Baker as he pulled the flask of schnapps from his jacket pocket and took a swig. "Now." He wiped his mouth with his sleeve. "Let's start with the basics. I'd like to know who you are, who sent you, and why."

She continued to scowl.

"Pretty please?" he asked in mock sweetness.

The beautiful stranger turned away.

"Come on, lady," Baker said. "Make this easier on yourself. I'm a detective, you know. For the LAPD. I could have you run in for threatening an officer of the law."

The woman snorted. "They'd probably thank me for it. You are a Jewish policeman, which means you are not the same as a regular policeman. You are an outsider, no? Just like during the war."

Baker's confidence faltered. How did she know who and what he was? Unless she was a Huey, which would make no sense because HUAC didn't employ dames as field agents.

"How did you—?" He cut himself off as she shrugged off her trench coat to reveal a beautiful satin dress that was cut just above the knees. Black leather high-heeled shoes wrapped themselves around her feet. *Who is this woman?*

He tried again: "How did you know I am Jewish?"

"S'iz du an untersheyd vi ken ikh?"—Does it matter how I know?—

she asked in perfect Yiddish. The ensuing silence was all-encompassing. He could hear the faint Swing coming from the Huangs' apartment.

"So." His mouth was suddenly dry. "Ir zenen oykh a yid?" You are a Jew, too? She just stared at him with those resiliently green eyes. "Well," continued Baker. "In any case, your Yiddish is impeccable." He hadn't spoken it with anyone for over a decade.

The woman picked a piece of lint off her dress and flicked it into the detritus of Baker's apartment. "Look," he began, not knowing what to say. Something deep down was telling him this woman wasn't a threat; that he could trust her. "I believe we got off on the wrong foot. What if...?"

"I know about Cronkite and Huston, Detective Baker," she said suddenly. "I need you to let me go. I am not your enemy. In fact, I am probably your only hope of staying alive."

It wasn't said with malice or anger. She spoke with unemotional finality, like someone discussing an undeniable axiom. Like the fact that Alger Hiss was fried in the electric chair. Or perhaps that Richard Nixon had been awarded the vice presidency for sending Hiss to such a shocking fate.

"I never said you were my enemy," mumbled Baker in the tone of a child caught in wrongdoing. "But I am a bit curious why you've been tailing me and held a gun at my face. And what's this about you helping me stay alive?"

She stared at him again, her bright eyes seeming to bore into his haunted brown ones. Then, without warning, she smiled and hung her head in surrender. Her smirk seemed to light up the room, which was fast filling with early-evening shadows.

"I'm sorry about that. It's been a very long couple of days, and I was getting a little desperate. I need to know if either Cronkite or Huston left anything behind, a note, a tape, a film reel even. Anything. You need to tell me, Morris."

She stood up and took a tentative step toward him. Baker half-heartedly raised the gun, but it fell limply to his side after a few seconds. Satisfied that he wasn't going to shoot her, the woman crossed the room until she was a foot away.

"I know you are a good man, Morris Baker, and I will tell you all I know if you can do me the simple courtesy of trusting me. A shlekhte sholem iz beser vi a gute milkhome. Yes?"

"A bad peace is better than a good war," he repeated in English. "Of course," he whispered.

The woman took a deep breath as though preparing to dunk her head underwater. "My name is Sophia Vikhrov and I am with Russian intelligence."

Baker was so shocked, he actually tripped over a pair of unwashed briefs and slammed into the wall. "You're a fucking Red?" he exclaimed. The accent made sense now. "Why would they send a Red with a Russian accent over here? Wouldn't that blow your cover pretty quickly?"

Sophia blushed and spoke again in perfect English, with no accent this time. "Why, Mr. Baker, you look ever so pale. Would you like a capitalist pick-me-up? A doughnut or maybe a cup of black coffee? Isn't that what policemen here love? Doughnuts and coffee?" She laughed, a girlish giggle that made his heart flutter. "I didn't need to use my American accent in front of you, Detective."

"A Red, a fucking Red," spluttered Baker. "A Red in my fucking apartment! They'll fry me just for being in the same room with you!"

"Please, Detective, be reasonable. There is nothing to fear from a

Communist, just as there is nothing to fear from a capitalist pig such as yourself. I joke, of course."

Baker's mind was racing; nothing sobered a guy up faster than speaking with an honest-to-goodness Commie. Sure, he'd arrested Bolshies in this town before, but he'd never met a bona fide agent of the USSR.

Personally, Baker believed in no ideologies (especially not those spouted by McCarthy), but he'd lived in America long enough to be subconsciously inundated with the blanket fear of Marxist beliefs. He wouldn't turn her in, even if it was his civic duty to ring up Hartwell and Waldgrave. Who knew, he might even get a commendation as one of the good Jews—a good American.

Breathing slowly, he stuck out his hand. "Pleased to meet you, Miss Vikhrov. Look, I don't give a shit if you're for the workers or for the birds, I want to know what you know and what you were doing following me around. I want to get to the bottom of this thing, too."

Sophia shook his hand. Baker stifled a shiver of delight. When she spoke again, the Russian accent resurfaced: "I'm afraid you may want to sit down for this. It involves you most grievously."

Baker removed some grease-stained trousers from a nearby chair and sat down like an obedient canine. "What the hell do I have to do with all this?" he asked, thinking of the word *Baker* written on Cronkite's note.

Sophia sat back down on the bed and let out a reluctant sigh. "I am here, in this country, because in two days' time you are supposed to attack the city of Los Angeles."

Baker laughed and kept on laughing until his sides hurt. "I'm sorry, Miss Vikhrov, that's a good one. I wasn't aware the Reds had such senses of humor. What's the real reason you're here?"

"Just as I say," said Sophia. "We received intelligence that you are going to detonate some sort of bomb on the Fourth of July."

Baker wasn't laughing anymore. He felt the schnapps threatening to repeat on him. He took another long draw from his flask.

"That's the most ridiculous thing I've ever heard. I don't know the first thing about bombs."

"Yes, we came to the same conclusion," Sophia said. "You are—what is the word? A patsy."

"A patsy?" Baker repeated. "A patsy for whom?"

"I don't know much more than you. But there is an explosion coming in two days' time on your country's Independence Day. I was supposed to meet with Cronkite and Huston yesterday morning. I was on my way to the house when I saw all the policemen there. I went back to my safe house, relayed what I had seen to my contacts, and awaited further instructions. I was told by an informant in your police department that you and a Brogan Connolly had been on the scene until your government took control."

Baker sucked in a breath of musty air. The government's worst fears were realized: Commie spies in the echelons of government. Sophia continued speaking.

"I have been following you since late yesterday afternoon. I thought everything was finished when you crashed your car. But when you drove away, I followed and waited outside this building all night. I didn't want to involve you in this, but with Huston and Cronkite dead, I have no choice. I apologize for all the cloak-and-dagger charade. Time's running out and I needed to know if you had any leads to the bomb."

That's when the cracked lightbulb in Baker's head illuminated something else. Hartwell had said something about "blowing up" during their run-in at City Hall earlier that day. "HUAC must know about this bomb threat, then," Baker blurted out. "There's no other explanation for why those two schmucks keep popping up. But if so, why not just arrest and torture me for the information? It's standard operating procedure for them."

"They must think you aren't working alone," Sophia postulated. "They must be afraid that making a move on you might trigger the bomb. Any idea of who would want to frame you?"

Baker shook his head. Sure, the Hueys—and even his fellow cops—hated him, but would either group really go to such dramatic lengths to kill innocent people and drag his name through the mud? Once again, it just didn't feel like the work of HUAC. They always went for the simplest route whenever they wanted to tarnish someone's reputation or make them disappear. Why go to the trouble of building and detonating a bomb when they could just bring him in on fabricated charges? Then there were all the dangerous criminals Baker had put away over the years. Some of them probably harbored some resentment against him, but most (if not all) of them were still in prison or dead.

"What was the meeting with Cronkite and Huston all about? How are they involved?" said Baker.

Sophia chose her next words carefully. "Have you heard of an organization that calls itself the Liberty Boys?"

"Not that old yarn," chuckled Baker. "It's just a fairy tale McCarthy haters tell their kids before bed."

"I can assure you, Detective Baker, that the Liberty Boys are very real," Sophia said. "John Huston was among their ranks. He and another operative went rogue and contacted my government for help. I was to be fully briefed on the mission yesterday morning. Cronkite was most likely just Huston's backup plan. If we failed, Cronkite would break the news of the plot in an effort to draw out or deter the real conspirators. Clearly, someone got wind of what they were up to."

"Well, that solves one part of the puzzle," said Baker. The revelations he had experienced over the last few minutes were almost too outlandish to believe. The Liberty Boys? Real? "But why me?"

"Who better to blame than a Jew?" Sophia answered. "You are the perfect scapegoat."

"To what end?" asked Baker. "What would framing me accomplish?"

"We can only guess," replied Sophia.

"If this is all true," Baker began, "then why is Russia involved? Why even try to stop it? Your country would love to see America implode in on itself."

"Think, Morris. An attack by a Jew in your country is automatic grounds to blame my country. We don't want to see tensions rising any further than they currently are. Things are precarious enough already. Just look at what's going on in Korea."

"Then why not have Khrushchev warn McCarthy? Why all the sneaking around?"

Sophia snorted in derision. "Your President McCarthy is finding Communists in his cereal bowl, yes? Always asserting your country is in danger from my people? Had we gone straight to him, he'd think it was a trick or a plot to invade. Wouldn't you agree that would be the reaction of a man who let the Russian embassy in Washington be burned down by an angry mob? Whoever is actually behind the bomb probably wants your government to think you are working for mine. Maybe they're trying to start a nuclear war."

Baker rubbed the back of his head, trying to make sense of what he was hearing. Sophia was laying out some hard truths about America.

About what it had become since the end of the war—a pathetic and trembling creature scared of a red-tinted shadow.

"Khrushchev is stubborn and tough, but he is not stupid," she continued. "He does not want to see the world end any more than you or I. He has loved ones, too. We are not the heartless devils you think us to be. It was Khrushchev who authorized this operation."

Baker plunged his hand into his pocket and pulled out Cronkite's crumpled note. He held it out to Sophia. "Speaking of 'devils,' this was in Cronkite's hand when I visited the crime scene yesterday. I found it on him before the Hueys—er—government officers could. My last name is written at the bottom, but now I know why. What about the other three words, does 'Beat the Devils' mean anything to you?"

Sophia studied the paper. After a moment of what looked like intense concentration, she handed the paper back. "I'm afraid it doesn't," she said, "but I expect it has something to do with the bomb." She looked genuinely disappointed, even frustrated. Baker pocketed the note. "Although there is someone who might be able to make sense of it," she said.

"Who?"

"The other Liberty Boy who was working with John Huston. I was told to rendezvous with him tonight at some club."

"Which one?" asked Baker. "This town is full of clubs."

"La Espada Roja...why are you smiling?"

Baker couldn't help himself. "Miss Vikhrov, are you aware that you have just named one of the most dangerous gathering spots in all of Los Angeles?"

CHAPTER 12

The Red Sword, or La Espada Roja, wasn't just a club. It was also the official watering hole of the Pistoleros, otherwise known as the Gunmen, the most violent, short-tempered gang in all of Southern California. Come to think of it, they were probably the most dangerous gang north of the border. A fella—even one who worked on the right side of the law—would have to be downright crazy to set their pinkie toe inside La Espada Roja.

That is why Baker thought Sophia was off her rocker when she named this hot spot of criminal activity as the rendezvous point. She insisted that she had not misheard the name of the place, and when she finally lost her patience and shouted at him for repeating the question, Baker dropped it. The more he thought about it, however, the more he realized that the Red Sword was the perfect place for a clandestine meetup. Since cops and Hueys steered clear of the place, there'd be little chance of prying eyes and ears.

The meeting was set for ten thirty that evening, so Baker polished off his remaining schnapps, handcuffed Sophia to the radiator, handed her a

Hershey's bar, and flopped onto his bed for a quick nap. Baker wasn't sure he fully trusted Sophia yet and wasn't about to take any chances. What if he woke up and she was gone, or worse—he didn't wake up at all?

"Is this really necessary?" she asked, pulling at one of the cuffs around her wrist.

"Considering you're an enemy of the state, yes," he replied, throwing her the pamphlet on *How to Recognize a Communist in Ten Easy Steps.* "Here, you might find that interesting."

She flipped through it. "Step Five: The Workers' Rights Test," read Sophia.

"If all signs outlined in Steps One through Four indicate Communist leanings held by the person in question, employ a series of casual questions about the current state of workers' rights in the United States. Take, for instance, the following scenario:

"Joe: 'Good morning, Bob. Hear about that strike of steel workers out in Pittsburgh?'

"Bob has two ways of answering:

"Answer Number One: 'Sure did, Joe. About time, if you ask me. The conditions in those factories are deplorable and the pay just isn't high enough to justify the risk.'

"Answer Number Two: 'Sure did, Joe, and it makes me sick to my stomach. Ungrateful workers holding up precious time that could be spent growing our great economy.'

"If the person gives any indication of empathy toward the 'plight of the worker' (i.e., Answer Number One), they may very well be a member of the Red Peril. If so, proceed to Step Six. If they do not (i.e., Answer Number Two), they are a red-blooded American and you are in no immediate danger."

Baker turned over on the bed and placed a pillow over his face to block out any sunlight.

"See? Like I said, very interesting. Now be a good girl and I may not have to take such precautions in the future."

With that, he fell into an uneasy sleep.

* * *

Two children were crying in the distance.

All he could see from his infirmary bed (if you could call a lumpy, straw-filled mattress a bed) were the blinding incandescence overhead and some of the polished linoleum floor. They always kept the place so neat and clean, despite the vile things that went on in here.

He tried adjusting his position, but it was useless. They had tied him to the bed's flimsy metal posts. In a healthier state, he could break free of the minimal straps without a problem, but now he was weak. So weak. Besides, his head was heavily bandaged and... wait. Someone was coming down the ward. The sound of their shoes hitting tile reminded him of a horse's trot. Clip! Clop! Clip! Clop! Clip! Clop!

Then he saw who it was: an extremely handsome young man with wire-framed glasses and parted brown hair smiling down at him. His white lab coat was as pristine as ever, and he held the blazing stub of a cigarette between pointer and middle fingers. A jagged scar running up the doctor's left cheek gave his pernicious smile a gruesome lopsidedness.

"And how are we today?" he asked, consulting a clipboard. His Czech-oslovakian was flawless.

Baker did not answer. Would not answer.

"Did the ovens burn your tongue?" the man asked, still smiling. "Shall we switch to Yiddish?"

Still no answer. The man walked closer to the bed and leaned down. His breath reeked of peppermint sticks, which still failed to mask the aroma of cheap tobacco and fermented cabbage.

"Do you know what I could do to you, hmm? Are you aware that I could dispose of you right now? One injection is all it would take. Or perhaps I am in more of a prolonging mood. Perhaps I am curious about the effects of a gallbladder removal without the application of anesthetics. But I must refrain from those impulses. You see, the commandant believes we are wasting our time and resources waiting for you to recover. You are 'more insignificant than a fly,' he says. To this I agree, but we have much need of a specimen like you. You will be part of something great, mark my words. I see something special in you. Now, if you value your worthless life, you will answer my question. So, I ask again: How are we today?"

"Very well, Herr Doktor Professor," Baker muttered through gritted teeth. He was fuming. He cared more about living than pride. It hadn't taken much for him to break and respond to the doctor's question.

The children cried out again, this time for their mother. And someone was calling Baker's own name, but it was faint and quite disconnected from this mad hospital.

"Beruhigen, Kindern," called the doctor. "I shall be with you both in a moment." He was still leaning in close, and there was no escape from the stink of his horrible breath. "Remember what I tell you. Remember my face, for it is the face of Death. There is no need to fear me. After all, death is just another part of life."

And leaning even lower, he selected a spot on the upper part of Baker's left arm, a point just above the string of numbers tattooed there, and stubbed out his cigarette. Baker did not want to show any further signs of weakness, but he could not prevent an instinctive groan of pain that escaped his throat. Furious with himself, he looked up at the ceiling: anything to avoid the doctor's blue eyes, which were sparkling with malicious glee. The scent of his own charred flesh made his underfed stomach churn with hunger. Rational signals from his brain reminded him of what was causing the smell while a fainter signal— one that was almost comical—cautioned him that human meat was not kosher, according to the Torah.

The doctor straightened back up, now looking bored. He walked away toward the crying children. A pair of twins who would never see their mother again.

"Don't lose your mind yet," he called over his shoulder. "It gets worse."

And the doctor was right.

* * *

Baker shot up in his bed, drenched with sweat. Turning, he saw a scared-looking Sophia right where he'd left her, chained to the radiator.

"Are you all right?" she asked. "You were shaking horribly and muttering to yourself. I kept calling your name, but you wouldn't wake."

"I'm fine." He swung his legs off the edge of the bed and placed his head in his hands. It was now dark outside. "How long was I asleep?"

"Two hours, maybe. I'm not entirely sure, I nodded off myself for a bit, but was woken when I heard you thrashing around."

Baker got up and walked to the clock sitting on the kitchen counter. It was nine forty-five.

"Lang," she said softly.

"What?"

He turned around to look at Sophia, who appeared as a curved silhouette in the pitch-black room. Not wanting to spend another minute in the dark, he flicked on the light switch. His pupils painfully contracted as a bright-orange light filled the place before subsiding into a dull pallid glow.

"It's what you kept muttering," she said. "You kept saying 'Lang' over and over again. What is it?"

"Not what, Sophia. Who?"

He ignored Sophia's quizzical look as he splashed water on his face and stretched. Finally, he uncuffed her from the radiator. She rubbed her wrists and then slapped Baker sharply across the face.

"Chain me to something again, and you'll learn why I'm the Kremlin's top assassin."

"Fair enough," said Baker, rubbing his cheek.

* * *

They arrived in El Sereno around 10:20 p.m. Baker parked the Continental several blocks away from the club. This was one of the oldest communities in Los Angeles, dating back to the late eighteenth century. In English, its name translated to tranquility, *a rather humorous irony*, Baker thought.

The Red Sword was a squat building covered in neon lights that illuminated the motorcycle-lined street. A mechanical man affixed to the building's facade kept sheathing and unsheathing a red saber, courtesy of rusted gears and pulleys. As they neared the club, Baker heard the din inside. Music was playing, but he could not distinguish the song over all the shouts and laughter escaping into the thick evening air. An iron curtain of mugginess had settled over the city once the sun went down, making it a little hard to breathe. A large man in a wide-shouldered zoot suit stood at the entrance, glowering down at them. A flamboyantly yellow feather stuck out of his hat.

"Can I help you?" he growled.

"Yes, sir," started Sophia. "We were hoping to go inside, if you please."

She smiled at the beefy man, causing his glower to grow in size.

"Business?" he grunted.

"Um, business? Yes, we have a meeting at your establishment. We are a shade early, but—"

"This ain't no conference room, gringos," said the guard, placing a cigar the girth of an engorged tick between his teeth. He lit it with a dented Zippo engraved with skull and crossbones.

Sophia was not disheartened. "Look, sir. Uh, what's your name?"

"Edgar Ramirez," said the bouncer, puffing out large plumes of smoke like a dragon roused from a deep slumber.

Christ, thought Baker. *We're standing face-to-face with the Pistoleros' muscle.* He now wished he'd written a last will and testament like old Arty Scholz. If things went south, there'd be no protection for himself or Sophia.

"Look, Mr. Ramirez—er—Edgar," began Sophia, "it is of the utmost importance that we gain access to your establishment tonight. You can pat us down. We are not armed, and we can pay you handsomely."

Edgar's eyebrows shot up.

"Ah, I see you are a discerning businessman," she continued. "Just name your price."

Baker started to panic. The part about not being armed was true because he'd insisted on leaving their guns in the car (Sophia's piece was a Makarov pistol, as he learned on the drive over). But as for the bribe, he was pretty short on cash at the moment.

"Fifty dollars for each of you," rumbled Edgar, his fat cigar bobbing up and down as he spoke.

Sophia beamed up at Edgar. "Very good," she said, and reached inside her trench coat to extract a fat wad of American bills. She peeled two $50 notes from the top of the pile and handed them over to Edgar, who swiftly pocketed them. He then patted them down—with surprisingly tender hands—and waved them inside.

"Go on," he snarled. "Before I change my mind."

Sophia made to push open the swinging saloon doors, but Baker put his hand on hers.

"Are you sure you want to go in there?" he asked again.

"Enough with the sheepishness already, Baker. I'm beginning to think the file on you was inaccurate." She pushed open the doors and walked inside.

"You have a file on me?" he asked, trailing after her.

The bar smelled strongly of marijuana and beer. The grimy floor, which may have once been blue linoleum, was coated in a layer of sawdust, dried vomit, and the seeds and stems of desiccated marijuana plants. Vinyl-topped tables and red upholstered chairs dotted the room. Almost all of them were occupied. On a small metal platform in the front of the room, a Negro band was playing a jazzed-up version of the Coasters' "Down in Mexico." A bright-yellow legend plastered across the bass drum declared that the group was called THE TOUCANS. All of its members were dressed in silver dinner jackets and bright-red bow ties. Scantily clad women gyrated in time to the music as men threw dollars, pesos, and even cigarette butts at them. Others clinked foaming mugs of frosty beer, huffed on pungent cannabis cigarettes, or snorted fat lines of cocaine with rolled-up dollar bills.

"Where did you get all that money?" Baker asked Sophia, catching up with her as she scanned the crowd of gang members clad in black leather jackets patched with images of pistols and calacas. Everyone, except the band, was speaking Spanish.

"Oh, come now, Baker," answered Sophia with an airy chuckle. "You think the Soviet government would send me on a mission without any operational funds? I guess your file was wrong about you being an adept problem solver."

She moved on, once again leaving a dumbstruck Baker behind. He started to run after her and slid on the greasy floor. Baker and Sophia's presence did not go unnoticed as dozens of narrowed eyes—including those from a particularly nasty-looking group of men playing poker—swiveled around to gaze upon the newcomers. One of them sported a large eye patch with a grisly red scar running underneath it.

"Oi! Querida!" called out a chubby specimen at the poker game, who was pushing his leather jacket to its absolute breaking point. "Why don't you come over here and let Miguel show you a good time, eh? It's been a long time since I've enjoyed some white meat."

It happened in an instant. Sophia leapt like a tiger and the next thing Baker knew, Miguel was drowning in his own stein of beer. He flailed his pudgy limbs, trying to grab at her, but they were too stubby. Beer slopped all over the table, drenching the playing cards and floor before she let him go. Miguel came up for air, sputtering and wiping beer from his goatee and beady eyes, which now looked frightened.

The whole joint had gone silent. Even the band had stopped playing.

"You crazy puta!" Miguel spat at Sophia.

A manic glint in her eyes, she shouted to the bar at large, "Anyone else want to tangle with the gringos?"

The silence endured another moment before everything returned to normal. The band leader snapped his fingers and continued the song.

"That was brilliant!" exclaimed Baker in Sophia's ear as they walked away. "Maybe we won't die here after all."

She smiled and rolled her eyes.

"Say," Baker added, changing the subject. "Where is this contact of yours anyway?"

"Excuse me," whistled a reedy voice from behind them. They turned to see a diminutive, white-jacketed waiter standing behind them. "The gentleman in the corner there would like to buy both of you a drink." The waiter pointed to a small alcove with a table big enough for two or three people. It was already occupied by someone obscured in smoke and shadow.

Baker and Sophia allowed the waiter to lead them to the alcove. He settled them in chairs and took their orders: a glass of peach schnapps for Baker and a shot of chilled vodka for Sophia.

"And for you, sir?" asked the waiter of the mysterious individual.

"Another scotch and soda, if you please, Pablo. Thank you."

The stranger's voice was deep and clipped. His face was still hidden in the smoke cloud trailing from his cigarette, which sat in a thin ivory holder.

"Very good, sir," said Pablo, who left to get their drinks. When he was out of earshot, the man spoke again.

"Well, young lady. I must say that was quite the impressive performance. Ever thought of being in the motion pictures?"

"Not particularly," Sophia said. "I've never been much of a film fan. Don't get much of them from where I'm from."

"Oh, but my dear, motion pictures are the lifeblood of this town. Storytelling is a powerful thing!"

Pablo quickly returned with their drinks, and they all sipped in silence. The alcohol warmed the back of Baker's throat and was traveling to his head quickly.

"Well, Mr. Storyteller," began Sophia. "Why don't you lean in so we can get a look at your face? And no sudden movements or my partner and I will be forced to do something you might regret."

"Well, we can't have that, now, can we?" chuckled the man, leaning forward.

From what Baker could tell, Sophia's contact was somewhere in his mid-fifties. He wore a magnificent mustard-colored suit and thick, black-framed glasses. But the most notable part of his person was an imperial mustache that curled into slight spirals at each end. His face was somewhat mottled near the chin and around the mouth, as if some childhood disease or shaving incident had left permanent scarring.

"Better?" he asked Sophia.

"Much," she replied. "Now let's get down to brass tacks. What's our next move, now that Huston and Cronkite are dead?"

"May I answer that with a question of my own, Agent Vikhrov? Why are you bringing this man here when I was under the impression that we were to be the only participants in this meeting? How do I know this is not a setup and that he is not a HUAC inspector in disguise, ready to whisk me away to the nearest hoosegow?"

"And what grounds would I have for arresting you?" asked Baker.

"The ultimate sin, my good man!" said the man, gesticulating wildly with his cigarette. "The crime of standing up for the poor, downtrodden worker. Now tell me, when did that become an offense punishable by death, hmm?"

"Christ, you're one, too?" said Baker in an undertone.

While the alcove was quite isolated and the club's din obscured their conversation, the mustachioed man lowered his voice anyway. "Precisely!" he hissed.

"Then why admit it to me? You said I could be a HUAC inspector."

"Oh, I was only teasing. I know who you are, Detective Baker. I just didn't realize we were inviting you to the party after all. Please forgive me—my wife says I have a flair for the theatrics. From what I've heard, you have a good heart, despite your hardened exterior and, forgive me, quite the affinity for peach schnapps. I wouldn't dream of you turning in a harmless Communist such as myself to the proper authorities."

"So, everyone's an expert on Morris Baker then, huh?" Baker said, beckoning Pablo over for a refill. The man did have a point, though. Baker had met two Reds in one day and not once did he seriously think of turning them in, of reaping the cash reward that was paid for in blood. He'd become a top scholar on blind fear during the war. How it could turn your best friend into your worst enemy. He would not rat out Sophia or this strange man, this alleged Liberty Boy informant who spoke with such impassioned formality. They were not the soul-sucking monsters the government made them out to be. This internal thought process must have shown on Baker's face, and the man smiled knowingly.

"You see? I'm very good at reading people," he declared. "Even better at creating them!"

"Come again?" Sophia said, knocking back her vodka in one gulp and grimacing. She signaled for another. *Don't Russians love vodka or is that just another part of federal propaganda?* Baker asked himself.

"Scriptwriter by trade, my dear lady," said the man. "Nothing better on this earth than a warm bath and the smell of fresh ink in a typewriter." He stubbed out his cigarette in a crystal ashtray and loaded another into the ivory holder before taking a measured sip of scotch and soda. "I was disgraced by the industry I had helped make so rich. A sham hearing, a year in jail, a hefty fine, and no steady work. Quite a deal, wouldn't you say? I should consider myself lucky. This was before McCarthy became president and started executing every Communist he could find. If he wasn't imprisoning or deporting them for life, that is."

He laughed wickedly, then took on a more somber tone. "Of course, not all of us were so lucky. My good friend Maurice Rapf committed suicide rather than allow those HUAC fiends to drag him out of his house in the middle of the night. It didn't even matter that his father was a producer for MGM. They kick out the Commies and the Jews, the ones who built this damn town, and now what has the industry become? I'll tell you: complete and utter horse hockey. Not a creative story out there. Except for mine, of course."

"Wait, what do you mean?" asked Baker. "I thought you said you were blacklisted?"

"Oh, Detective. Have you two ever heard of the time-honored phrase *If you can't beat them, join them*?"

"Yes," replied Baker and Sophia together.

"Well, there you are. I apply that logic to making a living in this town when no one will hire me. A man and his family still have to eat. I've continued to work in the movie business, but not so you'd ever know it. Have you ever seen a little picture known as *Roman Holiday*?"

"You wrote that?" Baker said, impressed. He had seen it five years ago while still a rookie on the force. The film stuck with him as one of the better movies of McCarthy's repetitive moviemaking machine.

"The very one!" exclaimed the screenwriter, now twirling his mustache with a free finger. "Where is the best place to hide from your enemies? Right in plain sight. And when one works where one shouldn't, one hears things. Information that could be quite useful to individuals such as yourselves. Individuals against the accursed regime. It's how I got in touch with your superiors and brought you to our aid, my dear," he added, winking at Sophia.

He dropped the dramatic shtick and took on a more serious tone. "You must put a stop to this bomb business, both of you. We can still beat the devils at their own game!"

Baker was on the edge of his seat now.

"These are dangerous times, in which our leaders cannot see in front of their own faces," continued the screenwriter. "And when that happens, it is up to the people to make things right. Democracy isn't a gift. It's a responsibility."

Charles Ward's words rang in Baker's ears again: "*If we keep turning a blind eye, there's no hope for any of us... We could always use a little more truth in this world.*"

The screenwriter reached inside his suit jacket. After years of police work, Baker thought the man was going to pull out a gun. But it was only a sheaf of folded papers.

"What's that?" asked Baker.

"Insurance," said the screenwriter. "I do tend to talk too much, don't I? Writing is much more my speed. Glad I considered this little contingency in case you were followed here, which you were. Should you succeed in your mission, there may be hope for American liberty yet. As for me, I now 'exit stage left,' as they say in the biz. Good luck."

The man closed his eyes. Before either Baker or Sophia could pose another question, there was a loud *Bang!* The man's head exploded in a shower of red mist. His body slumped forward onto the table as blood and bits of brain matter spurted from his exposed skull and into the half-finished scotch and soda.

Baker instinctively ducked underneath the table and placed a firm hand on Sophia's back, forcing her to follow suit. The screenwriter's feet gave a final, spasmodic jerk and then lay still. Blood, brains, and bone fragments were plastered to the table and wall. Baker snatched the folded papers out of the man's hand and cautioned a look over the table. He briefly glimpsed a trench-coated figure forcing its way past the women and out the front doors. The coat's belt whipped around the corner and was gone from sight.

Pandemonium ensued. Half-naked women ran around aimlessly; the band cowered behind their instruments; and gang members drew their pistols and started to advance on the alcove where Baker and Sophia were posted up with a dead man. Edgar, a murderous look on his face, was bringing up the rear, a large purple lump forming on his temple.

CHAPTER 13

Baker stuffed the screenwriter's papers into his jacket and held his hands up to show he was unarmed. He urged Sophia to do the same.

"I was wrong. We *are* gonna die here!" he whispered.

"Stop being so dramatic!" she hissed back.

"Ay, gringos! Come out from under there!" someone shouted. "You think you can come in here and just start shooting whoever you like?"

Baker and Sophia slowly came up from beneath the table, hands up high, blood and gray matter speckled on their faces and clothing. Edgar was cracking his knuckles. Baker didn't blame him. The guard who didn't want to let them in to begin with would now get to kill them and keep their cash. Not bad for a night's work.

Miguel, still wet from his dip in the beer, looked ecstatic. "Oh, querida," he said to Sophia, his eyes alight with animus. "I'm going cut up that beautiful face of yours. Then we'll see if you try and drown me."

Baker and Sophia were finally on their feet, facing a dozen or so armed members of the Pistoleros. Some held guns, others brandished knives, and one individual even handled a pair of throwing stars (acquired in Chinatown, no doubt). *This is the end*, Baker told himself, *dying in agony at the hands of a gang with an insatiable bloodlust. Torn limb from—*

"Esperen—wait!" someone shouted to the crowd. "Don't shoot!"

Everyone turned to the stage where a woman stood, resolute. She had heavily lidded eyes, dark skin, and beautifully chiseled features. Her black hair cascaded down to her shoulders in shining ringlets. She looked familiar to Baker, though he couldn't immediately place her.

"And why," Miguel asked, "would we not shoot these good-for-nothing gate-crashers? Of course, I'd like to have some time alone with the girl first." He smiled to reveal a pitiful collection of rotting teeth.

"You will not shoot them because they are my guests," replied the woman. "They are here on my invitation." She did not sound frightened. In fact, some of the grizzled men seemed to be cowering under her intense gaze.

"Come on, Valentina," said one brave soul. "You can't have invited these two here."

"I did and if you don't mind, they will now join me in the back of *my* establishment. Will you please put those damnable guns away?"

Her glare turned into a warm smile as she looked at Baker and Sophia, beckoning them over with a curled finger. She also summoned Edgar. The beads at the end of her satin shawl made slight clinking noises as she turned. It looked like she was ready for bed, not a night of music and boozing.

Slowly, Baker and Sophia made their way over to Valentina, lightly treading past the horde of angry gang members re-holstering their weapons. Edgar came lumbering up behind them and had to take a knee to speak with Valentina.

"What happened, cariño?" she asked him.

"They came up from behind and hit me," he replied, pointing to the bump on his head, still swelling and now turning dark blue. "Pretty good hit, too. Knocked me out cold for a minute. Once they took the shot, they didn't waste any time sticking around. I'll ask around, but we all had our eyes on their table." He leveled a meaty finger at Baker and Sophia. "I doubt anyone noticed a face. Was probably wearing a mask."

"They wore a trench coat," piped up Baker. Valentina and Edgar looked at him.

"Ah, yes," said Edgar sarcastically. "A trench coat is such a rare piece of clothing these days. We're sure to find them in no time. You could be a detective with those deduction skills."

"Edgar," said Valentina calmly. "Take care of that bump, make sure that the mess is cleaned up, and please call Mr. Rich's wife. Then see to it that the guests are calmed down and ask if they saw anything of note. For good measure, tell them the next three rounds are on the house."

Valentina stood on tiptoe and gave him a kiss on the cheek, which caused the large man to blush. "You got it, boss," he said.

"Boss?" said Baker and Sophia together.

"Not here," said Valentina in response to their question. "You two follow me now."

She led them through a reinforced-steel door in the back of the club hidden by a curtain of slinking beads. They were ushered into a dark storage room before Valentina slammed the door shut. There was no light, but Baker heard the unmistakable sound of a bolt sliding into place. Back in the club, the band had struck up a muffled rendition of the Champs' "Tequila."

Baker then heard shuffling and a click. Light suddenly illuminated the cramped space, which smelled strongly of mildew. Beer kegs and several unmarked crates were neatly stacked against the cracked brick walls.

"Where...?" Baker and Sophia began to ask, but Valentina put a finger to her lips.

"Not here," she whispered again. "Come." She disappeared into a dark tunnel, and they followed in silence for about five minutes until Baker caught sight of a warm glow.

Baker and Sophia shielded their eyes as they emerged into a grandiose foyer of velvet carpets and chenille curtains. A bright crescent moon, framed by large bay windows, was weakly shining through the city smog. They heard a *slam!* and turned to see Valentina locking a second and thicker metal door than the one she'd led them through in the club.

She turned to face them and re-draped the shawl she was wearing around her thin shoulders. "Fools! Both of you. What were you thinking coming here?" Her English was immaculate, but much like Baker and his Eastern European lilt, Valentina could not fully hide her Spanish accent.

Then the answer came to him. "Scholz!" Baker exclaimed.

"What?" she asked, taken aback.

"Scholz," he repeated. "I knew you looked familiar, and I just remembered we saw each other this morning at the reading of Arthur Scholz's will."

He couldn't believe it took this long to recognize her, but her face had been partly obscured with a veil during their shared visit to City Hall. That, and so much had already transpired between the reading of Scholz's will and the screenwriter's death in the Red Sword.

"Oh, Artie," sighed Valentina, her anger giving way to sorrow. "Yes, I recognized you from the moment you walked in. If Artie trusted you, I knew I couldn't let them shoot you back there. I also know it was not you who murdered Mr. Rich."

"Who?" Baker asked.

"One of the club's best customers, the man currently lying in my bar without most of his head."

"Oh, we didn't get his name," said Sophia. "Where are we, anyway?"

"Why," said Valentina, a weary smile playing over her lips, "this is the most moderately priced whorehouse in all of Los Angeles."

"So, you own this place, huh?" Baker said. He turned in a small circle to better appreciate the lavish setting. "I always thought that..."

"What? That those idiotas with pistols owned it? Don't make me laugh," Valentina scoffed. "They're too busy shooting their pitos off to actually run a business. Ask one of them to file federal income taxes and you can almost see smoke coming out his ears. No, I run both establishments with my sister, Renata, although she doesn't like to spend time here. She lives near the border with one of her boyfriends. Vargas, I think his name is. A gringo raised by Mexicans. How's that for some family history?"

She led them to some overstuffed armchairs located in the reception area, where clients waited to be greeted by prostitutes. Tonight, Valentina said, the girls had been sent to bed early. She then left Baker and Sophia to fetch drinks and a small tray of tres leches cookies. Upon her return, Valentina insisted that the two of them have some mescal to settle their nerves. Baker, who had been steadily destroying his liver for over a decade, was surprised at the harshness of the tequila slithering down his throat. It was like ingesting raw stomach acid. Sophia choked on hers and had to be given a glass of water. At such close range, Baker realized that Valentina was much older than he initially realized, but beautiful in an elegant way he couldn't fully describe.

"You weren't really Dr. Scholz's maid, were you?" Baker asked, testing the waters. He stuck a Kool between his lips and set it ablaze, hungrily sucking in a lungful of menthol-flavored smoke.

"Ha!" Valentina laughed, lighting up a home-rolled cigarette. "Very good, Detective. There was definitely much cleaning to be done when we were finished with a room, but neither of us ever picked up so much as a feather duster... for cleaning, anyway."

She smiled and Baker was impressed (not to mention a tad uncomfortable) at how unabashed Valentina was when it came to discussing her love life with two complete strangers.

"Artie was a sweet man," the madam continued. "Not like some of the scum that comes here to beat up a defenseless woman after having his way with her." She spat some stray tobacco on the floor. "Artie was different. He was..."

"A Nazi," Baker blurted out. Sophia looked at him in shock. Valentina looked resigned, as if she knew this was coming. "His name was Adolf Lang, not Arthur Scholz, and he was a monster. Doctor Professor Adolf Xavier Lang of the SS," Baker said. "The bastard changed his name, didn't he?"

Valentina reached out to lay a comforting hand on Baker's knee, but he jerked his leg away. Hatred he had not felt in a very long time bubbled up inside his chest like liquid magma.

"I know," she said, solemnly. "He told me everything before he died, and you cannot believe the remorse he felt. Even I—who was closest to him—cannot understand how someone could have done such thi—"

"He had surgery done, didn't he?" Baker asked, cutting her off. "To fill in the scar on his left cheek and to give him a cleft chin. He also grew a mustache, which is why I didn't recognize him in those pictures he left me. Am I right?"

She did not reply. *"Answer me!"* he bellowed, standing up and kicking a nearby ottoman so that it skidded across the floor. It left irregular scratch marks in the wood. The madam nodded, still not breaking eye contact.

How was it fair that so many perished by Lang's hand, but he got to live a long life, enjoying adventures in Africa, a cushy teaching job at USC, and a beautiful lover like Valentina? There was no justice in the world. None.

"You knew what he was, and you still fucked him!" Baker screamed, unable to control himself.

Valentina didn't flinch. "The man I knew was not the one you knew, Detective. He was a sweet, kind man who..."

"Yeah, he was some man, all right," Baker said. Fuming, he left the foyer. He didn't know the layout of the place, but he did not want to sit in the awkward silence caused by his outburst; did not want to look at the woman who claimed to love something as inhuman as Adolf Lang.

"Morris!" called Sophia after him, her voice still hoarse from the mescal. But it was too late. He stalked out of the foyer, blinded by anger and bitter memories.

* * *

It was musty in the cathouse, as if years of degenerates' ejaculate hung in the air like steam from a boiling pot. Or maybe it was just the elder majesty of the place. Its velvet carpets and marble staircases might've been transplanted from some royal palace in Europe.

Baker found himself in a hallway that seemed to stretch on forever. Watercolor paintings of indescribable blobs lined the walls. They reminded him of the posters hanging in John Huston's home. Films of a bygone era that had fallen into obscurity.

"Señor Baker?" The voice was gentle, almost motherly. He turned around and saw Valentina standing in the entrance to the hallway. "I did not mean to upset you," she said.

Baker's anger fluttered and died. Directing his fury at Valentina would do no good for anyone.

"I know. I'm sorry," he began. "Please accept my..."

"No apologies necessary, señor," said Valentina. "I know what Artie did during the war, and I do not think there is proper forgiveness in this life or the next. I gave him a temporary refuge from the guilt, but his future was cursed as soon as he laid his fingers on the innocent. You, on the other hand, well, your future is just beginning. You can choose to let the past dictate your path in life or you can use it as a way to appreciate what you have in this world. Not forget it, never forget it. You cannot and should not forget such things, but harnessing it is something else entirely."

"Miss Vasquez, what did Lang do at USC? Did he teach medicine?"

She looked a little taken aback, as if he hadn't been listening to what she said. "As a matter of fact, he did," she said. "He also did research on nuclear physics for the government, but he was never allowed to tell me much about that."

"Busy guy."

"Smart guy. It was a shame a mind like Artie's was put toward doing the things he did."

"There's no telling what any of us are capable of," replied Baker. "Any idea how he died?"

"Fenwick said it was a heart attack, but I don't believe it," she said sadly. "I think Artie killed himself."

"What makes you say that?"

"He was with me a few nights before he died and was in a very strange mood. After we made love, he began to cry and laugh at the same time. I was frightened and asked him what was wrong. He would only tell me that he was about to find true peace for what he had done."

"You said he told you everything about his wartime activities before he died. What did he say about me?"

"To help you if you ever showed up here and to tell you that he was sorry."

"That's it? He didn't say why he was leaving me a photograph album in his will?"

"No, and I don't want to know any more. I've since guessed that Artie was involved with something bad, and now he's involving you in it. You poor man, after all you've been through."

Silence pervaded the hallway before Valentina spoke again. "You and the girl are welcome to stay the night," she said, her hand hovering just above his shoulder. There was an uncomfortable pause before the hand fell away. "I cannot stop you if you want to continue looking into whatever you think is going on. Just know some things are not revealed without a price..."

"Morris?" Sophia was at his side now, an intruder on the intimate moment. "I was just thinking. We should take a look at the papers you took from the screenwriter if we're going to get any closer to solving this thing."

Baker blinked. All he could remember was the scriptwriter's head exploding like a balloon full of red ink. Then it clicked. He reached into his jacket pocket and pulled out the crumpled pieces of paper flecked with the dead man's drying blood. Sophia stood by his side as they read what seemed to be an excerpt from a screenplay. And not just any screenplay; it featured Baker and Sophia...

4.

EXT. HUSTON'S HOME—NIGHT

The Camera Follows the team of an LAPD DETEC-TIVE, a haggard male, and a SOVIET SPY, a beautiful woman, as they enter the deceased director's home under the guise of darkness before we . . .

CUT TO:

INT. HUSTON'S HOME—CONTINUOUS

All is STILL AND QUIET in the house as the two creep down the hallway toward a modern-looking kitchen. Their reflections gleam eerily back at them from the various appliances.

INT. HUSTON'S KITCHEN—CONTINUOUS

DETECTIVE

Let's split up and search the place.

The Soviet Spy nods and they begin to
search the kitchen. They open drawers, cabi-
nets, and the oven. Nothing is found until the
Spy opens the icebox and recoils in disgust,
GAGGING.

DETECTIVE

What is it, sweetheart?

The Spy is too overcome with repugnance and cannot immediately answer. Revulsion and nausea
are plainly displayed on her pretty face.

The scene cut out there. Baker and Sophia looked at each other, confused. Baker riffled through the other pages, but there was nothing, except a preposterous treatment for a film about Israel that would never be made in McCarthy's Hollywood. As if anyone gave a shit about the Jewish homeland anymore. The president had immediately cut aid to the fledgling country the first chance he got, saying that the Rosenbergs' betrayal was on the shoulders of the entire Jewish population. Without the financial or military backing of the United States, the tiny, ten-year-old country had been locked in a bloody conflict with several enemy nations that went straight for the jugular after sensing a moment of weakness. An Israeli surrender was expected any day.

Baker turned to Valentina. "We'll have to take a rain check on that sleepover, Miss Vasquez. We've got somewhere to be. Thanks…for everything."

"Mind if I use the little girls' room before we leave?" Sophia asked Valentina.

"Of course," Valentina said. "Down the hall and to the left near the phone."

Sophia disappeared for ten minutes and reappeared, looking flustered.

"Sorry," she said distractedly. "Got turned around."

"You are always welcome here," said Valentina as she ushered them out the front door. "And Detective?" Baker turned around to face Valentina. "Be careful. Buena suerte."

A moment later, they were out into the muggy night and walking back to the car. "Do you really think I'm a sweetheart?" Sophia asked Baker as they hopped into the Continental.

Baker laughed and began the journey back to Echo Park.

CHAPTER 14

Altivo Way looked even more like a jungle now that it was dark out. The chirp of cicadas hiding in the trees was almost deafening. It should have taken less than half an hour to travel from El Sereno to Echo Park via the East Valley Boulevard at this time of night. However, the Continental's collision with a metal pole the previous day caused the car to stall several times as it puffed acrid plumes of black smoke into the already smog-choked sky.

It was past midnight by the time Baker and Sophia pulled up to the puzzle-box home of John Huston. The house looked as dead as its previous occupant, a collection of sharp angles sticking out of the darkness. Straggling bits of yellow police tape hung limply around the front yard, swaying with every merciful breeze that made its way down the street.

Although it was not cold, Baker shivered as he stepped out of the car and looked at Sophia. She was even more ravishing in the weak moonlight. "Well, better do as the script says," he whispered, his voice almost drowned out by the chorus of cicadas.

As they made their way up the stone pathway, Baker thought he saw a pair of flickering yellow eyes, which turned out to be two fireflies hovering close to the manicured lawn. He again reminded himself to keep an eye out for hungry tigers. Come to think of it, this whole case felt like a jungle, one that got darker and more dangerous the more he hacked away with his machete.

"Think it's locked?" asked Sophia when they reached the door.

"I doubt it," said Baker. "Hueys are sloppy. They barely remember to tie their shoes after leaving a crime scene."

He was right. The door silently swung inward. It was deathly quiet inside the house, and Baker could just make out the framed posters lining the entryway. He turned on the flashlight he had extricated from the Continental's glove compartment and stepped over the threshold. He was closely followed by Sophia, who clutched his elbow. Once inside, Baker closed the door noiselessly behind them.

The flashlight cast an ominous and concentrated beam down the hallway. He didn't need much light to see the place had been ransacked by the Hueys, but what the hell were they looking for? Again, Baker thought of those three words left by Cronkite. They subtly beat in his mind as his heart raced with adrenaline.

Beat.

the.

Devils.

"The kitchen's down here," whispered Baker as they passed the living room where the bodies of Huston and Cronkite had been discovered. He knew the two men were now lying inside refrigerated cases below City Hall, but even so, he didn't want to enter that room ever again. Who knew if that accursed record player would begin playing "Ride of the Valkyries," spinning with the help of spirits that would not let him rest?

True to Mr. Rich's screenplay, the kitchen was quite modern. Baker hadn't gotten a chance to inspect the entire house before Hartwell and Waldgrave showed up to oust him and Connolly the day before. The place was packed with high-end appliances: an Admiral icebox, Hotpoint oven, Arvin dinette set, and a Kenmore garbage burner. While he'd no longer been a Hollywood hotshot, Huston really knew how to live.

"I guess we already know where to look," said Sophia, who placed one hand on the polished handle of the Admiral.

"Wait!" hissed Baker, pulling his gun from its holster and sidling up next to her. "Okay. Now."

She tugged the door open and a fetid wave of air rushed out like a starved prisoner. Sophia doubled over, retching, then ran over to the sink and vomited. He heard her cursing in English as she ran the water to wash out her mouth.

"What the fuck!" she gurgled.

Baker smiled. She was still so young, so untainted by the horrific odors the world could produce, given the right conditions.

"Someone's unplugged it," he replied, looking at the blue and green lumps of what were once meats, vegetables, and blocks of cheese. "Everything's gone bad."

The horrible smell was fast pervading the kitchen. Baker decided against opening a window, in case their voices alerted a neighbor.

"And why," began Sophia, walking back to Baker's side with a napkin around her mouth and nose, "would someone do that?"

"The same reason you'd rub shit on yourself if you were being hunted by bloodhounds. To throw them off your scent."

She still looked confused.

"Would you pay much attention to a bunch of food that's gone bad?" Baker said. "Look how you just reacted. You'd want it shut immediately. A strong and confusing smell to throw off the hounds. Or Hueys, in this case. They like to get dirty, but they're not as tough as they think they are. One whiff of this icebox and they'd move on without a second glance."

"Well, there are those bright-as-the-sun detective skills I read about in your file," Sophia said. "Very impressive, but still I don't see why Huston would see to it that all this food went to waste."

"Don't you?" said Baker, his finger pointing to a white Entenmann's box sitting on the top shelf. "Care for some devil's food cake?"

Green mold covered the chocolate dessert through the box's plastic window. Baker lifted it out of the refrigerator and placed it onto the kitchen counter. He then closed the door, much to Sophia's relief. Opening the cake box, they found a note taped to the cardboard lid. Spores of newly sprouted fungus clung to the slanted calligraphy:

To My African Queen,

"When the Queen of Sheba heard of Solomon's fame...she came to test him with riddles."—Kings: Chapter 10, Verse 1
"I am become death, the destroyer of worlds."—J. Robert Oppenheimer

PS: Must remember to get in touch with Humphrey about new picture idea.

Baker read the note three times with Sophia looking over his shoulder. The first half of it was carefully written while the postscript looked to be a scribbled afterthought. Given the director's former cinematic projects, it was not hard to deduce the "Humphrey" to whom the note referred. It was the biblical reference and Oppenheimer quote that confused Baker.

"Any idea why he would quote that particular verse?" he asked Sophia.

"It's been a while since Sunday school, but I think Sheba was an Ethiopian monarch, which would explain the title of *African Queen*. Does Huston have a Negro wife?"

"No. She's Italian."

"What about Cronkite?"

"No clue." Baker recalled the picture of the two young girls he had seen in Cronkite's wallet. The thought of them crying over their dead father floated to the surface of his mind as the gloom of Huston's home threatened to crush him alive. Like the death grip of a massive python.

"Well, the Oppenheimer quote is easy," Sophia said. "It's what he said when America created the first atomic b—"

Crash!

Baker grabbed Sophia's hand. "Someone's outside. We've gotta go, now!"

He grabbed the devil's food cake note, stuffed it into his pocket, and grabbed his gun and the flashlight, which he flicked off. They sprinted through the house and into the night. The cicadas had reached the point of hysteria. Baker could hear the subtle *Pat! Pat! Pat!* of rubber soles running around the side of the house. Without a backward glance, they hopped into the Continental. Baker turned the key as the engine sputtered and died.

"Not now, you stupid piece of—" The engine miraculously roared to life and Baker slammed his foot on the gas pedal just as he heard the unmistakable sound of a gun's hammer being pulled back. They drove away from the curb in a screech of tires that was sure to wake the entire neighborhood. But it didn't matter. They'd be long gone before anyone had time to put on their housecoat and slippers.

Once they hit Valley Boulevard, the danger left far behind, Baker and Sophia stole a glance at each other and began to cackle like a pair of hyenas.

"I don't care what your government says about my people," said Sophia, running her hands through her hair as the breeze whipped it into a frenzy. "Who says Communists can't have fun?"

CHAPTER 15

Back in Chinatown, Baker took Sophia to The Golden Fowl, his favorite late-night eatery, which, in his humble opinion, made the best Peking duck in all of Los Angeles. Freshly dispatched waterfowl hung in the window like convicted outlaws of the Old West. It was well past one in the morning, but the restaurant was packed and alive with the sounds of merriment. Thick steam carried the earthy scents of soy sauce, ginger, and five spice out of the open kitchen where cooks prepared dishes over hot woks and yelled to one another in Mandarin.

The owner, Hollis Li, recognized Baker at once and ushered them to the detective's favorite table in the corner with a big smile plastered on his face.

"Ah, Baker," he said in his thick North China lilt. "So good to see you again. The usual?" His voice was light and airy like the bao pork dumplings they made here.

"You know it, Hollis," replied Baker with a wink.

As always, "Mr. Lee" by the Bobbettes was playing on a loop. Hollis never accepted Baker's reasoned protests that the song was not about

Hollis. This topic was broached at least once during the drunken conversations they would sometimes enjoy into the wee hours of the morning. Baker would always drink schnapps while Hollis sipped bathtub shaojiu, a beverage he could not import due to America's strict trade embargo on Communist China. In the early days of their friendship, the two had trouble understanding each other through their accents, but they eventually discovered a common language among the slurred consonants of seasoned drinkers.

"Very good," said Hollis. "If you don't mind me saying so, your companion is very, very pretty."

Sophia blushed. Hollis adjusted his wrinkled teal bow tie and ran off toward the kitchen, smacking a busboy in the back of the head for not moving out of the way fast enough. He returned moments later with two steaming cups of lavender tea and a large plate of fried duck, its dark and gamy meat separated from the crispy skin, which was presented on the side. Thin scallion pancakes and a tureen of warm hoisin sauce accompanied the dish. This was Baker's favorite meal in town, and he'd never introduced it to anyone else—not even to Liz or Connolly. Normally, a person would have to order the duck a day in advance, but there was always a spare mallard or two whenever Baker decided to show up unannounced.

"Hollis, you never fail to disappoint," Baker said, already assembling a little duck wrap and taking a bite. "Perfection. Will you ever share the recipe with me?"

"Oh, you know I cannot tell you, Detective. My mother's secret family recipe. It's forbidden to tell anyone, but always nice to get compliments from my favorite customer. Enjoy your meal."

Hollis bowed to them and walked behind the counter, his shouts mingling with those of the cooks.

"Eat," said Baker, pushing the plate toward Sophia. "I'm sure you're hungry after emptying your stomach back at Huston's place.

She just sat there, eyeing the food.

"What, never had Chinese before? Here." He took a pancake, placed some duck on it, dipped it in hoisin, and handed it to her. Sophia still looked skeptical, but her eyes lit up as she took a bite.

"See?" he said with an encouraging smile.

"It's delicious!" she said, quickly devouring the duck-filled pancake and assembling another one. "You wouldn't believe all the ways they've been able to work potatoes into every dish back home. It gets boring after a while."

Baker laughed and took a sip of tea. "And home would be...?"

Sophia shook her head. "A poor, no-name village near the Urals. Nothing but snow, and potatoes for dinner every night with the occasional luxury of rassolnik. Not so extravagant as what you can get here in America. Duck blintzes. Who would have guessed? I mean, you are from Eastern Europe yourself, Detective. What simple lives we once led, no?"

"The things they think of here never stop surprising me," answered Baker. He didn't really want to discuss his birthplace. He put his cup down and popped a crispy piece of duck skin into his mouth. "So," he continued, "what led Sophia Vikhrov, a girl from some no-name backwater town, to become a—you know"—he lowered his voice, although no one would care much in The Golden Fowl—"a Soviet spy?"

She smiled at the question, blushing again under the orange glow of the paper lanterns that hung from the ceiling. For a moment, Baker could see past the woman's astonishing beauty and catch a glimpse of the impoverished little girl who had grown up on the frigid and unforgiving Russian steppe. "Same reason you wanted to become an officer of the law. Escape."

"How do you mean?" he asked.

"Come now, Baker. I've read your file. I know about your life before you came to this country. The things you saw and experienced during the war. Well, most of it, anyway. Many parts were redacted."

Suddenly he wasn't hungry anymore. "I did what I had to in order to survive," he mumbled, bringing the teacup back to his lips.

"Exactly," said Sophia. "No one's blaming you. There are things in this world we do to survive and sometimes, we want to forget them once they're over. Escape the darkness of the past. How could we live with ourselves otherwise?" He did not answer, and she pressed on. "My childhood was not like the upbringings people enjoy here in America. There were no ice cream trucks or Peking duck. No radios, even. During the day, I worked hard on my family's farm, which was part of a collective in Stalin's Ten-Year Plan, and during the night, I cowered from my father. One thing all countries share in common is drunkards."

Baker remained silent. A few fingers of peach schnapps would really help improve his tea right about now. The usual cacophony of The Golden Fowl seemed strangely absent.

"My father had seen the czar fall to the revolution," Sophia continued. "He lost his family's factory to those who considered Jews to be subhuman long before Hitler came along. After all, it was the Russians who had put pen to paper and drafted *The Protocols of the Elders of Zion*." Baker's left forearm seemed to burn white hot. "My father didn't know what to believe in anymore after that, so he drank. Made his own vodka by illegally taking potatoes we grew on the farm. The penalty for shorting the government on crops is nothing less than arrest and execution by firing squad. If you're lucky, you get sent to Siberia for hard labor until your dying day. Since he couldn't use too much of the crop, he fermented the potatoes with turpentine. The concoction would drive him insane. He'd beat us senseless: my mother, my little brother, Yuri, and me. Our attempts to spill out the vodka only made it worse and on some of the worst days, he'd take me into the cellar and—"

"Don't say it," interrupted Baker. "Please."

"I'm sorry, I didn't mean to—"

"It's okay," he said. From the sound of it, Sophia's formative years hadn't been much happier than his own.

"Life only got harder when my father was arrested," she explained. "The first chance I got, I ran away from home in the hopes of finding a better life in Moscow. They laughed at first. A female KGB operative? I was told to go back to my potato farm, I was called horrible things, but I stayed and forced them to accept me. And once they saw what I was capable of, there was no more laughter. The little girl who had been beaten and molested, who had been frozen and starved half to death most of her life, became one of Russia's most effective agents. Stalin himself met with me a few months before he died. He said I should be proud of who I was and what I was doing for my country . . ."

Sophia trailed off and began nibbling on a piece of duck gristle. Her eyes seemed to glaze over, looking far away at an invisible horizon of memory Baker could not see.

"But sometimes," Sophia said, "before he started brewing the poison, my father, he'd sit with Yuri and me, and teach us Yiddish and tell us stories about the Golem of Prague and the Wise Men of Chelm. My mother was not a Jew and according to the laws of the religion, neither I nor my brother could be considered Jews ourselves. Nevertheless, he thought we should know these things, to pass them down. So they would not be forgotten. But that was when we were very young. Those memories of a loving father, of the things he once taught me, were all but gone until I met you, Morris Baker."

He could not look her in the face. How many things had he forgotten in the last thirteen years?

"The KGB taught me how to speak several different languages, and Yiddish was not one of them," Sophia added. "That latent connection to our shared heritage was waiting for the right moment to resurface, sealed off by that frightened little girl who wanted to be tough. To forget her past and start anew. But that girl was wrong to wish for such a thing because it was her past that made her the woman that sits in this restaurant before you. Until I met you, Baker, I'd forgotten who Sophia Vikhrov truly was."

Tears began to fall down her face, and she was powerless to stop them. Baker stood and crossed the small table, wrapping his arms around her. He knew all too well what it was like to feel like no one; to try to run from your past only to be consumed by it. There was no cure for the pain. You could only wait until it subsided into the throbbing numbness of a toothache that runs straight down to the nerve. You played a lonely waiting game until your entire sense of self, like Morris Baker's family, like six million others, was gone.

Ashes in the wind.

CHAPTER 16

The Paradise Apartments didn't feel as depressing as they usually did when Baker and Sophia went up to 2A around four in the morning. In an effect that had nothing to do with the heat of the California summer, everything appeared warm and blurred around the edges for Baker. He felt like he was drunk on several bottles of peach schnapps, but he hadn't imbibed anything since that shot of mescal at Valentina's brothel hours before.

Back inside his cluttered apartment, he removed his jacket and gun. Placing both on the kitchen counter, he turned up the volume on his Regency TR-1 radio, something he hadn't done in a long time. He'd splurged on the thing four years ago when transistor radios were first being mass-produced for public consumption. Like everyone else, he was swept up in the paranoid hysteria of wanting to be kept up to date on possible Communist invasions. Two civil defense frequencies would disseminate warnings in such a scenario, but so far, every station (save for some intermittent tests) had remained on the air since the CONELRAD program was first enacted.

Surprisingly, the batteries were still good, and a sad funeral dirge filled the room. *"And now,"* said a deep, garbled voice, *"we honor those individuals our so-called government has seen fit to silence through that tried-and-true method of cold-blooded murder: Ralph Flanders, Paul Robeson, Irving Lerner..."*

The list of names went on and on. For the first time, Baker listened intently to the Liberty Boys broadcast, understanding why so many looked to these messages for hope. "So, they're actually real, eh?" he asked Sophia.

"As a heart attack," she said.

"Any idea who leads them?"

"Not a clue. I was only working with a small rogue faction."

The transmission cut off and was replaced with the ethereal reverberations of the Flamingos' "I Only Have Eyes for You." Sophia sat on the edge of the bed, removing her shoes and tossing them away. She rubbed the soles of her feet with a moan of pleasure.

"Would you care to dance?" asked Baker.

"Not much of a dance floor," said Sophia as she picked up an empty schnapps bottle. A pair of old socks was sticking to its cracked surface. Despite her jest, she was already on her bare feet and gliding over to him with a teasing smile. A true thing of beauty. It was hard to believe they'd been pointing guns at each other just a few hours ago.

Baker took her hand in his, remembering the various sock hops and dance halls Liz had dragged him to over the years. They began a slow waltz around the apartment, sweeping the *Recognize a Communist* manual away with their feet.

Her scent was more intoxicating than lemongrass and stewed plums. He needed her more than he'd ever needed anyone. They'd only just met, but his lust for her went beyond rational logic. It was almost too much. They swayed back and forth, keeping in time with the song. Upon their second trip around the apartment, Sophia pulled her head away from Baker's shoulder and looked up at him.

Then he kissed her. Kissed her as though a missile were headed for Chinatown; as though the Hueys were about to storm the apartment and take them away to separate electric chairs. Sophia tensed for only a moment before wrapping her arms tightly around his neck. It did not even matter that they were both sweaty and covered in blood.

The out-of-focus lens through which Baker now saw the world intensified. It was just him and Sophia—a Jewish American homicide detective and a Russian KGB operative. All differences between their countries fell away in that moment, giving way to pure, animalistic desire. He pulled the straps of her dress away from her shoulders. Like a caterpillar's cocoon, the red fabric dropped to the floor to reveal something even more beautiful underneath: exquisitely curved hips, firm breasts, and flawless skin paler than an early snowfall.

Slowly and tenderly, he helped remove her brassiere, stockings, and garter. Each newly exposed piece of skin was bestowed with a delicate pressing of lips. Once fully undressed, Sophia did nothing to cover her naked body. She simply looked up at Baker with an unblushing confidence.

He'd lain with women before, but never this passionately. It was the kind of sex that made him understand why it was called making love. Baker's physical relationship with Liz was more predicated on fucking than it was on establishing a closer emotional connection. This was not the case with Sophia. Baker felt her body like a blind man reading

Braille, discovering all the intricacies and taking his time, as though he'd never get the chance again.

When they'd both finished, he lay there holding Sophia under the covers as she traced the numbers etched across his forearm. "What's this?" she asked, gently passing her fingers across a depression of wrinkled tissue.

"Long story. I'll tell you all about it sometime," Baker said, already half asleep.

They drifted off to the crooning of Little Anthony, whose voice became dimmer and dimmer. Baker wondered if the radio's batteries were finally failing as he allowed a shroud of pure bliss to take him away into blackness...

* * *

Shovel for an extra ration of bread. Shovel for a better place to sleep. Shovel to stay alive. That's how it was. The unspoken rule that he followed from the early morning to the dead of night. It was his commandment—from when the heat of the ovens first burned his face in the morning, to when he disposed of the ashes in a nearby lake at night.

Ksh! Ksh! Ksh! was the only refrain as he scooped piles of black powder from the crematoria. No other words. No other conversations. Just Ksh! Ksh! Ksh!

It was a sound that kept him alive as he shoveled the sooty remains of death into a wheelbarrow, but it was also the sound that would drive him to the brink of insanity and haunt him for years to come. The lives of hundreds (maybe thousands) condensed into one shovel blade. Children and adults. Doctors, lawyers, artists, rabbis, and writers. Mothers, fathers, brothers and sisters. Nieces and nephews. Uncles and aunts. Cousins, grandmothers, grandfathers, and friends. All people. People who had lived, loved, and laughed; wept and celebrated; choked and died.

Try not to think about it. Ksh! Ksh! Ksh!

"You, there! Jew!" A voice, angry and harsh.

"Yes, Herr Kommandant."

"Tell me, Jew." He's bored, wants to play with you. "Why is it that you have not yet cleaned out your assigned oven?"

"Apologies, Herr Kommandant." You were always sorry. It was always your fault. "A larger transport of the elderly came in today and..."

"I do not care if it was your fucking whore of a Jew mother who came in on the train today. I asked why this oven is not clear of its ashes."

"Apologies, Herr Kommandant. I will work harder from here on—"

Wham! An explosion of stars. A burst of searing pain. A trickle of blood.

"Work harder from here on out, eh?" The commandant was removing his gloves now. Don't look at him, it's what he wants. Keep your eyes on the ground. "Why were you not working harder from the day you were given this position, dog? You have been given better food and living conditions. Have we been so lax that you have been able to get away with being lazy right under our noses? To disrespect our kindness and generosity?"

A fist to stomach. Breath gone. "Yes, Herr Kommandant. I am sorry." Always validate them. Be their lapdog.

"Oh, so you agree, then? You admit you have been lazy right under my nose?"

Another punch. This one to the small of the back, the kidneys. Pain shoots up and down the body, weakens the knees. "I am sorry Herr Kommandant. So sorry. Please."

"Do you know what we do to lazy Jew filth around here? Hmm, do you?"

Don't answer. Never answer. Remain silent. Ignore the pain. Don't look up. Stay alive.

Ksh! Ksh! Ksh!

"One of my bullets is too good for you, but I know just how to force a lesson into that rat brain of yours. And let it be a lesson to all of you!"

The rest of them aren't looking. Their eyes are on their own work as they silently thank their lucky stars that the commandant has not chosen them as his plaything today.

The shovel. Then the darkness. It's where the world ended, but also where it began.

Ksh! Ksh! Ksh!

WASHINGTON WRANGLES WARNERS!

Former Hollywood studio moguls Harry, Albert, and Jack Warner were arrested by federal HUAC agents today in a raid conducted at one of the brothers' nightclubs in New York City. The establishment in question, The Hungry Locust, was suspected of serving as a crucial meeting hub for Communist and homosexual subversives on the East Coast of the United States.

"The investigation is still ongoing, but we have charged the Warners with several counts of racketeering and money laundering as a start," Melvin Purvis (formerly of the FBI and now head of HUAC's Manhattan office) said during a press conference held shortly after the arrests. "It seems they were running illicit funds, possibly for Communist purposes, through their club, as well as several movie houses they currently operate throughout the city."

The Jewish Warner brothers founded their namesake film studio in 1923. Prior to its absorption by the government-run United American Pictures in March of 1954, Warner Bros.—whose former premises now serve as the central home for UAP—produced such pictures as *Casablanca* and *The Big Sleep*, both of which featured Humphrey Bogart (star of recent box-office hits *The Communist Kind* and *St. Gallen*).

Making good on a campaign promise to purge the entertainment industry of all its Communist influences, President Joseph McCarthy established the Department of Motion Pictures, which assumed control of all Hollywood activity from the Warners and other Hebraic studio heads such as Marcus Loew and Louis B. Mayer (MGM); David Sarnoff

(RKO); Jesse L. Lasky and Adolph Zukor (Paramount); and Joseph M. Schenck and Darryl F. Zanuck (Twentieth Century Pictures)—among others.

Walt Disney Productions remains the only independent Hollywood studio since the nationalization of the film industry. Disney mainly produces cartoons, including its critically acclaimed animated shorts inspired by the traitors Julius and Ethel Rosenberg.

PART III

July 3, 1958

I want to emphasize at the outset of these hearings that the fact that the Committee on Un-American Activities is investigating alleged Communist influence and infiltration in the moving picture industry must not be considered or interpreted as an attack on the industry itself. Nor should our investigation be interpreted as an attack on the majority of persons associated with this great industry. I have every confidence that the vast majority of movie workers are patriotic and loyal Americans.

—J. Parnell Thomas (HUAC chairman)

CHAPTER 17

"M orris? Morris?...Morris! Wake up!"
Baker's eyes fluttered open to brightest sunlight. He couldn't remember where he was, but his tongue ached horribly and tasted of copper wire.

"Oh, thank God." It was Sophia.

"What...?"

"It happened again," she told him. "You were shaking terribly and I couldn't wake you. I think you bit your tongue, too. I couldn't get anything for you to bite down on in time."

Running his tongue gently across his teeth, Baker could feel the sting of two giant bite marks. He sat up and the blanket slipped off his naked body.

Shit. Not again. The darkness was getting worse, overtaking him more often.

"Have you seen a doctor about this?" Sophia asked. "These episodes that you have?"

"Don't trust those quacks. Not after Lang," Baker said. "Don't worry. I'm fine. Although I'll probably talk with a lisp for a week or two."

He got up and began to dress, snatching a quick glance at the calendar on his refrigerator. They had one day to figure this mess out and clear his name. "Hurry up and get dressed. We've got a long day ahead of us."

She draped the blanket around herself like a toga, scooped up her clothes, and went into the bathroom, turning on the shower. Hot steam began to curl around her like a supernatural mist. As it had the morning he was summoned to Echo Park, the phone began to ring. Baker sat on the bed and answered, hearing the gruff voice of his partner on the other end.

"Is coming in late gonna become a regular thing with you? Because if so, I want part of your pay."

"No, Brogan. Sorry," Baker said. "I've actually decided to take the chief up on his offer and take the rest of the week off."

"Sure, sure. If this is about you looking into You-Know-What, I don't want any part of it. Oh, and before I forget, Peterson said he was looking for you."

"Peterson? Did he say what it's about?"

"Something about a missing kid."

Baker froze. Peterson must have gotten the warrant, which revealed that his apartment had been the last stop on Oliver Shelton's delivery route.

"You still there?"

"Yes," said Baker after a beat. "Tell Peterson I'll be happy to speak with him once I'm back in the office or he can come see me at my apartment."

"Will do. Hold on, I heard a joke yesterday that you'd appreciate."

"Brogan..."

"Won't take but a second. What do you call a cheap circumcision?"

158

" . . ."

"A *rip-off*!" Connolly brayed with laughter, and Baker could almost feel his partner's spittle flying through the phone and onto his face. "Get it, Baker? A rip-off!"

"Hilarious."

"Ahhh, what do you know about comedy?"

"Pretty sure my people invented it. Can I go now?"

"Happy holidays, Half Dick."

He sat on the bed, unmoving, the phone's dial tone buzzing in his hand. He'd hoped that the long weekend would have pushed off the warrant by at least a few days. He should have just been open with Peterson. Now no one would believe his side of the story. And if his interaction with Shelton was common knowledge, he needed to move fast. It couldn't be a simple coincidence that the kid had gone missing immediately after delivering a letter from Lang.

Still, didn't the boy's poor mother deserve to know what Baker knew? Of course she did. But if Baker played his hand too early, he'd be arrested. The path forward, he tried to assure himself, would also lead to Oliver . . .

The annoyed voice of the operator derailed his train of thought.

" . . . I said would you like to make another call, sir?" she asked.

"Yes," he said, "put me through to the Ambassador Hotel."

"One moment, please."

The line rang for fifteen seconds before the peppy voice of the concierge answered. "Ambassador Hotel, how may I help you today?"

"Yes," said Baker, feeling a bit foolish for what he was about to say. "This is Bartolomeo Vanzetti calling for Nicola Sacco."

He expected the concierge to laugh him off the line, but after a few seconds, they said, "I'll connect your call now, sir."

"Morris, darling," Enrica Soma answered. "So good to hear from you. Any news on our dear mutual friend?" Her tone was casual, her word choice cautious. It appeared she knew how to play the game with the best of them.

"A bit," Morris said. "I'm calling to see if Joh—our friend ever mentioned something about the Queen of Sheba or an African Queen?"

"Hmmm. Nothing about a queen, but Africa rings a bell. He would talk about taking a trip there to do some research on a film project he was working on. I tried to dissuade him from such a dangerous expedition. They've got mosquitoes there the size of small dogs and they carry the most horrible diseases and—"

"You're sure there was nothing else?" asked Baker. "Not even what the project might have been about?"

"Like I said, he could be very secretive sometimes, especially when it came to his next film."

"What about the phrase *Beat the Devils*? Does that ring a bell?"

There was silence from Enrica for a moment. "You know, dear, I think it does. I'm pretty sure it was the name of a picture our friend was developing before the industry became regulated. I'm not sure what it was about. This was almost seven years ago, mind you."

"Okay. Thank you, Enrica. I'll call again when I know more. Please send my regards to Anjie."

"Oh, you are a sweet one. I will, darling. And, Morris, dear—" She dropped her high-society shtick for a moment. "Thank you for calling."

"Just doing my job."

Sophia came out of the bathroom wrapped in one of Baker's few clean towels, all her curves showing through the damp fabric.

"So, where are we going, anyway?" she asked.

He lit up a Kool before answering, "We're going to meet a celebrity."

CHAPTER 18

Once the epicenter of Old Hollywood (or as the government referred to it, "Jewish-controlled Hollywood"), Burbank was now the place where McCarthy's highly regulated entertainment machine cranked out overly patriotic, anti-Communist nonsense. If anything, the presence of a single, all-powerful studio made the film business even more exclusive than it was before.

In thirty minutes, the Continental was parked outside of United American Pictures, hidden by palm fronds and long grass in need of trimming. Baker and Sophia walked toward the front gates, the massive Warner Bros. water tower looming in the distance, the last remaining citadel of a once great empire.

As Baker and Sophia neared the small wooden guard's hut, Baker went over the plan they'd rehearsed on the drive. He'd arrested quite a number of con men over the years and was trying to think of how best to emulate their typically slick and oily demeanors. Keeping his accent out of the equation was key—something that would prove even more difficult with his injured tongue.

They first stopped at a dress shop, because Sophia's outfit from the day before was still covered in blood and brain matter. She took forever in the store, briefly disappearing among the racks, but they eventually settled on a dress in Whipped Apricot, a color that wasn't too harsh on the eyes and was appropriate for early July. Baker chose to wear one of his best blue suits for the occasion, a woolen number with a matching fedora. Cronkite's "Beat the Devils" note and diary of sign-off phrases had been transferred to the new suit, along with Huston's cryptic note from the moldy cake box.

Before the young studio guard, his face full of acne, could step out of the booth to ask what they were doing there, Baker grabbed Sophia's arm. She started to put up a convincing struggle.

"Mornin' sonny," Baker announced in a near-flawless American accent. "Beautiful day, ain't it?"

The guard readjusted his cap and stared at them. He wore a uniform adorned with a plastic gold badge that barely reflected the sun.

"C-can I help you, sir?" the kid said, his voice cracking nervously.

Oh, this was going to be easy.

"As a matter of fact, you can, sonny," Baker said, letting go of Sophia. "Don't go nowhere, darling." She glared at him, following the script better than Liz ever could. Baker reached into his pocket and whipped out his own badge, which gleamed brighter than the cheap trinket pinned to the guard's chest. He had it back in his pocket before the kid could get a good look. "Detective Andrew Higgins, Los Angeles Police Department. Seems one of your script girls here got loose and was attempting to sell some screenplays for a quick buck downtown. We picked her up at about six this morning, begging a poor old couple to put a down payment on a *gen-u-ine* Hollywood script. After booking her and taking her mug shot, I figured I'd bring her back here for you people to deal with. Say, who's the head honcho 'round here?"

The guard looked at them, jaw slack. Clearly, his brain wasn't capable of processing so much information at once. He rubbed the back of his sunburnt neck and said, "That'd be Mr. Kazan, Officer."

"Detective, actually," added Baker, improvising.

"Uh yes, Detective. Mr. Kazan's head of the whole studio. I can ring his secretary to let him know you're here. He likes to be kept informed of stuff like this. What's her name?" The guard nodded in the direction of Sophia with a smug look on his face as he ogled her body. He winked at Baker as if they were sharing a joke, and Baker fought an urge to knock the kid's lights out.

"It's Martha Bedford," replied Baker, who was already moving toward the gate. "But don't bother ol' Mr. Kazan with this nonsense. It's early and I'm sure a studio head's got more to worry about in his morning routine than some wayward script girl. Hey, here's an idea. Who's Kazan's second-in-command here—or better yet, who deals with infractions on and off the lot?"

"Well, second-in-command would be Kenneth Bierly," said the kid, scratching the meager facial hair sprouting from his chin. "He's head of production, but I think you want the chief of security. That's Obadiah Whitlock."

"Then Obadiah Whitlock is the man I'd like to deposit Miss Bedford with," answered Baker, grabbing Sophia's arm again. "Where's his base of operations?"

The guard perked up. "That's easy! Walk past all the soundstages 'til you get to the administration building. Can't miss the stages, they look like goddamn airplane hangars. Once you get to admin, ask Pauline at the front desk to show you to the security office, which is where you'll find Mr. Whitlock. You can tell them Charlie at the front gate sent you."

"Kid, you couldn't be more helpful if you tried," said Baker, who was now level with the gates, whose iron was still warped into the letters WB. Glancing into the guard hut as he passed, Baker could just make out a half-eaten Mars Bar and a nudie magazine poorly covered by a studio directory and the most recent issue of *Counterattack*.

"My pleasure, Detective!" said Charlie. He bounced back into the booth and pressed a small red button set into the wall. There was a mechanical buzzing sound and the gates swung inward, allowing Baker and Sophia to stroll onto the movie lot of United American Pictures.

* * *

Charlie wasn't blowing smoke, thought Baker. The backlot had the square footage of a small city. The soundstages were massive, half-moon Quonset huts made of steel and soundproofed aluminum. The structures were so massive, they blocked out the sun in most places. The water tower stood tallest among them all.

The strangest-looking groups of people made their way to and fro, paying no heed to Baker or Sophia. A squat woman carried a stack of gaudy furs while one man in a tight silk vest wheeled a collection of costumes behind her, shouting. "Edna, please slow down!" he called. "There's no rush. Call time isn't for another forty-five minutes." The woman snorted and quickened her pace. A few feet away, a tan fellow in a long robe led a pack of camels and sheep across the pavement with a crooked staff. Bringing up the rear were two men talking in hushed tones.

"Is that fat, Commie-loving fuck still in Europe?" one said.

"Of course," replied his companion. "The president won't let him back into the country. He's finished in this town. I hear the Spicks have agreed to finance his *Don Quixote* picture, which starts shooting next month..."

Leaning against one of the soundstages, a group of women, dressed in sequined leotards and ostentatious feathered headdresses, stood around smoking and gossiping.

"And then he said, 'Look sweetheart, it ain't gonna suck itself,'" said one of them.

"What did you say to that?" asked another.

"I gave him a blowjob," said the first. "A girl's gotta eat, right?"

They all crowed with laughter, crushed their smokes under their high heels, and walked away.

"Once you're done putting your eyes back in your head..." Sophia laughed at Baker, who had been staring at the showgirls. "We can get back to business."

"Whuh?" he replied dazedly as she pointed to a pair of soundstage doors displaying a large sign:

"Crimson Moonrise"

Call Time 9:00 a.m.
Dir.: Samuel Ashton
Assistant Dir.: Matthew Hanlon
Exec. Producer: Sid Purschell
Assoc. Producer: Albert Raneer
Cinematographer: Theodore Ryker
Lighting: Quentin Burlap
Sound Engineer: Wendell Dillwacker

PRINCIPAL CAST:
Humphrey Bogart
James Stewart
Ronald Reagan
Lolita Hayworth
Ruth Beotiger
Please present all production inquiries to Colin Peterson, PGA.
Otherwise—
Quiet on the set!

"How do we get in?" Baker asked Sophia.

Before he could protest, Sophia pulled open one of the doors that led into the depths of the soundstage. "Like this," she said, disappearing into the darkness beyond.

CHAPTER 19

As Baker soon learned, the inside of the hangar-like structure was not totally dark, just underlit. It took a few moments to adjust to the meek illumination given off by a string of bulbs that ran along a tunnel of crisscrossed wooden beams and pink fiberglass. Once his eyes were accustomed, he gasped. The tunnel had taken them to a space larger than a football field. It was totally enclosed, with no windows. The temperature inside was stiflingly hot, and Baker immediately took off his fedora, using it to fan himself.

"Not much of a cross breeze, is there?" he said.

"Oh, quit being such a baby," replied Sophia. "Come on."

They strolled across the concrete floor. Baker couldn't help but feel a little insignificant under the building's convex ceiling that stretched toward the very heavens. *Look at me*, it seemed to say. *I am surely the finest soundstage in all the land.* It reminded him of a memory from childhood. A story his father once told him about a group of mountains quarreling among themselves. In the end, it was the humblest and smallest of them, Mount Sinai, that God chose as the place where He would present the Ten Commandments to the Jewish people.

Shaking off the memory from that other life in Europe, Baker saw them. Two women (one older, one younger) standing together in a prairie field. They were weeping into each other's arms as an impressive crimson-colored moon rose high into the dusky heavens.

"Will they ever come back, Mama?" asked the younger woman. Her flowing curls shone in the red moonlight.

"I don't know. I don't think we'll ever know," replied the older woman. Her brown hair was done up in a bun and she looked out at the endless field, a deep sadness etched on her face. "Come, it doesn't do to dwell on the past, Regina. The Communist threat is once more kept at bay...for now."

"Cut!" yelled a man in a tan safari jacket and black leather jodhpurs. "Excellent all around. Lolita, I've got goosebumps. Ruth, oh my sweet, sweet Ruth. What can I say? I have tears. Real tears! But we can still do it better. I know we can."

The illusion was broken, and Baker noticed the group of men and women standing to the side of the crying women. Cameras and bright lights were pointed at their faces. The prairie was nothing more than an amalgam of plaster, wood, and paint.

Reality encroached further on the tableau as the two women broke apart and gratefully accepted glasses of water from jittery production assistants. Baker realized he was looking at Lolita Hayworth and Ruth Beotiger, two of the most famous actresses in McCarthy's Tinseltown. Both were famous for their looks, acting prowess, and unmatched skills at ratting out others as Communists in an effort to advance their own careers. They were two little-known dames with a string of flops who'd become overnight celebrities just by pointing their fingers.

"Sammy, must we do another? It's so hot in here," Lolita whined to the director in a breathy voice. *If a project about the life of Marilyn*

Monroe isn't in the works, there should be, thought Baker. *Hayworth would get the part in an instant.*

"No, Lolita," said the director in a coddling voice. "No, of course not. A perfect take as usual! Liam! Get Ronald ready for the next scene!" he called out in an impatient bark. "And can someone please tell Bogie to sober up? His next scene is in an hour. Just because there's a holiday tomorrow doesn't mean we can afford to dilly-dally. I'm trying to avoid a meal penalty here!" He wiped at his sweaty brow with an ivory handkerchief.

"Right away, Mr. Ashton," replied Liam, a pudgy man who waddled over to a handsome actor admiring himself in a handheld mirror. Baker experienced another jolt as he recognized the president of the Motion Picture Association, Ronald Reagan.

"Wow, they got all the stars for this one, huh?" whispered Sophia.

"I thought you didn't get many movies in Russia?"

"I'm well versed in the cultures of many countries, given my line of work."

"Fair enough," he said. "And now, we enact the second part of the plan, which is to..."

"Follow my lead," said Sophia. She was already walking up to the director like she'd lived on this soundstage all her life.

"Oh, Sammy, darling," she said in a convincing debutante imper-sonation. "So glad we caught you in between takes."

"And who might you be?" asked the director, none too kindly.

"So sorry, darling. Maria Hiller. But surely Kenneth told you Jonas and I were coming today?"

"No. Mr. Bierly didn't mention anyone by those names. What do you want? We're very busy here, as you can plainly see."

"How odd," said Sophia. "Well, no matter. The show must go on, isn't that right, darling?" When Ashton didn't answer, she continued, "Sammy, dear, this is Jonas van Bezooyen. Famed voice coach, known the world over."

"The world over, huh? Never heard of him. Now please get off my set."

"But Jonas and I are here for Mr. Bogart, Sammy darling. We were hired by the studio to give him voice lessons so that he may act at his fullest, even when inebriated."

Ashton looked up from the script he was examining and let out a neigh of cruel laughter. "Bogie? Act while drunk? Impossible!"

"Oh, but Sammy, darling. It's not impossible for Jonas here." She gestured to Baker, who, catching on to the act, took on the air of a haughty celebrity who's just been asked *Who are you again?* by the maître d' of a fancy restaurant.

Ashton walked over to Baker, his leather boots squeaking on the concrete floor. "I've been in this business a long time and I've never been able to rouse an actor from a drunken stupor. What's your secret then?"

Sophia cut in: "Jonas doesn't speak in front of everyone, Sammy darling. He saves his voice for the stars, you know. Jonas takes his craft very seriously. That's what he keeps me around for. To be his mouthpiece, in a manner of speaking."

She let out an over-the-top chuckle. Baker scowled at the director, crossed his arms, and nodded his head in agreement.

"Heather!" yelled Ashton.

At once, a dainty girl with horn-rimmed glasses hanging around her neck appeared at the director's side, a clipboard in her shaking hands.

"Y-yes, Mr. Ashton?"

"Escort Miss Hiller and her associate to Mr. Bogart's dressing room."

"Y-yes, Mr. Ashton. Right away."

"Good girl. Oh, and Mr. Beelzebub?"

"Van Bezooyen," corrected Sophia.

"Yes, whatever. If I don't see results in the next thirty minutes, I'll make sure you're both out on your asses before you can say *Action!* Understood?"

"Oh, you won't be sorry, Sammy dear," said Sophia. "Jonas has been called a miracle worker by all of his clients."

Heather ushered them away from the set and across the expansive interior of the soundstage.

"Nicely done," whispered Baker to Sophia, so low that Heather couldn't hear him.

"Nothing to it," she breathed back.

They walked in silence through a maze of dim tunnels until they came to a red door set into the hangar's aluminum siding. A sizable gold star had been carved into the wood, and below that a thin gold nameplate: H. BOGART. Below the nameplate was a piece of wrinkled paper covered in larger block letters that read: DO NOT DISTURB! and below that, AMSCRAY!

Heather turned to face them, looking more nervous than ever.

"He doesn't like visitors."

"That's all right, Heather dear," cooed Sophia. "We can take it from here. You head back and let Sammy know you showed us to Mr. Bogart's dressing room. That's a good girl."

Relief played on Heather's face. She scampered away. When the sound of anxious footsteps finally dissolved into the distance, Baker looked at Sophia.

"Well, here we are," he said, rapping his knuckles on the door. The knock's echo was the only answer. Baker tried again. This time, he heard a shuffling from within. It swung open quite suddenly and the deeply lined basset hound's face of Humphrey Bogart greeted them with a blast of frigid air.

"How many times I gotta tell ya, Heather? Don't disturb"— his trademark lisp and New York intonation turned the word into *distoib*—"me when I'm in—Oh..."

His eyes bulged when he got a good look at them. "Who the hell are you?"

Without waiting for an answer, Bogart staggered back into his dressing room, a decanter of whiskey in one hand and a lit cigarette in the other. He was wearing a stained velvet dinner jacket and an undone batwing bow tie that hung like a docile snake around his collar. A pair of scuffed and worn penny loafers sat snugly on the actor's dragging, sockless feet. He looked a far cry from the clean-cut macho characters he often played on the big screen.

Baker and Sophia crept into the room and quietly closed the door behind them. It was mercifully cool in here after the sweltering heat of the soundstage. Bogart plopped into a sagging Barcalounger. Next to the chair was a small side table topped with an overflowing ashtray of discarded cigarette butts. The actor was nearly sixty, but the ruggedness and determination of his healthier days had not left his face, even after a lengthy battle with throat cancer. However, it seemed that the removal of part of his esophagus did not rob him of his love for booze and smokes.

"Care for a drink? Pick your poison," Bogie slurred, bringing the decanter to his lips and taking a noisy slurp of whiskey. "We got whiskey, gin, rye, and regret." He laughed and whiskey sloshed onto his jacket and pants.

The space was less dressing room and more elegant study. It housed a cashmere-draped divan topped with a half-finished game of chess; a wooden Stromberg-Carlson television cabinet carved with intricate Chinese designs; and a four-speed Empire-brand phonograph. There was also a fully stocked wet bar set into the opposite wall and framed posters (like the ones in the hallway of John Huston's house) also hung here, but depicted Bogart's more recent works, such as *It Came from Planet Communist!*

Hung next to the movie posters was a grand oil painting of UAP president Elia Kazan. His painted gaze was unnerving; Baker half expected the eyes to start shifting back and forth. For all he knew, there was a secret chamber behind the portrait, where the handsome Greek could spy into Bogie's dressing room to make sure he was toeing the studio line. Portraits of Kenneth Bierly and studio chairman Joseph Kennedy (who had eagerly sold off his RKO stake to the government) hung beside Kazan's, as did the usual photographs of McCarthy and Nixon.

"Would you like to wet your whistle?" Bogart said. "It seems you folks are a few drinks behind. That's the problem with the world. Everyone's a few drinks behind."

"No thank you, Mr. Bogart. We're just here to talk with you," said Sophia.

"Speak for yourself," said Baker, striding over to the bar.

Sophia carefully placed the chessboard onto the television cabinet and sat down on the divan. Smoothing out her new dress, she gazed at the actor with a simpering, almost rueful grin that made Baker uncomfortable. He didn't dwell too long on the thought. He had just located the bar's reserve of schnapps and was pouring himself a healthy measure with no ice.

"A man after my own heart," piped up Bogart, lighting another cigarette even though he had not finished the one currently dangling from his lips. "I never trust a man who doesn't drink. Now." He turned back to Sophia. "What did you say your name was, sweetheart?"

"I didn't," she said. "But I'm Sophia and that there"—she pointed to Baker—"is Detective Morris Baker of the Los Angeles Police Department."

"Oh, I'm not under arrest, am I?" asked Bogart, putting up his palms playfully. Even drunk, the man was smooth as freshly churned butter.

"Nothing like that, Mr. Bogart," said Baker. He threw back the schnapps and poured more into his glass. He couldn't believe this was happening. Was he really tying one on with *the* Humphrey Bogart? "We are just here to ask you about an old colleague of yours. John Huston. Does that name sound familiar?"

"Why, yes, it does," Bogart replied, sounding a bit more lucid. "Say, that's quite an accent you got there. You ain't from the States, are ya?"

"No. Czechoslovakia. Jewish, too. Got a problem with that?"

Sophia made a movement like she was about to get between them, but Bogie just smiled and laughed, pointing his newly lit cigarette at Baker.

"Never met a Yid with that much noive. Don't get me wrong, pally, I love your people. In fact, I owe them a debt of gratitude. Was a Jew doc saved my life when the Big C came around and decided to do the Lindy Hop in my throat. That tumor swelled up nice and big like Peter Lorre before they had the good sense to cut it outta me."

He swung his head back to reveal a fading pink scar along the middle of his throat. It was a grisly thing, as though someone had tried to bleed the actor like a fish. "Sure, the makeup folks hide it well, but it's a reminder that I could be six feet under at the moment, drinking dirt cocktails with the worms," Bogie continued. "My ex-wife used to say it made me look distinguished. She was a Hebe herself. Boy, was Lauren a looker. Used to work in this crazy business, too, until McCarthy kicked them all out. Too bad the studio made me divorce her."

The actor spoke as though he was trying to justify his actions to some unseen tribunal. He took another swig of whiskey.

"Er, don't you think you've had enough to drink, Humph—Mr. Bogart?" Sophia asked, looking genuinely concerned. The actor eyed her menacingly but didn't stop. "Yes, well, Mr. Bogart," began Sophia again. "We were just wondering what you can tell us about John Huston."

This seemed to rouse Bogart back to coherence and a state of wistfulness. "Yeah, Johnny and I made some good pictures back during the war days. Ever hoid of *The Maltese Falcon*? Great mystery film. Great twist, too, and boy, was Astor something to look at," he said. "I played a private dick in that one. Film noir, the French called it. Was all the rage once upon a time. We sure don't make 'em like we used to. I loved playing gumshoes. Got a lot of target practice on those sets."

"Mr. Bogart," Baker said, sitting down on the divan next to Sophia, "did you know that John Huston is dead?"

Bogart looked up, his eyes unreadable in their deep sockets. "No, I didn't, as a matter of fact. We haven't—hadn't—spoken for several years now. What happened to ol' Johnny?"

"Shot in the chest," Baker answered.

His face still a blank and drooping slate, Bogart shook his head. "Poor Johnny. Hell of a director. *Hell* of a director. I'll drink to that!" He downed the rest of the decanter in one go.

Baker sat forward and laid out another question. "Do you know if there was anybody out there who would want Mr. Huston dead? Was he involved in anything illegal?"

"Of course not!" The actor sounded offended. "Johnny was a dynamite filmmaker and a well-rounded family man. A little goyle and everything. I mean, sure, he had his affairs over the years. So have I, but that's a given in our business."

Sophia looked disgusted at the mention of the actor's various flings.

"I was proud to call him my friend," finished Bogart.

Baker now tried the penultimate card up his sleeve. "Does the phrase *African Queen* mean anything to you?"

After a moment in which he seemed deep in thought, Bogart replied. "Why, sure," he said. "It was the name Johnny had for a picture a few years back, which might have been the last time we spoke. He wanted to get back into filmmaking and wanted me to play some boat captain in Central Africa. He said it could be the role that finally got me the Oscar. I told him no audience would want to see something like that in the current political climate and we went our separate ways. He was a dreamer, Johnny was, and a little too headstrong for his own good. Never could do what he needed to keep his job. Wouldn't give in to the changing times."

"What about the words *Beat the Devils*?" asked Baker. "Strike any chords for you?"

"Hmmm," said Bogart, scratching his chin. "Vaguely sounds like the name of another picture Johnny pitched to me *years* ago, but if I recall correctly, he wanted to base it on a novel written by a Red, which would never fly."

"Any idea what the book was abou—?" Baker began, but he didn't get to finish the question. Someone was hammering at the dressing room door, making them all jump.

"Humphrey! It's Sam!" came Ashton's muffled voice. "I have two gentlemen here who would like to have a word with dear Maria and Jonas. Open up now!"

"They know," hissed Sophia to Baker.

Baker turned to Bogart. "Mr. Bogart. We're trying to solve the murder of John Huston and we didn't exactly tell the truth to get onto the lot and into your dressing room. Now, I know this is a long shot, but is there another way out of this room? I've seen the movies. Any hidden passageways?"

"Well, sure," said Bogart, gesturing with the empty decanter. "There's one behind the bar. Just push the button underneath and it'll take you where you need to go. Out, that is."

"Much obliged," said Baker as the enraged director of *Crimson Moonrise* banged on the door again. Baker ran behind the bar, found the button, and pushed it. With an electric hum the fake wall slid into a hidden recess, revealing a secret passage beyond.

"Where does this lead?" Baker asked the actor.

"Takes you right past the front gate," hiccuped Bogart. "Good for quick getaways from the press and adoring fans."

Baker tipped his fedora in a gesture of thanks. "Quickly, Sophia! Was a pleasure meeting you, Mr. Bogart."

"Likewise, Detective. Good luck solving that case of yours. You find Johnny's killer or die trying, you hear now?"

As the wall slid back into place, they heard Bogart shout at Ashton. "For Chrissakes, Sam! Say it again, why don't you? I was napping!"

CHAPTER 20

True to Bogart's word, the tunnel led out into dazzling sunlight. Palm fronds and overgrown vines hid the exit from prying eyes. A hundred feet away from where they had come out, Baker and Sophia could see Charlie, the gate guard, being yelled at by a beefy specimen of a man whom Baker pegged as head of security, Obadiah Whitlock.

Poor Charlie would probably be out of a job before the morning was out, but there were bigger things to worry about. Like the familiar Cadillac V-16 parked right next to the guardhouse. Hartwell and Waldgrave were sniffing around here, no doubt.

"Come on," Baker whispered. "Don't run. Walk like we're just taking a morning stroll." He placed his arm around Sophia's and they casually walked across the road, past Charlie, who was too preoccupied with the verbal beating Obadiah was giving him.

"Christ, boy!" Whitlock screamed. "I thought you had more God-damn sense than that. You didn't even ask to see any form of identification? Do you know how negatively this reflects on me?"

"But, but, sir," bleated Charlie without any real conviction. "He...He had a badge. I saw it myself."

"Oh, he had a badge, did he? Did you mark down the number? Did you check it for any form of forgery like I would have done? Like I trained you to do? Did you call ahead to let me know a so-called cop was snooping around studio property without a warrant? Fuck's sake, Charlie! You're dumber than a sack of nails! I never would have thought it possible that..."

They left Obadiah to his stream of insults about Charlie's level of intelligence and made it back to the hidden Continental.

"I hope he doesn't get fired on our account." Sophia looked worried as she hopped into the passenger seat.

"You heard Mr. Whitlock. He didn't follow security protocol. Besides, sweetheart." Baker turned the key in the ignition, and the engine purred like a snoozing leopard. "This is Hollywood. You gotta play dirty if you wanna survive in this business."

* * *

He would not answer her questions when he removed Lang's shabby photo album from beneath the driver's seat and made her wait in the car while he went to make a phone call.

"Baker?" said Charles Ward over the crackling line. "What can I do you for?"

"I need the toxicology report on a stiff. USC professor by the name of Arthur Xavier Scholz who may have come in over the past few days."

"Uh, sure. Just give me a second. Does this have to do with the thing we discussed the other evening?" Charles sounded excited.

"Yes. Now less talking about that over the phone, and please go check if you don't mind. Time's running thin."

Charles came back on the line with good news.

"You're in luck, Baker. Body came in the morning after you were here. The deceased specifically requested an autopsy in their will. What do you want to know?"

* * *

After his call with Charles, Baker stopped by the North Hill Street library and ran inside. Around noon, he and Sophia were back in the relative safety of Chinatown. Only when they were finally tucked away inside a nondescript café (it had no official name but was unofficially known to locals as General Tso's Chicken & Tea Shop) nursing two cups of steaming oolong and a platter of crispy spring rolls, did he tell her about Lang's will and what had been bequeathed to him. The photo album now sat between them on the sticky Formica table.

"I'm so stupid," said Baker as Sophia watched him with rapt attention. "I should have remembered when we were in Huston's kitchen last night, but it didn't click."

"What didn't you remember?"

"Africa!" he said a little too loudly, causing the wizened café owner, who was filling out a crossword puzzle, to look up slowly like an old sloth.

"*Africa* is the key word," Baker continued in a softer voice. "Just like *Devils*, it keeps cropping up, but *Devils* is only part of it! The note in Huston's home was addressed to his 'African Queen' and mentioned a Bible passage about Sheba, who tested King Solomon with riddles. Then there was Bogart telling us about Huston wanting to make a film set in Central Africa as well as another picture he wanted to base on a book called *Beat the Devil*."

"Is that why we stopped at the library?" Sophia asked.

"Yes," he said. "They burned all copies of it, because it was written by a Communist named James Helvick. I was able to find a short summary of the book in some old records, and guess what it's about?"

"I'll bite," said Sophia.

"A rush to secure a uranium mine in—"

"Africa," she finished.

"Correct!" Baker responded in triumph. "Which also explains the Oppenheimer quote."

Sophia still looked a little confused. "I'm not seeing the significance of all this."

"And then there's this!" he added, slapping a hand on the photo album. "A photo album, containing pictures of Adolf Lang's adventures in—where else?—Africa. A trip he probably took after he escaped Europe."

It was hard to keep the contempt and pain out of his voice. Sophia put her hand on top of his. "I know you don't care much for this man, but remember what Valentina said. He felt remorse at the end. Maybe this was his way of making it up to you."

"He could never make it up to me," Baker snarled. "He just knew that maybe I would have a chance of stopping whatever is supposed to happen tomorrow. I'm not entirely sure how he was mixed up in all of this yet, but I think he and Huston are connected somehow. Lang didn't die of old age. He was poisoned, but I think suicide by poison was much more likely the cause."

He recounted the postmortem report that Ward had relayed over the phone.

"Cyanide?" Sophia asked.

"Potassium cyanide, to be more precise," said Baker. "A Nazi's favorite escape route."

"Not just Nazis," said Sophia. "We have to carry capsules around with us on every mission in case we're captured by enemy forces. False molar. But why would Lang want to kill himself? If he knew something, why not just go straight to you? Why not go to your press?"

"These days, our press is just as censored as yours is," answered Baker. "A major paper does bite on a controversial story every once in a while, but I think whatever's going on here is just too dangerous. Even the free press has its limits these days, especially if you're trying to paint McCarthy in a negative light."

"Then why did Huston bring in Cronkite if CBS wouldn't want to risk angering the government?"

"I think Cronkite was operating outside the network's authority. My secretary spoke to the head of CBS, who said that Cronkite was supposed to be on vacation, which means he wasn't in town on official business. As for why Lang didn't just come to me, who knows? Maybe he was too ashamed to make contact with me ever again. Maybe he thought he'd put me in more danger if he did."

"All right," said Sophia. "One thing at a time here. Why did Lang kill himself?"

"Lang probably didn't want to go on the lam. He was tired of running from things, just like Valentina said. Besides, I think whoever was coming for him could have found him, no matter where he went and no matter how far. He was part of something big and someone was ready to kill him to keep it under wraps."

"You really think so?"

"I'd stake my badge on it. And what's more, I think he hid evidence of what he knew somewhere before taking himself out of the equation. Why else would he bring me back into his life? He probably knew I would never speak with him face-to-face, so he left clues like this." He patted the photo album again. "If my theory is correct, Huston and the screenwriter were also working to point me in the right direction. I've got a pretty good idea what some of this bomb business is all about. Lang was a doctor, but he was also an expert in nuclear physics."

"The bomb!" squeaked Sophia. "It can't be an—"

"Yes," Baker said. "The person—or people—trying to frame me have some sort of A-bomb, and Lang helped them build it. If *Beat the Devils* is any indication, they got the uranium in Africa and had Lang refine it."

He rolled up his left shirtsleeve to show Sophia the string of spidery blue numbers on his skin, and just above that, a ghastly-looking crater of pink scar tissue.

She put a hand to her mouth in horror. "It looks worse in the light."

"They called it Special Field Test Experimentation Number Six Sixty-Five," Baker began quietly.

"I'd been hurt, a head injury while working as a Sonderkommando in the crematoria. Instead of just gassing or shooting me, they treated me back to a relative state of health and used me for testing. That son of a bitch Lang was in charge of it. They wanted to see what effects radioactive material had on the human body. This was near the end of the war. Hitler knew about America's bomb and was afraid of what would happen if it were dropped on Berlin or Munich or Nuremberg. They didn't have time to make their own, so there was a rush to find out how its effects could be mitigated. They used the material they had from their own abandoned nuclear program.

"There were twelve of us from the start. Six died of radiation poisoning within the first few days. They were the lucky ones. Have you ever seen what intense exposure to radiation does to a person, Sophia? It eats away the body from the inside out. We were already malnourished and weak, but the radiation added diarrhea, vomiting, swollen hands, and gangrenous sores. Being in that room, which smelled of our own waste for days on end, drove some of the subjects mad. They screamed and cried for their mothers until the scientists could no longer stand the noise. Those men were quickly shot."

Sophia looked like she was about to cry. A bell tinkled somewhere as the café door opened, but Baker did not notice it. Now that he was telling the story, he could not stop. No one had ever heard it, not Brogan, not Liz, not Hollis, and most certainly not the West German courts that kept haranguing him for testimony.

"After six weeks of that hell, there was only one person left. I can't remember how or why I survived. To this day, I'm still not sure, but it all ended when I developed a tumor the size of a grapefruit on my left arm, which was my ticket out of that room. I was taken to surgery, where, without the use of any anesthetics, Lang removed the tumor with a dull scalpel. He wanted to study it further. You can't imagine the pain, and no one should have to imagine it. As the Americans approached the camp, many of the Germans fled and left me to die on the operating table. I should have died of radiation sickness or cancer or infection long ago. Yet here I sit."

Baker looked down as bitter tears of memory dropped into his teacup. *Drip drip drip.*

"I was—*am*—ashamed of it all. Of working in their employ, of lying and leading my brothers and sisters to slaughter, of shoveling their ashes just to keep myself alive. Part of me knows I deserved the punishment of that experiment, but another part knows that nothing could ever completely atone for what I did. That is why I came to this country and became a homicide detective. I could never make up for my sins, but I could do some good in this world—try and stop those who would want to take the lives of others."

Sophia's look of horror had been replaced by one of pity. She held his hands tightly in hers and tried to lock eyes with him, though he wasn't ready to meet her gaze just yet. "Morris," she began, "you can't blame yourself for what happened. It was war, it was a confusing time. There was no way—"

"I could have refused," he said in a hoarse voice. "I could have told those monsters to go fuck themselves. That I'd rather have them put a bullet in my skull than be a cog in their murder machine. It was people like me, Jews like me, who let it happen. And if by some chance a God does exist and He forgives me, I never will."

"Morris. Please."

"I thought I could do it," he said. "I thought I could try and do some good, but nothing changed. I was still broken inside, still complicit."

That's when he told Sophia about the Liu family. How they had been taken in the dead of night by HUAC inspectors. How he had heard their screams, so like the screams of his family back in Czechoslovakia; of the people choking to death in the gas chambers. Instead of standing up for the Lius, he retreated further under his blanket like a child—like a spineless coward.

The silence between them hung heavier than the café's ever-present curtain of wok-fried grease, but Baker was all right with a little awkwardness. He'd finally lifted a weight from his shoulders for the first time since 1945. He did not feel absolved of wrongdoing, only relieved that he could admit to someone else that it really did happen. The darkness seemed to ebb away from the rocky corners of his mind where it always threatened to spill over and take control. Not gone completely—it would never be gone completely—but it had been lashed back by a temporary dam of admission.

"Morris," Sophia said gently. "You mustn't let the blame rest solely on your shoulders. People did what they could, so they could survive and tell their stories just like you've told me. Bearing witness to evil after the fact is just as important as fighting it head-on. In that way, you help make sure it never happens again. As for that poor family, what could you have done? Try to be the hero and end up taken away with them? No, you lived to fight another day. To win the battles that *can* be won."

Her words fell like drops of soothing ointment onto a stinging burn.

"Thank you, Sophia," he said. "I mean it." Baker was finally beginning to understand what Valentina meant about harnessing the pain of past events.

"Don't mention it. We seem to be helping each other a lot, don't we?"

"It would seem so."

"I'm real glad we met each other. Now, what were you saying about the photo album Lang left you?"

Baker slid his chair around to Sophia's side of the table and flipped open the photo album. The golden letters that spelled out MEMORY MAKERS flashed in the rays of sun filtering in through the shop's smudged window. Light fell upon sepia-tinted photographs of sweeping African jungles and savannas; Lang holding up the pelts of vicious-looking predators; Lang standing arm in arm with unknown men in many-buttoned safari costumes; Lang waving from atop a basket trussed to an elephant's back; a blurred something just out of focus with bright orange blotches. Like the film had been exposed to light before it could be properly developed.

"Aha!" said Baker, running a finger over the picture and feeling a noticeable lump behind it. He easily peeled back the photo, as the adhesive holding it to the yellowing page was already beginning to lose its stickiness. Where the blurry photograph had been a second before, there now sat a two-pronged brass key. Below that, a piece of paper no bigger than a postage stamp, which contained three lines of faded ink:

Bank of Los Angeles, Brentwood
   Safe Deposit No. 613
31.12.56

Baker turned to Sophia and smiled. "Care to make a withdrawal, Comrade Vikhrov?"

CHAPTER 21

Brentwood was most famous for its Country Mart, which had opened ten years before. The prominent and barn-like shopping center was often used as the perfect example of "Capitalist Idealism" in Southern California. Although people always seemed to forget (or purposefully omit) the fact that it was constructed by a Jewish-owned company, the Baruch Corporation.

Baker and Sophia found the Bank of Los Angeles, Brentwood branch, situated a few blocks away on San Vicente Boulevard. The financial institution resembled the one-story buildings that were once fixtures of the American frontier. Places where desperadoes went to steal burlap sacks of money emblazoned with large dollar signs.

It was nearing one o'clock when Baker parked the Continental in the Country Mart's spacious parking lot. He and Sophia started their walk to the bank, but stopped in their tracks when the door to a department store across the street swung open. A screaming woman, flanked by two HUAC inspectors, was dragged outside and violently thrown onto the sidewalk. Her bags split open, revealing a collection of brassieres and other undergarments.

"My husband isn't a Communist, I swear!" cried the woman, whose skirt had hiked up to reveal the tops of brown stockings. She was desperately trying to cover up her purchases in vain as the two Hueys laughed derisively. "He's just an accountant for the city!"

"An accountant who's been embezzling funds for known subversive groups," sneered one of the inspectors, kicking a box away as the woman reached for it.

The street was busy with foot traffic, but no one seemed interested in the scene. Men lowered their fedoras and quickened their paces, while women chatted with one another in exaggeratedly loud voices that did not completely drown out the woman's pleading. Every person gave her a wide berth, as though she were a contagious leper.

Sophia made a slight move, clearly ready to cross the street and offer some help. Baker grabbed her arm in a pincer-like grip before she could do so.

"Don't," he whispered as Sophia gave him a look of helpless fury.

"Please! He's not a Communist! He's not! He's just an accountant! Just an accountant!" the woman cried again, mascara-smudged tears now streaming down her anguished face.

"We'll see about that," said the other Huey, hungrily eyeing the tops of her pale thighs. He and his partner grabbed the woman under the arms and dragged her away to a waiting car. The undergarments were left in a dusty heap on the sunbaked concrete.

Finally, Baker tore his gaze away from the unpleasant scene and left a horrified Sophia staring across the street. A department store employee emerged to clear away the brassieres and girdles. Soon, it was like nothing had happened.

Baker was about to tell Sophia they had to go when a nearby phone began to ring. No one came to answer it. Baker walked over to the booth and lifted the receiver.

"Hello?"

A deep, unfamiliar voice addressed him by name. "Morris Baker," it said. "Tread carefully."

"Who is this?" he asked.

"You're all over the CONELRAD station. You're wanted for questioning by HUAC. Stay out of trouble and get to the bottom of this thing. We'll meet soon. Good day and good luck."

The line went dead and Baker's mouth dried up. The phone booth suddenly felt like a coffin. He quickly scanned the streets but didn't see anything or anyone unusual. Hanging up the phone, he casually walked back to the car, Sophia on his heels, and rotated the radio dial until it was on the CONELRAD station, which confirmed the caller's warning:

"...Repeat. Morris Baker of the Los Angeles Police Department is wanted for questioning by the House Un-American Activities Committee. Baker, who is of the Hebraic persuasion, is considered armed and incredibly dangerous. The subject drives a pale-green Lincoln Continental. If you happen to see Baker, do not try to apprehend him yourself, but contact your local HUAC office at once...Repeat. Morris Baker of the Los Angeles Police Department is wanted for questioning by..."

Sophia looked at him, eyes wide. "What are we going to do?" she asked him.

"Be quick about our bank visit," answered Baker, draping the Continental in the waterproof tarp he kept in the trunk in the unlikely event of rain. "Come on."

* * *

Henry Lincoln IV was more toad than man, but a genial fellow nonetheless. The Brentwood bank had been a part of his lineage since the mid-1800s. His family was, as Henry liked to tell everyone who ever stepped foot in his establishment, distantly related to Honest Abe himself. While *that* part of the family went into politics and abolishing slavery, Henry's side proved itself naturally adept at personal finance. Henry was the sixth Lincoln to run the bank.

He was short and heavyset, and looked downright comical in an ill-fitting three-piece suit—complete with a pocket watch and magnifying glass that dangled from golden chains on his inflexible waistcoat. The small pair of glasses delicately perched on his face looked even tighter. At such close proximity, Baker could make out the kidney-shaped dimples they dug into the bridge of Lincoln's globoid nose as he spoke.

"...So, you see, President Lincoln was allergic to shellfish and cowered in fear every time he saw shrimp in the White House," said the nasally banker. "Not many people outside my family know that. So, what can I do for you today, Mr. and Mrs. Baker?"

Baker and Sophia had decided to pose as a couple so as not to arouse suspicion. Luckily, it sounded like Lincoln didn't listen to the radio during work hours or their plan would have fallen apart before it began.

"Well, Mr. Lincoln," Baker said. "My wife and I recently suffered a terrible loss. My great-uncle, Arthur Scholz, passed away."

"Oh, how awful," said Lincoln, taking off his glasses and massaging the dimples they'd left behind. "How awful indeed."

"Yes, he was like a father to both of us. And he was a very learned man, a professor at USC, no less."

"Indeed?"

"Oh yes. The academic world has lost a great mind, but we're not here to bother you with tales of Uncle Artie's eventful life," Baker continued, borrowing Valentina's pet name for the man. "The fact of the matter is that he always hinted to us that we had been written into his will. And sure enough, at the reading of his last wishes just a few days ago, the lawyer called us out by name. Now, we're not well-to-do people, but we're not poor, either. We didn't expect anything from Artie, but imagine our confusion when the attorney hands us a key for a safe-deposit box at your bank?"

"Well, I imagine you were very shocked indeed."

"Yessir. Isn't that right, dear?"

Sophia nodded and said, "Artie was never one for jokes, I'm afraid. A sweet man, of course, but never one to do something so... mysterious."

"Indeed," intoned Lincoln. "We never truly know the ones we love until they are gone."

"That's what I was telling Morris just before we walked in."

"Indeed?"

"Well, Mr. Lincoln," Baker forged on, "we know it's unorthodox and all, but we were wondering if it would be possible to see what's inside my uncle's deposit box."

Lincoln fingered the pocket of his waistcoat for a moment before speaking. "Well, Mr. Baker. You are correct. The circumstances are quite strange. Quite strange *indeed*. But you two seem like a nice couple with capitalist ideals. We don't put up with any Communist chicanery around here. No sir indeed. And as a fellow supporter of capitalist ideals, I will help you to the full extent to which I am able. Please give me a moment to pull Mr. Scholz's file."

With some effort, he extricated his large bottom out of his high-backed leather chair, then walked into a back room and out of sight. The door clicked shut behind him.

"Communist chicanery?" Sophia asked quietly. Baker stifled a laugh.

For five minutes, there was nothing but the whoosh of the ceiling fan overhead and the impatient sighs of a single bank teller assisting an elderly man who seemed to have forgotten his account number. When Lincoln finally returned and plopped back down, he was holding a beige folder and wearing a large smile.

"Well, Mr. and Mrs. Baker. You are, indeed, in luck." His pudgy hand flipped open the folder. "It seems your uncle knew what he was doing by leaving you that key to one of our safe-deposit boxes."

He slid a piece of paper across the desk. It was an affidavit, instructing the bank to grant Baker access to safe-deposit box number 613 if he ever showed up after Scholz's passing. It was co-signed by Laremy Dinsmore Fenwick, Esquire, and dated April 15, 1956. Lang had known of Baker's existence in Los Angeles for over two years now—perhaps longer.

"Wow," said Sophia.

"Indeed," said Lincoln. "Now, I'll just need proof of identification and you can go open your box."

Baker passed over his badge and license without thinking. He immediately wished he hadn't produced the license. Lincoln used his magnifying glass to inspect the document and narrowed his eyes in suspicion when they fell over the words INDIVIDUAL OF JUDAIC ORIGINS. Baker's fist curled and he was visited by an overwhelming urge to knock the pudgy banker into next week. Lincoln looked reluctantly satisfied. He pulled a massive rubber stamp from inside his desk drawer and squashed a large AUTHENTICATED on top of Lang's affidavit.

"Very good, Mr. Baker. Very good indeed," he said, handing back the license and badge. "If you will both follow me."

Some of the geniality had left Lincoln's voice and he made a big show of wiping his hands on his trousers after handling Baker's personal items. He got up again with great difficulty and led them to a thick metal door, which he unlocked with a large brass key of his own. They stepped into a room that Baker initially mistook for a small morgue. Hundreds of closed lockers lined the walls, from floor to ceiling. Lincoln waddled over to the only wall devoid of lockers and pulled out a small metal inspection table.

In clipped tones, he pointed to the corner of the room. "Your box is over there," he said, eyes narrowed. "You may inspect its contents on this table in privacy. I'll be waiting outside if you require further assistance." *But since you're a filthy Jew, you better not require any further assistance from me*, his tone seemed to imply. Lincoln left the room and closed the heavy door behind him.

Silence prevailed as Baker walked over to the door. He put his ear to it, making sure Lincoln wasn't listening in on the other side. Not hearing the banker's heavy wheezing, he crossed the length of the room to Lang's safe-deposit box with Sophia at his side. Upon seeing the tarnished numbers of box 613, he began to laugh.

"What's so funny?" Sophia asked.

"It's just that there are supposed to be six hundred and thirteen commandments according to Jewish tradition." Yet again, here was another ancient artifact from that other life; the one he'd enjoyed before the war. "I wonder if Lang knew that and wanted to make a little joke at my expense."

"I think I remember my father telling me about that when I was very young."

"Well," Baker said pulling the safe-deposit key from his pocket, "joke or no, let's see what the hell the doctor left behind for me." The *thunk!* of the lock's tumbler sounded rusty, but the box slid out with relative ease and Baker hefted it over to the inspection table. The box itself was heavy and slippery with accumulated dust. The lid almost slid out of his grip when he opened the container to reveal...

What had he been expecting? Glimmering jewels? Wads of cash held together by shriveled-up rubber bands? An SS cap with a death's head insignia? None of the above were inside. The box only contained paper—and lots of it. Memoranda, letters, reports, dossiers, photographs, legal contracts, and more from various governmental branches. The State Department, Pentagon, United Armed Forces, Joint Chiefs of Staff, FBI, CIA, State-War-Navy Coordinating Committee, Joint Intelligence Objectives Agency, and Office of Scientific Intelligence were all mentioned. Baker picked up a poorly photostatted page from the summer of 1945 and began to read:

CONFIDENTIAL
MEMORANDUM FOR JCS

FROM: Major Robert B. Staver
SUBJECT: Exploitation of German Specialists in Science and Technology in the United States

In light of Germany's unconditional surrender, it is time to consider America's future and her inevitable conflict with the Soviet Union, which can no longer be considered an "if," but a "when." It therefore stands to reason that whichever country has the superior science will win the coming war. There is also the continuing skirmish in the Pacific Theater to consider.

Adolf Hitler was in possession of some of the world's greatest minds who could have given him the world. One wonders why Germany, with its possession of superior scientific knowledge (in numerous fields such as rocketry, medicine, and chemistry) did not come away victorious. The very thought of a Nazi victory is chilling, given all the evidence we are continuing to discover about the heinous crimes perpetrated by the Third Reich during the course of its 12-year reign.

Nevertheless, it is not up to generals and other military men to ponder the inner workings of fate, destiny, or even God Himself. Many of these rare minds (and the thousands upon thousands of documents they could not destroy in time) are now in our custody and more are being tracked down as of this writing. We have won the war, but it is now imperative that the United States begin to use the deep pool of German intelligence before it is monopolized by Russia. If steps to this end are taken, the double purpose of preventing Germany's resurgence as a war power and advancing our own industrial and military future may be served. Evacuating these men (and, in some cases, women) from Germany and putting them straight to work in the US is crucial to ensuring a brighter future. The moral trappings of the former Nazi affiliations of these people will no doubt cause difficulties, but delay on a decision could prove, I believe, to be disastrous for America and her citizens.

June 1, 1945

CONFIDENTIAL
MEMORANDUM FOR JCS

FROM: Dr. Howard Percy Robertson
SUBJECT: Exploitation of German specialists in
science and technology in the United States

It is preposterous and downright heinous to entertain the idea of trusting these people with special allowances—let alone permanent residence—in the United States. They are nothing but unscrupulous opportunists who were (and are) hostile to the Allied cause. Consider the hypocrisy as we prepare to put their very leaders on trial for war crimes in Nuremberg. I support using the scientists' knowledge to advance our own military, naval, and aviation preparedness, but once they have given us all they can, they should receive a one-way trip back to their beloved "Fatherland."

July 6, 1945

CONFIDENTIAL
MEMORANDUM FOR SWNCC

FROM: JCS
RE: Exploitation of German specialists in science
and technology in the United States

Exploitation of German scientific knowledge approved. No known or alleged war criminals, profiteers, or ardent Nazis shall be included in this operation (henceforth called "Overcast"). All military agencies seeking to hire specialists must submit requests to assistant chief of staff, G-2. Only the most compelling argument should bring a German specialist to this country. Once here, they are to remain in protective military custody. All hiring will, per previous suggestions, be temporary.

Proceed accordingly.

August 23, 1945

CONFIDENTIAL
MEMORANDUM FOR G-2

FROM: JIC/JCS
RE: German specialist requests

All military agencies interested in hiring German specialists must direct requests to the newly created Joint Intelligence Objectives Agency. No exceptions are to be made.

September 1, 1945

CONFIDENTIAL
MEMORANDUM FOR JIOA

FROM: John C. Green

SUBJECT: Exploitation of German specialists in science and technology in the United States

Having these experts work in our country on a short-term basis is not enough. They have families in Germany and unless they and their loved ones can be promised American citizenship and long-term contracts with the military (or even private) sector, their performance and morale may decline. Without family support, they could become depressed or even suicidal. Sending them back to Germany is counterproductive thinking. It would just turn them into easy targets for the Russians. In addition, the Department of Commerce sees this as a ripe opportunity to explore the practical, industrial, and economic advantages of German discoveries. We are prepared to establish an oversight committee that will weed out the "bad" Germans from the "good" ones.

Please find my full proposal attached.

September 12, 1945

CONFIDENTIAL

FROM: JIOA
RE: Citizenship for German specialists in science and technology

Secretary Wallace has endorsed Mr. Green's American citizenship and family relocation proposal for eminent German specialists.

Proper requests have been sent to State Department for approval on fast-tracking visa application process. Stand by for further information.

September 20, 1945

CONFIDENTIAL

FROM: JIOA

First contingent of German specialists (rocketry team led by Wernher von Braun) has arrived safely at Fort Strong in Boston Harbor. Six of them will be transferred to Aberdeen Proving Ground for document translation and cataloging. Von Braun to be escorted to Fort Bliss for V-2 recreation and testing.

November 1, 1945

CONFIDENTIAL

FROM: JIOA
RE: Slowdown in "fast-tracking" of German specialist visa applications

Problem has been identified as Samuel Klaus, a JIOA State Department representative (and former head of "Operation Safe Haven"), who has denied every application request so far. Klaus has been outspoken about operation from the beginning. He declared at a recent meeting that "less than a dozen German specialists would ever be permitted to enter the US." He has also compared the program to "making a deal with the Devil for national security gains."

Klaus now requesting in-depth dossiers for each applicant so as to properly conduct thorough background checks for Nazi-related affiliation and fanaticism via military government in Germany and document center in Berlin. He is also demanding that each candidate undergo mandatory denazification courses. It is the belief of this agency that Klaus's Jewishness may possibly be getting in the way of America's scientific progress.

November 6, 1945

CONFIDENTIAL
MEMORANDUM FOR: JIOA

FROM: JIA
RE: Slowdown in "fast-tracking" of German specialists visa applications in State Department

Per previous memo, attached is second slate of German scientist, engineer, and technician files.

Axter, Tessman, Huzel, Rees, Lindenberg, Ambros, Strughold, Richkey, Debus, Kneymeyer, Dornberger, Rudolph, Osenberg, Blome, Gehlen, Putt, Knerr, Shlicke, Ziegler . . . Lang.

Hundreds upon hundreds of names specializing in rocketry, medicine, biology, chemistry, missile guidance systems, jet propulsion, virology, aviation medicine, aeronautics, nuclear physics, and more. But it wasn't just a list of names. Each "specialist" came with their own corresponding dossier and photo—all of them making up an abhorrent set of trading cards (collect them all!). Their files told horror stories of unimaginable depravity:

- Concentration camp inmates frozen to death to see if Luftwaffe pilots could be revived after being shot down over large bodies of water.
- Other inmates forcibly exposed to the fatal effects of high altitude and decompression to see how much a pilot's body could endure before completely giving out.
- Jews exposed to deadly and infectious pathogens like bubonic plague for testing in Himmler's secret biological weapons program.
- Romani and homosexuals gassed with volatile and hitherto unknown nerve agents.
- A contest at Dachau to determine the efficacy of competing desalination methods on prisoners.
- Gruesome medical operations that seemed to serve no purpose whatsoever.

Soon, the correspondence was becoming more and more feverish, sent single days or even hours apart:

Requesting Klaus's immediate removal from visa office. The threat of Communism is becoming too great and his obstinance is standing in the way of this operation and the safety of American lives. He is now citing refusal on grounds of SS and SA membership on the part of German specialists. More scientists will be recruited by the Soviets if action is not immediately taken.

An internal memo circulated among the top JIOA staff:

The alleged past misdeeds of these brilliant authorities can and must be overlooked in the face of the growing Russian threat, which is expected to reach capacity for total war against the United States by 1952 (see: JIC intelligence report 250/4). The knowledge culled from Hitler's brightest minds is most important in effectively fighting the conflict to come. Thanks to their association with National Socialism, many (if not all) of these individuals are already avid anti-Communists. Klaus's removal from the visa office is integral to the operation's overall success.

A proposal on providing the scientists with cleaner identities has made its way among the desks of this agency. For the time being, please flag more "alarming" dossiers with a small paper clip. These files will be held for State Department review until the sanitized portfolio plan is approved and the Klaus problem can be dealt with properly.

Secretaries Patterson and Byrnes are currently working to resolve the latter.

Another internal note came a week later stamped with large black letters:

HIGHLY CLASSIFIED
DESTROY AFTER READING

Klaus effectively relieved of JIOA visa oversight responsibilities. Per the proposal mentioned in the last memo, expunging Party membership and activities during wartime will not be difficult.

Highly revised biographies will now be attached to scientist dossiers before they are submitted for visa review and approval. However, it will take some time to amend the backgrounds of all these men after seeing the number of "paperclip" hopefuls flagged in the last week alone.

HIGHLY CLASSIFIED
DESTROY AFTER READING

I must say, this system of revised backgrounds for Nazi scientists is ingenious. Begin the same process with CIA-recruited German scientists and informants.

—Hillenkoetter

January 3, 1946

HIGHLY CLASSIFIED
DESTROY AFTER READING

FROM: JIOA

Attached is a recommendation for bringing one thousand additional Germans to US for weapons-related research. List compiled by General Joseph T. McNarney of USFET.

September 3, 1946

HIGHLY CLASSIFIED
DESTROY AFTER READING

President Truman has officially given his support to operation (henceforth called "Paperclip"). Recommendation for one thousand additional scientists and technicians to emigrate to the US is now No. 1 priority of this administration.

A one-page telegram sent by a West German prosecutor named Bauer in the summer of 1947:

- Witness accounts of life in the underground Nazi rocket factory beneath Harz Mountains (Thuringia) are ready for trial.
- Accompanying Nordhausen-Dora concentration camp (aka Mittelbau-Dora) liberated by American Allied forces in April 1945.
- Vast subterranean tunnel system for rocket production was dug with bare hands by slave labor (culled from Jewish, French, Polish, and Russian POWs) supplied by the SS from conquered nations and eastern network of concentration camps (e.g., Buchenwald, Gross-Rosen, Auschwitz).
- V-1 and V-2 rockets assembled via slave labor in underground Mittelwerk arms factory during war. Shifts ran for 12 hours, 7 days a week.
- Living conditions deplorable: no sunlight, ventilation system, or proper washing facilities.

- Camp's estimated 20,000 deaths stemmed from combination of overwork, malnutrition, typhus, dysentery, pleurisy, pneumonia, tuberculosis, beatings, and public hangings.
- Said hangings (inflicted upon those charged with sabotage and revolts) were conducted with a crane directly above assembly lines to ensure worker compliance via intimidation.
- Von Braun (among others) implicated.
- Full list of names attached. Their presence at upcoming trial is strongly requested.

Bauer's telegram went completely unanswered. Instead, there was a panicked memo from JIOA deputy director Bosquet N. Wev to FBI director J. Edgar Hoover:

HIGHLY CLASSIFIED
DESTROY AFTER READING

The results of the Dora-Nordhausen trial could be potentially embarrassing for Operation Paperclip and its participating agencies. Moreover, we cannot send the requested men to Europe, where they'll be vulnerable to the Soviets. The trial will have to go on without them and on the recommendation of Colonel Holger Toftoy, it is strongly requested that the trial record be classified once the proceedings are over.

A short response from Hoover promised that it would get done, no questions asked. All damning documents from the trial would be sealed until 2025.

The most recent piece of correspondence came from the chairman of the House Un-American Activities Committee, Francis E. Walter, dated November 1, 1955, only two years after he had taken office. As with so many other documents in the safe-deposit box, this one was also ordered to be destroyed once it was read:

There is no doubt that Operation Paperclip has been and con-tinues to be successful for this country and its battle against the USSR and its diabolical spread of Communism all over the world. We have broken the sound barrier and discovered a way to mass-produce the deadly, German-created nerve agents known as tabun and sarin. We have learned about the destructive power of the hydrogen bomb and the devastating effects of biological weapons and high-altitude conditions on the human body. We even expect to put a man on the moon within the next several years. University laboratories and private defense contractors have benefited greatly from the scientific secrets these men and women have unlocked for us.

Should the United States be forced to engage in another global conflict, the president is confident that America will come out victorious thanks to the work of these brilliant minds. History will remember them not as instruments of Adolf Hitler's war machine, but as heroes of democracy and capitalism. That being said, the American public may not see it that way, even though they have prospered and grown fat on the nectar of Nazi discoveries.

Will the denizens of this great nation embrace what was done in the name of their protection or will they hang their heads in shame? We are optimistic it will be the former. After all, the best way to treat a wound is not always the most comfortable. Pouring iodine on a cut is painful, but it is the most sensible course of action. Hindsight is our greatest ally.

Nevertheless, with the war in Europe still so fresh in our collective memory, it is too great a risk to rely on the current citizens of this great country (particularly those of the Judaic persuasion) to understand what this government has tried to do by recruiting these scientists and putting them to work in the name of making American greater than she already is.

In other words, the wound is still too fresh for the metaphorical burning to abate, should the details of this operation become public knowledge. As of this moment, all government agencies involved with "Operation Paperclip" are henceforth ordered to purge their document inventories of anything pertaining to said operation. This includes but is not limited to: memoranda, contracts, telegrams, dossiers, photographs, letters, and recorded testimony. Failure to comply with this order will result in heavy penalties...

* * *

The paper clips were the key. They had unlocked the floodgates of evil, allowing an embarrassment of toxic filth to spill onto American shores. Before McCarthy came to power, Baker always admired the United States. It wasn't perfect, but no country was. He admired the Constitution's Bill of Rights that, until recently, allowed anyone to walk down the street without fear that they would be dragged away without due process and never heard from again.

Now Baker knew the horrible truth. That his adopted homeland, the country that helped liberate Europe from the yoke of fascism, had welcomed monsters like Adolf Lang with open arms. Instead of facing retribution, these people were rewarded with citizenship and generous compensation.

How many American soldiers perished on the battlefields of Europe with the idea that the German bastards would be punished for every acre of land stolen, every piece of art pilfered, every gold filling ripped from the mouths of dead Jews?

Lang's escape from justice, Baker now realized, was the symptom of a much larger disease. Sure, he knew that many guilty parties evaded retribution after the war, but not to this degree. The sound of his heart beating in his ears was like a cruel joke. Why was he even alive? He'd become a police officer to do some good in the world, but why bother when these people had not faced a single repercussion?

These men were the reason he would black out and hurt himself without control. They were the reason he had not slept soundly in over ten years. They were the reason his family, his entire town, no longer existed. They were the reason he hated the world.

Baker felt a vindictive pleasure bubble up inside him and was now glad for his ambivalence over answering the influx of letters from West German courts that wanted his testimony against potential war criminals. They would not be allowed to make a farce of his suffering if this was the way in which justice was meted out.

For many years, Baker knew that the world was a backward and upside-down place, but until this very moment, he did not understand just how morally bankrupt it truly was. Nothing he did could make any difference to the contrary. His mission as an officer of the law now felt like a hollow sham—a one-man performance in a run-down theater.

And why did Lang leave all of this for him to find? Was it a final act of sadism from beyond the grave to show him that the Reich had won in the end? Or was it an admission of guilt? Was Lang, like Valentina claimed, actually penitent for his crimes? If that was the case, then what did he want Baker to do with these documents?

No newspaper would ever publish something that made McCarthy look bad, and Baker would probably be killed by the Hueys if he tried. Lang was either taunting him or asking for his help; either way, it angered Baker beyond words. He wasn't inclined to follow the orders of the man who had helped destroy his entire will to live.

"Morris?" Sophia's hand was on his shoulder. "I know learning about all of this must be awful, but..."

"Spare me your justifications, Sophia," he said. "We were all taken for suckers. The greatest joke is that we believed this country actually stood for something. Come on, let's get out of—"

The sight of one last piece of paper at the bottom of the safe-deposit box gave him pause. He pulled it out and began to read the cursive that wove around the page like ivy. The document was a deed for thousands of acres of land in something called the Great Rift Valley in British East Africa. The document had been drawn up and signed by none other than Laremy Dinsmore Fenwick, Esquire, while the land was in the name of one Arthur X. Scholz.

"Beat the Devils," Baker whispered. "Okay," he said, turning to face Sophia. "It's time to visit my lawyer."

CHAPTER 22

Baker stopped at another phone booth outside the bank and asked to be connected with Fenwick's office. There was no answer. He tucked the business card the lawyer had given him the day before back into his wallet.

He figured it was a wise move to leave all the papers (with the exception of the African land deed) at the bank. The safe-deposit key now rested snugly inside his sock. The incriminating evidence against the federal government would be safer under the watchful eye of Henry Lincoln IV. Safer, indeed.

The picture was beginning to come into focus, though Baker was still puzzled about Lang's connection to Huston. Both had pointed him in the direction of Africa. And what about Cronkite? Was he, one of the last decent journalists left in America, brought in to expose this Operation Paperclip as well as the bomb plot Baker was supposed to be perpetrating tomorrow?

All that fit. But there was one question still nagging Baker: Who was behind the deaths of these three men? With the government documents in play, the Hueys were beginning to seem like the obvious answer. Were they picking off anyone with knowledge of Lang's cache? But that didn't explain who was behind the bomb.

Baker felt like he was attempting to solve a Chinese puzzle box, turning all of the clues this way and that, looking for the right combination that would turn the rudimentary tumblers and reveal the reward inside. Every time he seemed close, he'd hit a dead end and would have to start over.

* * *

He and Sophia didn't have all the facts, and the white-hot anger he felt over learning about Operation Paperclip was making it hard to concentrate. As such, he drove past the law offices of Fenwick, Marter & Hepworth twice without realizing he had done so. For all the attorney's pomp and circumstance, Fenwick's office was located in a run-of-the-mill limestone building in Van Nuys. While there was a good chance Fenwick had already taken off for the holiday weekend, Baker theorized that Lang's death would be keeping the lawyer pretty busy, especially if the doctor's death was part of something larger.

A charter airplane putt-putted overhead, coming in for a landing at the local airport as Baker parked in a side alley that would be easy to miss if you weren't looking for it. So far, their luck was holding: No one had recognized his car. He and Sophia walked up to the squat office building, which announced itself as THE SYCAMORE on a weathered slab of granite that sat next to a revolving door.

Inside, they found a tasteful lobby where naked porcelain cupids endlessly pissed jets of water into basins lined with palm fronds and

California poppies, the state flower. It looked like a dream sequence ripped straight out of a Shakespeare play.

Although still furious over what he'd discovered at the bank, Baker found himself calming down a bit. Whether it was the soothing sound of running fountains or the subtle opioid effect of so many poppies in one place, he couldn't tell. This was most likely intentional in a building where angry people came to get divorced or sue the California Highway Patrol for outrageous speeding tickets.

Sophia looked over at him, smiling serenely. "Just like *The Wizard of Oz*," she said dreamily. "I'd say we're getting close to the Emerald City."

"More like the Wicked Witch of the West. Your understanding of American culture continues to impress, Comrade Vikhrov."

As chance would have it, *The Wizard of Oz* was one of the few pre-McCarthy pictures he'd seen after his arrival in the country. The thought of Margaret Hamilton shouting "Poppies! Poppies!" made him smile.

"I already told you, Detective," Sophia replied. "You've got to have an understanding of American culture if you want to visit the United States without stopping by the electric chair on your way out."

Baker kissed her on the lips right then. "If they send you to the electric chair, sweetheart, they'll have to get me one next to yours."

"Oh, Morris," giggled Sophia. "Your morbidity is *sooo* romantic."

They called the elevator and stepped inside, listening to Frankie Lymon play over a pair of speakers. The metal grille closed them off from the outside world, and the slow-moving lift made Baker feel claustrophobic. Fortunately, Sophia made the experience more bearable.

Lymon's extended "tell me whyyyyy" was cut off by the lift's ominous juddering as it hit the third floor, which housed the legal offices of Fenwick, Marter & Hepworth. The elevator doors opened to reveal a quiet reception area carpeted in periwinkle blue.

Baker pulled the grille aside and extended his arm. "Vayber Ersht, maydl," he said in Yiddish. "Ladies first, miss."

Sophia gave him an exaggerated curtsy of thanks and stepped out. Baker followed and that's when he heard it—softly at first, then growing in magnitude. A terrifying winged beast taking flight. He froze in place and felt warm beads of sweat breaking out on his forehead.

"Morris? Morris, what is it?" asked a concerned Sophia. The carefree aura of the poppies was now wearing off.

"It's nothing. Just some music," Baker said, swaying slightly. The elevator door clanged shut behind them and began its descent back to the lobby. "Let's find that lawyer now, shall we?" His voice was louder, shakier. He wanted to faint right here in the hallway, but the urge to know, to learn the truth, kept him going.

Sophia gently roped an arm around his own and helped him take the first step down the hallway. The walls were painted egg-yolk yellow and mounted with beautifully rendered oil paintings of some of the greatest legal battles ever argued on American soil: the Scopes Monkey Trial, *Dred Scott v. Sandford*, *Gibbons v. Ogden*, *Marbury v. Madison*, *Plessy v. Ferguson*, *Hiss v. United States*.

"And here we are," Sophia announced.

The ink painted onto the door's frosted glass proclaimed the office of L. D. FENWICK, ATTORNEY-AT-LAW, and it was behind this door that the music had reached its horrible crescendo.

"Bom Bom Bom bom bom bom bom bom bom bom bom bom bom bom bom bom bom bom BOOOOMMMMM!" went the voice of Laremy Fenwick in

time to Wagner's "Ride of the Valkyries." From the sound of it, the attorney was drunk as a skunk. Everyone seemed to be hitting the bottle pretty hard today.

Baker knocked with a tightly curled fist, which caused the glass to shake in its frame. There was the sound of papers shuffling on a desk and the quick opening and closing of a drawer.

"Huh—Hoo izzitt?"

Baker opened the door, which swung inward with a slight creak of hinges to reveal a good-sized office. A large oak desk, metal filing cabinet, and curio case of various tchotchkes were among its most prominent furnishings. Atop the curio case stood an old gramophone playing a large 78, slowly bobbing up and down with each rotation.

Fenwick's law degree from the Southern University Law Center in Baton Rouge was affixed to the wall behind his desk, along with photos of him shaking hands with California governor Goodwin Knight and Vice President Nixon. It was the sanctum of a man who likes to surround himself with the illusion of power and celebrity, all the while knowing that he will never truly achieve either. As for the bombastic lawyer himself, Fenwick was sitting as close to the desk as his large belly would allow. Today he wore a suit of a shocking-pink fabric and a checkered red, white, and blue bow tie.

Despite the air-conditioning, Fenwick's pudgy face was beet red and perspiring like a cold glass of Cherry Coke at Merv's Diner. In one hand, he held a tumbler of clear liquor, which helped to explain why he was sweating so much. His other hand was hidden behind the desk, something that Baker's instincts as a veteran cop picked up on right away.

"Ah," said Fenwick when he saw Baker. "Oh!" he exclaimed as Sophia stepped into view. "I know you, Detective, but who's your ravishing friend?" He laughed heartily and took a large swig of his drink. "Can I offer either of you some gin? I'd offer you a sweet tea or mint julep like my mammy used to, but gin is the nectar of the cultural socialites, wouldn't you agree? A Southern gentleman like myself must keep up appearances out here in the land of glamour."

"Yeah, I guess," said Baker. His head was still buzzing from the music. He pointed to the phonograph. "Can you please turn that off?"

"Certainly," replied Fenwick. He put down his glass, swung around, and pulled the needle off the record. His other hand remained hidden from view. "I hope you can excuse the volume. Everyone is out of the office for the holiday. I just thought I'd get into the spirit of our great nation's birthd—"

"Shut up!" shouted Baker. "I'm here to talk, Fenwick." He sat down in the smaller chair reserved for clients. Sophia put a comforting hand on his shoulder.

"We'll talk, if you like," slurred Fenwick. "I enjoy talking to a man who likes to talk."

"Stuff it and listen."

Baker reached into his pocket and saw Fenwick's eyes widen with fear as his hidden arm twitched like a dying insect. If the time came, Baker was ready to draw his own gun at a moment's notice. He extracted the African land deed and slid it across the desk.

"Explain."

Fenwick looked down at the paper, then up to Baker. "My word, Detective. Wherever did you find this?"

"Never mind where I found it," said Baker. "I thought you dealt in wills."

"I . . . well, I dabble in many types of law, Detective," sputtered the attorney. His drunkenness betrayed itself again with the arrival of a large belch. "'A man cannot live on bread alone,' as the Bible tells us. Besides, it would be an affront to lawyer-client confidentiality to say another word about this document."

"Save the legal bullshit for someone who cares," spat Baker, reaching into his pocket again and prompting another spasm from the fat lawyer. Baker pulled out his cigarettes, lit one, and offered the box to Fenwick, who respectfully declined with a small shake of the head.

"Lang is dead, you don't owe him jack shit," Baker continued. "And don't try playing dumb, saying you've never heard that name before. I know you helped change his name to Scholz."

Tears began to pour from Fenwick's eyes. "I'm sorry," he moaned, over and over.

Sophia made a movement, as if to cross the desk and console Fenwick, but Baker stopped her by holding up his hand. "No," he said. "He's made his bed."

Baker plucked the lit Kool out of his mouth and flicked it at the lawyer. It bounced off Fenwick's sweaty white shirt, burning a small hole in the fabric. The blubbering Fenwick patted the hole with a beefy hand to keep his shirt from going up in flames.

"You can save the waterworks too," added Baker. "I have no sympathy for whatever you've gotten yourself into. But I want to know why Lang bought up all that land in Africa and for whom. What is or *was* on that land? What's happening tomorrow? And most important, what's it got to do with me?"

While he was sure of some of the answers, Baker needed to hear them from Fenwick's mouth. The lawyer sniffled, dabbing his eyes and mucus-coated nostrils with a monogrammed handkerchief. When he spoke, his voice was slightly hoarse.

"You must understand, Detective. It was a different time when Adolf Lang became my client."

"You mean he was fresh out of murdering hundreds of people in the camps," said Baker.

"Morris, let him speak," said Sophia.

"Thank you, miss. Um, yes," blustered Fenwick. "As I was saying, those days were confusing. He was employed by the government and then USC. His references were impeccable. How was I supposed to know I had taken on a former Nazi as a client? I didn't pose too many questions when he asked for my help in changing his name and setting up a foreign land deal that he promised would pay enormous dividends. If I had known what I was agreeing to, that I'd be working on their behalf, I never would have done it. Believe me."

"'*Their* behalf'?" repeated Baker. "So, Lang wasn't buying this land on his own?"

"Oh, heavens no," wheezed Fenwick. "It was...a group of investors, shall we say, who put up the funds to buy all those uranium fields."

Baker froze in the act of lighting another Kool, his hunch confirmed. "Uranium?"

"Yes, uranium. Africa's an untapped gold mine of the stuff, don't you know? They bought up as much of it as they could."

"Who is '*they*'?" asked Baker, somewhat afraid of the answer.

"Please, Detective. You must understand, I didn't know going into it. I didn't. They threatened me, but that came later on. At first, they promised to make me rich, which they did. I was struggling financially at the time. I..."

Baker held up a hand to stop the lawyer's rambling. "Who is '*they*,' Fenwick?"

Fenwick's mouth gaped. He looked a lot like a bloated fish trying to breathe on land. But before he could speak, there was a screeching of metal from down the hall. The elevator. They all glanced at the door as if they could see through it.

Baker rounded on Fenwick, pulling out his gun. "Expecting someone?"

Fenwick clapped a hand to his mouth and squeaked in horror. "What time is it?"

Baker looked down at his watch. "Three thirty," he said.

"Oh dear. Oh dear. Oh dear," moaned the attorney. "It's *him*."

Fenwick's foreboding emphasis on the word *him* made Baker's stomach drop. This didn't sound like the lawyer was meeting with an ordinary client, which meant that he and Sophia couldn't just casually walk out of the office.

"*Fenwick! Quick!*" hissed Baker. "*We need somewhere to hide!*"

Moving with a swiftness that did not seem to match his weight, Fenwick jumped to his feet, revealing the snub-nosed police special he'd been concealing behind the desk.

"*Behind here!*" he whispered, leaning against the curio case, which noiselessly moved aside on a set of hidden tracks. Just then, there was a sharp rap on the office door. "One moment please, old boy!" called Fenwick over his shoulder before turning back. "*Inside. Now!*" he sibilated.

Behind the case was a hidden alcove just big enough for one large person or two smaller people, if they didn't mind being packed together like sardines. Baker and Sophia quickly squished themselves into the concrete space, which housed a combination safe. They could barely utter whispers of thanks before Fenwick slid the case back into place, cutting off all light. Baker's mind flashed back to the war, when he would hide in the homes of non-Jews. In the end, they'd all been discovered, and no one was saved.

From the other side of the curio case, he and Sophia heard the muffled creak of the desk chair as the lawyer sat down. "Come in!" he called out. "Ah, Rudy. Thank you for being so patient, old sport. I had a little lunch fiasco and needed to change my trousers. That's the last time I ask for extra catsup on my hot dog."

Even in the hiding space, Baker could tell that the lawyer's ensuing attempt at a mild-mannered chuckle was hollow and forced. Being farther away, the newcomer was a little harder to hear, but Baker and Sophia held their respective breaths to catch every word.

"Quite," the stranger responded. "You Americans with your Würstchen drowned in sauces." Baker let out a small gasp before Sophia responded with a near-silent "*shhh!*" The harsh voice of the newcomer sounded eerily familiar to Baker.

"Mmm, yes," said Fenwick. "So, Rudy, what can I do for you today on the eve of our great nation's birthday?"

"'*Our*'?" asked Rudy with contempt in his voice. "I do not consider this land of excess my home, Herr Fenwick. My glorious homeland is across the Atlantic Ocean and it shall soon be redeemed."

"Yes, as you have said before. In any case, how can my legal expertise be of service to you and your colleagues today?"

"Lang," said the stranger. "Even from the grave, he continues to be a thorn in our side. Wernher says that everything will work out, but I do not share his blind optimism. So, I come here of my own volition to settle this matter once and for all. As I told you during our conversation after the reading of Lang's will, we know he accumulated sensitive information, which he placed in a safe-deposit box at a bank not far from here. I asked you to give us access to said box, but you claimed Lang did not use you as executor on that particular matter. I now know you have not been completely honest with us. One *persuasive* interview with the bank manager revealed that you *were* present at the deposition during which he bequeathed the box to the Jew, Baker. He also told me Baker was at the bank not an hour ago to have a look at the box's contents. Now I ask you this, Herr Fenwick, and I expect you to be forward with me because I will tolerate no more insolence from you. Where would be the next logical place for this noxious Jüdische Scheisse to go after seeing what was inside that box?"

"I-I-I," stammered Fenwick. "I haven't the slightest idea, Rudy."

"I thought I just requested that you be forward with me. Time is running thin and we can't have the Jew-dog mucking things up for us. Now I ask you again, and this time I will be more direct. Where is the Jew-dog? I know he and the whore are around here somewhere."

"Rudy, why don't you put that thing down before someone gets hurt."

"My patience is evaporating quickly, Herr Fenwick. I have been against your participation from the start. You are a fat man who has squandered the wealth we have given you on worthless American trinkets and your precious hot dogs. I have always said this, just as I have always asked you not to call me Rudy. My name is—"

"Go to hell, you Hun bastard!" screamed Fenwick.

There were two loud bangs and a pair of resulting *thuds!* After a minute of silence, Baker maneuvered his body against the wall of the alcove and pushed the curio case along its tracks. Light filtered back into the cramped hiding space and he squinted.

"See anything?" he asked Sophia, who was closer to the opening.

"I think they're both dead."

Baker pushed the case completely aside and the two of them staggered back into the office on numb legs. One look at the room proved that Sophia was only half correct.

The legal mind of Laremy Dinsmore Fenwick, Esquire, was now

splattered all over the back wall of his office. In some cases, sharp bits of skull fragment had cracked the frames. The lawyer was still in his chair, his body bent backward from the force of a point-blank gunshot. One thing was certain: Laremy Fenwick would not enjoy a seersucker suit or hot dog ever again. Sophia took a horrified glance at the gore on the walls and what remained of Fenwick's head before running over to the wastebasket to vomit for the second time in twenty-four hours.

Meanwhile, Baker, gun still in hand, crept around the desk to where the other man called Rudy lay on the floor. He sported a mid-contour haircut that was once so popular with National Socialists. A vivid red stain was blooming across his chest like a freshly cut rose.

Even with the obvious signs of cosmetic surgery—the chin shaved down, dueling scars filled in, nose flattened, and hair dyed brown— Baker recognized the man for who he really was. Rudolph Rascher, the concentration camp commandant who had once beaten him senseless with a shovel. A man who had committed a hundred other unspeakable acts in the name of his Führer's Final Solution.

How could he not have recognized him at the reading of Lang's will? He seemed vaguely familiar then, but now that Baker was so close to the man, there could be no question.

Rascher coughed up a mouthful of blood. His shocking-blue eyes fluttered open. The hatred, the current of evil running through them, had not waned over the intervening years. Rascher's fingers twitched in an attempt to grab the Luger he had used to shoot Fenwick, but Baker kicked it out of reach. His heart pounded in his chest as adrenaline filled his body. After all these years, he would finally have his revenge.

"Do you know who I am?" Baker's voice cracked with rabid anticipation.

Rascher tried to laugh but could only manage a pitiful gasp. Blood bubbled at the corners of his mouth. The ragged whistle of his breathing told Baker that Fenwick's bullet had punctured a lung. If something wasn't done soon, the former commandant would drown in his own blood.

"Sophia, come over here. Help me get him up."

Sophia hurried over to help Baker get Rascher into a sitting position against Fenwick's desk, then opened a window. The office now stank of blood, vomit, and shit. The late Mr. Fenwick had vacated his bowels in death, but Baker hardly noticed. A ghastly euphoria was ebbing through his veins. After more than a decade of numbing the pain with alcohol, he realized that retribution was what he really needed. What he craved. What did the Bible say? An eye for an eye? Well, he'd take both of Rascher's eyes just to be sure. Maybe an ear and his pecker, too.

"Do you know who I am?" asked Baker again, snapping his fingers in front of Rascher's face, trying to keep him awake.

"Yes," breathed Rascher in another whistle. The color was fast draining from his pale face. "I'm surprised you did not recognize me yesterday, but I have had some cosmetic work done since the old days."

"I am going to kill you. Do you know that?"

"I would expect nothing less, Herr Baker. It is your right, I suppose."

"First, I want to know who helped Lang buy all that land in Africa. Who do you work for?"

Rascher tried to laugh again but doubled up in pain. Whatever discomfort he was feeling, Baker knew it was too good for the likes of him.

"Still so much you do not understand, Jew," rasped Rascher. "The Fatherland will rise again like the mighty Valkyrie. The Americans.

The Russians. Running around, spying on each other like headless chickens. They could only stop the Reich's destiny for so long."

"Who do you work for?" shouted Baker. His voice cracked on the last syllable. Rascher chuckled in response, finally managing a true laugh. Sticky, warm blood poured out of his chest and mouth. His tongue flicked back with practiced speed and popped the false molar out of place. Before Baker could stick his fingers into the man's mouth, Rascher bit down on the concealed cyanide capsule. As white foam began to pour from his lips, he gurgled his last words. "Heil Hitler."

Rascher's body convulsed, his chalk-white face contorting into a rictus of agony. After fifteen seconds, he was dead, along with Baker's chance for revenge. Baker closed his eyes and heard an animal-like roar of rage and pain, only to realize that the noise was coming from his own throat. Looking down, he saw Rascher's face resembling a pile of chopped meat. In his rage, he'd attacked the former commandant. Bits of Rascher's flesh and blood were mixing with Baker's stinging knuckles. Tears streamed from his eyes as Sophia led him out of the room, down the hall, and back toward the elevator.

CHAPTER 23

Rascher had gotten the final word in the end. He, and so many others like him, had escaped justice. Sophia was jabbing a finger onto the elevator button when Baker's anger began to recede and he was able to think clearly again.

"Wait," he said, looking down at the blood on his hands and clothes. For the second day in a row, one of his best suits had been ruined by a violent death. He turned around and began walking back toward Fenwick's office. Sophia ran over and grabbed his arm.

"Morris, enough!" she screamed. "There's nothing for you back there. What good will come from—"

"The safe."

"What?"

"The safe," he repeated. "The safe hidden behind Fenwick's case. It might hold some answers. We need to open it."

* * *

The top-of-the-line SentrySafe was made of twenty-four inches of reinforced fireproof steel, complete with a combination dial and five-spoke handle. It had more in common with Henry Lincoln IV's bank vault than it did with a personal safe.

"We need the combination," Baker said. "Look in the desk for a manufacturer's manual or something that will help us. I'll check Fenwick's pockets."

Trying hard to avoid touching the lawyer's corpse, Sophia opened the desk drawers and riffled through Mr. Goodbars; unfinished wills; wells of black, blue, and red ink; and pornographic magazines that promised SALACIOUS SOUTHERN GIRLS within their pages.

"Ugh," said Sophia.

"His brains just repainted the wall and you're disgusted by the fact that he decided to rub one out every once in a while?" asked Baker, plunging his hand into another pocket.

"Just saying," said Sophia, sounding a little offended. "He seemed so...I don't know...cultured."

"Anyone who works for Nazis can't be all that cultured."

Baker's search yielded a sizable ball of lint, another monogrammed handkerchief, and a melted Mr. Goodbar. Wiping the sludgy chocolate on Fenwick's pant leg, he stood up and swore in Czechoslovakian. "Find anything, Sophia?"

"I think so." She was rummaging around in a drawer full of paper clips and brought out a small white booklet titled *SentrySafe Owner's Manual*. "Aha!" She flipped through its pages before throwing it on the desk in exasperation. The manual hit a concave piece of Fenwick's skull, causing it to spin like a top. "Worthless. The page on combinations isn't there."

Baker swiped up the dog-eared manual and took a look for himself.

Sure enough, the page titled "Setting Your Safe's Combination" had been ripped away from the words at the top. He dropped it on the floor and cursed again. The booklet flopped onto the yellow-handled snub-nosed revolver Fenwick had used to put a hole in Rascher's chest.

"It's fine," began Baker. "Even if it was in there, we'd still need the exact combina—" Hold on. Yellow? The handles of snub-nosed police specials weren't yellow. They were typically made of wood or plain metal unless they had been altered on the black market or... Baker bent down and gently picked up the gun by its barrel.

"That sly bastard," he said with a whistle.

The missing page of the safe owner's manual had been taped around the gun's handle with the flip side facing out so the text wouldn't be ruined. Nevertheless, Fenwick's large and sweaty paw had soaked it through, causing some of the type to run in places. Baker slowly peeled off the page, careful not to rip it. Once free of the metal handle, the paper attempted to curl in on itself.

Baker smoothed it out on the desk and began to read. Scribbled below the instructions on how to reset the combination were six numbers: 4-7-1-9-5-8. Baker got down on one knee and began turning the safe's dial. After he reached 8, the tumbler gave way with a hard metallic *clonk!* and the steel door swung outward with a well-oiled squeak.

Baker and Sophia gasped. A small pyramid of solid gold bars sat on the safe's bottom shelf. Baker reached in and picked one up, but nearly threw it across the room when he saw what was deeply engraved into its gleaming surface. An eagle clutching a wreath inlaid with a swastika. The symbol of the Third Reich.

"'Enormous dividends,'" said Baker. "Probably made from the gold fillings of dead Jews. Do you know that's what they did, Sophia? They made us pull the fillings out with rusty pliers after the gas had done its work. After a week of reaching into people's mouths, your hands would be stained blue from the Zyklon B."

Sophia looked horrified but said nothing.

"I asked you a question," hissed Baker through gritted teeth. "Did you know that?"

"Yes," she whispered, not looking him in the face.

"What was that?"

"Yes!" she shouted, and now there were tears forming in her beautiful, doe-like eyes. "Yes, Morris! I know it. Fenwick knew it and that man over there"—she pointed in the direction of Rascher's corpse—"knew it, too. In fact, the whole world knows it. But what will taking it out on me solve? It won't bring those poor people back. All we can do is keep moving forward and try to stop whatever these people are up to. That's how you'll get your revenge. By saving those who can still be saved. You heard Rudy, he sounded scared, which is all the better for us. It means we're getting close. I know you suffered, and nothing can ever make up for what you went through, but we're still here to make sure it never happens again. We have to be on the same side because if not, they've already won, and I hitch the next boat back to Russia."

Baker turned the gold bar over in his hands. It was one thing to survive on your own, but it was another to turn on those you cared about. In the camps, it was so easy to keep your nose clean when you were only looking out for number one. It was the ultimate test of courage to stand up for others, to join forces with like-minded people and spit in the face of evil. Even if it meant you were hastening your own demise.

Baker turned to her and said, "You're right. I'm sorry, Sophia. I didn't mean it."

"I know you didn't. Now, let's see what else is in this safe. What's that under the gold?"

As it turned out, the bars served as expensive paperweights for several documents.

"Look at this," said Sophia, pulling out a plane ticket to Baton Rouge scheduled for that evening.

"Guess he wanted to skip town before the bomb went off," guessed Baker.

Sophia also pulled out a manila folder marked *Lang-USC Correspondence*. Inside were three letters. Baker picked up the first sheet that was topped with USC's crest of torches and roses. It was dated June 28, 1958:

Dear Mr. Fenwick:

Thank you for the deposition on Professor Scholz's mental state of mind. While I have no doubt that he is brilliant as ever, there is still the matter of him missing eight classes in a row this past semester for a course that only meets once a week. Furthermore, there is the issue of Professor Scholz's incident with a student shortly before Christmas vacation. After consulting with the Board of Trustees, we have come to the conclusion that Arthur Scholz is no longer mentally fit to teach at our university. That being said, we are extremely grateful to him for his years of faithful service to the school and his contributions to the biology and physics departments. His papers on human anatomy and atomic power are invaluable gifts to aspiring doctors and scientists the world over. Moreover, we will never forget his help in the establishment of our Health Sciences campus in 1952. We believe our retirement offer is more than fair and want Professor Scholz to know that he can always count USC as a second home, should he ever care to visit or give a guest lecture after honoring the three-year grace period. We wish him nothing but the best and hope he can find peace of mind once the burden of teaching has been lifted from his shoulders.

Sincerely Yours,
Norman H. Topping
University President

The next letter was a short note from Fenwick to Topping sent two days later. The lawyer informed the president that Lang would be pursuing litigation against the university on the grounds of "unrightful removal."

The third and final piece of correspondence was written by Lang to Roger Danforth, head of USC's biology department. Hadn't Danforth come to collect the academic papers the old Nazi left to the school? The final letter was dated July 1, the day of Lang's death, and looked as though it was written on a poorly tended typewriter:

Dear Roger,

I cannot say that I have made many acquain-
tances since I came to this country, but I
count myself lucky to call you my friend. Your
friendship has meant more to me than you know.
You put up with my various neuroses and quirks
that may have driven another person away. As
you have no doubt heard, Topping and the board
are pushing me toward an early retirement.

My attorney is already preparing a lawsuit
against the school, but I don't really see a
point to it. It is my own fault that things
have gotten this far and to be quite frank, I
am rather relieved. The assault on that student
was an egregious mistake and I deserve to face
the consequences.

I have been distracted as of late and that
unfortunate incident was simply a culmination
of the things weighing on my mind these last
few years. Believe me when I say that I am not
as mentally sound as my deposition claims.

Don't worry, Roger. I assure you details of
my madness and true identity will arise very
soon if I have my way. Sins take their toll.
Remember that.

I am writing this letter on a typewriter my

```
father gave to me when I was just starting out
as a medical student at Humboldt University in
Berlin. I write this in the hope that I can
recapture the innocence of that young man who
wanted to save lives once upon a time.
```

```
Always Your Friend,
Arthur X. Scholz
```

```
PS: Die Luft der Freiheit weht
```

"Die Luft der Freiheit weht," said Baker. "The wind of freedom blows. Lang used the same phrase in his will."

"What do you think his attack on the student was all about?" Sophia asked.

"Not sure, but I know someone who will," Baker replied, unconsciously placing one of the heavy gold bars into the pocket of his suit jacket. Its weight caused the garment to oddly droop to one side. He scooped up the university letters. "Come on. We're going back to school."

CHAPTER 24

Time was running out, but they were both starving and decided to stop for In-N-Out burgers on the way to USC. Since Baker was currently a wanted man, they couldn't pick up their meal at the drive-in. Sophia went to get the food while Baker parked in the lot of a nearby department store. As luck would have it, there was another pale-green Continental already there. He pulled up beside it, remembering what the screenwriter had said about hiding in plain sight.

Baker listened to "Earth Angel" by the Penguins and tried to piece everything together. Not an easy feat when his stomach kept rumbling every two minutes. His reverie was broken by a light tap on the car window. He looked over, expecting to see Sophia with a bulging bag of burgers and two Cherry Cokes. Instead, he felt his hunger evaporate like droplets of water on a hot skillet. It was Liz. She was holding a purchase wrapped in brown paper and looked worried. He rolled down the window and gave her an ingratiating smile.

"Liz!" he said, trying to sound casual. "What're the odds?"

"Morris!" she exclaimed, looking over her shoulder. "You're all over the radio. I've been worried sick."

"Oh, the CONELRAD thing? It's nothing."

"Being wanted by the Hueys isn't nothing, Morris."

"I'm working a case and would rather not spend the holiday weekend having my fingernails pried loose. Look, Liz, this isn't exactly the best time."

"Morris? They were out of fries, so I got onion rings. Is that—?"

Sophia had returned with the food. She looked even more beautiful, like some patron goddess of full stomachs. Liz looked from Sophia to Baker. A meltdown was imminent.

"Morris," she muttered through gritted teeth. "What's going on here?"

"Um…" He had to do some quick thinking through his food-starved fog. "She's my…cousin."

"You expect me to buy that?" Liz said in a choked voice. "If you wanted to see other people, you should've just said so, Morris."

"Liz, I…"

"Save it!" She turned to Sophia, who looked wrong-footed. "Have fun with him," Liz said, and stormed off.

"Should I ask?" Sophia said as she passed him a burger through the open window.

"Nope," he responded, taking a much-needed bite.

* * *

It was close to six and still terribly hot when they strolled onto the USC campus. With summer classes available, there was a chance Danforth would still be around and able to answer a few questions.

As they coasted into visitor parking, Baker wedged the gold bar and African land deed under the driver's seat, which already concealed Lang's scrapbook. While it was late on a summer afternoon on the eve of a national holiday, there was a sizable group of students holding an antiwar protest on the red-bricked quad.

"Hey! Hey! McCarth-ay! How many kids have you killed today?" chanted the students.

They held up signs that declared:

END THE WAR IN KOREA BEFORE IT ENDS YOU!

END THE UNJUST WAR IN KOREA AND THE COMMUNIST WITCH HUNTS AT HOME!

I DON'T GIVE A DAMN ABOUT UNCLE SAM, I AIN'T GOING TO KOREA!

Freedom of expression and peaceful assembly were still technically upheld by the First Amendment, but the McCarthy administration was doing its damnedest to get around it. By nightfall, a battalion of Hueys was sure to descend on this gathering. The students would ultimately spend their vacation in a holding cell. They knew this and didn't give a shit. Fighting "the establishment" was in vogue for many young people these days. As for Baker, he wanted to be long gone before any federal agents hit the scene.

He removed his jacket and slung it over his shoulder, feeling just like James Dean in *Rebel Without a Cause*, one of United American Pictures' biggest regrets. Instead of the country's youth seeing the movie's protagonist, Jasha Sernestky, as a lazy, morally decayed Communist, they admired his nonchalant attitude. What was meant to be a cautionary tale about falling prey to the listless Bolshevik lifestyle turned into a phenomenon of teens emulating Sernestky by wearing red jackets and tight jeans, smoking cigarettes on the football field instead of going to class, and racing stolen cars.

Baker approached a young man in a V-neck sweater vest and tapped him on the shoulder. "Uh, excuse us," he said.

The boy stopped chanting and turned around. "Yeah?" he snorted.

"We were just wondering how to get to the biology department," replied Baker.

"Why should I tell you? You could be Huey pigs for all I know."

Baker whipped out his badge. "I'm LAPD. You're standing in the way of an important investigation, son."

"So? You're still working for The Man," said the kid in a raised voice. Some of the other protestors stopped chanting and looked over. "And what's with the goofy accent, Daddy-O?"

Baker smiled. "Okay. You want to play it like that?" He began to reach for his gun when he heard a thud and a wheeze. Looking up, he saw the boy on the ground with Sophia's heel on his neck.

"You gonna tell us where the biology department is, or am I going to have to make you eat some dirt first?" Sophia whispered into the boy's ear.

"Okay! Okay!" he screamed. He lifted one arm with difficulty and pointed to a rectangular building that looked a lot like a giant harmonica. "The College of Letters, Arts and Sciences."

"Thank you," said Sophia, taking her foot off his neck. "Was that so hard?"

A girl holding a LONG LIVE THE LIBERTY BOYS! sign took a step toward Sophia. Her eyes were alight with wonder. "Can you teach me how to do that?"

* * *

They found Danforth's office door on the fifth floor. Sophia gave Baker's arm a reassuring squeeze and he knocked. There was no answer.

"Probably went home for the holid—" began Baker, but before he could finish the sentence, the door flew open.

Danforth looked even more unkempt than he had yesterday at the reading of Lang's will. His unshaven stubble had turned into a curly neck beard, and his eyes were tired and glassy. The man needed a shave, shower, and shut-eye, in that order.

"Yes?" he said, crossing his arms. Baker noticed an elbow patch was missing from Danforth's shabby tweed jacket.

"Dr. Danforth?"

"Yes? Do I know you?"

"Not exactly," said Baker. "My name is Morris Baker."

"The fellow they keep mentioning on the radio?" Danforth inquired, now looking a little nervous. "Say, you look familiar. Have we met before?"

Baker explained their tenuous connection through Arthur Scholz. When he was finished, the doctor sighed and nodded gravely.

"Look, I don't know what you think I can do for you. Yes, Arthur was my friend, but he was also extremely secretive. Brilliant, mind you, but terribly introverted. I'm afraid I don't know any more than you d—"

"Please," said Sophia, and she reached into Baker's pants pocket and brought out Danforth's letter. "He obviously trusted you. Can you at least explain what happened with the student?"

Danforth read the letter before asking, "Where did you get this?"

"Dr. Danforth, please," she implored. "Something is going on and we need to get to the bottom of it. All we ask for is five minutes of your time."

Danforth sighed. For a moment, it looked like he wanted nothing more than to tell them to fuck off and slam the door in their faces.

Then, with a resigned slump of his shoulders, he said, "If you must. Come in and close the door behind you."

The office resembled a magnificent library. It was dimly lit with a high ceiling surrounded by walls that were stuffed to the teeth with medical journals, textbooks, and jars of formaldehyde where strange, pickled creatures floated ghoulishly. Danforth's desk was as disheveled as his appearance—littered with un-graded papers, letters to colleagues, empty bottles of Coca-Cola, and scraps of paper covered in notes and calculations. Baker was reminded of his own apartment and felt a certain kinship with the man's disorganization. A muffled ringing sound rose up from the clutter on the desk, and after shifting a few objects onto the floor, Danforth unearthed a black rotary phone and answered it.

"Roger Danforth speaking...Yes? How did you know?...I see... I...Yes, yes of course, Norman. You have a lovely holiday as well." He hung up and looked at Baker and Sophia. "University president just making sure I lock up before I head out. Now, how can I help you two?"

"We know Professor Scholz was starting to slip mentally over the last year or so," began Sophia. "What can you tell us about that?"

"I started to notice that Arthur seemed...'distracted,' we'll call it, as early as the spring or early summer of 1956," Danforth said. "He'd gone on holiday to visit the German village where he grew up as a child. He was only there for a few weeks and when he came back, he was...different."

"Different how?" prompted Baker.

"Well, like I say, Arthur was a private man, but I'd known him since 1950 when he first came to the school. He opened up to me after a while. I was about the only person he was actually friends with.

We'd get together every week for brandy and cigars in this very office. Following his visit to Europe, however, Arthur began to say he was too busy to meet up. Not long after that, he began missing department meetings and classes as well. I didn't press him too much because he said he was working on some big project. That's academia for you."

"But it wasn't just some project, was it?" asked Baker. *What happened to Lang in Germany?* he wondered.

"I never found out for sure, but no, I don't think it was," said Danforth. "If he came in to work at all, he'd spend entire days cooped up inside his own office. Finally, the president and board of trustees got involved and said that if his performance didn't improve, he'd be asked to leave his post. That was before the incident with Miles Brewster..."

"Was that the student?" asked Baker.

"Yes," said Danforth sadly. "You see, Arthur was improving, little by little. He'd join me for lunch once a month or go on a stroll with me around campus for some fresh air. He'd apologized profusely for his behavior. He claimed it was a small bout of melancholy that was finally abating. Then, right before Christmas break this past year, he had a meeting with a student, Miles Brewster. It was about some assignment or other and Arthur... well, he just snapped. He sent Miles to the hospital."

"Oh my," said Sophia.

"I know," Danforth said. "I'd never, in all my years of knowing Arthur, seen him become violent, but he apparently did on that day. Luckily, Miles only ended up with a broken arm and some cracked ribs. The way Miles tells it, though, Arthur became like a rabid animal. He'd simply lost control and that was the end for him. Topping and the trustees wanted him out and to be honest, I don't blame them.

Miles's father was threatening to sue the school unless Arthur was sacked. Arthur didn't seem too upset about it, though he no longer reached out to me. I was sure he was ashamed and embarrassed of what he'd done to poor Miles. And so I lived my life, giving him space, until a few days ago when I heard he was dead. I could hardly believe it."

"Wow," said Sophia. "That's quite a story."

"It sure is," said Danforth, twisting open a fresh bottle of cola and taking a large gulp.

"Just two more quick questions," Baker said, leaning forward. "What does 'Die Luft der Freiheit weht' mean to you? Beyond the literal translation, I mean."

Danforth smiled, perhaps remembering better times with Lang. "Arthur was quite fond of that phrase," he answered. "He'd often say it was a pity we didn't teach at Stanford. It's their motto."

"I see," said Baker. "He ever say why he liked that particular phrase?"

"Oh, I think it reminded him of home and also the freedom he found in America after the war. He was a refugee. Did you know that?"

Baker decided not to correct Danforth. "Last question, Dr. Danforth. What did Brewster do that made Scholz lose control like that?"

Danforth, who'd been nursing his soda bottle, put it on the desk. "Well, it was common knowledge that Arthur was from Germany and his accent was pretty thick. Anyway, Miles got fed up and called him— well, I don't usually like crass language like this, but he called him a 'fucking Nazi.' Miles didn't mean it, but you know how teenagers can get when they're angry. Now if that is all, I really must be getting home for the holiday."

"Thank you so much for your time, Dr. Danforth," Sophia said. "We really appreciate it."

"Always happy to help out a police investigation," he replied, smiling a little sadly. "I'm sorry for what comes next."

"For what?" asked Sophia as the office door burst open, nearly flying off its hinges.

"No sudden moves, Baker!" someone yelled.

About two dozen men in trench coats were standing outside the door, aiming their guns into the room. It was a small army of Hueys. Baker turned back to face Danforth with an expression of disgust.

"That wasn't the university president who called when we got here, was it?"

"I'm afraid not, Detective. They asked me to keep you busy while they got here."

"You son of a bitch," said Sophia.

"I truly am sorry," said Danforth, and he looked down at his bottle.

Two large Hueys grabbed Baker and Sophia, slamming them against the wall and handcuffing their wrists. That's when Baker heard Hartwell breathing in his ear.

"End of the line, you nosy fucking Hebe. Detective Morris Baker, you are under arrest on the grounds of harboring Communist sympathies and intentions to subvert American law and order. You will hereby submit your firearm to us and be escorted to HUAC headquarters, where you will be processed and interrogated."

"Bullshit!" grunted Baker. "I'm not a Commie and you know it."

Hartwell laughed. "Oh really? Your girlfriend says otherwise."

"Girlfriend?" a confused Baker repeated. "What the hell are you talking about?"

Hartwell leaned against the wall and lit a cigar. "You know I've been waiting to smoke this all day, Baker? Real Cuban, almost impossible to find these days." He contentedly puffed away for a minute before continuing. "You were good but couldn't hide from us forever. We got a call an hour ago from one Elizabeth Short. She reported your car, see? She also let us in on those red skeletons in your closet. Looks like all that proletariat pillow talk finally caught up with you."

Hartwell laughed and all the other Hueys joined in. The game was up. He and Sophia had run out of road just as they were nearing the heart of it all.

Baker went for the Hail Mary play. "How do you know I'm working alone, Hartwell?"

The Huey tapped some cigar ash right onto Baker's face. "I'm listening..."

"The bomb that's set to go off tomorrow. Do you really want to risk bringing me in and have one of my associates trigger it?"

"Nice try, Baker, but we've let you have your fun. It's time to pay the piper. Besides, you're not just wanted for being a no-good Red. Your fellow officers at the LAPD want to question you about the disappearance of a kid named Oliver Shelton. Seems he delivered something right to your front door two days ago and was never seen again."

"Outrageous!" shouted Baker. "I don't know what happened to him."

"Like I'm going to believe a Jew like you. Oh, and if you weren't in deep shit already, Baker, you've *also* been poking around a federal investigation, asking questions about a deceased pair of lavender lad subversives. Cronkite and Huston were part of a Russian sleeper cell right here in California. They were buddies of yours, right?"

"I'd never met those men in my life!"

"You've had quite the day, haven't you, Baker?" Hartwell said, clearly not listening. "You gave us the slip out in Burbank and then at Van Nuys." He clicked his tongue in mock admonishment. "Two bodies in the office of Laremy Fenwick. Messy, *very* messy. Come on, Baker—

what man runs from a crime scene if he's innocent? And what man goes running around with a Russian spy if he's a patriotic American?"

Baker stopped struggling, his eyes widening with fear. Hartwell's face lit up with fiendish ecstasy. "That's right," said the Huey. "We know all about your sordid love affair with Miss Vikhrov here." He leaned over to Sophia, whispering sensually in her ear. "You're going down, sweetheart. A real shame because you're a Grade-A piece of meat. Hmm, I wonder what fried Russki smells like."

Sophia spat in his face and Hartwell struck her. Sophia cried out in pain.

"I'll kill you!" snarled Baker.

"Tell it to the judge, Groucho. Take 'em downstairs, boys!" Hartwell said, wiping spittle from his nose, no longer merry. "These traitors are starting to stink up the place. And make sure they don't travel together."

"No!" Baker had begun struggling again. "Please! I can explain!"

This is exactly what Hartwell wanted—for him to scream, to beg for mercy—but Baker didn't care. The only other time he'd been this desperate was shortly after Lang removed the tumor from his arm. When he'd begged for a swift death. Now he was begging that none of the Hueys would lay another finger on Sophia.

"Sophia!" he yelled as they were being forcefully yanked in opposite directions. "Sophia, it'll be okay! You'll be okay!"

"Morris!" she called back. The sound of his name on her terrified lips tore at his insides.

"Be strong, don't tell them anything!"

"Don't that just break your heart, fellas?" said Hartwell, relighting his cigar and throwing the match over his shoulder. "Throw them in with the other fuck-ups!"

CHAPTER 25

Just as Baker suspected, the antiwar protesters had also been arrested. For thirty minutes, he'd been cramped next to four of them in the back of a converted Ford Interceptor, which bore the HUAC symbol on both passenger doors. A siren sat on the roof, flashing red, white, and blue. Hartwell drove, while his partner pointed a pump-action shotgun at the prisoners for the ride to Echo Park.

After being apprehended at USC, Baker was practically carried outside by the gorilla-like Waldgrave and stuffed into the back of the car with the students. He didn't know their names because they'd been given strict instructions not to talk or, as Hartwell put it, "the back window would be painted red."

"You guys like Bobby Darin?" called out Hartwell as "Splish Splash" came on the radio. "Aw, hell—I don't give a fuck what you guys think!" He dialed up the volume knob to ear-bursting levels and cackled like a madman. "You know what they say, Gene," he said to Waldgrave. "If ya do what you love, you'll never work a day in your life!"

Baker tried his best to tune out the music and Hartwell's off-key singing. He needed to think, he needed to get out of here, and he needed to stop the bomb from going off. But most importantly, he needed to make sure Sophia was all right. His position as a cop wouldn't protect him, not in McCarthy's America, where a Jew got the shit kicked out of him first and asked questions later.

Getting in touch with Chief Parker or Connolly would do no good, other than implicating them in this colossal mess. As a Soviet spy, Sophia was as good as dead, and it was all his fault. The first genuine human connection he'd had in years was about to be severed.

He vowed not to give anything up, but for how long would that promise remain steady once they started pulling his teeth out with a pair of rusty pliers?

They could punch, kick, and humiliate him all they liked. He was used to that. Compared with his time spent as a guinea pig during the war, this was going to be a piece of cake.

CHAPTER 26

Baker suspected it was past eight in the evening when they arrived on Temple Street, right outside the former Los Angeles Public Library: Echo Park branch. In a few hours' time, it would be the Fourth of July. Something bad was going to happen, although he had no idea when or where it would occur. Or by whom, for that matter.

The automatic gates lined with barbed wire swung inward to let the car pass. "All righty," announced Hartwell. "Last stop. Everyone out!" As soon as he said it, both doors of the car were wrenched open and its occupants—save for Hartwell and Waldgrave—were forcibly tugged out. Baker got a brief glimpse of the cake-like structure of the building before entering.

* * *

With no bookshelves or books left to occupy the place, the ex-library felt empty and wrong. The very nature of the building had been corrupted by federal interlopers. Still handcuffed, Baker emptied his pockets at the security checkpoint in the lobby. His wallet, badge, and car keys, along with Danforth's letter, Huston's cake note, and Cronkite's booklet of sign-off phrases, were all placed into a metal tray. A Huey sweep team was probably searching his car at this very moment, but he hoped they wouldn't discover the stash of findings under the driver's seat.

After the on-duty guard haphazardly inked his name (and those of the protesting students) into a massive logbook, Baker was shepherded along. Once inside, he saw an entire command center where the library's literary guts had once been housed. About a hundred tightly packed desks covered the main floor, and the phones sitting upon them were ringing nonstop. Each call was answered with the same greeting: "HUAC Echo Park. What Communist or deviant activity are you reporting this evening?"

It was the eve of a holiday, but every desk was filled. When a call came in, the tip was scribbled onto a notepad and the caller was graciously thanked for reaching out and assured their tip would be investigated immediately. There were many scenarios that might lead a person to call HUAC: A woman gets in a spat with her neighbor, makes one phone call, and *poof!* no more neighbor. A greedy business owner is jealous of the successful Jew running a store next to his. *Ring Ring.* Yes, hello? No more Jew. The competing business is theirs.

A large banner took up the entire back wall, hanging from the railing of the library's upper level. It showed a massive fist containing the Stars and Stripes splashed across its curled fingers, a blown-up version of the pin every HUAC agent wore on their lapel. Underneath, in garish red lettering, was the organization's corny motto: FIGHTING FOR WHAT MAKES AMERICA GREAT SINCE '38!

The remaining walls, once covered with posters that extolled the virtues of reading, were now plastered with anti-Communist propaganda posters. One showed a pretty woman pinned underneath a boot. The words IF RUSSIA SHOULD WIN were written at shin level of the massive leg. IS THIS TOMORROW? read another, showing a group of Americans being terrorized by goblin-faced Soviets in full military dress as the US flag burned in the background. A third depicted two men in lavender-shaded jumpsuits holding hands and giving each other simpering looks of affection. DEVIANCE IS A DANGER TO DEMOCRACY, read the caption in frilly neon-pink letters. REPORT ANY SUSPECTED HOMOSEXUAL ACTIVITY TO YOUR LOCAL HUAC OFFICE.

A fourth poster showed a gargantuan skeleton in a Russian army uniform holding a bayonet in one hand and a machine gun in the other. The bony soldier was standing atop a burning rendition of the earth. The planet's surface was branded with a yellow Star of David that contained the hammer and sickle. BOLSHEVISM UNMASKED! it proclaimed in flickering orange letters.

This poster was, of course, just an Americanized version of the one created by Goebbels's Ministry of Propaganda in 1939. Once again, the Hueys showed their utter lack of originality, as well as their nauseating debt of gratitude to a Reich that fell just 988 years from its projected goal.

As he and the other detainees were ushered farther into the building, Baker saw that not every worker was answering phones. Some people had headphones over their ears and sat near large, box-like devices where spools of magnetic recording tape slowly turned like hypnotic merry-go-rounds. Every so often, the people staffing these machines would jot down a note or two and run them over to a superior. Baker realized they were listening in on individuals who had been bugged: celebrities, an irate employee thinking of going on strike, and maybe even the LAPD chief of police.

Baker must have been staring, because he received a painful blow to the back of the head. "Move it!" barked the Huey who had pulled him out of the car. He was pulled through a side door, down a poorly ventilated stairwell, and into a dimly lit hallway lined with what he knew were soundproofed interrogation cells. These rooms had not existed when HUAC took over the building.

The Huey unlocked a cell at the far end and threw him inside. Baker covered his ears as the heavy metal door slammed shut. Once the noise subsided, he stood up and looked around the room, which contained a dusty lightbulb on a chain, a metal chair bolted to the ground, and a mirror, which he suspected was two-way. He'd gone through it all before as a cop but knew this was nothing like LAPD headquarters, where a detective might offer the suspect a cup of coffee or cigarette while the person waited for their lawyer to arrive.

This was the kind of place where suspects were deprived of food and sleep to make them more susceptible to questioning. The Germans had perfected this strategy, fine-tuning it like an old radio. The Hueys wanted Baker to sit in the chair, rest his feet awhile, and get nice and tired, but he wouldn't play their sick games. He went to the corner and sat on the cold stone floor, which was dotted with dried flecks of blood. Not cleaning the cell was another form of intimidation. The latest victim was forced to wonder what happened to the last poor schmuck. Baker spread out his legs and forced himself to stay alert when a voice squawked from a speaker hidden somewhere in the room.

"*Sit in the chair, please.*"

"I'm comfortable here, thanks," Baker replied cheerily.

"*That was not a request,*" squawked the hidden voice again. "*You have ten seconds to comply.*"

"Oh, a challenge!" squealed Baker in mock delight. "Here's one for you. You've got ten seconds to go fuck yourself."

On the word *fuck*, the door opened and the massive form of Waldgrave entered the room. His crew cut brushed the low concrete ceiling. Walking over to the corner where Baker was seated, he drove a large fist into the detective's face. Baker felt his two front teeth come loose and thought of Sophia before passing out.

* * *

He didn't know how much time had passed when he woke up in the metal chair, bound with rope. His mouth and nose were crusted over with dried blood.

"Wakey, wakey, eggs and bakey," cooed Hartwell. "Gene really did a number on your mug there, huh?"

Baker tried to fire back an insult, but all he could manage was a low groan of pain.

"Yeah, I thought as much," replied Hartwell. "Now, here's how it's going to go." He began to pace around the room. Through his agonized haze, Baker saw the Huey swinging a cracked Louisville Slugger back and forth like a metronome. "You're going to tell me where the bomb is hidden and in return, I won't bash your head in like a rotting pumpkin on November first. Sound good?"

Baker ran a tongue across the gaps where Waldgrave had punched out his teeth and hot rage bubbled up his throat. "Counteroffer," he managed to say, the word coming out as a whistle. "You drop your pants, bend over, and I shove that baseball bat so far up your ass, you'll start singing 'Hound Dog.'"

"You're a feisty one, Baker, I'll give you that. You know in all those old gangster movies they don't make anymore, when the mobster says that someone's got moxie? Then they'd say something like, 'Too bad I'll have to beat it out of ya'...? I used to love those pictures."

Hartwell adopted the cheery voice of Walter Winchell: "It's a beautiful day here at Los Angeles Memorial Coliseum, folks, and the Dodgers are down four-to-nothing against the Phillies." He moved closer to where Baker sat and took the classic batter's stance. "Morton Hartwell steps up to the plate, a rookie and one of the first to play as a Los Angeles Dodger. It's history in the making, ladies and gentlemen. Here comes the windup aaaand..."

It was a home run. Fingers snapped Baker awake, but he wished they hadn't. In addition to his busted nose and missing teeth, his midsection was on fire. Hartwell had hit him straight in the abdomen.

"Ah, there's our golden boy. Feel like talking yet, Baker?" asked Hartwell, gently tapping Baker's head with the end of the bat. "Just tell me what I wanna know and you can go home. Hell, I'll tuck you in myself. Tell me where the bomb is and how Huston and Cronkite were involved with this Commie shitstorm."

"What makes you think I had anything to do with them?"

"A good question," said Hartwell, pacing again. "You see, Huston was a known person of interest. We were keeping an eye and an ear on his place. Not long after we got a tip-off about your little bomb scheme from a credible source, we intercepted a call to Huston's house from one Arthur Scholz. He spoke in some kind of code, but there was one word we managed to catch. You know what that word was, Detective?"

"Was it *Baker*?" said Baker.

"Congratulations, kiddo. You win the grand prize!" exclaimed

Hartwell in a mock announcer's voice. "Now, why did your name come up, do you think? Why is everyone associated with you dead or disappearing, Baker?"

"Maybe it's because I've got such bad breath." He spat a gob of saliva and blood onto Hartwell's wing-tipped shoes.

The Huey actually laughed, clearly impressed despite himself. "What'd they do to you in that camp, Baker? Install a pair of brass balls between your legs? What about Vikhrov? Think about her. You wouldn't want us to carve up that pretty face of hers like a Thanksgiving turkey, would you? Or I could let Gene here take a shot at her with his trouser snake. I know it sounds hard to believe, but Inspector Waldgrave usually has trouble with the ladies, so he practices on the ones we bring in."

The image of Waldgrave mounting a struggling Sophia made Baker feel sick, but also helped clear his head. Any promises they made to him about her safety would be a lie. She'd be beaten, raped, or both before being sent off to the electric chair. Where were they keeping her, anyway? In another cell like this one? She was a professionally trained KGB agent, who was prepared for something like this, but what if...? Baker's stomach contracted violently as he wondered if Sophia had already bitten down on her cyanide capsule. The thought made him retch, and Hartwell jumped back in surprise.

"Whoa, now!" he yelled. "Don't be spewing up your lunch on me, Baker. We're not at that stage in our friendship just yet. Of course, I might be a little more forgiving if you were to offer up the information I want."

Baker looked up at Hartwell, trying his best to convey just how much loathing and contempt he felt for the man.

"Believe it not, we've been doing it the easy way so far. You leave me no other choice." Hartwell turned to his partner and said three words that turned Baker's blood to ice: "Get the girl."

Smiling like an idiot, Waldgrave left the cell and came back at top speed with a frightened Sophia. He held a gleaming switchblade against her throat.

"Give me a reason," breathed the hulking Huey. "Any reason and I'll spill all of her Bolshie blood right here."

"Don't tell them anything, Morris!" Sophia shouted.

"Feeling chatty now, Baker?" countered Hartwell, wearing a triumphant grin. "Tell me what I want to know, and maybe I'll let her live. Where is the bomb and who else knows about it? Did the Russkis put you up to it?"

There was nowhere else to hide, no tricks left to play. The trail of bodies had led Baker to this very moment, when he would be forced to make a choice. The Hueys always got what they wanted in the end. They always broke their man, and now Morris Baker would collapse like a house of cards during a California earthquake. His pledge to remain steadfast was as good as worthless.

"I don't know where the bomb is, you schmendrik," he finally said. "I was just trying to clear my name. You should be looking for a group of ex-Nazis, not Reds! I'm pretty sure they've got some sort of A-bomb. They built it with uranium they mined in Africa!"

"What?" said Hartwell, who was in the middle of lighting another cigar. "Nazis? You're really gonna and try and blame this on some Heinies?"

"I'm not lying," breathed Baker. "Scholz's real name was Lang, and he was caught up in some sort of—I don't know—plan formulated by a group of Nazi scientists that the government brought over here via Operation Paperclip."

"Impressive, Baker," Hartwell said. "It is true what we say about you people. You are sneaky and well informed, but so what?"

"I've got a box of proof," Baker pressed on. "About all the murderers the government brought over here."

"Now we're getting somewhere," Hartwell said, blowing a lazy smoke ring. "Once you tell me about the location of the bomb, you're going to tell me where I can find that box."

Near the door, Waldgrave was playing with Sophia's hair as she whimpered. The blade was pressed all the way up against her jugular now. It would only take one good swipe to open the vein.

"Are you deaf?" exclaimed Baker, struggling against his bonds. "I've just told you the truth."

"Where's that bomb and your other collaborators?" Hartwell asked again. "Huston, Cronkite, and Scholz are all dead. Who else are you protecting? Surely, it ain't Charles Ward."

Baker looked up at Hartwell. "What did you do to Charles?" he said.

"Sorry, Baker," Hartwell said, not sounding very apologetic. "The queer should have known better than to go against our investigation."

Baker was shaking with rage. He wanted nothing more than to rip out Hartwell's throat with his bare teeth. Not Charles. Poor Charles, who championed truth in a world so bereft of it. And suddenly, Baker remembered another person he'd seen in the last two days, one who was also missing.

"What about Oliver Shelton?" he asked. "You kill him, too, and now you're trying to pin it on me?"

"Christ, Baker," parried Hartwell. "Just because Jews like killing babies for their flatbread recipe doesn't mean we all do. What do you take us for? Monsters? We would never harm a child."

"Small comfort," spat Baker. "There, now you know everything I know. I'm not the enemy here."

Hartwell sighed and bit down a little too hard on his cigar, cleaving it in two.

"Ah, fuck," he cried out, spitting a mouthful of wet tobacco onto the floor. "You made me waste my Cuban, Baker. And worst of all, that was your last chance to come clean. Gene, make sure the girl's watching this."

"Nooo!" screamed Sophia.

"Well, ladies and gentlemen, Hartwell is up at bat once again, but can he pull off another stunning hit like the one we saw from him just a few innings ago? Will he help the Dodgers make the World Series this year? And the windup, here comes the pitch, aaand..."

Baker was unaware that he had cried out.

"Baker? Baaaaaaaaker? We need you here with us, Baker. What does 'She-ma Yis-roel' mean? Baker? Gene, get the bucket."

Iciness jolted Baker back into the waking world. He sputtered as the cold water cascaded over his head, drenching his hair and clothes.

"'She-ma Yis-roel,'" Hartwell repeated. "What does it mean?" Is it some code word?"

Baker did not answer. He was weak, shivering, and sore all over. Hartwell's denial of his admission proved that they'd rather kill him than open their eyes to the truth.

"What does it mean?" Hartwell asked again, nearly shrieking the question. "Gene, make him talk!"

Waldgrave walked over to the metal chair, pulling up Baker's limp right hand and holding the pinkie finger apart from the other digits.

"Out with it, you foolish kike," he growled. "No? Okay..."

Waldgrave snapped the finger, breaking the bone like a dried twig.

Baker cried out again and this time he heard himself say it. "Shema Yisroel Adonai Eloheinu Adonai Echad!"

"See? What the fuck does that mean, Baker?" Hartwell asked. "Just tell us and the pain will stop."

Baker just stared at Hartwell, panting hard and trying not to pass out again.

"You do this to yourself, Baker. Gene?"

Waldgrave snapped Baker's ring finger and he cried it out again, reiterating the ancient Hebrew words embedded deep within his psyche. "Shema Yisroel Adonai Eloheinu Adonai Echad! Shema Yisroel Adonai Eloheinu Adonai Echad! Shema Yisroel Adonai Eloheinu Adonai Echad!"

Over and over, he shouted the ancient prayer of a people he no longer considered himself a part of.

"Gene, shut him up!"

And then the all-consuming darkness.

* * *

The sounds of gunfire and screaming were all around him, but he was too weak to lift his bald head and take in what was going on. Even the simple act of opening his eyes was difficult. When he managed to do so, unfocused blurs swam in his line of vision. Lights popped and exploded as entire galaxies were born and died in the span of seconds. How lucky was he to bear witness to such a rare spectacle? But he was also thirsty. So damn thirsty. And the sensation of his parched tongue came back to him as it ran slowly across the cracked sandpaper of his lips.

The bullets and screams were getting closer. He didn't know much English but understood some of the curses bellowed over the gunfire. Now his fingers and toes were twitching, although he still did not possess the energy to actually get up and survey his surroundings. Where was he and why did his arm hurt so much?

The sound of running footsteps, someone yelling about the place being deserted.

"Jeezum Crow!" The blurred outline of a person stood above him, an amorphous blob that refused to come into focus. "Juarez, get over here!"

More footsteps and a second voice: "Ai Dios mío! What the fuck did they do in here, Captain?"

There was silence now. The screaming and gunfire had abruptly vanished. It was impossible that a person could feel this thirsty. Baker licked his lips again.

"Christ, this one's still alive," said the captain. "Looks like shit, though. Who knows if he'll make it? Go get a medic and tell Hirschberg to bring one of the guards in here, too."

Juarez's footsteps receded.

"Christ," said the remaining figure as the sweet aroma of burning tobacco filled Baker's nostrils. "Just hold on there, fella. We got a doc on the way. Hold on."

It could have been a minute, an hour, or possibly ten lifetimes later when more people finally entered the room.

A new voice exclaimed in Yiddish, "My God!" and then in English, "Captain, what the fuck did they do?"

"That's what we're gonna find out, Hirschberg. Once you get yourself under control."

Hirschberg was making horrible gagging noises.

"Over here, Doc," continued the captain. "This one's the only one in here who's still kicking and he's in a bad way. See what you can do for him."

Footsteps and another vaguely defined shape was looking down at him. "Captain, your canteen. Quickly!"

Water, glorious water, poured over his cracked lips and into his mouth. He couldn't swallow it fast enough and nearly drowned. He was so eager to slake his profound thirst. After drinking his fill, the space became a little clearer, but the popping stars and galaxies continued to block out most of his vision. He could just discern four blurry figures standing over him, three of them dressed in olive green and one in steely gray.

"Can you hear me?" said the medic's voice. "Uh, Hirschberg, would you mind translating?"

Now someone was speaking Yiddish directly beside his ear: "Can you hear us?"

Somehow, he was able to manage a weak nod.

"Christ," said the captain again. "Whaddya think, Doc? He gonna make it?"

"I don't know," answered the medic. "He's severely dehydrated and malnourished and look at his left arm. That wound, whatever caused it, is badly infected. We might have to amputate and even then, there's no guarantee he'll survive. Christ, what a fuckin' mess."

"You can say that again. All right. Go get a stretcher and Juarez will help you carry this poor soul out of here. Goddamn—this whole place stinks to high heaven."

"Yes, sir," replied the medic, and he ran out of the room.

"Okay, Hirschberg, bring that piece of shit over here where we can have a nice little chat."

There was the sound of scuffling and a whimper.

"First ask him if he speaks English."

"Sprichst du Englisch?" asked Hirschberg, his voice undeniably shaking with rage.

This time, a new voice spoke out, and it sounded like its owner had a chicken bone lodged in his throat. "Ein Bisschen."

"He says he speaks a little."

"All right, now tell him to take a good look around this infirmary."

"Werfen Sie einen Blick auf diese Krankenstation."

A moment passed.

"Now ask the Kraut bastard what he sees."

"Körper...uh, bodies," replied the German guard in heavily accented English.

"Bodies?" asked the captain. "No, son. These aren't just bodies. Take another look at what's been done to them. In all my years of service, I never seen anything like this. Hirschberg, ask him what they did in here."

"Was wurde an diesem Ort gemacht?"

Silence. Then a kick and squeal of pain.

"Was wurde an diesem Ort gemacht?" asked Hirschberg again.

"Ex-ex-experimente," replied the guard in a choked voice. "Medizinische experimente. Bitte."

"Halt die Klappe!" shouted Hirschberg, now crying as he told the guard to shut up. "Medical experiments, Captain," he sobbed.

"Yeah, I gathered as much," said the captain. "Ask him why."

"Warum?"

"Bitte," squeaked the guard again. "Sie waren nur Juden."

"They were just Jews, eh?" said Hirschberg, sounding quite deranged. "Guess what, buddy, you're looking at a Jew who's about to kill you and every fucking Kraut who ran this place."

"Bitte! Bitte! Bitte!" wailed the guard over and over.

The captain flicked away his cigarette in disgust and left. The medic returned with Juarez, and they lifted Baker onto a stretcher. He felt a tiny pinprick in his arm and experienced a comfortable, painless warmth spreading throughout his body.

A sleepy darkness enveloped him, but not before he saw Hirschberg carefully close the door to the infirmary. The guard was screaming in rapid German, begging for his life to be spared. Neither the medic, Juarez, nor the captain looked back as the rifle went off.

* * *

"Fucking Christ, he's apoplectic."

"Not apoplectic, you moron. *Epileptic!* Hurry, stick something in his mouth before he bites his damn tongue off! He won't be able to tell us anything if that happens. Then we'll really be fucked!"

Baker's jaw was suddenly wrenched open and something hard stuck between his teeth. He was convulsing worse than ever, but was finally coming back to his senses, which meant the gunfire he could hear was not just a memory. It was real.

"Fuck fuck fuck," said Hartwell, repeating the word as if it would magically set things right. "We're under attack! We gotta get outta here, Gene... Gene?"

A shot rang out inside the room. Even in his semi-lucid state, Baker knew that he'd be hearing a ringing in his ears for several weeks to come.

"Gene!" Hartwell cried out as two more shots went off in quick succession. "You bitch!" he screamed. "You utter bitch!"

Someone was patting his cheek now and anxiously whispering his name. "Morris... Morris, I need you to wake up. We have to get out of here."

Sophia's voice had a medicinal quality, slowly coaxing Baker out of his stupor. Outside the room, something exploded, and he heard muffled screams. It sounded like the HUAC building was being bombarded with artillery fire. When the convulsions finally subsided,

Baker opened his eyes and received a shock. Waldgrave was dead, most of his head gone. Next to the hulking corpse was Hartwell, attempting to crawl away with no kneecaps, which had obviously been blown away by the smoking .44 Magnum Sophia held in her hand.

Despite the direness of the situation, she smiled at his expression. "I got it off the big one when you started seizing. Now get that out of your mouth."

He reached up and pulled Waldgrave's switchblade from between his teeth. Its wooden handle was splintered from the force of his bite.

"Are you okay?" he asked Sophia, gently reaching out to caress her face. "Did they hurt you?"

"Yes, I'm fine," she said, smiling morosely. "Looks like you took most of the beating." She tore off part of his shirt and used the fabric to quickly bind his broken fingers together.

"I've been through worse," Baker responded, the *s* sound whistling through the gap in his teeth. Pocketing the knife, he got up. "Let's get the fuck out of here."

Simon:

Thank you so much for sending over those documents on Eichmann. The mamzer's in South America, all right, and your hard work is going to help Mossad catch him.

As for that side project you had us working on, none of our investigations have unearthed any proof in support of your ODESSA theory. The idea of an underground network of high-ranking SS members would make for a good potboiler novel, I'm sure, but it seems a little too far-fetched in reality. I will concede that part of your theory does hold up. The sons of bitches had plenty of pilfered gold with which to purchase new identities. And we know that <u>Perón</u> (yemach shemo) gave them sanctuary after the war, but I'm having trouble fitting in the rest of the pieces.

I mean, Eichmann is living in some shack and working at a car factory, right? If he had access to the vast network of wealth and connections that you claim exists, then don't you think he would be enjoying a nicer life? No. It just doesn't make any sense.

Still, I will admit that telegram you received from your African contacts was rather suspicious. I've got some of my people looking into it now. For the time being, however, I urge you to keep your eyes on the prize, Eichmann, and let this ODESSA thing drop to the wayside. There are plenty of these men and women still at large (and we'll catch as many as we can), but it is the predominant theory of this agency that former Nazis are *not* working together.

Chag sameach! Oy, my stomach is already dreading the thought of eating matzah for a week.

Your friend,
Isser Harrel

The above letter was mailed from Tel Aviv to the Jewish Historical Documentation Centre in Vienna hours before Simon Wiesenthal and his family were gunned down while enjoying a Passover seder. The crime was ruled a home invasion.

PART IV
July 4, 1958

We cannot defend freedom abroad by deserting
it at home.

—Edward R. Murrow

CHAPTER 27

They stepped over the sobbing Hartwell and left the interrogation room, allowing the door to slam shut behind them. The din in the hallway was much louder. Either the building was under attack by a small army or someone was celebrating the Fourth a little early with high-grade fireworks.

"This way," said Baker. He easily found the stairwell, and they began to climb. Would the top part of the building still be standing? The cellar-like addition they were now leaving had been built after the library. Ironically, the torture cells were much safer in the event of a catastrophe.

But there was no need to worry. The structure was still intact when they arrived back in the main command center, which was devoid of workers. Aside from that, however, everything looked as it had when they first arrived earlier in the evening. The building rocked once again with the sound of an earsplitting explosion that didn't seem to physically exist. No balls of fire appeared; none of the masonry transformed into deadly hot shrapnel.

"What the hell?" said Baker. He didn't have long to ponder the mystery. Sophia was already making a beeline for the exit.

"Come on!" she shouted over her shoulder. "Do you want to get out of here or do you want to start redecorating the place?"

"Wait," he said, dashing over to the guard station and mentally thanking the Hueys for their unparalleled laziness. His personal effects were still in the metal dish where he'd deposited them hours before. Checking his watch, he saw it was three in the morning.

He'd been tortured and/or unconscious for the last seven hours.

* * *

They burst out into the oppressively humid night, which was ablaze with light. The Ford Interceptor that had brought Baker and several USC students here was on fire. The unmistakable sounds of a war being fought had evaporated—replaced with the chirping of crickets and steady crackling of the automotive blaze.

"What do you think happened?" Baker asked. "Where is every-one?"

"They went out the fire door on the other side of the build-ing. Had to use one of my last grenades, but I'd say it was well worth it," said an oddly recognizable voice from the shadows of the parking lot.

Sophia held up Waldgrave's gun. "Who are you? Show yourself!"

"Of course," replied the stranger. Their hands facing upward, they slowly stepped into the glow cast by the fire, and Baker's jaw nearly hit the pavement when he saw who it was. Standing there, the usual Camel cigarette held between his fingers, was Edward R. Murrow. His face was eerily bathed in the flickering, hellish glow from the burning Interceptor.

He took one look at Baker and his pouchy face broke out in a warm, fatherly smile. "Christ on a cracker, kid," he said. "You look a little worse for wear. What do you say to getting a cup of coffee?"

CHAPTER 28

"But... you're dead," Baker heard himself say. "It was all over the papers for weeks!"

"Cover story," replied Murrow, inhaling the final remnants of his cigarette and flicking it away. He was dressed in his famous attire: white shirt, rolled-up sleeves, loosened tie, and suspenders. "Couldn't let that son of a bitch McCarthy force me into an early retirement. Being dead allowed me to recruit a few like-minded people who could help me take him apart, piece by piece."

And then it clicked for Baker. "You're behind the Liberty Boys?"

"Guilty as charged," answered Murrow.

"And you called that pay phone in Brentwood to warn me that the Hueys were looking for me," Baker continued. He remembered how the mystery caller used a variation of Murrow's famous "good night and good luck" sign-off phrase.

"Guilty again," said Murrow. "I was sure you'd be too busy with your investigation to pay attention to the CONELRAD frequency. Now, I'm happy to answer any other questions you may have, but I'd prefer to do it somewhere safer than this. The fire department is probably on its way, and the evacuated HUAC employees won't stay outside forever."

"How did you get them to leave? It sounded like you were shelling the damn place."

Murrow beamed and lit another Camel. "My career was made in the audio space, Detective. I know all the tricks of the trade: hijacking radio signals, augmenting my voice, and fooling the human ear."

He directed their attention to a 1957 Chevrolet pickup truck parked several feet away, which had a pair of massive loudspeakers strapped to its bed. They were pointed right at the HUAC building. "Okay, Ralph," Murrow said, "let her rip."

Someone sitting in the cab gave the thumbs-up signal, and a second later the sounds of a battlefield erupted from the speakers. The ground shook with seismic reverberations.

"Pretty neat, eh?" Murrow shouted over the false explosions.

"Yes!" said Baker and Sophia in unison, covering their ears. "Please turn it off!"

Murrow shouted to Ralph again and the babel stopped. "A contact of mine in Northern California rigged these up for me," he explained. "They're prototypes, not even patented yet."

"Great," said Baker, "and who's Ralph?"

"All in good time, Baker," Murrow said. "Why don't we get that cup of joe, eh?"

* * *

Ralph turned out to be one of Murrow's two bodyguards.

"Recognize these two gentlemen?" asked Murrow when they all met outside Merv's Diner twenty minutes later.

"You two were Hueys," Baker said, astonished. "Kirk and Weston. But Hartwell said you were reassigned to the Midwest office."

"Bullshit," replied Ralph Weston, a tall and soft-spoken young man with quiffed auburn hair. "They couldn't let the public get wind of two of their own defecting, so they just said we were sent to another part of the country."

"We both realized just how corrupt and amoral the entire organization had become," cut in Gerald Kirk, the stockier of the two. "We joined HUAC to protect our country from foreign invaders, but when it became clear that the only people causing trouble were our fellow agents, we cut and ran with as much incriminating evidence as we could."

"So, what?" Baker asked Murrow. "You got an army of Liberty Boys at your disposal?"

Murrow laughed at the question. "No, Detective. An army would be rather hard to conceal. Ralph, Gerald, and I are the only...I guess you could call us field operatives. The others in our employ make up a nationwide network of informants."

"And how did you fake your death?" Baker continued, feeling like a lawyer cross-examining a witness. "To operate under that kind of secrecy, you'd need a new birth certificate, Social Security number. Everything."

"Ah, I'm rather proud of myself for that little bit of Machiavellian trickery," Murrow declared. "I found a drifter riddled with cancer who, in exchange for making his final months as comfortable as possible, allowed me to assume his identity."

It was almost too surreal to be true. Murrow was a man best suited to reporting on wars, not taking part in them. Nevertheless, he gave off a reassuring aura with his deep, measured way of speaking that made you trust him without question.

"Who is your ravishing friend?" Murrow asked Baker, taking Sophia's hand and bestowing it with a light kiss.

"Sophia Vikhrov of Russian intelligence," she answered with a smile. "Pleased to make your acquaintance."

"So, Johnny and Dalton really brought the Soviets into this one after all?"

* * *

They sat in a corner booth farthest from the front door, smoking and drinking coffee. Ralph and Gerald were a few booths away, playing a game of Old Maid. It was nearing five in the morning and the place was pretty much deserted, save for a haggard cabdriver getting off his shift. He barely paid them any attention, slurping down a bowl of oatmeal before heading home to get some sleep.

Upon seeing Murrow, Merv (whose prosthetic leg was barely stable on the best of days) nearly sustained third-degree burns when the fresh pot of chipped beef he was carrying threatened to topple over. Walking around the counter, he vigorously shook the journalist's hand.

"I'm a big fan of yours, Mr. Murrow. A *big fan*," he said. "I knew you wasn't dead. I just knew it! Any enemy of McCarthy eats at my diner for free—for life!"

"That's mighty kind of you, Mr. Pachenko. Say, would you do me a small favor?"

"Name it," Merv said, beaming like a kid on Christmas morning.

"Would you mind putting up the CLOSED sign for an hour or two? I'd rather not be disturbed. I promise not to overstay my welcome."

Merv saluted and without another word, stumped over to the door and flipped over the OPEN sign to CLOSED. Murrow thanked him and walked over to the jukebox, inserting a dime and selecting "Silhouettes" by The Rays.

When they were finally seated, Murrow interlocked his fingers and spoke to Baker. "I'm sorry you had to be involved in all of this, Detective Baker. But the clock is ticking and with most of my people in this town dead, you and Agent Vikhrov here are about the only ones who can help me stop the Black Symphony."

"The what?" Baker and Sophia asked together.

Murrow took a long draw on his Camel before answering. "Crazy bunch of bastards. An organization of ex-Nazis employed by the United States. 'Ex' doesn't really apply here because they're just as fanatical about the Third Reich as they ever were. They've been operating unchecked within our borders for years, and now that they've consolidated their power, they're looking to influence American political policy."

"Influence political policy how?" Baker asked.

"Use that detective's brain of yours, Baker," Murrow said. "Things are already tough for your people in this country. Imagine how much worse it would get if a Jew was found responsible for blowing up a major metropolitan area? It would make the Rosenbergs look like the Lindberghs. Those rumors about reopening the Jap internment camps wouldn't just be talk anymore. McCarthy will start rounding up the Hebes left and right, and the Symphony will celebrate a toast to turning the clock back thirteen years."

Baker felt like he'd been hit by Waldgrave again. Of course. The plan was so simple, yet so elegantly devastating. "How'd you find out about the Symphony?"

"America and Russia have spies, so why not the Liberty Boys?" shrugged Murrow. "They're backed by the ODESSA, the network of former SS members, who used all the gold and artwork they stole during the war to set up cushy lives for themselves in South America. Wiesenthal got wise to them, so they killed him and his whole damn family. These are very dangerous people we're dealing with here."

"And why do they call themselves the Black Symphony?" Sophia asked, grasping her mug with two hands.

"It's an ironic little pet name they've cooked up for themselves. In 1944, a group of Wehrmacht officers conspired to assassinate Hitler."

"If I recall correctly, that mission failed," Baker said.

"Horribly," Murrow replied. "Dozens were executed, including Rommel. The Gestapo labeled all of the conspirators 'Die Schwarze Kapelle.'"

"The Black Orchestra," breathed Baker. "Jesus."

"Glad to see you're following along," said Murrow. "These scientists think they're being cute by naming themselves after Hitler's would-be assassins. Well, sort of. An orchestra's just a collection of people, but a symphony, that's something more complex. It's what an orchestra can accomplish once assembled. As for this bomb plot of theirs, they call it Valkyrie."

"After Wagner, Hitler's favorite composer," Baker said.

"Not just that," cut in Murrow. "The assassination plot in '44 was also called Valkyrie. The Black Symphony is being cute yet again."

"Wait a second," Baker interjected, remembering something else. "'Ride of the Valkyries' was playing on Huston's record player when I showed up at his house three days ago."

Murrow let out a jagged laugh and lit another cigarette. "Johnny was being cute right back at those Jerry bastards. We kept an open radio frequency to his home and three nights ago, we heard that fuckin' Wagner opera coming over the channel. It nearly blew Ralph's ears out, but I'm positive it was a mayday signal that the jig was up."

A minute passed. Baker, Murrow, and Sophia just sat there, as if they were a group of friends enjoying an early breakfast without a care in the world. Finally, Murrow broke the silence. "I reported on one of the camps at the end of the war, Baker. I know what these monsters are capable of and so do you. Our own counter-operation must thwart them at all costs. I think the name we've chosen is very fitting." He took a sip of coffee and a long drag on his cigarette. "We call it Beat the Devils."

CHAPTER 29

Everything made sense now. Baker told Murrow about the note he'd found in Cronkite's hand three days earlier.

"Johnny and Dalton wanted to involve the press, but I said it was too dangerous to involve civilians, and I was right," Murrow said. "Walter didn't have to die. I knew him from the old days; he was a great journalist. Johnny always was a little headstrong and cut off direct communication with me two weeks ago. Then he and Dalton went off script and ended up dead. They showed their entire hand to the Symphony. I didn't realize they'd bring in the damn Russians, though. No offense, miss," he said to Sophia. "That was all Dalton and his Communist connections, I suppose."

"Sorry, who's Dalton?" asked Baker.

"Dalton Trumbo. The man you got killed at the Red Sword."

"Hey!" Baker shouted. His knees knocked together under the table as he tried to stand up in indignation. "You can't blame me for that. I didn't know someone followed us there. Speaking of, why didn't you make yourself known to me as soon as you knew the Symphony was looking to frame me?"

"I'm sorry, Baker. We were hoping to have this whole thing settled before it got out of hand. If the bomb didn't go off, you would've been none the wiser, unaware of how high the shit pile goes."

"You said you had a spy who alerted you to the Symphony. Where is he now?"

"Dead. His cover got blown and they cut his head off. Before that, our man was able to tell us that they were smuggling enriched uranium over here for some kind of new A-bomb, but without its location, we're up the creek. Any ideas, Detective?"

"None," said Baker.

"Damn, I was hoping you'd have the key to that particular lock after your adventures yesterday."

"And where were you all of yesterday?" Baker asked, not able to keep the annoyance out of his voice. "We sure could've used some backup."

"I didn't want to add more questions with your plate already so full," Murrow answered. "Thought you could handle yourself. Glad I decided to have you tracked, though. How else do you think we knew where to find you tonight? You're welcome, by the way."

Baker and Murrow glared at each other until Sophia broke the glacial silence. "Is the measuring contest over, boys? Maybe we can get back to business."

"Very well, then," Murrow said. "The second and less pressing matter is where the hell they got the uranium in the first place. If some foreign government is colluding with the Symphony, it needs to be dealt with after we find that bomb."

"That," said Baker, "I do have the answer to." When the Liberty Boys commander raised his eyebrows expectantly, Baker pressed on. "They bought hundreds of acres of uranium-rich land in Africa."

He told Murrow how Lang's photo album and the note found in Huston's icebox had led him to Humphrey Bogart and the Helvick novel. He also mentioned the land deed Lang left for him to find and his theory about how the old Nazi must have gone turncoat after getting cold feet about the bomb plot.

"Well, I'll be damned. My own men working with a member of the Symphony? Even I couldn't have called that one," said an excited Murrow. "Calling this operation 'Beat the Devils' was Johnny's idea in the first place. That was Johnny for you, a storyteller through and through. You have proof of the land purchases?"

"Yes, I do. It's in my car under the driver's seat. Or I hope it is. The Hueys probably searched it when they took us captive. They may have found it."

"We'll see about that," said Murrow. "Hueys are as sloppy as they are dumb."

Murrow called over Ralph and instructed him to get all the evidence out of Baker's car.

"How'd you find out Trumbo was dead, anyway?" Baker said.

"How else?" replied Murrow. "I called his wife."

Ralph soon returned with the items requested: Lang's scrapbook, the bar of gold stamped with the Nazi insignia, and the African land deed.

"Whoever finds out too much about the plan has a nasty habit of turning up dead," said Baker. "Lang, Huston, and Trumbo knew their time was limited, which is why they left clues for me."

"If that's true," Murrow said, "then they should have left some indication of where the bomb is being kept."

Baker smiled. "Well, Mr. Murrow, the good news is I'm pretty sure of the answer to that."

CHAPTER 30

The location of the bomb had been with Baker for two days now. Only after Ralph had brought his belongings into the diner did the revelation come to him.

"Open the photo album to the first page," Baker instructed. Murrow pulled the album toward himself and flipped it open. The cigarette perched on his lips fell into his lap and he had to pat it out with a few choice swear words. After the potential conflagration had been dealt with, he looked up.

"It's that simple?"

"It's that simple," parroted Baker. "The bomb is at the Griffith Observatory."

"The Griffith Observatory," echoed Murrow. "The balls they've got on them never ceases to amaze me. And you're sure?"

"Quite," answered Baker. "At first, I thought it was just some meaningless keepsake that got stuck in the book." He spun the photo album around and pried the postcard loose. "You can buy them anywhere in town, so I didn't think much of it until now. Think about it: Lang didn't originally come to this country wanting to be an American. He was a proud German and Nazi when he first got here. I don't know what changed his mind when he went back to Germany, but he despised everything this country stood for. Besides, the postcard shows no signs of age at all. The cheap paper always turns yellow after the first few months."

He held it out to Murrow, who took it for further inspection. "Which means," Baker continued, "that the postcard is relatively new, maybe even purchased a few days before Lang committed suicide. He wanted me to know about the uranium in Africa and he wanted me to know about the Griffith Observatory."

"I'll be damned," said Murrow. "And he made it so goddamn hard just in case it fell into Symphony or Huey hands, I suppose. Take care of that brain of yours, Baker. If we survive this, it's taking you places. Now comes the simple matter of getting our hands on the explosive and clearing your name."

"Speaking of which," said Baker. "What kind of bomb are we dealing with here? An ICBM?"

"Jesus, no," Murrow said, looking shocked. "As crazy as they are, the Symphony's not looking to irradiate all of Southern California. Excuse me, I need to call my nuclear expert. They're based right here in Los Angeles."

Murrow slid out of the booth and walked to the phone on the other side of the diner. His bodyguards immediately gave up their card game and followed him. Baker got up to stretch his legs and get a refill on his coffee.

"It's almost over," he said to Sophia. "Any idea what you want to do afterward? If we survive, that is."

"Well," she said, lying down in the vacated booth and closing her eyes. "I've never been to the beach."

"You're kidding!" he said.

"Nope. Not many beaches where I come from. I hear the Pacific is beautiful."

"Once we sort out this bomb business, I'm driving you straight to Santa Monica," he said. "Corn dogs, cotton candy, funnel cakes, and an ocean view. The whole shebang."

"That sounds nice," Sophia said, her eyes still closed. Before he knew it, she was lightly snoring, rocked to sleep by the idea of crashing waves and warm sand. Baker removed his jacket and placed it over her shoulders like a blanket.

Murrow returned a minute later wringing his hands together. Baker held up a finger to his lips and pointed to Sophia. Murrow nodded and whispered, "My expert is on the way. Once they're here, we can figure out a plan of attack."

The sun was starting to rise when Murrow's nuclear expert got to the diner. Baker's jaw threatened to hit the floor once again when he saw her. It was his and Connolly's secretary, Gladys Hargrove.

"Hi, Morris," she said rather sheepishly. "Guess the cat's outta the bag, huh?"

"You were having me watched?" Baker rounded on Murrow.

"For your own safety, Detective." He lit up another cigarette. "This here is Joanna Rapf."

"Joanna? Her name is Gladys."

"That's a fake name, actually," said Joanna. "My father, Maurice, was blacklisted for being a Jew. He was rather outspoken about criticizing the government and had a HUAC warrant put out for his arrest. But sadly..." Her eyes turned foggy. "...my father killed himself before they could come for him. I joined the Liberty Boys as soon as I graduated college. Maybe we can change it to the 'Liberty People' soon, Edward."

Murrow rolled his eyes in jest.

"A woman studying nuclear physics?" Baker asked.

"No one knows more about splitting the atom than Joanna here," Murrow said. "Let's get down to brass tacks, shall we? Joanna is going to explain the bomb that the Symphony's constructed."

They moved to another booth, allowing Sophia to sleep a little longer. Once Joanna began to talk science, Baker felt rather guilty for all the reports he'd asked her to type, and for ogling her body. It was clear she was a lot more knowledgeable than he was.

"We're in uncharted waters here, Morris," she explained. "We have reason to believe that the Black Symphony has developed an entirely new breed of atomic explosive. I've dubbed it a radiological dispersal device because its whole purpose is to explode and spread radioactive material over as wide a radius as possible."

"The Griffith Observatory," offered Murrow. "That's where they have it stashed, Joanna."

She nodded her grave understanding. "A smart move on their part," she said. "From that height, they'll basically be creating a cloud of radiation across the entire city. The devastation will be terrible if they get away with it."

"They're just like Huston and Trumbo," said Murrow, peeling the cellophane off a fresh pack of Camels. "They don't want to be subtle about it. Can't resist going for the grand effect."

"So how do we deactivate it?" Baker asked.

"Unfortunately," began Joanna, "we have no idea what this thing looks like or how it works. That's why you'll need to secure it before it goes off and bring it back to me, so I can find a way to render it inert."

"How heavy do you think it is?" Baker asked. "Will I be able to carry it by myself?"

"Again, the unknowns are against us here," Joanna said. "But this bomb is as crude and dirty as they come. If I had to guess, I'd say it's just a few sticks of dynamite strapped to several kilos of enriched uranium."

"And there's no risk of getting radiation sickness?" Baker said. The darkness of the past called out to him. He forced himself to remain present and not let Murrow or Joanna see him seizing up.

"If the Symphony has done their homework, there's no chance of it," she said. "The weaponized materials need to be encased under a thick layer of lead so they can be safely loaded onto the bomb."

Baker's relief must have shown on his face, because Joanna gave him a warm smile. "You'll be fine," she said. "I'll be on the radio if you have questions."

"That's all great, but I don't think they'd leave a weapon like that unattended," pressed Baker. "I won't be able to just walk in, pick up the bomb, and walk out."

"Leave that part to me," said Murrow. "We're good at making distractions, as you saw earlier." He looked at his watch, a jeweled Bulova. "Only one question remains: When do they plan to blow the damn thing up?"

They sat in silence as Merv wiped down the counter, pretending not to eavesdrop. Baker looked at his own watch and saw it was six in the morning. That's when the latest epiphany jolted him to speech.

"My God," he said, remembering Fenwick walking up to him in City Hall and whispering the time of Lang's death: 6:00 p.m. He relayed the story to Murrow and Joanna.

"This Lang sounds like one sly fox," Murrow said. "But all those Krauts were pretty slick once Hitler decided to call it quits, weren't they? I say we get a few hours of shut-eye, give them some time to set up, and then crash the party. Let's meet back here around one o'clock."

With a groan, Murrow got out of the booth, hands on his lower back. The chief Liberty Boy leaned away from the table and cracked his spine. It seemed to relieve him greatly. "Much better," he said. "Those booths are murder on the lumbar."

Baker opened his mouth to speak and, somehow reading his mind, Murrow answered: "I know what you're gonna say, Baker. That we should hit them right now, but who knows if the bomb's even at the observatory yet. They may not transport the thing until the very last minute to prevent any interference. Don't worry, we'll get there with plenty of time, so long as they don't know we're coming."

"Okay. I'm going back to my apartment then," said Baker, yearning for a shower and some sleep. Murrow clapped him on the shoulder and went to thank Merv for his generous hospitality.

Baker went over to Sophia and tenderly roused her. "Come on," he said. "Wouldn't you prefer to get some rest on an actual mattress?"

CHAPTER 31

North Hill Street was ominously quiet when Baker and Sophia arrived at the Paradise Apartments. An oppressive haze of tension hung in the air of Chinatown. The usual presence of rickshaws, playing children, and street peddlers was at a minimum this morning. Xenophobic raids always spiked on holidays, and Baker knew that the gun-wielding men and women just out of sight were holding their collective breath in anticipation of the worst.

While always a mess, Baker's apartment had clearly been searched—most likely by the Hueys. The mattress was turned up against the wall, dresser drawers had been pulled out and left on the floor, and the lid of the toilet tank sat in the shower with the full contents of his medicine cabinet.

The cracked bathroom mirror showed Baker a swollen face stained with rings of black and blue. Too tired and hurt to actually clear the shower and bathe properly, Baker washed up in the sink with warm water, wincing as he splashed at his bruises with two broken fingers. He then walked back into the main room, his foot making contact with a half-full schnapps bottle. Baker downed the entire thing in one gulp. The booze offered a bit of relief, but not much. He gingerly undressed, extracting Lang's safe-deposit-box key from his sock and stashing it in a kitchen drawer.

Since both of them were too tired to make love, Sophia gave him a quick kiss, which painfully reminded Baker of his missing teeth. She went to take a shower as he flipped his mattress over with a protest from his beaten abdomen and flopped onto it facedown.

Despite all he'd been through over the past twenty-four hours; despite his anxiety over having to retrieve an atomic bomb from a group of dangerous Nazis; despite his aching body, sleep came easily.

* * *

He was so cold and yet so hot at the same time. It was agony, being stuck in the purgatory between these two extremes. And just when his body would begin to settle on one, it started to convulse—along with the added bonus of uncontrollable vomit.

No matter how much they fed him, it always came back up. All they gave him was a watery broth akin to the kind he had been fed as an inmate. The only difference was that this broth had some actual flavor to it. The Americans learned the hard way what happened when you fed a starving individual too much too quickly. The only reason Baker had not died this way was because he was too weak to greedily munch on Hershey's bars and K-rations when the soldiers first arrived at the camp.

In fact, he had barely been conscious.

So, the broth and vomit arrived. One after the other, like old friends.

An indeterminate amount of time passed this way in a haze of blurry shapes until his surroundings slowly came into focus. Then, one day, he could lift his head up. Lifting himself up on his pillows came next. The pretty nurse taking care of him had given him a little peck on the cheek for this. Swinging his legs off the cot and standing up had caused him to faint, but at least he was regaining his strength.

He'd come very close to losing his left arm where the tumor had been excised and the resulting wound left to fester. The doctor called it a miracle, a word Morris Baker no longer believed in. Miracles had been shoveled into the ovens along with the bodies. When a rabbi came to his bedside, Baker refused to speak, turning away from the man. How could anyone still believe after all this? It wasn't possible to believe anymore. The numbers and injury on his forearm would always be proof of that.

The wool had been pulled from his foolishly naive eyes.

There was no forgetting.

There was no forgiveness.

There was no God.

* * *

Sophia tapped him awake. "Morris," she said. "It's twelve fifteen. We should probably get dressed."

"That time already?" Baker said, clearing phlegm from his throat. "It feels like I just closed my eyes." He groggily pulled himself up from the mattress and looked around. The place looked even messier in the light of early afternoon. "Twelve fifteen, you said?"

"Uh-huh," Sophia replied. She was lying next to him wearing her bra and panties.

"Well..." Baker said, "Merv's isn't that far from here and we've still got some time to kill. No sense in...coming early..."

Sophia giggled as he rolled on top of her.

* * *

Twenty minutes later, they were fully dressed and heading down the hall. Sophia was back in the dress they'd purchased yesterday, while Baker went for plain slacks and a short-sleeved shirt. If he was going to be hauling an atomic bomb around in the heat, he at least wanted to be comfortable. He also had his gun tucked into his waistband and Waldgrave's switchblade hidden in his sock.

Mrs. Huang, his landlord's wife, stood in the doorway to her apartment as they passed. Baker could hear a Mandarin cover of "It Don't Mean a Thing if It Ain't Got That Swing" crackling from somewhere inside. He gave her the most innocent smile he could muster and said, "Afternoon, Mrs. Huang. Enjoying the holiday?"

She continued to stare and then said, "What happened to your teeth?"

"Oh, you know, baseball accident."

"You're late on rent this month, Baker," she said, not offering any sympathy for his injury. "I don't care about the holiday. I want your rent tomorrow." She retreated into her apartment and slammed the door. As if the world were settling back into itself like a creaking old house, Baker heard the familiar muffled shouting between Mrs. Huang and her husband.

* * *

Liz was waiting in the lobby, wearing a horrendous excuse for a dress, which seemed to be fashioned out of an old American flag. Flinging her arms around his neck and peppering his cheek with short kisses, she shouted with anxious glee.

"Morris! Oh, thank God! You look dreadful! I'm so sorry. I was angry and hurt when I made that call."

"Liz!" he said, at a loss for words. "What are you wearing?"

"What, this old thing?" She released him and smoothed out the creases in her dress. "I figured I'd be a little festive."

"Look, Liz..." he began, but she cut him off.

"I know what I did was inexcusable. It's just that..." Liz stopped talking when her eyes fell on Sophia.

"Oh..."

"Liz, please. This isn't the best time. I've got, uh, a big errand to run."

"I can see that," she said, still eyeing Sophia. "So, this one's a keeper, then?"

"Liz!" Baker barked at her. "This is really not the time! I promise we'll have an actual discussion about where we stand soon. But right now, we really need to go."

"Don't bother!" Liz shouted after them as they left the lobby, tears streaming down her cheeks. "We're through!"

Once they were safely in the car, Sophia said, "Who would've known? Morris Baker: heartbreaker."

"Cram it, Commie," he shot back, turning on the radio. The El Dorados began to sing about a "crazy little mama."

Sophia burst out laughing. It wasn't long before Baker joined her.

* * *

Murrow, Ralph, Gerald, and Joanna were already at the diner, waiting for them. Despite the job ahead of them, they all looked rather chipper.

"You two ready?" asked Murrow. Baker and Sophia nodded. "All right then, we'll take two cars and rendezvous at the end of North Vermont Ave—"

"Wait a minute," said Baker, smacking himself in the forehead. "Those sons of bitches."

"What is it?" asked Murrow.

"It was on the radio three days ago. The roads leading to the observatory were closed off for construction. They've been here this whole time."

"Well, you know what they say about crying over spilled milk," Murrow said. "Let's get moving."

CHAPTER 32

The Griffith Observatory was completed in 1935 with funding from a man who'd been given one of the most unfortunate names in human history: Griffith J. Griffith. Upon Griffith's death in 1919, his will instructed that the observatory, complete with planetarium and exhibit hall, be built on a patch of land he had donated to the city in 1896. The philanthropist's goal was to make astronomy more available to the public.

The intentions were good, but what Griffith did not account for was the near-constant layer of smog that made it impossible to see the stars most nights. People mainly visited the place for its picturesque view of the Los Angeles Basin, especially in the evenings, when the setting sun turned the city into a beautiful watercolor painting of oranges, reds, greens, browns, and yellows.

It was still too early in the day for such a romantic view to present itself when they arrived, half an hour later, at the end of North Vermont Avenue. The dusty road was cordoned off with traffic cones and heavy construction equipment. Baker parked his car, and Murrow's party did the same thing with their pickup.

"Looks like you'll have to walk up the rest of the way, I'm afraid," Murrow called over to Baker and Sophia. "We'll try and move that stuff out of the way, but you should get a move on and secure the bomb. Joanna, tell them what they've won."

Joanna walked over to the Continental and handed Baker a walkie-talkie, which he affixed to his waistband. She also brought out two grenades and handed them to Sophia.

"For emergencies only," she said.

"We'll be right behind you," Murrow added. "Now get going and drop us a quick line when you get up to the observatory, so we know you're not dead. Good luck."

Baker shook hands with the ex-journalist, and Joanna gave him an encouraging nod. With that, Baker and Sophia set off up the hill.

* * *

They made it up West Observatory Road with no problems, passing nothing but trees and dehydrated scrub. Baker could now view the entire city, just as he had from John Huston's home an eternity ago.

The boiling sun was high in the sky, but up here, away from the hustle and bustle of Los Angeles, it was rather peaceful. Baker thought of all the innocent people below, swimming and barbecuing—unaware that they might be covered in radioactive fallout in a few hours' time. It was a false normalcy that only mutually assured destruction could create. You told yourself everything was fine when two angry men stood between your perfect suburban world and an apocalyptic wasteland.

After ten minutes of walking in silence, they reached the crest of the hill where visitors could park their cars before trekking over to the observatory itself. Preferring not to walk straight toward the building, Baker and Sophia stuck to the periphery of the surrounding grounds. Anyone looking out of the front of the building would not immediately see them coming. The structure was clearly in sight now, its domed roofs resembling a collection of holy mosques in some far-away country.

When they were close enough, he and Sophia darted off to the left and sidled along the building's east side. Baker unclipped the radio from his belt and held down the TRANSMIT button. "It's Baker. We just made it to the observatory."

He took his hand off the button. The device beeped a second later and Murrow's deep voice arrived via a short squawk of static. "Excellent. I'll be placing you in Joanna's capable hands from here on out. Over."

"Thanks," replied Baker. "Over."

He was clipping the walkie-talkie back onto his belt when he heard a rustling sound from around the corner. Sophia moved closer to him as he reached for his gun, only to find that it was no longer in its holster. He looked over and saw her holding it.

"Now, that'll be far enough, Detective." Humphrey Bogart was walking toward them and pointing a gun right at Baker's stomach. He was dressed in loose-fitting slacks and a piqué polo shirt drenched with sweat. "Hands where I can see 'em. Don't get any smart ideas."

Baker thought the haze of the California sun was pulling tricks on his weary brain. He wanted to laugh. Here he was getting stuck up by the world's most famous movie star.

"This can't be real," he said out loud.

"It is," said Bogart. "And you're going to lead me to the Black Symphony's bomb."

Was the world going insane? None of this made sense. Still, Baker played along and kept his hands raised. Luckily, Sophia had his gun.

"Shoot him first chance you get," he whispered out of the side of his mouth.

"Pipe down, Baker, she ain't gonna shoot me," Bogart said. "You don't wanna end up like your friend at the Red Sword, do you?"

"You killed Trumbo?"

"Bingo."

"You killed Huston and Cronkite, too, didn't you?" The look of disappointment on Huston's face illuminated in the flickering lights of the morgue made sense now.

"What a smart cookie you are, Baker. Too bad I never cared much for cookies."

"But why kill Huston? You said he was your friend."

"And he was," Bogart said. "One of the best friends I had both behind and in front of the camera. No one wrote dialogue quite like John. Except he was narrow-minded."

"He suspected you of going over the deep end," said Baker. Now he understood why Bogart was mentioned in the note he and Sophia discovered in Huston's icebox. The actor's claim that he and the director had not spoken in years was a lie. They had remained in contact and Huston must have sensed that his old collaborator could no longer be trusted; that if he ended up dead, Bogart would help point the way.

"He failed to grasp the bigger picture," retorted Bogart. "The times are changing and sometimes, even I feel like I don't know what it's all about anymore."

"How so?"

"Communists. Nazis. Capitalists. It can make a fella's head spin. Tenuous treaties, nuclear arms, collapsing governments. The world ain't what it used to be and it's teetering on the brink of destruction. People need someone to believe in, someone who will lead them out of the clusterfuck we've gotten ourselves into. That's where I come in."

"What? Being a hero in the movies isn't good enough anymore?"

"The pictures are nice, but the title of 'American Savior' is a bit nicer, wouldn't you agree? People can escape to the theater for an hour or two. But what about when they return home to their crummy lives, where an atomic bomb could wipe them out of existence at any time? What then? They need a hero in real life as well as in the moving pictures. McCarthy's promised me the kind of fame you can't get from acting. That's why I killed Johnny and his pals. Those HUAC numbskulls were bungling the job anyway. I couldn't even fill them in when they came snooping around the studio after you left. That's how secretive my mission is. It comes straight from the top. And now I'll become the most beloved person in the country once we go in there and you lead me to the bomb."

"You're delusional," said Baker. "Sophia, shoot him."

No answer from Sophia as Bogart's smile grew wider. The cancer scar on his neck stood out horribly, like a rope burn from a hangman's noose.

"Sophia?"

"I told you, Detective, she ain't gonna shoot me. Come here, sweetheart."

With a shuffling of feet, Sophia walked over to stand next to the actor, not looking at Baker.

"Sophia, what's going on?" Baker was having trouble keeping his voice under control. He dreaded what came next. Bogart put an arm around Sophia and kissed her hard on the mouth.

"Detective, I'd like ya to meet Faye Dalton, a bright-eyed girl from

Minneapolis with big dreams of becoming a movie star. She came off the bus with ten dollars in her pocket and a willingness to do anything to make it in this town as an actress. And I mean *anything*. She's also my blushing bride-to-be. Ain't that right, doll face?"

"Yes, Bogie," said Sophia softly.

Baker's world was slipping away. The bomb, the Symphony, the mission lost their urgency in the fallout of the explosive Bogart had just detonated right here in the shadows of the Griffith Observatory. Baker tried to swallow and found his mouth bone-dry.

"You're . . . you're lying."

"Am I? Or is it that my fiancée here is one hell of an actress? All it took was access to some of your personal information and she was able to tailor the character of Sophia Vikhrov specifically to your liking. Of course, she needed some language and combat lessons to truly win you over with some Yiddish, a phony-baloney accent, and a passing knowledge of hand-to-hand combat. It's been over a year of planning."

Baker looked at Sophia, a pleading look on his face. He was begging her to tell him it wasn't true. He needed to hear her say it.

"What? You thought she was actually falling for you?" Bogart laughed cruelly. "Oh boy, you've been alone longer than I thought if one night with a fake Russian dame could fool you that easily."

The man bore almost no resemblance to the drunken slouch they'd encountered on the UAP lot the day before. He was now sure-footed, calculating, and very much off his sagging Barcalounger. It was as though some monstrous breaker had been flipped in the actor's brain. It reminded Baker of a painfully obvious truth: Bogart was both an experienced drinker and a performer. A person capable of feigning sloppy inebriation if he had to.

"How could you?" Baker asked Sophia, the question encompassing all the pain, betrayal, and shame he now felt. She was still looking down at her feet and did not answer. Her silence was enough of a confirmation. How could he have been so stupid? The signs had been there, presenting themselves plainly one after the other. But he'd been unwilling to listen to his instincts.

This explained that horrible, simpering smile she'd given Bogart in his dressing room; why a Russian agent had a flawless American accent and perfect knowledge of American culture. It also explained why a toughened assassin and spy had vomited twice at stimuli a person of her stature would almost certainly be trained to withstand. He'd been played like a cheap jazz trumpet. Baker swayed where he stood, cursing himself with every swear word he knew (and in every language he knew) for allowing himself to be so trusting. Of course the world was just as unfair and backward as it had always been. Nothing had changed.

"Now," said Bogart. "Let's go take a stroll inside, shall we, Detective? You're going to help me land on the right side of history."

With Bogart's gun trained on his back, Baker was slowly led to the front entrance of the Griffith Observatory. The view of the city from here was incredible, but Baker was in no state of mind to appreciate it. All the resentment he'd felt since his liberation at the end of the war began to creep out of the dark and slimy hole in the back of his mind. What did it matter if the Black Symphony set off the bomb? Most of the country thought Jews were not to be trusted anyway. He could just walk away and let the villains win like always. But there was no walking away from a gun pointed at his back.

"That's it, Detective," said the actor. "Nice and slow." When they reached the front door—where a sign declared the place closed for the long weekend—Bogart spoke over his shoulder to Sophia. "All right, toots, you stand here and keep the coast clear. I don't want you gettin' into any trouble with those Krauts. After you, Detective."

Baker felt a sharp poke from the gun's barrel and began to reach for the door when she finally spoke up. "Don't hurt him."

"Heh?" said Bogart, turning around fully to face the woman called Faye.

"Don't kill Morris. There's enough blood on our hands already."

"Does it matter at this point? Look, baby, we do this and we're set for life. We'll have anything we could ever want. No one will be able to touch us, understand? So, stay here and stay out of my goddamn way!"

Baker heard Bogart's hand make contact with Faye's cheek, heard her yelp in pain and surprise. "Now, as I was sayin'... after you, Detective."

* * *

Mythology and science overlapped as Baker and Bogart entered the observatory's chapel-like rotunda—a marble hall of murals painted by Hugo Ballin. The cosmic deities of Greek and Roman traditions populated the domed ceiling while fresco paintings of man's scientific discoveries circled the walls.

Bogart whistled as they looked around the hall. The shrill sound eerily rebounded around the empty room. "Nice place," he said. "Never had the chance to make it up here before. Ever visited, Baker?" Baker nodded his head slowly, his mind still focused on Sophia's betrayal. He'd spent one enjoyable spring day here several years ago with Liz. "Well, tour's over," Bogart continued. "Let's get going. And don't think just because I'm an actor, I don't know how to use this thing. I got plenty of target practice on all those old noir and gangster pictures, even if I was just holding props. You run and I'll put three bullets in your back before you can say *Howdy Doody*." He prodded Baker in the back again. "Move."

"So that was you at Huston's house two nights ago?" Baker asked.

"If you were any more right, Baker, you'd be going left," said Bogart. "Faye put in a call to me right before you left that cathouse."

"Why follow us there, if you weren't actually going to kill us?"

"Ah, that's the thespian in me," Bogart said. "Had to set the scene and ramp up the stakes, so you'd keep digging into this thing. It's like a movie, Baker. You have to put the hero's life in danger to drive the plot along. The threat of death is the best motivation."

They continued into the South Gallery, which linked all of the structure's halls to the planetarium. The largest dome of all.

"I think that's where the bomb is," Baker said. "They're looking to spread nuclear material as far as they can, and the planetarium is closest to the city. Their plan probably includes turning this whole building into an avalanche of irradiated debris."

"Not a bad theory. Let's go get it," said Bogart.

"Not that simple," Baker replied. "This thing could be heavy. We'll need something to roll it out on. Try to find a custodial closet or something."

Bogart eyed him suspiciously. "All right. But we look together. I'm not letting you out of my sight."

"This way." Baker really wanted to forestall the moment when they finally walked into a den of highly dangerous Nazis in the hopes that he could somehow overpower Bogart and get his gun. He didn't want to enter the planetarium defenseless if he could help it. Together, they walked into a side hall that had restrooms, a stairwell, and a small door marked JANITORIAL STAFF. Baker tried the door and was not surprised to find it locked.

"Shoot it open," he instructed Bogart.

"Okay, but I'm serious about shooting you if you run."

"I won't run. I want to stop them just as much as you do."

Bogart nodded. "Step back."

Baker did as he was told, and the actor pointed the pistol at the door's lock. He fired once. The sound of the bullet tearing through the mechanism rang throughout the empty space, and for a moment the two men held their breath, waiting for someone to come running. After a minute, nothing happened, and they relaxed. Bogart kicked the door open to reveal a shabby concrete room filled with mops, brooms, various cleaning supplies, a few mousetraps, and a flatbed cart.

"Get it," said Bogart. He trained his gun back on Baker, who walked into the musty room and wheeled the cart out into the hall. The rusted wheels squeaked on the polished marble floor.

"Fair warning," said Baker. "They'll probably be more than ready to put up a fight. You may have to point that gun somewhere else very soon."

"You think I don't know that? I just gotta make sure you don't pull a fast one on me before we get in there, that's all. Let's get going—actually..." Bogart reached into his slacks with a free hand and pulled out a metal flask, unscrewed the top with two fingers, took a swig, and then held it out to Baker.

"Care for some liquid courage, Detective? It's your favorite, if I recall correctly. Peach schnapps."

Baker looked at the flask, feeling the need to suck the alcohol down as if it were mother's milk. He felt himself reaching out for it until he reeled his arm back in with a great deal of willpower. "No thanks," he said. "I'm gonna need my wits about me."

"Suit yours—" Bogart dropped his gun and looked down to see a red stain spreading across his chest. Shock and confusion were etched across his face as he toppled forward. Baker dove for Bogart's gun, but he wasn't quick enough. He felt something hard collide with the back of his skull and everything went fuzzy. He collapsed onto the floor, his body slowly sinking into a dark abyss.

CHAPTER 33

They said he was free to leave the camp once morning came.

It was early evening in late summer, and he was taking a walk around the perimeter of a place from which he couldn't wait to escape. A place where his life had become a living hell. He'd been here nearly three months, recovering from malnutrition, dehydration, typhus, septic shock, and a nasty bout of the flu. He'd been able to walk on his own again for the last week and now spent as much time as he could outdoors, bringing up his strength—not wanting to spend any more time in a hospital bed. Most of his hair was back and his weight was finally stabilizing after endless bars of Hershey's chocolate (his new favorite snack). A full recovery like this was nothing short of a medical anomaly, according to Dr. Elijah Mayhew.

The Americans had taken over the camp and turned it into a base of operations for displaced persons of war. Eisenhower insisted on erecting heated hospital tents for the former inmates, refusing to let them return to the diseased and lice-infested barracks to which they had been confined for so long. The general also gave strict orders to his subordinates now running the camp not to destroy or raze any structures, preferring that they stand as a monument to what had occurred there.

While Baker was unconscious, the Americans forced the citizens of the local hamlet to tour the camp, its death facilities, and the pile of bodies stacked by the entrance. Baker wished he could have seen their horrified faces.

He'd grown fond of Nurse Perkins and Dr. Mayhew these last few months. They'd started him on the path to speaking English, and he was proving adept at picking up the new language. Using their influence, he secured himself a spot on a naval battleship carrying a few hundred American soldiers home the following afternoon. There'd be a short stop in London and then the boat would head across the Atlantic to New York City. The thought of leaving Europe frightened him somewhat.

New York was a place he'd only ever heard about in exaggerated stories: buildings that disappeared into the clouds, bright lights that could drive you blind, and restaurants that served hundred-pound steaks.

Despite his apprehension, there was nothing left for him here. Everyone and everything he ever knew or loved was destroyed or dead. America was the place they called the "land of opportunity." He wasn't entirely sure what that meant, but it didn't matter. He just wanted to forget the past and start anew. Maybe America, where no one knew his name or personal history, would give him just that.

In the meantime, he spent his days walking around the camp or listening to the news coming out of Nuremberg about the "trial of the century." What he wouldn't give to have a front-row seat to the proceedings. Watching Justice Jackson and the other tribunal members judging Bormann, Jodl, Göring, Frick, Speer, and the rest from on high. The age of the kangaroo court in Germany was finally over and those who hid behind the Reich's sham concept of law would feel the full force of American, Russian, British, and French justice.

In the back of his mind, though, he was bitter about the upcoming trials. Were hearings held for the millions of people killed in camps like these? Of course not. Why not just shoot these men and be done with it?

He passed the outer edge of the camp, walking past Zeishe Malamud. The former inmate was reciting mincha, the afternoon prayer, with his eyes closed, his lips moving soundlessly, and a knit skullcap sitting on his skull-like head. Nine other men in baggy clothing (some of them US soldiers, some of them former inmates wearing striped camp uniforms) had joined Malamud to form the required minyan of ten men.

Baker snorted to himself. What a load of dreck. Zeishe had a tattoo on his forearm just like the rest of them. Zeishe had been tortured, his family killed. And yet, Zeishe still believed. The thing that allowed him to continue to place his faith in God—a God who had remained silent for a dozen years—remained intact. For Morris, that thing inside him was irrevocably broken.

He walked away as everyone in the group began to solemnly speak the mourner's kaddish. "Yit'gadal v'yit'kadash sh'mei raba . . ."

Morris did not give the obligatory "amen" at the end of the hymn.

No more Judaism. No more religion. He was going to be an American and didn't need this nonsense anymore. Feeling a twinge of regret at what his mother and father would say if they heard him renouncing his five-thousand-year-old faith, Baker strolled by the barbed-wire corral in which the German POWs—many of them former guards of this very camp—were still being held.

Three months had passed since Hitler put a bullet in his brain, and there were more displaced soldiers of the Third Reich than the Allies knew what to do with. They could not be released—not after Himmler and Mengele had been erroneously identified. It didn't matter that for every two hundred men, only one was an actual war criminal. Each and every individual needed to be evaluated and cleared.

Baker looked down at his arm where fresh pink scar tissue was beginning to form above the tattooed numbers. He rubbed it, thinking of Lang. Where had the doctor gone once the fear of the advancing Americans became too great? Was he somewhere in Poland? Germany? Another continent entirely? Baker's guess was as good as anyone's.

Dozens of refugees came through the camp every day looking for their loved ones. Baker saw the faces of desperation, the sunken eyes and loping gaits. They knew that the person or people they were attempting to locate were long since dead, but they could not stop searching. Giving up that sense of purpose would rob them of whatever meaning they had left in the world.

"Psst."

Baker looked up from rubbing his arm and saw a man in a filthy Wehrmacht uniform looking at him from behind the tangle of barbed wire of the Pig Pen—as some of the Americans referred to it. It was essentially a paddock for captured Germans, a large square of several acres surrounded with barbed wire and watched over by GIs in guard towers. Tents, latrines, freshly laundered beds, and mess tables were placed every hundred feet or so. During the day, the POWs lounged around, smoking American cigarettes, eating American candy bars, and gambling with American playing cards. They got three square meals a day, warm blankets over their bodies, and as many Chesterfields as their lungs could handle.

In short, they had it infinitely better in captivity than their victims ever did.

"Ist es wahr?" asked the soldier. Is it true?

"Is what true?" Morris said, keeping his distance.

"Japan. Die Amerikaner. Ist die Bombe, von der sie sprechen, echt?"

Morris now understood. For days, wild rumors were flying around the camp about some kind of "super-weapon" the United States had dropped on Japan.

"They say it's true," he replied in German. "And I have no reason to believe the Americans would lie about something like that."

"Mein Gott. They say it wiped out hundreds of thousands of people in a single second."

Morris shrugged. He didn't much fancy having a conversation with this man, but he did not recognize him as a camp guard, so he humored him for now.

"Bist du ein Jude?" Are you a Jew?

He nodded.

"Das ist eine Schande."

"What's a shame?" Morris prompted him.

"Well, you're part of an endangered species, aren't you?"

"And what would you consider Nazis?" countered Morris.

The soldier shrugged back. "I did what they asked of me," he said, dodging the question. "I served my country."

"Where did you serve? Wehrmacht? Kriegsmarine? Schutzstaffel? Einsatzgruppen?"

Just because the man was wearing a German army uniform didn't mean he had actually served in the army. Plenty of guilty men would don the steely gray tunic in an attempt to blend in with the innocent. If any German could be innocent, that is.

"As if I'd tell a Jew like you," said the soldier, pulling out a pack of cigarettes and lighting up.

"And yet, you're the one behind that wire now. Isn't that where they usually put the endangered species? Behind a fence?"

The German shrugged again. "Temporary, this." He drew an imaginary circle with his smoke. "It won't hold us. It's all a show for the Jewish bankers in America. We'll be out of here in no time."

"You so sure about that?"

"Even if we're not, there's still a Germany. Where's your country, Jew?" The soldier leaned against the barbed wire so that it dug into his hands and cheeks—blood trickled onto the parched summer grass. His teeth were bared in an abominable grin. "I will get out of this cage, but what about you? Will you

ever truly escape this place? Eh? It does not matter what your American and Jewish overlords say. We live on."

"Who lives on?"

"The Führer. The Reich. The Fatherland. Take your pick. You will never be rid of us. Never. What we did is only the beginning."

Morris turned away. He suddenly felt extremely dizzy and on the verge of collapse.

He turned around and started walking back toward the camp.

"You cannot run from us, Jew!" shouted the German. "We will get out and you never will! Remember that!"

"We'll see about that," was all Baker could manage as he stumbled back to the medical tent and fainted.

CHAPTER 34

"A fiery chariot, borne on buoyant pinions..."

At first, Baker thought he was imagining the voice ringing inside his head.

"Sweeps near me now! I soon shall ready be to pierce the ether's high, unknown dominions. To reach new spheres of pure activity!"

Very slowly, Baker opened his eyes. His line of vision was blurred, but he could tell that he was in the observatory's planetarium. Its massive roof was open, offering a glimpse into the hazy evening sky. Even with fresh air streaming in, the room was stiflingly hot. Los Angeles didn't really cool down until the sun had completely set—and even then, the humidity could still make its grand entrance.

"Ah, so nice of you to join us, Herr Baker," said a man standing in front of him. "I knew you would come in the end. Are you an admirer of Goethe?"

Baker did not answer.

"Are you all right, Herr Baker? I do hope that little blow to your head didn't result in any lasting cognitive damage."

The man moved closer and slapped him gently on both cheeks, returning a modicum of visual clarity to his waking state. Baker grunted and tried to move, only to realize he was tied to one of many chairs placed all around the auditorium where people could sit and watch the stars on those rare nights devoid of smog. The stranger stood directly in front of him, stooping down to grip the detective's immobile wrists. Now that the man was standing still, Baker registered a stern face and neatly parted, sandy-blond hair streaked with silver.

"I need you to understand," said the man, breathing the scent of stale tobacco into Baker's face. "I need you to understand before you die. Which"—he took his hands off Baker's wrists and stood up—"should be very soon."

"I've seen you on television, haven't I?" Baker said. "Explaining how rocket ships work?"

The man laughed heartily and began to sing "When You Wish Upon a Star" in a merry tune. The Disney song sounded wrong in his voice, a grim reminder that not all wishes were pure of heart. "Wernher von Braun, at your service," he said with a theatrical bow. "You like my educational programs on space, Herr Baker?"

Baker's head was still throbbing, but the blurriness was thankfully starting to abate, allowing him to notice the dead-eyed lens of a film camera perched atop a tripod. A surly-looking woman adjusted the tripod's legs, while a man standing next to her fiddled with a fuzzy microphone on a long black pole.

Baker snapped his attention away from the camera and glanced around the room, finally spotting his target. It wasn't exactly as how Joanna had described it, but it came pretty close. The bomb resembled a large drum of oil covered in sticks of wired dynamite. If he didn't know what kind of destruction the thing was capable of, he'd have compared it to the explosives used in construction.

"So that's it, huh?" Baker nodded in the bomb's direction.

Von Braun smiled. "You are astute as ever, Herr Baker."

"And Bogart's dead?"

"Ja," replied von Braun. "Dear Humphrey fulfilled his part beautifully."

"His part?"

The scientist began pacing, hands linked behind his back. He wore a crease-free suit of a mud-brown fabric and burgundy penny loafers. "Humphrey Bogart was ours from the beginning, a tool of the Schwarze Symphonie. In fact, it is because of *us* that you are here tonight."

"What the fuck are you talking about?"

"Tsk, tsk. Such language," said von Braun. "But not unexpected from Jewish vermin like you. Yes, Baker, we have been pulling the strings from the start. When it became clear that Lang left behind a trail of breadcrumbs for you to find, framing you was no longer enough."

"You keep saying 'we' and 'our,'" said Baker. "Where's the rest of the Symphony? Your ramshackle film crew"—he nodded toward the camera and microphone operators—"can't be the only members."

"My dear Baker. They have been here the whole time." He pointed across the planetarium to another cluster of chairs where a small collection of people sat in shadow, their faces obscured in the darkness cast by the open dome. "Meet the Black Symphony."

"If the Americans were so good to you, why turn on your new masters at all?" Baker asked. Surreptitiously knocking his shins together, he could feel Waldgrave's knife still resting in his sock.

"For a time, we were content here," von Braun said. "We worked for this country and reveled in the good old days over drinks after long hours in the laboratory. Things got even better when that fool McCarthy became president. We thought he might even pursue the Führer's vision of ridding the world of Jews and other undesirables."

"Except that he didn't?" mused Baker in a casual tone.

"The president and his Hueys, as you like to call them, got close, but still needed a nudge in the right direction," replied von Braun. "That's when a plan began to form in my mind, and the Symphony quite agreed with it. If we could frame a Jew for a terribly violent act, then McCarthy would finally do what needed to be done. The ODESSA put up the funds and everything fell into place. The land in Africa was just waiting to be plumbed for its uranium. We built centrifuges on the same land and bribed customs agents to look the other way as we smuggled the enriched material into America. All paid for with gold smuggled out of Germany. Gold melted down from the teeth fillings of Jews we had disposed of in our noble conquest. Perhaps even gold from your own family members."

Von Braun held up a bar of gold stamped with the Nazi eagle clutching the swastika. "We found this in your car. Tell me, Herr Baker. Do you have any gold in *your* teeth?"

With one fluid motion, the scientist swung his hand forward and Baker felt his jaw crack in an explosion of white-hot pain. Several more of his teeth skittered to the floor in a spray of blood. Von Braun bent down, picked them up, and tossed them up and down in his palm as if playing some perverse game of jacks. Baker panted as his brain sent wave after wave of agony to a mouth currently filling with blood.

His mind tried to tell him something about the gold bar, but nearly all rational logic had been driven from his brain.

"You... you said framing me wasn't enough?" he managed to say with his now-fractured jaw. "What did you mean by that?"

The German smiled and let Baker's teeth fall back onto the floor. "You are a resilient one, Herr Baker. I had to see for myself, and you do not disappoint."

"Get on with the story," Baker said, spitting a gob of blood into his lap and inching the knife out of his sock. "What happened with Lang? He lost his nerve for the whole Nazi shtick. I've already worked that out for myself."

"I told him, Germany—the real Germany—no longer existed and there was no point in going back, but he wanted to see his hometown against our wishes. So, he went, and do you know what happened, Baker? My worst fears came true: A filthy Jew recognized him. And do you know what this Jew said to Adolf? He said he forgave him for everything. Can you believe it? What seemed like a bullet dodged soon became a pain in the Symphony's side. Lang came back with strange notions. He began to wonder whether we were doing the right thing. That Jew planted something in his brain that could not be reasoned away. He nearly ruined all."

"Why not just kill him to keep him quiet?"

"He promised me he was still committed to the cause and like a fool, I believed him. Even so, I wisely decided to keep a close eye on him. Rudolph Rascher came up from Argentina to monitor him from morning until night. We threatened to kill Lang's sons and their families. Aside from teaching classes, he was under near-constant house arrest and told nothing more of the plan. But these measures were clearly not enough. Lang was secretly in contact with those meddlesome Liberty Boys. The damage was done. By the time I discovered what he'd been up to, it was too late. Our plans had to change. You see, I knew of Adolf's guilty fascination with you. That disgusting brothel he frequented has thin walls."

Von Braun turned around. "Eichmann," he said. "Would you come over here, please?" One of the silent and shadowy audience members got up and walked across the room and into the light. Eichmann was an owlish man who barely fit into his own suit. He held a cardboard box in his hands and looked at Baker with academic curiosity. "I suspected the remorse and psychological burden would become too great for Adolf. That he might one day remove himself from the board and draft you in his stead," von Braun said, reaching into the box and pulling out a piece of poorly photostatted paper. He held it up close to Baker's face.

The detective's heart skipped a beat. He recognized it as one of the documents in Lang's safe-deposit box. Smiling maliciously, von Braun reached into the box again and brought out something that made Baker forget about his growing list of injuries: Lang's scrapbook. That's what his brain had been trying to tell him when von Braun hit him with the gold. The Symphony had found the safe-deposit key and his stash of items underneath the Continental's driver's seat.

"But...how?" was all Baker could manage.

"You see, Bogart was only one part of our master plan. He was meant to rid us of the tiresome Liberty Boys and guide you in the right direction. But to make absolutely sure that you would find this evidence for us, you needed a foil." Von Braun turned around to face the Symphony members and called out, "Miss Dalton, if you would?"

It was Sophia. She still wouldn't meet his gaze.

"No," Baker heard himself say. "No."

"Yes," von Braun countered. "You see, Miss Dalton has been in our employ for quite some time."

Here it was, the last piece of the puzzle—the missing connection that brought the entire case into crystal-clear focus.

"You were never supposed to meet with Huston and Cronkite, were you?" Baker said to her. "Lang somehow figured out who you really were and blew your cover that night, which is why Bogart was sent to kill them. Huston probably would have tipped me off. Trumbo didn't know yet, but he would probably get wise."

That's why Charles had found faint traces of radiation on the bullets used to kill Huston and Cronkite. Bogart was using a gun provided to him by Nazis working around uranium. Once the actor had done his part and silenced all the meddlesome parties that might have exposed Sophia, it was her turn to ensure Morris tracked down all the incriminating evidence.

"I was the final loose end," he added. "How could I have been so stupid?"

"Your reputation precedes you, Herr Baker," replied von Braun with a small golf clap. "You really are an exceptional detective, even if you were a little slow on the uptake. Faking her credentials as a Soviet spy and linking her up with that fool Trumbo was simple. Leaking her name to HUAC would remove any further doubt. If only impatient Rudolph had listened to me, he might still be alive. He didn't approve of Miss Dalton, but you did just as I predicted. You fell for her innocent-lamb act . . ."

"Hook, line, and sinker," Baker finished angrily. "And what if HUAC got to me before I found all the evidence? What then?"

"I was partially counting on it," answered a delighted von Braun. "Either you found that safe-deposit box, brought it to us, and took the blame, or you died under HUAC interrogation and took the blame. It was a, how do the Americans say? A win-win."

"So, you kept them informed of our movements?"

"I'm a betting man by nature," said von Braun. "I knew you were smarter than those government buffoons, which is why we kept them apprised of where you were headed. Whenever you fell asleep or let her out of your sight, Miss Dalton was feeding us information that we simply passed along to the proper authorities. I wanted to see if you'd cross the finish line first, and while you stumbled near the end, you still won. Congratulations."

"And that Oliver kid paid the price just for being in the way, I expect?"

"A regrettable but necessary action. We did not know how much the boy knew and just couldn't take the risk. Speaking of which, that Danforth will have to be dealt with, too," said von Braun. "Thank you, Herr Baker. Thank you for delivering everything Adolf Lang left behind on a silver platter. Do it, Eichmann."

Eichmann placed the cardboard box on the floor, pulled a box of matches out of his pocket, struck one, and set the documents ablaze. Baker felt numb with shock. The whole time he'd been working for the Black Symphony, whose members were now laughing and jeering with savage pleasure from the shadows. He had been used and tossed aside by a group of Nazis, just as he had had been during the war.

"Why, Faye?" he asked the woman he knew as Sophia. "Why did you do it?"

"I'm sorry, Morris," she said to the floor. "They threatened to kill my whole family. I had no choice."

"And now," von Braun pressed on in a business-like tone. "The time of Valkyrie is nearly upon us." The scientist violently grabbed Sophia and held a gun up to her temple. "Herr Baker," said von Braun, reaching into his pocket and pulling out a piece of tightly folded paper. "You are going to read this message into the camera. If you do not, I will blow Ms. Dalton's head off."

The camera operator stood at attention and made some final adjustments while her assistant began to lower the boom pole near Baker's head. Wernher von Braun walked over to Baker and placed the paper in his tightly bound hands.

"Read it!" he barked.

It read:

I am Morris Ephraim Baker. Until today, I was a homicide detective for the Los Angeles Police Department. I have never much thought of myself as an American and it is with great pride that I announce myself as a Jewish liberator and Communist subversive. It was I who detonated the radioactive bomb at Griffith Observatory in an effort to bring the country's attention to the plight of my people. Long live the Jewish cause, long live Communism, and down with McCarthy.

"You're crazy if you think I'm going to say this shit," Baker snarled at von Braun.

"Then I kill the girl." Von Braun violently grabbed Sophia and placed the gun against her temple.

"Do it," Baker said. "She means nothing to me."

Sophia's eyes went wide, and she began struggling against her captor. "I'm sorry, Morris!" she screamed. "I never would have done it if I knew it would lead to this. I swear!"

Baker's callous statement wasn't entirely true. Even if Sophia was just a character, didn't he still have feelings for the person who brought her to life? He needed time, time to think; time to get Waldgrave's switchblade out of his sock and cut himself free.

An explosion—or maybe just the illusion of one—rocked the

building, rattling the planetarium and causing von Braun, Eichmann, the camerawoman, and the microphone operator to wobble comically.

"Don't be alarmed!" von Braun called out to the crowd of Symphony members shouting in surprise. "There is nothing to worry about."

The distraction allowed Sophia to free herself from von Braun's grasp and pull a grenade from her pocket. One of the grenades Joanna had given her.

"Nobody move!" she said, pulling out the pin. "Or we all go kablooey."

While he now knew that she'd never been trained by the KGB, Baker saw a flicker of the wild abandon he had come to know from the apocryphal Sophia Vikhrov. Perhaps not all of it had been an act and there was more to Miss Dalton than met the eye.

Her grenade threat distracted the Symphony and gave Baker a chance to reach for the knife. So far, he'd managed to loosen his right hand during his little chat with von Braun. If he could just lift his foot up a bit more...

The rocket scientist looked murderous and ready to shout himself hoarse, but what came out of his mouth was surprisingly calm. "Miss Dalton, please," he said. "Put the grenade down. I am sure we can come to amiable terms on this." Baker's partially freed hand snaked its way down to his foot like a soldier crawling under barbed wire. At last, it reached the knife, flicked the blade into the open, and began slicing through the ropes. "Miss Dalton," cooed von Braun. "Surely there is something that can be done here. Something you must want."

"Yeah, there is," she said, catching Baker's eye. He nodded.

"Name your price," said von Braun.

318

"I'll let Morris lay down my demands."

Baker jumped free of his seat and drove Waldgrave's knife into the center of von Braun's back up to the splintered wooden handle. Letting out a shocked screech of pain, the scientist desperately grabbed at the knife he could not reach and fell backward onto the floor, driving the blade further into his body. The Symphony members were all scrambling out of their seats and filing out of the room through a hidden door.

"As a mutual friend of ours liked to say, Wernher," Baker whispered to the dying von Braun, "Die Luft der Freiheit weht."

"Freedom is what we say it is, Baker," von Braun coughed, a trickle of blood moving sluggishly down his chin. He then raised his gun and fired a round into Sophia's chest. Letting out a subdued yelp, she dropped the live grenade she was holding and fell to the ground.

CHAPTER 35

The grenade rolled toward the nuclear bomb. Baker left von Braun to die alone on the marble floor as he lunged for the explosive. He flopped onto his stomach, which gave his cracked ribs an excuse to scream in protest. His body was so full of adrenaline, he barely sensed the shrieking pain, and it was with great relief that he felt his hand close around the grenade. Muttering "shit! shit! shit" to himself, Baker wound back his arm, as though about to pitch a baseball, and lobbed the explosive out through the open planetarium roof. It barely cleared the lip before detonating. Large chunks of white brick rained down to the floor and a cloud of black smoke blossomed up into the early evening sky. Standing over Sophia, Baker shielded his face until he was certain the whole place wouldn't come tumbling down on them like the walls of Jericho.

There wasn't any time to relax, because Sophia was losing a lot of blood. Elevating her head in his lap, Baker placed pressure on the gunshot wound, but it was no use. The warm, crimson fluid poured between his fingers at an alarming rate. How many people had he seen die these last few days? Why was he always the last one standing? The final witness to the unending sorrows of the world?

"Try not to speak," he said tenderly. "You really saved the day."

She smiled. "After messing it up in the first place. Morris, I'm so sorry about how things turned out. I just wish we'd gotten to know each other under better circumstances."

"Me too, Sophia," he said, gently kissing her cheek. Tears poured down his face and onto hers.

Sophia reached up to touch his cheek and left bloody smears wherever her quivering blue fingers met flesh. "You really are a good man," she rasped, grimacing in pain. The end was near. "And it's true what I said about going to the beach. That wasn't a lie."

"We'll go," Baker choked. "Corn dogs, cotton candy, funnel cakes, and an ocean view. The whole shebang. Just like I said." He didn't know why but he was laughing now, too—the heartache was crossing wires in his brain.

"I'd like that."

Faye Dalton took one last shuddering breath and was gone.

* * *

Baker wept over her body for a quarter of an hour before grabbing the walkie-talkie to inform Joanna and Murrow that the bomb was secure. He made sure no pain came through in his voice.

"Good," Murrow said, his voice crackling over the channel. "For a second there, we thought you let the Symphony blow the damn thing up."

"No, that was just a grenade. I took care of it."

321

"And Agent Vikhrov?" Murrow asked. Even through the static, Baker could hear concern in the man's voice.

The question nearly caused Baker to break down again, but he remained calm.

"She...didn't make it," he replied.

"I see," said Murrow. "I'm very sorry to hear that. We'll be right with you."

Murrow, Joanna, Ralph, and Gerald arrived within ten minutes, pushing the janitorial dolly Baker and Bogart had planned to use. Without asking for any details about what happened, Murrow removed his jacket and placed it over Sophia's body, while instructing his bodyguards to dump von Braun's corpse outside.

"Let the birds and coyotes have at him."

The ex-Hueys started to lift von Braun when Joanna called out.

"Wait!" She walked over to them and without any hesitation, started sticking her hands into the various pockets of von Braun's crinkled and bloodstained suit. "Aha!" she said at last, finding a rectangular black box studded with a row of white buttons. "Just as I suspected." Baker cocked his head in question. "If they wanted to taunt you first, Morris," Joanna explained, "they needed a way to set off the bomb from a safe distance once they made their escape. This remote control would have set off the device with a special radio frequency. Okay, boys," she said, turning to Ralph and Gerald, "now you can dump the son of a bitch."

Murrow's bodyguards took von Braun outside and returned to help lift the bomb (disarmed at this point) and Sophia onto the dolly. Meanwhile, Joanna did her best to clean up the smoldering remnants of the box containing Lang's evidence against the Black Symphony. She also had the good sense to wipe up all the blood that coated the floor, which looked like some macabre piece of impressionistic art. On the way out, they picked up Bogart's corpse and headed into the Fourth of July dusk, where the crickets chirped a song of tranquility.

"They got away," said Baker, breaking his grieving silence. "The other Symphony members. They played me, Huston, and Trumbo. Even Lang."

"Don't you worry," Murrow said, lighting up another Camel as though he didn't have a care in the world. "Leave them to us. We'll see if we can't smoke 'em out."

They loaded the bomb and two bodies onto the flatbed of Murrow's truck in silence.

"Well," said the chief Liberty Boy at last, wiping his hands on his pants. "That settles it. The question now is, what the hell do we do with this thing?" He pointed toward the inert bomb.

"I've got a pretty good idea," said Baker.

CHAPTER 36

Hollis Li, proprietor of The Golden Fowl, answered his call on the third ring. In the background, Baker heard the usual sound of the Bobbettes singing in harmony.

"Oh, Detective," said Hollis. "So good to hear from you. I was going to close early, but can whip something up if you'd like to come in."

"No time, Hollis," breathed Baker. "Look, I need every able-bodied fighter you can spare over at Merv's Diner as soon as possible."

"I don't know," Hollis replied, sounding tired. "It's a holiday, Detective."

"Don't give me that, Hollis. Those people never leave their posts. I could really use your help here. It's the Hueys—they're after me."

Hollis took a long time to answer. "You got it, Detective," he said at last. "Twenty minutes, tops."

"You are a lifesaver, Hollis! I owe you big-time!" Baker shouted, already hanging up so he could ring the madam of a certain whorehouse.

* * *

It was dark, a mesmerizing fireworks display erupting on the horizon, when Baker got to the diner. Murrow, Joanna, Ralph, Gerald, and Merv were waiting outside, smoking. Merv was still fawning over Murrow, who seemed to be enjoying the attention after spending so much time undercover. Five minutes later, Hollis arrived with a militia of fifteen men and women. One of them was a stooped old lady, a Kalashnikov confidently grasped in her gnarled hands. The rest wielded M60 machine guns, with bandoliers strung around their necks and over their shoulders like deadly scarves.

"What's this all about, Detective?" Hollis asked.

"Hollis, meet Edward Murrow. Edward Murrow, meet the best crack shots in Chinatown."

"Pleasure," said Murrow, shaking Hollis's hand. Turning back to Baker, he added, "You think it'll be enough to keep the HUAC pricks at bay?"

"It will be if we're involved!" called a gruff voice behind them. Baker turned and saw the broad-shouldered Edgar Ramirez, head of security for the Red Sword. He was joined by a group of leather-jacketed Pistoleros behind him, including Miguel, the man Sophia nearly drowned in his stein of beer the night before. Nunchucks, spiked clubs, and medieval-looking maces were just a few of the weapons carried by the rugged delegation. "Valentina said you might need a hand, Baker," Edgar said.

Baker smiled and shook the bouncer's meaty paw. "Thanks for coming."

"Hold on just one blasted second!" called Merv Pachenko, stumping out of his diner with a sawed-off shotgun pointed into the air. "I want a piece of the action. Don't shoot till you see the whites of their eyes, boys!"

"Whoa, Merv," Baker said, placing a calming hand on the proprietor's shoulder. "There won't be any shooting if all goes according to plan."

"No shooting?" squawked several people at once. "Then why are we here?"

"I need an army of my own if I'm going to negotiate with the US government," said Baker, pointing up the street, where a motorcade of Cadillac V-16s was zooming toward the diner.

"How'd they know to find you here?" asked Murrow.

"How else?" Baker replied. "I called them!"

The HUAC vehicles stopped fifty feet from the diner, creating a cordon that blocked off the entire street. Hueys in dark suits, trench coats, and fedoras extricated themselves from the cars as the motley crew of soldiers from Chinatown and the Red Sword readied their weapons. Baker realized this might be the start of the citywide revolution Chief Parker had been tasked with preventing all this time. It looked like things were about to change forever.

Baker casually strolled in front of the gathered Hueys. "Which one of you is in charge?" he asked.

"I am," said a particularly mean-looking Huey with a pompadour and sideburns. "I'm Chief HUAC Inspector Lonergan. I run the Echo Park branch."

"How's Hartwell?" Baker asked lightly.

"He may never walk again, but he'll live. More than I can say for Waldgrave. Now, if we're through with the pleasantries, you're under arrest, Baker."

"Oh, I don't think so, Inspector."

"You hear that, boys?" Lonergan called to his men. "This shylock doesn't think so."

They all laughed sycophantically.

"You heard me right," said Baker. "You Hueys are going to drop the charges against me."

"And why would we do that?" shot back Lonergan. An angry red flush was creeping up his neck. He clearly wasn't used to getting lip from the Hebrews.

"Because I'm going to hand over the bomb I was supposed to detonate today." Baker signaled to Ralph and Gerald, who effortlessly carried over the Nazi device.

Lonergan looked at his former underlings with revulsion and hatred.

"So," he said to them. "This is what you traitors have been up to since you cut and ran, eh? Helping a goddamn kike perpetrate mass murder? Guess Baker won't be the only one I bring in tonight."

"No, you won't, Inspector," replied Baker, rapping the oil drum with his knuckles, which caused Lonergan to glance down at the barrel-like explosive.

"What the fuck is this?" he asked. "Some kind of Jew tomfoolery?"

"I assure you, Inspector, that this is the bomb your men were looking for. If I was as guilty as you presume me to be, why would I just hand it over?"

"Don't ask me to ponder the way a Jew's mind works," blustered Lonergan. "You could be trying to pull a fast one on us. We won't know until I've interrogated you at headquarters."

There was an uproar from the small army standing behind Baker. Some of Lonergan's men stepped back, pulling out their guns. The negotiations were about to take a turn for the worse if someone didn't defuse the situation. That someone turned up in a gray 1957 Eldorado.

"Just what in the ever-loving Christ is going on here?" boomed the distinctive voice of Brogan Abraham Connolly. "Baker? Oh, I just knew you had to be behind this."

"Brogan, what're you doing here?"

"I was on my way to get more hamburger buns. My kids are fuckin' eating machines. Fucking Christ, Baker"—a quick cross—"you look like you got eaten by a tiger and shit out the other side. I told you to stop digging on the Huston-Cronkite case. Didn't I tell you?"

"Good to see you, too, you Irish son of a bitch," said Baker.

Lonergan cleared his throat loudly, causing Brogan to look around, annoyed. "And who might the fuck you be?"

"I am Chief Inspector Lonergan of..."

"Oh, a Huey," scoffed Brogan.

"Excuse me," Lonergan said, looking madder than ever. "I could have you arrested for talk like that. You're lucky I'm busy at the moment, taking care of this loudmouthed Jew."

"What he do?" Brogan asked, flashing his police badge to Lonergan.

"He killed a HUAC inspector and escaped custody."

"You have concrete proof of this?" Brogan continued.

"Well...no," Lonergan said. "I don't think I need...I mean to say Baker here is supposed to detonate some kind of bomb tonight."

"This bomb," Baker said, pointing out the Nazi device to his partner. "I was turning it over to the good people at HUAC since I'm innocent."

"Well," said Connolly. "It sounds like he's off the hook then."

Lonergan's face was beet red and it looked as though his head were about to explode. "This kike is coming with me whether you like it or not, Detective Connolly."

Brogan looked from Baker to Lonergan and then to Baker again before pushing his partner behind his back. "No, I don't think we have a deal, fella."

"Then you'll both be coming with m—"

Lonergan didn't get to finish. The unlikely battalion in front of the diner began to hurl insults at the Hueys. Many of them began to advance and Hollis even fired some bullets into the air, lighting up the night sky alongside the distant fireworks. Muttering among themselves, Lonergan's men began to retreat in earnest. The chief inspector was no fool and knew he was outnumbered. He jabbed a sausage-like finger at Baker.

"This isn't over. Larry! Charles!" he called to a pair of cowering Hueys. "Quit pissing your pants and get this thing loaded into one of the cars."

The oil drum affixed with dynamite was hoisted into one of the Cadillacs and as the Hueys began to drive away, Joanna stepped beside Baker. She gave him a celebratory kiss on the cheek and said, "I hope you didn't tell them we removed the uranium."

"Didn't see the need to burden them with the information," said Baker, who—relieved, heartbroken, and sore beyond all measure—passed out and into Connolly's arms.

WESTERN UNION TELEGRAM

FROM: A.E.

Los Angeles, California, July 5, 1958

TO: B.E.

São Paulo, Brazil

Valkyrie failed—STOP—

Von Braun dead—STOP—

Baker still alive—STOP—

Bomb no longer in play—STOP—

Awaiting further instructions—STOP—

Heil Hitler—STOP—

PART V

July 27, 1958

Justice can span years. Retribution is not subject
to a calendar.

—Rod Serling

CHAPTER 37

It took all of his willpower to knock, but he knew it had to be done. How did that old Jewish proverb go? "If not now...when?" So many things from his past life had started to come back to him these last few weeks. Giving up the peach schnapps really did wonders for clearing up a guy's head.

Liz opened the door and smiled with gleeful surprise. He caught a tiny glimpse of her sparsely furnished studio apartment—one that was kept much tidier than his own.

"Morris!" she exclaimed. "You didn't tell me you were coming. Would you like to come in?"

"Uh, no," said Baker. He attempted to smile back, only managing a grimace that made it look like he had a toothache. "I can't stay long."

If he crossed that threshold, the cycle would probably start all over again. He'd paced the apartment lobby for a quarter of an hour, preparing himself for this very moment.

"Liz, I—" Baker began.

"Morris," she said, cutting him off. "I just want to reiterate how sorry I am for my behavior. I flew off the handle and went crazy there for a second. They could've killed you! I'd understand if you didn't want to see me anymore after that. To be quite frank, I didn't think I'd ever see you again after what I did."

"It's okay," he replied. "I appreciate the space you've given me these last few weeks. I should have been a little more up-front with you from the start. You had every right to be angry at me for... well, for being with... her."

Liz's smile disappeared. "Is she waiting for you downstairs?"

"No," he said, his throat becoming tight with anguish. "No, she's not. That's over."

"Oh," replied Liz, doing a poor job of hiding her pleasure. "I'm... sorry to hear that."

The time to do it was now. If he didn't, he never would. "Look," he began, "there's no easy way to say this, but I came by to say that... well, you've been swell. It's just that things never would have worked out between us."

"What are you saying?"

"I'm saying it's time for us to go our separate ways, Liz. All the time we spent together was nice. Real nice, actually. I don't think I would've made it these past ten years without you. But whatever this was"—he ran his hand between the space that separated them—"has run its course."

"I... I don't understand," she said. There weren't any tears yet, but her eyes were definitely threatening them. "Is it because you're Jewish and I'm not? You know that doesn't matter to me, whatever the government says. Morris, I... I love you."

There they were: the three words he'd been dreading.

"That's why this thing needs to end, Liz. I just don't feel the same way about you. I care for you, but I don't..."

"Love me," she finished.

The tears arrived, right on cue.

"I'm truly sorry, Liz. I can't keep leading you on anymore, making you think that there's some sort of future with us. Your company was . . . a salve of some kind. Sleeping with you, spending time with you, was— I don't know—a distraction for me. The deeper I got, the more I convinced myself that I would learn to love you, but that just wasn't the truth. I know now that trying to run from my demons won't solve a thing. You deserve someone better than me, someone whole."

"Sounds like you've given this a lot of thought," said Liz, her eyes red and puffy. "You really mean it, don't you?"

"I do," he said, resisting the urge to step into the apartment and hold her close.

"What if I convert? I could convert. I'll do anything."

She was becoming hysterical, but who could blame her? Baker had been steadily making this uncomfortable bed for over a decade, stuffing the pillows with straw and tucking rocks under the mattress. Now he was going to lie in it.

"Goodbye, Liz."

He turned away from the open door.

CHAPTER 38

The pews were made of wood and the scent of their varnished mahogany hung in the small chapel like a protective cloud in the desert. The back wall consisted of a large stained-glass depiction of a burning bush. Shafts of California sunlight brought the mosaic to vivid life, making it seem like an everlasting conflagration.

For all Baker knew, it was the same bush through which God had spoken to Moses, distilled into a hundred pieces of glass and affixed into this synagogue with mortar. Perhaps the same mortar the Jews had used during their time as slaves in Egypt. The sparks coming off the glass flames were arranged in such a way that they spelled out the Hebrew word for truth: *emet*. It was tastefully done, Baker decided when he first walked into the fort-like building.

A towering wooden ark stood at the front of the room where, although he could not see it, there undoubtedly rested a velvet-covered Torah scroll or two. The ark itself was a thing of simplistic beauty with beseeching hands carved into its sides. Hands waiting to accept the Ten Commandments on a mountaintop from God Himself. Or maybe the hands were waiting to accept a bowl of watery soup from a surly camp guard, who could pretend to dole out a ladleful and beat you when you asked him why. Baker could not decide which seemed more likely. In his experience, he'd only ever seen the latter.

This thought kick-started some part of his mind, a part he thought dead with so many other things. He remembered the beautiful synagogue of his home, his first home. A small town on the Czechoslovakian-Hungarian border that no longer existed. But he remembered it like a child does after waking from a particularly fanciful dream. For just a moment, he was a young boy again, clutching his father's hand and looking at that magnificent old synagogue in the town square for the very first time. He felt pride in the new Sabbath clothes his mother sewed just for him.

Inside, the chapel was a humble structure of weathered wood and flaking paint erected hundreds of years before when Jews spread across Europe in the wake of the Spanish Inquisition. He heard the solemn intonations of the "Lecha Dodi," the joyous prayer that welcomes the Sabbath like a groom greets his bride. He saw the men singing with what they called "kavanah," conviction. Singing praises to a God who would forsake them soon. But for now, that God was content to take their prayers. They did not yet know it, but these people were doomed. No, *that* was a lifetime away, an eternity, really—a nightmare fomenting in the mind of Western Europe. A virus that had yet to spread to this little shtetl with its simple, traditional people.

A small and doe-eyed Morris Baker watched with awe as the men shuffled back and forth with their long black overcoats, curled sideburns, and tasseled prayer shawls. Oh, how he envied the prayer shawl—a tallis. His father had promised him his very own shawl when he turned thirteen and became a bar mitzvah. And he would get it, the same year a madman would seize power, vanquish his political enemies, and set his sights on the world.

As Morris read from his Torah portion about Balaam, a man hired to curse the Jewish people, Röhm was shot in a Munich prison cell; von Schleicher was gunned down in his own home; Strasser bled to death for over an hour; von Kahr was cleaved with an ax; Klausener was gunned down in his office; Jung was dumped in a ditch near Oranienburg . . .

On and on it went—each note, every stressed syllable and word, punctuating the blows of murder that echoed across the valleys of time and space like long, sharpened knives. God would send no talking donkey, no voice of reason to Hitler like He did for Balaam. This time, the Jews really were cursed, and no one could save them.

During his youth, Morris learned about praying to the souls of righteous men, who could act as intermediaries between the living and the Almighty. He'd tried it a few times when the Storm Troopers goose-stepped into town. He tried again when the Torah scrolls were stolen and the synagogue burned to cinders. He tried again when his father was savagely beaten, his beard shorn for the simple crime of being a Jew.

The prayers began to peter out when Morris was shoved into the back of a crowded cattle car that stunk of feces, urine, and vomit. A single prayer came when he saw the sunken and skeletal faces of the inmates who yanked him out of the boxcar when it first arrived at the concentration camp. When he discovered the blank-eyed expression of his younger sister, Magda, who had starved on the trip. Sweet Magda, of whom he had never spoken aloud since.

A silent kaddish for the dead arrived a year later when he learned of his parents' deaths in the gas chambers. Some halfhearted intonations came as he hoisted members of his own community into the ovens as a member of the Sonderkommando. The penultimate prayers came when a Ukrainian inmate told him that his older brother, Ze'ev, had been killed clearing mines for the Germans on the Eastern Front, while a rabbi from a neighboring town informed him that one of his elder sisters, Ana, had been raped and thrown from a building.

By that point, however, Morris was out of conviction. The prayers rang hollow. Survival had become his only deity, and his invocations were the refrain of a shovel digging into an endless pile of human ashes. A final prayer came after Adolf Lang removed the tumor from his arm. Except this time, it was not a request for the righteous to intervene on behalf of the suffering Jews, but a selfish, simple plea for it all to end. Even then, it seemed as though the righteous were out to lunch.

"I'll be locking the place up in a few minutes, but you're welcome to stay as long as you like and take the fire exit when you're ready to go," said a voice from behind the pew in which he was sitting.

Baker looked over his shoulder to see who had broken him out of his reverie. A kind-faced man in a double-breasted brown suit and a black skullcap was picking up stray books with his right hand from the benches and placing them into the shelves lining the chapel. The left sleeve of his suit was rolled up and pinned to the side of his suit jacket. He looked to be about Morris's age—maybe a bit younger.

"Please accept my apologies if I interrupted your prayer. I didn't expect anyone to be here today. It is a fast day, after all."

"Is it?" asked Baker, a little abashed as he remembered the coffee, eggs, and bacon he'd eaten that morning.

"Yes, Tisha B'Av," said the man. "The ninth day of the Hebrew month of Av. Some call it the saddest day in Jewish history."

"Is it?" asked Baker again, annoyed that he couldn't think of something else to say.

"Oh yes," replied the man, unfazed. Baker was surprised to hear an accent similar to his own. "Both of the Holy Temples in Jerusalem were destroyed on this date. The First Crusade commenced on the ninth of Av, and so did Spain's expulsion of the Jews during the Inquisition. And more recently..." His smile faded a little. "Hitler provided the go-ahead for the Final Solution on this day in 1941. Exactly one year later, deportations to Treblinka from the Warsaw Ghetto began."

"Wow," said Baker, who had a vague recollection of observing Tisha B'Av as a boy. He realized he was involuntarily rubbing his left forearm and stopped.

"At least God had the good sense to put everything on one day. Makes it easier to remember that way." The man's smile returned. "No food or water in the middle of summer, though. No wonder nobody came in today. They usually stay home and watch television or some such to occupy themselves. Helps take their minds off the hunger and thirst."

"I'm sorry," began Baker, "but..."

"Oh, my apologies," said the man, and he held out his right hand. "I'm the rabbi of this congregation. Jacob Kahn."

Baker shook the rabbi's hand and was surprised that he was not asked for his name in return. "Your accent," Morris said. "Forgive me for saying so, but it sounds familiar. Are you from Czechoslovakia?"

"Oh yes! Are you?"

"As a matter of fact, I am," said Baker. "A small shtetl that no longer exists."

"That's how it is for most of us," said Rabbi Kahn sadly. "Let Zion weep bitterly and Jerusalem give forth her voice...For You, O Lord, did consume her with fire."

"Trying out some beat poetry on me?" asked Baker.

Rabbi Kahn laughed. "No, no. I'm no, what's his name? Ginsberg? Yes, that's it. That was an excerpt from *Eicha*."

"I've been away from this stuff for a while, Rabbi," said Baker.

Kahn chuckled kindly. "It's a book we read from on this holiday. *Eicha* means 'lamentations' and it tells the story of the Babylonians besieging Jerusalem and destroying the first Temple. Such a beautifully written piece of poetry that tells such an awful story. It compares the city to a grieving widow who has been betrayed."

"Wow," said Baker.

"Quite," said Kahn. He took a break from collecting prayer books and sat down next to Baker. "If there's one thing we Jews know how to do, it's suffer. We've perfected the art ever since Abraham gave himself a circumcision and sat outside in the boiling desert heat."

Baker winced at the thought. "Why us, though?" he blurted out, surprising even himself. "Just because we're good at suffering doesn't mean we deserve it, surely?"

Kahn was silent for a moment before answering.

"Better men than I have asked this question many times over the centuries and not even they could answer it, I'm afraid," he said. "The best answer I can give you is that it's our lot in life, just as it is the lot of a cow to be slaughtered, so that it can nourish others. Everything in this world has a function, but no one ever said each function would be positive. A spider has venom so it can eat, but that venom can also kill a human being. Do we berate the spider for possessing deadly venom? The poison within the spider's fangs is meant, not for a man, but for the capture and incapacitation of pests that would otherwise bother a man. It is like the song we sing on Passover, 'Chad Gadya.' Everything in life has a natural, unavoidable progression. Once things are set in motion, there is nothing we can do, except wait until things reach their eventual conclusion."

"But what about the war? The camps? Are you saying those things were natural? That they couldn't be helped?"

Kahn smiled. "Of course not. The intellect of man is a lot like the spider's poison. It can be used to solve the issues that plague us all, or it can be used for senseless violence and killing. Would you blame a scientist for using his mind to cure a deadly disease or create a faster automobile? Surely not. It all comes down to the intent of the function. I know that isn't really an answer to your question, but I suppose it's also about the perspective one takes on suffering. Perhaps it serves a function indiscernible to anyone but Hashem—er—God."

Baker looked at Kahn like the man was crazy. The rabbi laughed once more.

"I know that's somewhat of a, what's the phrase Americans use? Cop-out! That's the one. Think of it like this . . ."

Kahn looked over his shoulder before awkwardly reaching into his jacket pocket and bringing out a battered, mustard-colored book titled *The Golden Apples of the Sun*, a story collection by Ray Bradbury.

"My congregants don't know this, but between you and me, I'm something of a science-fiction nut. A lot of people would say it's not a clergyman's job to be reading mind-numbing pulp; he should keep his nose in a Bible at all times. But they fail to realize the intriguing existential arguments these writers think of. They're like modern-day scholars applying the lessons of today to what could be. Just like the old Talmudic authorities. There's a fascinating story in this book about a wealthy time traveler who pays an exorbitant amount of money to go back in time so he can kill a dinosaur. Except he loses his nerve when the beast shows up. The terrified man strays off the predetermined path and accidentally kills a butterfly. It sounds inconsequential, stepping on a small insect like that, but when he returns to the present, there are egregious differences in political outcomes—in the very construct of language itself. Just think what ramifications the suffering of the Jewish people could be having. No one said you had to like it or that it was fair or that it even has to make sense, but, paradoxically, it's the only way it could make sense. The only way you can stay sane," he finished, placing the book back inside his jacket.

"You were in one, too, weren't you?" Baker asked quietly.

"Theresienstadt," replied the rabbi. "I was on wood-cutting duty until I showed up to roll call late one day." He rolled up his left sleeve, revealing to Baker why part of the jacket was pinned up. Kahn's hand had been cut off just below the string of numbers tattooed on his arm. In its stead was a puckered stump of scarred flesh. "They gave us blunt axes so the work would be harder. It took the commandant about fifteen swings with mine until he could separate my hand from my arm as a punishment. At least that's what I was told when I woke up hours later. I passed out after the ninth swing."

"How could you believe in God after that?"

Kahn rolled his sleeve back down. "For a while, all I believed in was anger. The thought of revenge was the only thing that kept me going when my wound turned septic. I was very near death, even ready for it. I begged for God to claim me and take away the suffering when I heard someone speaking in my ear. 'Your name is Jacob Kahn. Your name is Jacob Kahn,' they kept saying over and over again. You see, my name was not always Jacob. I was born Eliezer Kahn. However, it is traditional in Judaism to change a person's first name when they are in a life-threatening situation in order to trick the Angel of Death into thinking they have the wrong person. It sounds silly, I know, but that voice stayed with me until my fever broke and the infection passed. When I regained consciousness, I learned from the inmates in my barracks that it was an elderly rabbi. He sat by my bunk, day and night, praying on my behalf, keeping me nourished and hydrated with his own meager rations and repeating my new name. The night before my illness passed, they told me, he had been placed on a train for Auschwitz. One of the final shipments."

Kahn's voice broke. He brought a silk handkerchief to his eye.

"When the Russians liberated us, I looked for this rabbi, although I did not know his name. I didn't even know what he looked like, due to my delirium. All I knew was the sound of his voice. Finally, certain he had not survived, I decided to honor his memory by becoming a rabbi myself. I wanted to inspire the same selflessness in others that had been shown to me. Now I'm married and have two wonderful children. That's the greatest revenge, Detective: survival."

Baker looked up in surprise. "You know who I am?"

Rabbi Kahn smiled and placed his hand on Baker's shoulder. "Officially, no. But unofficially, every Jew in town knows who you are. Thanks to the Liberty Boys. You're a bit of a hero to us. The downtrodden people of this country now know they can count on you for help when they're in trouble."

"I don't know about that. I was just doing my job."

"So were the commandants and guards at the concentration camps. Forget suffering for a moment. If we can choose to make the right choices in the face of suffering, then it matters not what someone can do to you. It makes all the difference in the world. Now..." Kahn stood up with a small groan and brushed dust off his suit. "I would not blame or judge a person for abandoning religion after what we went through. And I certainly wouldn't expect them to come back."

Baker looked down at his shoes.

"That being said," continued Kahn, "I'd love to see you in here again—or if you're up to it, we could have more chats like this one. It's always good to catch up with someone from the old country."

"I'd like that," said Baker. He whipped out the notebook he sometimes used on crime scenes and jotted down his home number, handing it to the rabbi. The notebook was returned to his jacket, where it sat next to Walter Cronkite's diary of sign-off phrases.

"Excellent. I'll be in touch, Detective Baker. Please feel free to stay as long as you like. Just don't forget to take the fire exit when you go," Kahn finished genially, gesturing toward the fire door, a reinforced hunk of steel that looked more like the entrance to a bank vault. A thought, brought on by the rabbi's final words about helping people, began to take root in Baker's brain. Kahn was nearly out of the sanctuary when he called to him.

"Uh, Rabbi Kahn?"

"Yes?"

Baker raised a hand to his breast pocket, where a collection of letters from West Germany sat. He decided that they finally deserved replies.

"Have an easy fast."

EPILOGUE

Do not choose your future profession for money.
Profession should be chosen like a wife—for love.
　　　　　　　　　　　　　　　　　—John Huston

August 4, 1958

The joint funeral for John Huston and Walter Cronkite—their fates having been so intertwined that a shared ceremony was only natural—was held at the Hollywood Forever Cemetery on Santa Monica Boulevard. Opened at the turn of the century, when the film business was just in its infancy, the cemetery was now filled with the rotting remains of some of the industry's finest: Valentino, Arbuckle, Fairbanks, Fleming, and Lasky.

It was a fitting resting place for industry veterans, especially since the pre-federalized Paramount Pictures had once operated down the street. Tall palm trees were planted every few feet, separating the cemetery's unique collection of obelisks, mausoleums, reflecting pools, and sarcophagi.

Dalton Trumbo, the talented screenwriter gunned down by Humphrey Bogart at the Red Sword, had been interred here two weeks earlier to no fanfare. Even in death, he remained a blacklisted pariah.

Bogart's funeral had been held at the Forest Lawn Memorial Park cemetery the previous week. The event drew in mourners from all over the country, and they came in droves, clogging the city with even more traffic and smog than usual. Kenneth Bierly had delivered a fiery eulogy (no doubt written by McCarthy's own speechwriters), extolling Bogie's presence on the screen and stating that Hollywood would not yield in its battle against Communism. The search was now on for a new star to be the face of the propaganda machine. Bogart, who was willing to murder for eternal fame, had gotten his wish...as a martyr.

* * *

"...They were men unmatched in their respective fields of motion pictures and journalism," droned the priest, who was officiating the joint funeral. "Men whose lives were tragically cut short in their primes."

Cronkite's and Huston's family members and colleagues were in attendance, but members of the press were noticeably absent. Not very surprising. The only account of what had occurred in early July came from Murrow's broadcasts, which made it easy for the government to downplay Operation Paperclip and the Black Symphony, especially since all the physical evidence had literally gone up in smoke.

"Russian spies looking to sabotage the US space program" were blamed for the untimely death of Wernher von Braun, who received a glowing, six-page obituary that hailed him as "the father of space travel." There was no mention of the man's use of slave labor during the war. Huston, Cronkite, and Trumbo, on the other hand, were still being branded as Red sympathizers by HUAC, which continued to chalk their deaths up to vigilante justice.

Baker continued to keep his trap shut about all that occurred. The previous month had passed in a blur of letters, telephone calls, and one delicious apple pie baked by an admiring fan in Glendale. Jews from as far away as New Jersey were taking the time to write and call to thank him for doing something that didn't officially take place.

More depressingly, Baker had endured an uncomfortable meeting with Oliver Shelton's mother, Jane, who sobbed the entire time. He didn't blame her. Oliver's body had not yet been located, although Baker hoped to give the distraught woman some closure by offering the usual empty words. Of how Oliver was a good kid, how he had refused Baker's efforts to tip him. Through snot-filled gasps, Mrs. Shelton thanked Baker for visiting her. Oliver was given an honorary headstone at the Shelton family plot in the Angelus-Rosedale Cemetery, his grave sitting in the merciful shade of an aged holly oak.

The body of Charles Ward was found in his one-bedroom apartment in Long Beach. The word FAGGOT was scrawled on the wall against which his corpse rested. He was buried at the Forest Lawn Memorial Park in Hollywood Hills. Since Charles was unmarried, it fell to his sister and widower father from Sonoma to oversee the burial arrangements.

Baker attended the small memorial service and placed a bottle of disinfectant on Charles's freshly filled grave. It was something he knew the germophobic medical examiner would probably find ironically comical during his long dirt nap. Just as he was about to leave, a burly man with a bushy beard embraced him without warning. Tears dripping from his eyes and into his beard, the large man released Baker.

The stranger tenderly placed a wreath of white roses on Charles's grave and left without a word.

While the funeral for Cronkite and Huston took place in the morning, it was already shaping up to be another brutally hot day. It reminded Baker of the morning when he was first dragged into the mess with the two dead men.

Even after all that had happened, life continued as it was. McCarthy was still in office, hoping for a third term and doubling down on anti-Communist and anti-Semitic messages. Not to mention the fact that the Black Symphony was still out there. Baker reminded himself that he needed to be careful. With their plan foiled and leader dead, revenge was probably the next item on their agenda.

Rarely is there ever a happy ending, Baker thought to himself as the priest began the usual prayer about "ashes to ashes, dust to dust." *I know better than anyone else what it's like for the bad guys to walk away without so much as a scratch.*

And yet this bleak thought did not fill him with the dread and resentment it once had. Not even the darkness threatened to cloud his mind and drive him incoherent. The American public was now a little more informed, a little more aware of what those in power could do without consent. If it sparked just a little more hope and resistance around the country, then it was all worth it.

"Now let us bow our heads in a moment of silence for the deceased," finished the priest, closing his leather-bound Bible. Everyone closed their eyes and looked down, solemnly. Everyone, that is, except Baker. He'd been a homicide detective for nearly a decade and still felt uncomfortable in cemeteries. They were too pristine, too well manicured. Rarely was death ever this organized.

Baker took one last look at the two coffins (festooned with exotic flowers and dazzling shreds of gold leaf) and slipped away from the crowd. He strolled among the tombstones, passing the cenotaph for Terry, the dog that portrayed Toto in *The Wizard of Oz*. Wandering into the Beth Olam section, he came across a relatively new tombstone with a Star of David carved into its front.

ALBERT AKST (1899–1956)

MOTION PICTURE EDITOR

BELOVED FATHER, HUSBAND, AND BROTHER

אַל תִּירָא מִפַּחַד פִּתְאֹם וּמִשֹּׁאַת רְשָׁעִים כִּי תָבֹא

DO NOT FEAR SUDDEN TERROR OR THE DISASTER OF THE

WICKED WHEN IT COMES

Baker read the epitaph three times over. Once again possessed by the ingrained traditions of his formative years, he bent down, knees cracking in the summer stillness, and ran his hand over the perfectly tended grass until his fingers came across a smooth stone. He stood up and delicately placed it atop the headstone of Albert Akst.

A soft breeze rolled through the cemetery, faintly rustling the grass. The floral aroma of late summer reminded him of Sophia. His love for her, unlike the woman, had not perished. Almost nothing had changed, but the world felt different to him now. Sophia, however fictional she may have been, taught him that there was more to the world than lies, pain, and anger. Her memory alone was enough to give him the courage to ask Shira Abramovich, a pretty member of Rabbi Kahn's congregation and a survivor of Auschwitz, out to dinner.

No one had come looking for Faye Dalton. Her body ended up in the city morgue, which was now under the jurisdiction of Interim Medical Examiner Thomas Noguchi.

The eternal detective, Baker did some digging and anonymously called Faye's family in Minneapolis. The news hit Mrs. Dalton pretty hard, despite her admission that she and her daughter had not spoken in quite some time. The anguish coming through the other end of the phone was almost too much for Baker, who considered hanging up right then and there. But he willed himself to provide a semi-true account of how Faye died. She was murdered, he said, trying to protect her country; her remains would be shipped home from California.

He added that Faye cared more for them than they knew and hung up before her mother could provide any details on where a funeral service might be held. He knew that if she told him, he'd be on the next flight to Minnesota. But he was not in love with Faye Dalton, he was in love with Sophia Vikhrov, and therefore did not deserve to share in the family's sadness.

"Well, you did it, darling."

Baker was so engrossed in thoughts of Sophia that he didn't notice Enrica Soma and her two children standing right in front of him. Even in mourning, she was a stunner. Looking at her, Baker knew she was going to be okay. A woman like her didn't just give up in the face of tragedy. She had plans, though what they were was anyone's guess.

Anjelica, hiding behind her mother's legs as usual, looked nice in a dark-blue dress with her hair done up in the pageboy style. Anthony, whom Baker had not previously met, looked like his father, minus all the lines of age. As all frustrated young boys do, he made a show of scuffing his shoes by kicking up loose dirt clods.

"I suppose I did, Enrica," Baker said. "It was a lovely service, by the way."

"Yes," she said drily. "Personally, I find funerals to be a bit passé, but Johnny was an excellent showman, so it's nothing short of what he deserved as a final send-off. He protected us, after all—sending us away just before he died. Anyway, I came over to let you know that the kids and I are moving to New York to live with my father. There's nothing left for us in this town. The stink of Johnny's murder will hang over it worse than the smog. Not good for the children, you know? It's been very hard on them. Especially Anthony." She whispered her son's name with a small jerk of the head in the boy's direction. "Anyway, I hope you take care of yourself, Morris, darling. Do keep in touch. Come along, children."

Enrica turned and so did her children. They were about ten paces away when Anjelica turned back and ran to Baker, wrapping her arms around his legs. He was shocked and stood rooted to the spot as Enrica gently guffawed.

"Thank you for catching the bad people who hurt my daddy."

"You are quite welcome, Anjelica," he said, crouching down to give her a proper embrace. He smiled at her with a full set of teeth. The ones knocked out by Waldgrave and von Braun had been expertly replaced by a dentist named Bagley who refused to charge Baker for the service.

They broke apart and the young girl scampered back to her mother. Soon, all three Hustons were out of sight.

Smiling, Baker patted Cronkite's notebook in his pocket and strolled out of the cemetery, whistling some long-forgotten Yiddish tune his mother would sometimes hum to him before bed. He'd attempted to give the notebook to Cronkite's widow, Mary Elizabeth, but she simply refused, pushing it to his chest with a choked word of thanks.

He was unlocking the Continental when a familiar voice shouted, "Baker! Hey, Baker!"

Andy Sullivan came running over, sweat rolling off his face.

"Whaddya say to an exclusive one-on-one interview for the *Times*, eh? Think about it. Big front-page splash with your face and a big ol' swastika right next to it. 'Los Angeles Police Officer Restores American Faith in Jews.'" He ran his palm through the air as if the words would suddenly appear in big, bold font. "Snappy headline, eh?"

"No thanks, Andy," Baker said, pulling the door open. "I'm out of the policing game."

"What?" exclaimed Sullivan, jotting down Baker's words so frantically that ink splattered across the page of his notebook. "Where are you going? What will you do?"

Morris got into his car and turned the ignition. "You'll be able to find me on Wilshire Boulevard. I'm opening my own private investigation service. Less people breathing down my neck. I can do more good that way," he added, more to himself than to Andy.

Lonergan was demanding that Baker be terminated from the force, but Parker, as always, refused. To save the chief any more headaches and to forgo the hate-filled looks and slurs thrown his way by Dashiell Hanscom and countless others within the department, Morris submitted his resignation the very next day. A certain member of the typing pool had also quit.

"If you need me, feel free to make an appointment with my secretary, Joanna," he said to Sullivan. With Huston and Trumbo now dead, Murrow agreed it was a good idea to have his nuclear expert (who had drowned the Symphony's uranium off the Santa Monica Pier in the dead of night) keeping an ear to the ground in Los Angeles.

"That's swell," said Andy, still writing feverishly. "So how about this headline instead: 'Legendary Cop Gives Up Police Work for Private Sector.' Whaddya say, Baker? It might even nab us the Pulitzer."

"You know, Andy, you've been a putz from the moment I first met you and I have a feeling you'll always be a putz. Goodbye."

"So that's a no, then?"

"It's a no."

"At least tell me why, Baker."

Baker twiddled the radio knob and the Belmonts' "I Wonder Why" fortuitously came over the speakers.

"Well, for starters, I don't like you very much," said Baker, remembering a particular sign-off phrase he'd come across in Cronkite's notebook. One of the few ideas not crossed out by the late journalist. "And that's the way it is."

Acknowledgments

Acknowledgements are always the most boring part of any book, so I'll try to make this as quick and painless as humanly possible, folks. Still, things like this don't occur in a vacuum. As much as I'd like to take all the credit for myself and call it a day, that would be incredibly insulting to all the amazing people who supported me along the way.

First off, a *massive* thank you to my literary agent, Scott Miller of Trident Media Group, who completely understood what I was going for with this novel. The night he called me with an offer of representation remains one of the most thrilling moments of my life. Hearing another person—one I'd never met—affirming the merit of my creative idea is something that truly goes beyond words.

You spend so much time alone with a book that you don't know how others will receive it.

By the time Scott got in touch, I'd already been rejected by dozens of other agents (thankfully, Brad Meltzer gave me some encouraging words to keep persevering).

All it took was one reader to see the potential of Detective Morris Baker and the world he inhabited. Scott, your enthusiastic support for *Beat the Devils* helped me realize a lifelong dream of becoming a published author, and for that I will forever be in your debt.

Next, I'd like to thank my amazing editors over at Grand Central Publishing, Ben Sevier and Wes Miller, both of whom helped me crack the narrative nut of this labyrinthine project. Their feedback and suggestions helped transform *Beat the Devils* (originally titled *In My Hand* until Ben had the good sense to talk me out of it) from a rough manuscript into a book you'd actually want to read. The original draft was about a hundred pages longer, with the climax set at a boardwalk amusement park, until Ben, yet again, thankfully convinced me to dial things down a bit.

Ben's incisive feedback made me realize the story was not about raising the stakes or starting a food fight at a drive-in (which was also in that earlier draft). The crux of the story is, first and foremost, about Baker and his journey of adopting a new worldview. To uncover a sense of agency and optimism after so many years of wallowing in bitterness, self-pity, and peach schnapps. I didn't need an over-the-top standoff in Santa Monica to drive that home. (I can't speak for later books, though.)

Wes, meanwhile, was always available as a sounding board for any questions—both big and small. He taught me that if something is bugging you, bring it up before it's too late. Thanks so much for putting up with all my emails and neuroses, Wes! You're a real champ.

You can also thank Laura Jorstad, Carmel Shaka, and Bob Castillo—whose amazing editorial and typesetting work turned *Beat the Devils* from a hefty Word document into a beautiful addition to your personal bookshelf.

Before all the exciting developments with Scott and Grand Central came along, I had my loyal beta readers who provided some of the earliest feedback when I finished the very first draft back in the fall of 2017. Thank you to my mother, Hillary Givner, Josh DiCristo, Ethan

Riback, Phoebe Burnstein, Mark Koh, and Caroline Leavitt. You were all willing to read a 430-page manuscript when you probably had better things to do. Not many people have the patience to do that, and I'm incredibly grateful to you all for taking the time.

To my wonderful fiancée, Leora Rychik: Words cannot fully express how grateful I am to you for being so patient with me throughout this entire process. Your ability to put up with all the time, energy, and anxiety attacks I poured into this book is worthy of a gold medal. I love you!

To my wonderfully supportive siblings—Shani, Noah, Ari, and Rob: Thank you for being the best cheering squad a guy could ask for.

To David Dahan: Thank you for finally getting around to reading the book after a busy tax season. To David Klein: Thank you for helping me hone the Yiddish. *Zei gezunt!* To Tsofia Gabay: Thank you for polishing up the German. To Valeria Berlfein: Thank you for double-checking the Spanish. And to Mark Greaney: Thank you for fact-checking the armory.

Also, a *big* shoutout to my father, William Weiss, for hammering out all the legal details—pro bono, of course. Then come those teachers who, if you're lucky enough to get them on your course schedule, will push you in the best way possible. Thank you to Dr. Eileen Watts, Barry Kirzner, and Dr. Jordan McClain. If I could, I'd give you all an A.

The same goes for my amazing team over at SYFY WIRE: Alexis Loinaz, Trent Moore, Caitlin Busch, Dennis Culver, and Adam Pockross.

Lastly, I'd like to make note of individuals I don't know personally—authors like Annie Jacobsen, Eric Lichtblau, Andrew Nagorski, Paul Roland, and Anthony Read. Their exemplary histories of Hitler's

ACKNOWLEDGMENTS

Germany and the fate of Nazi war criminals and scientists post–World War II served as the basis for many of the revelations found within *Beat the Devils*.

As the grandson of a Holocaust survivor (upon whom Morris is partially based), it seemed important to at least present that tumultuous period as accurately as I could. To show that despite the court trials held after WWII, dozens of offenders slipped through the cracks, undetected.

Some didn't even need to slip through the cracks. The United States knew about the murderous pasts of many of these men and women but put them to work anyway—all in the name of fighting the growing scourge of Communism. These former Nazis enjoyed cushy lives of wealth and adulation until the government finally owned up to its mistake in the late 1970s, when brave individuals like Congresswoman Elizabeth Holtzman began to speak up, prompting the Department of Justice to form the Office of Special Investigations.

This office tracked down war criminals living in America, hoping to strip them of citizenship and accolades before deporting them out of the country in disgrace. By that point, however, these men and women had already grown fat on the allowances of a nation that had turned a blind eye to their heinous crimes. A nation that had dived headfirst into a global conflict to end the fascist ideas to which these people had once so easily subscribed. Ideas that led to the industrialized genocide of 11 million people (6 million of them Jews).

Sure, Wernher von Braun's revolutionary work in the field of rocketry helped us reach the moon in 1969, but was winning the space race worth the cost of ignoring the horrific system of slave labor used during the war to make V-1 and V-2 rockets for Hitler's relentless war machine? As poor Samuel Klaus said, it was like "making a deal with the Devil for national security gains."

The central question is this: At what point does a country compromise its own moral values for the sake of progress? Moreover, what does that look like in a version of the United States consumed by the rabid hatred, xenophobia, and suspicion so often associated with Nazi Germany? When a government protects genuine offenders and goes after those they deem to be "Other"?

Well, we don't really need to peek into an alternate reality to receive an answer to that question because it's essentially what happened at the height of Joseph McCarthy's political power. The individuals who helped perpetrate the Holocaust got a free pass while the "Big Bad" Communists—suspected or otherwise—were exposed with a malicious fervor.

Lives were destroyed, regardless of proof, and *Beat the Devils* simply dials up the mania of that era to an 11 1/2. For instance, the motion picture industry never came under federal control, but I'd like to think that if it did, every single Jewish person (from the most powerful executive to the lowest camera operator) would have been ousted without a second thought. Not only that, but I think people suspected of being even remotely Jewish—like Darryl F. Zanuck, who was actually not a Member of the Tribe, if you can believe it—would be too.

It is almost impossible to fathom how America went from boldly stamping out Nazism, a wicked ideology that turned a nation against its own citizens, to embracing similar tenets found in McCarthyism just a few years later.

If you'd like to delve deeper into the topics of the Nuremberg Trials, Operation Paperclip, and the search for Nazi fugitives after the war, I highly recommend checking out the following titles: *Operation*

Paperclip: The Secret Intelligence Program that Brought Nazi Scientists to America, by Annie Jacobsen (Little Brown & Company); *The Nazis Next Door: How America Became a Safe Haven for Hitler's Men,* by Eric Lichtblau (Mariner Books); *The Nazi Hunters,* by Eric Nagorski (Simon & Schuster); *The Nuremberg Trials: The Nazis and Their Crimes Against Humanity,* by Paul Roland (Arcturus); and *The Devil's Disciples: Hitler's Inner Circle,* by Anthony Read (W.W. Norton).

About the Author

Josh Weiss is a first-time author from South Jersey. Raised in a proud Jewish home, he was instilled with an appreciation for his cultural heritage from a very young age. Today Josh is utterly fascinated with the convergence of Judaism and popular culture in film, television, comics, literature, and other media. After college, he became a freelance entertainment journalist, writing stories for SYFY WIRE, *The Hollywood Reporter*, *Forbes*, and Marvel Entertainment. He currently resides in Philadelphia with his fiancée, as well as an extensive collection of graphic T-shirts, movie posters, vinyl records, and a few books, of course.